'Has all the elements of
packed with ... ..., revenge ... ... 'th'
Historical Novels Review

'Stand aside *Gladiator*, the real classics are coming'   *Independent*

'Where Manfredi excels . . . is in his mastery of detail'
Sunday Express

'Moving at a blistering pace . . . A good introduction to the life of a legend'   *Herald*

'It's a rip-roaring, page-turning yarn, full of Oriental mysticism, Roman values and old-fashioned adventure'   *Yorkshire Evening Post*

'An exciting, fast-paced and atmospheric novel'   *Choice*

'A great Roman smorgasbord of a novel that both encapsulates and celebrates the genre . . . Manfredi has this genre off to a finely honed art . . . The background to this ambitious and impressive novel is always delivered with maximum verisimilitude'
Barry Forshaw, *Good Book Guide*

'Written in an easy-read style, this epic tale is a real page-turner, full of bravery, love, myth and magic'   *Belfast Telegraph*

'He's the hottest writer of ripping historical yarns right across Europe and is catching on fast here . . . Find out what the excitement's about with this rip-roaring archaeological adventure that makes *Indiana Jones* look kind of slow'
Peterborough Evening Telegraph

WOLVES OF ROME

VALERIO MASSIMO MANFREDI is an archaeologist and scholar of the ancient Greek and Roman worlds. He is the author of seventeen novels, which have won him literary awards and have sold 12 million copies. His Alexander trilogy has been translated into 38 languages and published in 62 countries and the film rights have been acquired by Universal Pictures. His novel *The Last Legion* was made into a film starring Colin Firth and Ben Kingsley and directed by Doug Lefler. Valerio Massimo Manfredi has taught at a number of prestigious universities in Italy and abroad, and has published numerous articles and essays in academic journals. He has also written screenplays for film and television, contributed to journalistic articles and conducted cultural programmes and television documentaries.

Also by Valerio Massimo Manfredi

VALERIO MASSIMO MANFREDI

WOLVES OF ROME

Translated from the Italian by Christine Feddersen-Manfredi

PAN BOOKS

ISBN 978-1-5098-7899-4

3 5 7 9 8 6 4 2

A CIP catalogue record for this book is available from the British Library.

Typeset in 11/13 pt Dante MT Std by Jouve (UK), Milton Keynes
Printed and bound by CPI Group (UK) Ltd, Croydon, CR0 4YY

Visit **www.panmacmillan.com** to read more about all our books
and to buy them. You will also find features, author interviews and
news of any author events, and you can sign up for e-newsletters
so that you're always first to hear about our new releases.

To Alessandro

Thereupon appeared a young man of noble birth, brave in action and alert in mind, possessing an intelligence quite beyond the ordinary barbarian; he was, namely, Arminius, the son of Sigmer, a prince of that nation, and he showed in his countenance and in his eyes the fire of the mind within.

Compendium of Roman History (Book Two)
by Velleius Paterculus,
translated by Frederick W. Shipley

Prologue

Three horsemen armed with swords, spears and shields made their way slowly along the shore of the pitch-black swamp. The sun had begun to set, its light silhouetting the dense forest that lay beyond the swamp, thick with colossal oaks and fir trees as black in the twilight as the brackish water and the far-off mountain peaks. Two of the men were escorting the third, a warrior prince no longer in his prime; strands of white hair mixed with his long blond locks.

He was wearing his best armour and his long sword hung from a silver baldric. As the sky darkened in the west, the prince urged his horse on, suddenly eager to quicken his pace. The autumn rains had swollen the swamp, causing it to spill out onto the lowlands all around it, and it was taking far longer than he had expected. He would arrive at his destination neither by day nor by night, but with the false, deceptive light of the gloaming, when reality blended into dream or nightmare, when the forest filled with ghosts.

A rock at the side of the road bore signs of ancient runes, once carved deep but faded with time so they could no longer be deciphered. Nonetheless, they told the prince that he was on the right path.

'How far do we have to go, my lord?' asked one of the two young warriors, the best of all his guard.

'Not much further,' he replied. 'When the shadow of that mountain peak reaches the edge of the swamp, we'll be there.'

The two youths fell silent. They clutched their swords tighter and their eyes strained to miss no movement in the half-light, every sense as taut as a bowstring. The prince began to ascend the slope of a small hill. He was the first to reach its top and he waited for his warriors to join him, one on each side. He pointed at a spot in the direction of the setting sun and said, 'It's there, that cave belongs to the Germanic oracle.' The long deep whistle of an owl sounded from the boughs of an oak tree.

The two warriors shivered but their hearts did not falter. 'Let us go first. We've sworn to keep you safe.'

'No. It is I who must do battle with the virago within the cave. She is huge and horrible to see. It is said that she never misses.' It wasn't clear whether he meant with the deftness of her blows or the truth revealed in her utterances. 'To hear her words, one must first contend with her. Many men have died trying.' The prince drew his sword, dug his heels into his horse's flanks and began to descend the slope alone.

All at once a creature, a feral beast, came out of the mouth of the cave, so enormous that she looked like a bear. She threw a great bundle of sticks onto a fire that had been smouldering just outside the entrance, giving rise to a flurry of sparks.

The fire reflected in the faces and the eyes of the two young warriors as they sought their next move. They wanted to gallop straight at the awful hag but they dared not disobey the command of their lord. He couldn't have been clearer: only if he fell were they allowed to come to his aid. They were not to attack unless his life was at risk. But they did draw closer, so they could see and hear whatever was about to ensue.

When the giantess realized that a warrior with his un-sheathed sword stood before her, and that two more warriors were close behind him, she let out a roar that dwindled slowly to a hoarse rasp. The two warriors were stunned to hear her voice begin to take on a human tone.

'Hermundur,' said one to the other. 'She just said, "Who are you?"'

'You don't recognize me?' said the prince, looking straight into the virago's eyes. Her face contorted and the raw animal hides that only half covered her let off a disgusting stench. She gave out another roar and lifted her axe as she croaked, again in Hermundur, 'What do you want?'

'Give me your prophecy,' replied the silver-baldricked horse-man as he swung his blade. Axe and sword met with a loud crash and one of the two young warriors lunged forward but his companion stopped him.

'We promised. He has to fight her alone.'

The blows came fast and strong, blades clashing with vio-lence. As the fighting grew harsher, the prince could hear that the frightening hag was beginning to groan. Certainly no one had come to challenge her for a very long time. The strength she had once been able to depend on was failing her, but her sheer size made her indomitable still. She lurched at her quer-ent with a burning stick from the fire in one hand and her axe still in the other. He dodged her blows, twisted around and rammed at her with all his might. She was thrown off balance, threw up her hands and sank to the ground on her knees. He pushed the tip of his sword into the small of her throat. 'The revelation,' he hissed.

The virago resisted defeat. She shook her head and her shaggy tangled hair covered her face.

'Don't you know me? Pronounce the prophecy for me now!'

The Germanic oracle finally spoke and the two young warriors sheathed their blades.

They could hear the voice of the ogress but they couldn't understand a word. They saw the tears of their lord and heard a wailing first and then a long agonized shriek that echoed from the mountainsides. The silver-baldricked prince took his sword then and plunged it deep into the throat that had spoken and the virago collapsed face down on the fire she herself had lit. She burned under the horrified eyes of the two warriors.

When the prince turned towards them his eyes were full of darkness.

PART ONE

Forest of the Cherusci, Germania, 3 BC

1

Two boys, running through the forest.

Sparkles shot through their hair as they slipped in and out of shadow and met the sun, flashing gold. They flew, light as the wind that touched the fronds of the trees, light as the scent of resin that wafted among the giant firs. They never hesitated, never slowed as obstacles appeared, not even for any of the giant forest creatures who might suddenly emerge. Pure joy in their every movement.

Wulf and Armin their names, noble their stock.

The boys reached the top of the Hill of Echoes just as the sun was flooding the great clearing.

Armin stopped. 'Listen!'

Wulf stopped as well. 'What?'

'The hammer. It's the hammer of Thor.'

Wulf listened hard. Deep bursts of thunder, accompanied by pounding water and the endless echo of the same.

'Are you trying to scare me?'

'No, not yet.'

'Where's it coming from?'

'From the right. Behind the oak wood.'

'Shall we go?'

'Yeah, but careful, though. It's not really Thor's hammer.'

'What is it, then?'

'I told you . . . I'm going to show you the road that never ends.'

Armin motioned for his brother to follow as he began to move forward, cautiously, among the oak saplings and ash trees. Armin wasn't hard to follow. Taller than any boy his age, his red and silver tunic could be seen from afar, like the bronze reflections in his hair.

Armin finally stopped. Wulf drew up alongside him and what he saw left him dumbstruck. A road paved with polished stones, almost thirty feet wide, perfect in every way, dry and straight, constant in its dimensions and complete in its structure. It was as beautiful as if the gods themselves had built it. Wulf followed it with his eyes until he saw it disappear behind the oak wood.

'You said the road that never ends.'

'I did. Follow me.'

They scrambled down the slope of the Hill of Echoes and there was the road again, straight and flawless.

'See?' said Armin.

The road stretched on and on to the edge of the Great Swamp, which reflected the disc of the sun like a mirror, but it did not end at that enormous expanse of water. It skimmed the swamp's still, liquid surface, continuing on straight to the middle, where it stopped at a distance of at least three miles from the shore.

'How can that be . . .' whispered Wulf.

'Look, down there, by that little island,' replied Armin. 'See those wooden towers? Each one of them is manned from the inside by at least fifty soldiers. They activate a mechanism that raises a two-hundred-pound mallet thirty feet in the air. It's let loose on a stake that's been planted into the soil bed underwater, driving it further and further down. Look closely. You'll see a double row of those stakes emerging just slightly over the surface of the water, see? Beams are pounded into the stakes, and then oaken planks are placed over the beams. Sand is spread over the boards and then stones to cover. Every piece of wood, from the stake to the beam to the plank to the pegs securing them, is cooked first. They use a mixture of oil and pitch so that the wood can last centuries under water. A road that never stops, no matter what obstacle it finds on its way. A forest, a lake, a swamp, even a mountain.'

A Roman road!

'How do you know all these things?' asked Wulf.

'I just do, that's all.' Armin cut him short. 'We have to go back home now. Father will have our hides for disobeying.'

'We'll never get back home before sunset,' said Wulf.

'I'm not so sure. We're good runners and there's plenty of reason to be home in time.'

'Wait,' said Wulf. 'Hear that?'

Armin stopped in his tracks, then scowled, peering hard in the direction the rhythmic sound was coming from.

'It's a Roman legion. On the march. Down, get down!'

Wulf dropped to his stomach. 'What are they doing here?'

'Shhh! Don't make any noise and do as I do.'

Armin covered himself with leaves, making himself invisible in the underbrush and Wulf, obedient, did the same. The cadenced beat of nailed boots drew closer until it was next to the two brothers. Under the leaves, Armin felt for Wulf's trembling hand and squeezed it hard. The trembling stopped and the pounding began to fade until it disappeared into the distance.

Armin lifted his head, but the sight of two Roman nailed boots at an arm's length from his face made him jump with shock.

'Well, look who I've found!' exclaimed a hoarse voice in Latin. A switch flicked through the dry leaves.

Armin jumped to his feet, shouting, 'Go, run!' The two boys took off in headlong flight without a second look. They alone knew every corner of the forest, every nook and cranny, every light and every shadow, and would reach a safe haven in no time.

Centurion Marcus Caelius Taurus did not go to the bother of shouting or cursing. He simply made a gesture with his hand and five horsemen – three Romans and two Germanics – set off at a gallop, managing to swiftly block the boys' flight and cut off any route of escape. All five slipped to the ground at once and surrounded the two brothers who stood tall, back to back, and pulled out the daggers they wore at their belts, pommels pressed to their chests.

'Those two,' hissed Wulf, nodding towards the Germanic soldiers. 'They're like us. Why are they trying to get us?'

The two brothers wheeled slowly, facing towards their enemies. 'Traitors,' Armin replied. 'They've sold themselves to the Romans and fight by their side.'

Their attackers pounced from every direction but the two boys defended themselves ferociously: they struck out with their blades, kicked, punched, bit. Five robust men struggled to best the two barely adolescent boys. In the end they pinned them to the ground, tied their arms behind their backs and dragged them off on two ropes tied to the horses.

The patrol chief approached the centurion. 'They're like wild animals, those two. It took all five of us to overpower them.'

'Do you know who they are?' asked the centurion.

One of the Germanic soldiers nodded. 'They're the sons of Sigmer, the chief of the Cherusci.'

'Are you sure?'

'Without a doubt.'

'Fine catch. You'll be rewarded. Don't let them escape or it's me you'll have to answer to. At least until tomorrow.'

Armin and Wulf were put inside a tent surrounded by armed guards. Two mattresses had been rolled out onto the ground. A slave brought them roasted meat with bread, a jug of beer and two glasses, as well as an oil lamp to light after dark.

'They're treating us well,' said Wulf.

'That's a bad sign,' replied Armin. 'It means they know who we are.'

'What do you mean?'

'They can't treat all their prisoners this way. If they're being nice to us, it means they're going to try to get something from our father.'

'What could they want from him?'

'Rome wants one thing: submission. They call it alliance but both sides know that's not what it is. Allies know they can never trust one another, and so the stronger one – Rome, that is – demands some kind of guarantee.'

'What guarantee?'

'We're it. You and me. Hostages.'

'Our tribal chieftains do the same.'

'They do. But it's completely different. An exchange of hostages doesn't imply submission; it ensures peace between the two tribes. Now naturally, the Romans won't use the word "hostages"; they'll talk about education, training for military command, studying, learning Latin and maybe even Greek. In truth, though, hostages are what we will be. May be.'

Wulf dropped his head and for a while there was total

silence in their little tent. The wind outside carried the voices of the sentries as the new shift came on duty.

'Help us, powerful gods,' he whispered.

SIGMER, SUPREME CHIEF of the Cherusci, had spent a sleepless night. When his boys hadn't come home by sunset he sent squads of scouts riding out on horseback, carrying torches to comb every path of plain, hill and swamp, without finding any sign of them. The search continued the next day, fresh squads replacing those who returned exhausted. Finally, one of the men arrived at Sigmer's house at a gallop. He sprang to the ground and was brought immediately into the chieftain's presence.

'It was the Romans,' he said in a single breath.

Sigmer did not rage or curse. 'How do you know?' he asked.

'One of their auxiliaries, he told me himself. He was born in my village. It was the boys' curiosity that got the better of them. They made their way to the road that crosses the swamp and were surprised by a Roman cavalry patrol that was reconnoitring the service roads where supplies are brought in for the roadworks. They were unlucky. It was the old fox Centurion Marcus Caelius Taurus of the Eighteenth Legion *Augusta* who found them.

'I know for certain they're being treated well, but they're guarded day and night; it's impossible to get close. A raid would be a mistake for now, too dangerous for the boys. It seems, however, that Centurion Taurus will ask you to receive him so he can relay a message from Terentius Niger, the legion's legate.'

'Yes,' replied Sigmer. 'I'm prepared to do anything but I want proof first that my sons are alive.'

'You will get it,' assured the scout. 'And very soon. But now you should get some rest.'

Rest . . . how could he do that? His boys, the light of his eyes, were in Roman hands and no one could say what destiny might await them. Would they be taken away? One of them? Both? Would Rome accept a ransom? But what could he offer? Flocks and herds? Horses? Sigmer felt impotent, shattered. The Cherusci were the most powerful of all the Germanic tribes and the most numerous but they could never challenge the Empire of Rome. It was said that it extended from one end of the world to the other, from the southern sea to the ocean . . .

He'd challenged the Empire, once. He'd tried to kill one of their commanders, young Drusus, who at the age of twenty-four had been conducting a fleet of one hundred battleships down the Rhine. Sigmer remembered the canal that Rome had dug to make that possible, eighty leagues long, stretching from the bend in the Rhine to the northern lagoon. Rome reigned over seventy million people and there was nothing it could not do: Romans brought land where there was water and water where there was land. Now Rome had his sons.

CENTURION TAURUS ARRIVED two days later, escorted by a squad of cavalrymen and a Germanic interpreter. He asked to be admitted to the presence of the sovereign of the Cherusci. Sigmer received him seated on a wooden throne adorned with gold, surrounded by his most imposing warriors wearing their finest armour. All of them wore their hair loose to the shoulder, blond as gold. Sigmer's younger brother Ingmar was also present.

'What is the reason for your coming?' asked the sovereign.

'I must arrange for a meeting between you and the legate of our legion, Terentius Niger. It will take place on neutral ground, at the clearing of the four oaks. Each of you will be escorted by a maximum of thirty men. You and the legate will be unarmed.'

'Will my sons be present?'

'Certainly. You must understand that they are being treated with all of the respect due their rank. What shall I tell the legate?'

'That I accept,' replied Sigmer in a low voice.

Taurus mounted his horse and rode off with his escort.

Sigmer lowered his head with a sigh.

THE ENCOUNTER TOOK place as arranged two days later at mid-afternoon, at the clearing which took its name from four colossal trees that were probably centuries old. Sigmer was shaken at the sight of the hemp ropes binding the wrists of his two young sons to prevent their escape. The interpreter was ready, on his feet.

'Is this how you treat my sons?' Sigmer exclaimed. Ingmar laid a hand on his brother's shoulder in warning.

The legate advanced to the centre of the clearing, on his horse, and Sigmer did the same.

The legate replied, 'I'm sincerely sorry, but your princes mean too much to us. We cannot afford to untie them, under these circumstances.'

'I am willing to pay any price to have them back,' said Sigmer. 'I will give you everything I own.'

'I understand you, noble Sigmer. I would do the same in your place but I have no authority to negotiate a ransom. Caesar is very interested in meeting these young men and he wants them to experience Rome in all its greatness. He wants to meet them in person, you see. Rome needs a new generation of soldiers who will learn our ways and who can defend our world, and a new generation of commanders and also magistrates who can govern Roman Germania, when the moment arises.

'They will be returned to you at some point, and you will be proud of them. You will see what a great advantage it is for you to respect the terms of our alliance. Your sons will not be hostages, but guests. You can believe me, Sigmer.'

Not much remained to be said. It was clearly evident that, even if this man called Caesar had his plans for Wulf and Armin, the boys were hostages and if their father challenged the terms of his alliance with Rome in any way they would suffer the consequences. Sigmer had no alternative but to accept the conditions and renew his promise of loyalty.

The meeting was over.

'May I say goodbye to them?' Sigmer asked the legate of the Eighteenth *Augusta*.

Terentius Niger nodded. 'Certainly.'

Sigmer walked slowly towards his boys, who waited without moving, without displaying any emotion. His own face did not show any signs of turmoil, although his blue gaze went dark like a stormy sky.

He stood in front of his sons, so close he could touch them. A shock seemed to run through his soul. Then he suddenly lifted his hand and slapped them violently, one after another. It was like slapping two trees. Neither one moved, nor changed expression, nor reacted in any way.

'Now you know why, when I give you an order, you must obey.'

The boys' heads dropped before him. Sigmer touched the head of Armin, and then Wulf. 'Farewell, my sons,' he said. 'Never forget who you are and who your father is.'

He stood still, never taking his eyes off them, until they disappeared over the hill.

Only in the deep of night, in the most complete solitude, did he weep.

2

SIGMER AND INGMAR turned north without ever looking back, without ever calling the boys by name. They were lost. Gone.

They advanced in silence, the only sound coming from their horses' snorting. They had nothing to say; there was no course of action to be discussed. They knew what they needed to know. Back at home they would take up their work, face their difficulties, nurse their troubles and their hidden wounds.

The few times their eyes met they were inexpressive and cold. There were no messages, nor feelings, to communicate. Their forebears and now their people were accustomed to dealing with death and with life's hardships, used to revealing nothing of what they felt inside. No laughter or tears. Because, every day and every night, they knew they had to survive the cold and the heat, the insects and wild animals, the pounding rains, the mud, the damp, the snow and the chill that sank into their bones.

Sigmer did not relish the power he wielded. It was more of a burden to him, sometimes a curse. Women had filled up his life for a long time, but that changed when he married Siglinde, daughter of a Sicambri chieftain. With light blonde hair, and eyes the colour of the sky, Siglinde was like a forest spirit, delicate and ethereal. She was also very sensitive and did not always succeed well at hiding her most secret emotions.

He loved her, in his own way, as one could love a bride in a marriage arranged for reasons of state. But she had given him two sons and now he was returning home with neither. Siglinde surely knew that children belong to their mothers only as long as they are small and helpless, like puppies. When they reach the threshold of adolescence and learn to reason and to speak for themselves, they are passed on to the father. It is he who decides their destiny, he who prepares them to live, and also to die.

Of the two boys, it was more often Armin who sought his mother out; he was more like her and they shared the same disposition and sensitivity. He never missed saying good morning to her. He would bring her pretty blossoms at the beginning of spring and one day in May he brought her a gift: a little cage made with reeds that held a nightingale he had taken from its nest and raised. Its song was as intense and poignant as that of a poet but that was an illusion: in reality, it was an air of defiance. Sigmer knew she would miss Armin terribly.

He knew that she would not react with screaming or crying. But her long silences cut as deeply as a blade.

He thought he would have been more suited to a passionate, ardent, sensual woman. There was one, in particular, who had penetrated his heart like an enemy's sword.

It had been many years before. It was the night that Sigmer had dived into the Rhine from the eastern bank and attempted to swim across the great river. His aim was to reach the flagship of the Roman fleet, with General Drusus aboard, and kill him, to win the war with a single stroke.

A fish had stopped him. It was a gigantic sheatfish, scraping up hard enough against his skin to make him bleed. He knew he was lost. Those repugnant creatures would be shortly coming at him from every direction, attracted by the odour of his blood, and they would devour him, ripping him to shreds.

The chill of death sank into his bones and he realized that, as close as he was to the flagship, he would never board it, never reach the Roman side of the river. But just as his nostrils were filling with the stink of more of those huge muddy beasts, an arrow tore through the air dense with fog and sank into the monster's body. Sigmer himself was pulled aboard the huge, gleaming battleship that smelled of pine and oak and tied to the mast, the trunk of an enormous larch tree.

Whoever had let the arrow fly hadn't killed the sheatfish to save Sigmer's life but to open the way for a boat that was making its way by dint of its oars to the flagship. It bore a litter that was covered and shrouded, and pulled up alongside the larger vessel. The litter was hoisted onto the deck at the bow. From it emerged the most beautiful woman that Sigmer would ever see in his life, more captivating than any dream or imagining, more desirable than Freya, the goddess of love. She was Antonia, the young wife of General Drusus.

He would learn that they had been married for a couple of years and that they loved each other so intensely that they couldn't live apart for longer than the briefest of periods. All Drusus needed to do was send word and she would leave the comforts of her villa, face hardships and danger to be with him wherever he was.

Her head was veiled when she stepped away from the litter but her body swayed under a light gown, blown by the evening breeze. Sigmer breathed in her scent when she passed; he'd never experienced anything like it. No forest flower, no springtime zephyr was so magical, so pure. The women he'd known mostly smelled of the stables. The light fragrance of girlhood lingered with them for too short a season.

Over the years he had often tried to understand what was in the scent that wafted in the air as that sublime creature went to meet her beloved spouse. Perhaps the fragrance of remote valleys, of salty shores, of honey and of lilies.

One night he saw them, or rather their shadows, cast by the lamp light onto the fabric of their tent at the stern. Bodies clinging to one another in a delirium of love, mouths breathing into one another, lips burning. Sigmer felt hopelessly unhappy. He realized that, although he was a prince, the difference between their life and his own was so great that it could never be bridged. Sigmer dreamed of Antonia at times, dreamed that he could win her for himself as a spoil of war. The dream only made him feel bitter when he shook himself awake at dawn. He couldn't begin to express the emptiness she had aroused in him; he didn't even have the words.

The Romans had rivers of words. The commander and his wife even had a poet on-board for the sole task of delighting them with his song. He was something like the bards of the Germanic peoples but his voice was lighter, while the stories that inspired him were more intense. He sang of emotion and the musicality of his words was fascinating. In just a few months, Sigmer began to understand the sounds of that language as the meaning of its words opened up to him, never to be forgotten.

During his long stay on the flagship, he had to remind himself that it was he who'd swum across the gelid current of the Rhine with the intention of driving his dagger into Drusus's heart and thus instantly winning the war for his people. Over the months, he began to feel something very different, something closely akin to friendship for the youth who was exactly the same age. He admired Drusus's intelligence, his courage, and his ability to make thousands of men obey a single word from his mouth. His men thought of him as something close to a god.

Time and time again, Sigmer had thought of escaping, but he never went ahead with it for one reason: because he knew he'd be robbed of the sight of Antonia. In the end he managed to break the spell and win back his freedom, so he could continue to fight for his people against the Romans and against General Drusus. And yet, in great secret, the two young men continued to meet up from time to time. They sat facing one another and talked. Actually, Sigmer would ask question after question and Drusus would talk about his world. His house in the countryside with a garden full of silver-fronded trees, his hunting dogs, a little lake where he could take his bride for a row under the summer moon.

Even now, Sigmer still thought about those moments, of his secret talks with the commander of Rome's Army of the North, of the sensation that they were peers thanks to the intimacy of their friendship and that he, too, was one of the most important men in the world.

Now many things had changed and yet, when he felt sad or tired or incapable of making a decision, he went back to mulling over the days of his youth.

He recalled the first time he realized that despite the enormous distance which separated Rome from his own nation, he was still a prisoner. The Roman fleet of the Rhine had sailed down the canal, which Drusus had built to join the bend of the great river with the northern lagoon. It was then that Sigmer realized that he knew things that the Roman general was completely unaware of, or that Drusus had never seen and may have only read about in books. Foremost among these was the great tide. One night the water withdrew by two hundred leagues or more, and all of the Roman ships ran aground in the mud. The Germanic army, who had been waiting in the coastal forests for such an opportunity, were ready to launch the attack and destroy them all at once with their flaming arrows.

How could it be that Drusus did not seem worried? How could he not realize the huge danger he was in? He remained calm even as thousands of Germanic warriors began to leave the cover of the forest, brandishing bows dancing with flames.

Yet Drusus was right to be calm for three reasons. The first was soon evident: a troop of Frisii horsemen raising lit torches in their left hands and steel swords in their right. It was with them that Drusus had entered into an alliance before he had set off with the fleet – a people who inhabited those lands and who now patrolled the coasts. They would be the bulwark between the ships beached like dying whales and the Germanic army lying in wait in the woods. From the bow of the flagship, Sigmer saw a snake of fire quickly spread across the beach from west to east.

But the Germanic warriors instantly understood what was happening and they reacted, taking off at a gallop on their swift horses to take control of the beach in front of the Roman ships before the Frisii could manage to occupy it and cut off their attack.

The second reason was that in the bilge of every ship was a machine run by four men which was designed to suck in water and shoot it back out through a fabric hose, in any direction. When the first incendiary arrows plunged into the resined wood, the crew turned their hoses towards the flames and put them out immediately. Sigmer had seen nothing like it his whole life.

He understood the third reason when an artillery crew on the flagship, at a sign from General Drusus, removed the oil-cloth covers from six big machines positioned at the bow, three on the left and three on the right. The men fed heavy iron bolts into the grooves, tightened the steel bands that primed the bows, took aim through the sights and fired them off one after another, at the centurion's orders:

'*Prima, iacta! Secunda, iacta! Tertia, iacta!* . . .'

The bolts taking off with such deadly precision were like the one that had saved his life when the sheatfish in the Rhine was about to devour him. Where they landed they ripped through flesh, tore through trees, took off the heads of men and horses. From the ground, the Romans were invisible, unlike the Germanic warriors who could be seen clearly from the ship, riding white horses, holding torches and firing fiery arrows from bows. In no time, terrified, they were forced to retreat into the forest.

The Frisii rode back and forth on the beach all night, torches held high to illuminate the banks. When the tide began to come in, the ships were set afloat as if nothing had ever happened and resumed their navigation towards the mouth of the Elbe, the river which would mark the new border of the Roman Empire.

Once Sigmer actually asked Drusus why he would face such great danger, risk getting killed himself by spending nights out in the open, fighting on the front line and chancing wounds and disease, when he could have stayed in his own palace in the great marble city, or in his country house alongside his bride.

Drusus had answered him: 'To serve the State.'

'And just what is the State?' asked Sigmer again.

'The State is everything for us. It encompasses our lives, our family and our people. If I fight on the banks of the Rhine, I'm defending my wife who lives in Rome, and my children, even if you have done nothing to harm me. Because if I don't do it now, one day your horses' hooves will trample the ashes of our marble city. One of our greatest poets has said so.

'Serving the State is the greatest honour for us. Giving our life for the State is the most glorious fate. The emperor represents the State and every nod from him is law for us.'

Sigmer remembered the conversation very well and he remembered that it was clear for him then why their relationship had continued for so many years: because that strange friendship overcame their differences of origin, tradition, language and blood.

Drusus continued to fascinate him with the stories he told of his country. The miracle of how a village of huts – which were very similar to the ones the Germanics still lived in – had become the centre of almost the whole known world. The Empire of Rome contained two seas and was bordered by the two greatest rivers in the world, along with a third river, in the south, tens of thousands of leagues long and populated by monsters, that ran powerfully enough to fill the southern sea. And yet in that land it neither rained nor snowed; almost all of the territory was covered with burning sand and no one knew where all the water came from. This was the greatest mystery of that enigmatic land, whose inhabitants considered their river a god.

Drusus himself had been given the task of moving the border of the Empire eastwards, past the Rhine, into the beyond, to the Elbe. It was the emperor who demanded it, the most powerful man in the world, the man whose wish was law.

'Why?' Sigmer had asked Drusus.

'Because you Germanics are the only people remaining on the face of the earth who are worthy of being part of the Empire. First you will be our friends and our allies, and then you will become like us. You will live like us, fight in our army; you'll become notables, commanders, magistrates. You will raise great cities, and with us you will build the roads that never end. The world cannot be Roman forever if you are not a part of it.'

'But what if we don't want to?' asked Sigmer.

Drusus stared at him with an almost incredulous expression, and then continued coldly: 'Then it would be a battle to the last blood, as it was between us and the Celts two centuries ago. Every spring two consuls and four legions made their way up the valley of the Po River and took on the tribes of the Boii and the Senones. The Celts even look a lot like you do: blond with blue eyes, big builds. We crushed them, exterminated them. In the end they were on their knees, begging for mercy. We chased the survivors over the Alps, all the way back to their ancestral lands.

'Is this what you want for your people, Sigmer? Be careful what you wish for. We were living in huts like yours eight centuries ago. But it could take you almost as long before you become like us, and maybe even then it won't be enough.

'If, instead, you join us, the wars will end, for centuries perhaps. Or, who can say . . . forever maybe.

'We'll cultivate art and law together. We'll practise agriculture. The roads that never end will reach every village, even the most remote. We'll build ships capable of navigating the ocean. The armies will serve only to protect the borders of our immense State and tend to order within. The *Urbs* – the city – will be the State and the State will be the world. And the world will be blond and dark. Can you understand, Sigmer? Do you understand me?'

General Drusus's voice had started low, but rose as he was speaking, until it sounded as if he were reciting poetry.

'If only you could see Rome, you would understand.'

Sigmer didn't ask further questions. He was disturbed and yet fascinated by Drusus's words and he decided for the time being to support his friend's vision. This resulted in many advantages for his people and his family, and his closeness to power gained him a newfound respect from other chieftains who had been hostile to him in the past.

Their meetings continued, deep in the forest of the bison. One day Drusus confided he'd had a dream that had shaken him badly. He couldn't get it off his mind. He had heard that there was an oracle, the Germanic oracle, who was reputed to speak the truth. He asked Sigmer to help him consult it.

What the Romans called the 'Germanic oracle' was said to be found in a cave in the Black Forest where no one was allowed to enter. Sigmer agreed to go with him and also to teach Drusus the words in the ancient Germanic language that had the power of rousing the oracle and calling it out through the portal to the underworld.

Sigmer stood back as Drusus approached an opening covered with moss and decaying tree trunks, scattered all around with human bones. There the Roman stopped and shouted out the ancestral formula three times. They waited.

The silence was broken by the sound of heavy footsteps, trampling putrid leaves and rotting branches.

'Immortal gods,' whispered Drusus. 'It's a giant.'

'We can still go,' said Sigmer softly.

'No,' replied Drusus. 'I haven't come this far to leave now.'

A creature wearing a long robe of goat pelts emerged, its bulk filling the mouth of the cave. When it saw them it let out a deep groan first and then a shrill scream, as strident as the cry of a falcon. It was a woman! She was gigantic and she wielded a battleaxe that made a dull rumble as she whirled it in front of her.

'You have to fight her,' said Sigmer. 'If you win, she will pronounce a prophecy. If you lose, she'll kill you. The bones you see all around are from those who sought to interrogate the oracle and were defeated.'

General Drusus unsheathed his sword. It was a weapon he'd had forged for himself which was longer than any gladius – to compensate for the greater reach of the large northern warriors. He scrutinized the axe and saw that it was cast from rough, impure metal. Its only strength was in its weight. He could win.

It was she who struck first. Drusus dodged the blow, and the axe pounded into a stone and exploded into a thousand incandescent shards.

Drusus crept up on the oracle, threatening her with the sharp tip of his sword, but she threw off her black mantle and hurled it at him to ensnare his weapon. The arms she uncovered were covered with coarse dark hairs. The Roman's blade flashed bright and sliced the foul mantle in two. She let loose with what was left of her axe but he leapt out of its path and then, as he was landing on his feet, twisted back and with a mighty blow chopped the axe's handle in half. He spun around and stood tall, sword in hand, facing the horrible virago.

Perhaps for the first time ever, she felt threatened and the feral look on her face resembled fear. She held out her hands and moved them downwards as if miming a surrender of her weapon to the ground. Her fear became panic. Drusus gripped the haft of his sword ever tighter and advanced imperceptibly.

She suddenly spoke out in a deep, raucous voice, in Latin, 'How far do you want to get, Drusus? To the ends of the earth?'

Sigmer was astonished, but Drusus, without any show of emotion, answered, 'To the current of the Elbe, to mark the furthermost confines of the Empire.'

Sigmer couldn't understand his every word, but he did understand the sense of what Drusus was saying.

Night was falling and the air had become cold but the face of the Germanic oracle dripped with sweat. Only three words left her mouth, deep and low: 'You'll die first.'

THE TWO MEN'S lives took separate paths after this, and their armies began once again to clash, but before long Sigmer realized the cost of war with Rome was too high. The sentence of the Germanic oracle continued to ring in his ears. Secretly, in his heart, he refused to believe it. He couldn't stand the thought that Drusus was condemned to an early death. They stipulated a truce and a pact of mutual non-aggression. As the centre of Germania, the territory of the Cherusci, became more peaceful, Drusus moved north, until one day when, after a skirmish, he fell off his horse and hurt himself badly.

Since he'd suffered no visible wounds, he neglected the consequences of his fall, which was so serious that it had, in fact, shattered his thigh bone. He was so convinced that final victory was near that he was unwilling to curtail his activity for any reason in the world, much less some ill-considered recommendation from his doctors.

3

FOR DAYS THE COLUMN of Roman horsemen and Germanic auxiliaries crossed the forests and swamps that Sigmer's sons were well familiar with. Armin and Wulf proceeded on horseback as well, at the centre of the squad escorting them. Their father had sent them garments and footwear before their departure so their appearance would befit their rank of princes of the Cherusci people. And so that they would stay warm on the snow-covered plains beaten by frigid winds. The only thing they were not allowed was their weapons. Their minders had already been introduced to the boys' expertise in their use.

At every setting of the sun, the Roman soldiers and the Germanic auxiliaries pitched their tents and Centurion Taurus instructed the scouts to reconnoitre the territory in every direction to identify possible threats or dangers.

He always preferred to position the camp on elevated terrain which allowed a good view of the surrounding areas, and he would send out mixed groups of Roman and Germanic horsemen, mostly Hermunduri, Chatti and Cherusci. The latter were easily recognized by the boys.

Wulf turned to his brother one day. 'How can Taurus trust these men who speak our language? They could easily free us if they wanted to. They could take us back to our father, who would pay them a rich reward.'

'I wouldn't be too sure about that,' replied Armin. 'If it were so easy, they would have already done it.'

'What do you mean?'

'Taurus speaks our language well enough, and he understands the others who live on these lands. He knows exactly where we are every time we stop. Have you ever noticed that thing he wears around his waist in that little leather case?'

'Yes, it looks like a little roll of leather. He unrolls it and then does it back up again after he's done looking at it.'

'That's right. That little roll is called a *tabula*.'

'What does that mean?'

'It's Latin, and it means a drawing of the earth with all its mountains, rivers, lakes and the distances between them. When Taurus moves anywhere on our territory he even knows where the legions are garrisoned and where the cavalry units are and he knows how far away that is. He can measure time, what hour of the day it is, with great precision. He can send off light signals using a polished metal plate. Our Germanic auxiliaries must know there's no way they could get away with it.'

'So we're not going to do anything to try to get free?' asked Wulf.

'I didn't say that. Our freedom is what's most precious to us and I wouldn't want to lose it for anything in the world, but we have to wait for the right time.'

Wulf said nothing. If Armin, who was the wilder of the two, suggested waiting, that was good reason for him to be careful. He didn't even have a plan for running away.

On the fifth day of their march, they arrived at the foot of towering, snow-covered mountains. Taurus said that it was there that the Rhine and the Danube, the two greatest rivers of the world, had their sources. The Rhine then went north towards the ocean, while the Danube turned east to fill a closed sea called the Pontus. They had been travelling on one of the roads that never end and they stopped for the night in a place where there was a stone house, a well for drawing water and a stable for the horses and mules.

'What is this place?' Wulf asked one of the Germanic auxiliaries. The Hermunduri warrior said nothing.

Taurus broke in: 'The Germanic auxiliaries are not authorized to speak to you. This is a *mansio*, a changing station. There's a tavern that serves hot food, with beer for the barbarians and decent wine for us. There are bedrooms, a bathroom with hot water you can pay to use, latrines with running water and soldiers on guard. There is one of these every twenty miles on all of our roads.'

The two boys exchanged an amazed look. They'd never seen or heard of such a place in all the territory of the Cherusci, and these people had one every twenty miles.

Smoke was coming out of the chimney, and they could smell meat roasting. There were a number of slaves, both men and women, who were busily lighting lamps, fetching firewood, baking bread and carrying big wine jugs up from an underground room.

A full moon was rising, and the snow-covered mountains stood out like ghosts against the deep blue sky that glowed turquoise around the silvery moon. Very few constellations could withstand the bright light but those that did seemed like coins hung by a goddess in the firmament. The mountain spurs gave way to barren cliffs, pillars rising in the night.

'Great Thor . . .' said Wulf in a whisper. 'I've never seen anything like this.'

'What are you thinking about?' asked Armin.

'I'm thinking that . . . I think that if we'd remained in our village, we never would have seen the road that never ends, or the mountains of ice, or the way the moon makes them shine like silver.'

'We have the moon that shines in our rivers and that mirrors itself in our lakes . . . Wulf, are you forgetting our own land?'

'I'm trying to suffer a little less. What's wrong with that?'

'You're resigning yourself to your prison? A warrior learns to suffer without complaining or cursing fate. He grits his teeth and swallows his tears.'

'We didn't even say goodbye to Mother.'

'It was better that way. She would have cried.'

Taurus walked up, flicking his switch against the palm of his hand. 'What do you two have to talk about?'

'I didn't know it was forbidden,' replied Wulf. 'Where we come from brothers talk to one another. Sometimes they hit each other or bite each other's ears. Now we're talking. Later we'll see.'

'Don't get smart with me, unless you want a taste of this. Go inside now, it's time for dinner. Then off to sleep. Tomorrow we'll be leaving before dawn.'

They walked in towards the tavern. The northern wind had carried the stink of the stables and mouldy hay into the courtyard, but all they needed to do was turn back towards the gate and everything changed: the fragrance of the mountain and its flowers blended in a harmony that made them remember the lands they came from. Besides that, the aroma of meat roasting on dwarf pine branches and of freshly baked bread reminded them that they were famished adolescents.

'Do you even like that stuff?' Armin asked his brother.

'The bread? It's fantastic,' replied Wulf. 'I would eat it every day. I never get tired of it because it tastes good with everything. If we could find the seeds, I'd plant wheat, but I'll bet you the weather where we come from is too damp and too rainy for it to grow.'

Armin abruptly changed the subject. He pointed at one of a group of cliffs that towered at the lower part of the mountain, before the snow-capped peaks. 'Wulf, look. There's a path up there. There, where the spire that looks like a bull's horn is. It's a hidden path. You know how good my eyesight is.'

Wulf shook his head. 'I don't want to hear about it. Armin, you said we had to wait.'

'We've waited long enough. Taurus and the auxiliaries won't be able to use the horses; they are too bulky and heavy to chase us up that way. The mules are still all loaded up so they can't use them either. All we need is a little food in our knapsacks and some warm clothes. When they get tired of looking for us, we'll make our way down the other side and we'll be back home before long.'

'Right, and Father would send us back with a beating. You know he can't afford to go to war with Rome.'

'He wouldn't turn us away.'

'If you're so sure he won't, then go. I'm not.'

'When we were little we swore we would never separate.'

'We aren't children any more.'

'All right. I'll go on my own.'

'Can we at least have dinner together?' asked Wulf with a wry smile.

Armin smiled too. 'A promise is a promise, isn't it?'

They walked into the tavern where Centurion Taurus was already sitting with the chief of the Germanic auxiliaries, a giant over six feet tall with a bushy blond moustache. Armed with a long sword, he slapped it down on the table with the evident intention of making Armin and Wulf, who'd sat down opposite him, jump. Neither boy flinched in the least. Armin looked straight into his eyes with a defiant expression.

'What nice-looking boys!' sneered the warrior. 'On your way to see the world?'

'We're not allowed to speak with the servants,' said Armin. This time Wulf jumped. The giant got to his feet, grabbed the hilt of his huge sword in both hands and raised it as if he would use it to cut Armin in two. Taurus barked out an order in Latin, but the sword was already descending. The blade stopped at a finger's span from the boy's head but Armin neither blinked nor took his eyes off the warrior's.

Taurus stood in front of the giant, the veins on his neck bulging.

'He offended me!' bellowed the Germanic chief.

'He's a child,' replied the centurion. 'Take it out on someone your own size, if you're looking for a fight.'

'I said it,' said Armin. 'He's a servant.'

The giant, who had been turning to walk out of the room, wheeled around brandishing the sword in his hands again. A heavy blow landed between the two boys, cleaving the solid fir-tree table in two. The food-filled plates, the cups of wine and the jugs of beer crashed to the floor in a huge mess.

In the confusion no one was watching Armin. When the situation finally calmed down he was already in his bedroom, along with Wulf.

They stretched out next to one another on the two beds and remained there listening to the noises coming from the ground floor and from the woods surrounding the *mansio*.

After a short while, Wulf's heavy breathing made it clear that he was sleeping deeply.

Armin shook him. 'You're not going to fall asleep on me, are you?'

'Brother, I told you that your plan of escape does not interest me. It's stupid and foolhardy. You should sleep too. Tomorrow they'll be getting us up early and we'll have another long march ahead of us.'

'Wait,' replied Armin. 'Look.' He took the lamp, raised the flame and laid something out on the floor: Taurus's *tabula*. 'I took advantage of the yelling and confusion to slip it away from him.'

Wulf nodded. 'So you started the fight with that yellow-moustached boar?'

'Something like that. But look what it got us! We won't get lost with this, and if we leave right now, they'll never find us. The path we need to take is marked here, see? It's the thin red line that goes between the mountains. By the time they realize we're gone we'll be at the foot of the bull-shaped cliff. There's no snow up to that point so we won't leave footprints. The full moon and the reflection of the snow will help us to find our way easily. We'll stay hidden up there until the Romans and the Germanic auxiliaries get tired of chasing after us. Then we'll go down the other side of the horn and three days later we'll be home.'

'If it were really so easy, I'd be right behind you,' said Wulf. 'But these things only turn out well in fables.'

Armin sighed. 'You do what you want. I'll go alone.' He glanced over at the light. 'If you want, you can help me by creating a distraction. Look, right under the window there's a pile of straw for the mules and hay for the horses . . . count to fifteen after I'm gone and then drop the lamp. It'll get the guards' attention and I'll disappear in the other direction. Farewell, brother!'

'Goodbye,' said Wulf in a low voice.

Armin put on his heaviest clothing and boots and jumped

down onto the pile of hay, making sure the guards had just passed on their rounds. Wulf started counting and peeked out of the window. Armin had sprung to his feet and was running along the wall of the stable, until he disappeared around the corner.

'Seven . . . eight . . . nine,' counted Wulf and with every number he became more regretful that he hadn't jumped with his brother. He saw him reappear at the far end of the stables – 'ten . . . eleven . . . twelve' – and climb up the enclosure wall until he'd made it to the top. 'Thirteen . . . fourteen . . . fifteen . . .' Wulf tossed the lamp on the hay, which went up in a burst of flame. Armin flattened himself on the top of the wall so he wouldn't be seen. The glow of the fire spread and cries of alarm resounded all over the courtyard. The neighing and scuffling of the frightened horses and mules added to the atmosphere of confusion and fear.

Taurus, his legionaries and the Germanic auxiliaries were already at work. They swiftly formed a chain from the well, passing buckets full of water from hand to hand, from one end of the courtyard to the other all the way to the foundations of the *mansio*, where the fire was burning. The wind carried clouds of sparks towards the stable.

Wulf had dressed as well and shoved the leftover food he'd brought back to his room into a knapsack. He moved out into the corridor and ran quickly down its length. The pounding of nailed boots up the wooden staircase promised trouble so he opened a window and leapt out onto the boughs of a huge, ancient oak tree. He crouched for a while among the branches until the soldiers had moved on. He then carefully made his way down one of the big boughs that stretched towards the enclosure wall until he was close enough to make another leap onto the roof tiles covering it. He dropped off on the other side and set off running as fast as he could possibly go in the direction of the mountain, turning back now and again to catch a look at the *mansio*. What had looked like a blazing fire at first soon dimmed into a faintish red halo. He could almost hear the pounding gallop of the Germanic horsemen filling his ears and the jangling of the Roman cavalrymen's weapons as a furious Taurus led them in the chase.

'Armin! Armiiiiin!' he cried out, trying to make his voice heard over the hissing wind. All at once, he fell to the ground and tumbled almost all the way down to the edge of the rocky path.

His brother's voice sounded, angry and close. 'Idiot! Follow me.'

He got to his feet, sore all over. 'It was you! You tripped me!'

'It was the only way to stop you. Come, now!'

Wulf found his place at his brother's side, running.

'They're already after us, they're catching up,' he shouted, panting. 'Maybe I should have counted to thir—'

'Just keep running,' said Armin, interrupting him. 'Up there, look, the path cuts away from the road. The horses won't be able to keep up with us if we make it that far.'

'Do you think they've spotted us?'

'With this moon? You can be sure of it.'

The path that was cut into the rock of the Great Horn cliff shone white in the moonlight and the two boys ran uphill with every bit of energy they had. Armin couldn't stop himself from looking back to see how far their pursuers had got and what they were doing.

His heart was pounding so furiously in his chest that it felt like it skipped a beat entirely when he saw that a group of sharpshooters had climbed up the side of the cliff and were loading their slings. One was let loose with a dull whistle and a lead shot hit the rocky ground just by his foot.

'Careful!' yelled Armin to his brother, who wasn't aware of the danger and was still trying to catch up with him as quickly as he could, not bothering with cover. Just then another shot hit Wulf in the calf and sent him tumbling to the ground.

The pain was so acute that it skewed his perception of time and place and while he thought he could reach the base of the cliff, in reality he was crawling towards a precipice. A hail of sling shots kept Armin pinned down in a shelter he'd found at the side of the cliff, but he could see Wulf slipping further and further towards the gorge. He waited for the onslaught to lessen and he started crawling towards his brother who'd been hit again in the back and had completely lost all control of his movements. He grabbed him by the hand just an instant before he was about to plunge below.

A curt order sounded and the hail of stones stopped. Armin turned and saw Centurion Taurus standing wide-legged in front of him.

'Help me . . .' he managed to croak out.

'You are the one who dragged your brother into this. Now it's you who's responsible for his life.'

Armin realized that Taurus had no intention of lifting a finger. With every bit of his strength he sought to pull his brother to safety without letting the boy's weight drag both of them down together. He pulled, grinding his teeth and ignoring the cramps that were tormenting his muscles.

His heart felt like it would burst from his chest with the strain until he finally realized that Wulf's body was no longer falling. He gripped him tight and then collapsed breathlessly on top of him, as if to shield him. The world dissolved into darkness.

The bitter cold jerked him back into consciousness and he realized that he was half naked and bound to two iron pickets driven into a rock. Wulf was not in his line of sight.

Taurus's jeers echoed nearby. 'You look like Prometheus, chained to that rock in the Caucasus!' The centurion was rhythmically flicking a vine-shoot switch at the palm of his left hand, skin rough and calloused.

'You pay for your mistakes,' he said with a voice sharper and colder than the wind. The first lash fell on the boy's naked back, lacerating his flesh to the muscle. That was followed by a second and a third. Armin had often experienced his father's riding whip, but the vine shoot was much rougher, knottier and crueller. He gritted his teeth as he was used to doing and Centurion Taurus heard only a dull, stifled mewling.

ARMIN AWOKE IN his bed, the room barely lit by a smoking lamp, just enough light for him to take stock of his wounds.

Wulf lay on the other bed, unmoving.

Armin reached out a hand to his brother's neck to feel for the pulsing vein that reveals life. He found it, and the pain that seemed not to spare a finger or toe melted away with relief. Wulf's fingers uncurled and he showed Armin a lead bullet.

'What is this?' he grumbled from swollen lips.

'It's the ammunition shot by a sling,' replied Armin, with no less effort.

'But it says something . . .'

Armin took it and held it up to the light. 'It's Latin.'

'So what does it say?'

'Shove it up your arse.'

Wulf tried to laugh, but his chuckles were transformed instantly into a whimper of pain.

4

AT DAWN TAURUS ASSEMBLED his men and the two boys in the *mansio* courtyard. Armin and Wulf could barely stand on their feet; maintaining an upright position set off painful contractions and the rubbing of the coarse fabric of their clothing against their wounds was possibly more torturous than the whipping that had caused them.

Taurus took slow steps while reviewing his troops and stopped in front of the two boys. 'Now you know what Roman discipline is,' he said, speaking in the Germanic language. 'This iron rule, which everyone must obey without questioning, is the reason our armies, made up of small, dark-skinned men, crushed the giant blond Celts, the Cimbri and Teutons who are no less courageous or valorous in battle. Those who tried to resist were crushed. Caesar was responsible for one million deaths in Gaul and now that land is the most loyal and the most prosperous of our provinces; its young men are proud to enlist in our legions. The Teutons were butchered on the banks of the Rhone until its waters flowed red with blood. They had promised to reach Rome and fuck our women. Now their corpses fertilize the vineyards of Aquae Sextiae. The Cimbri suffered the same fate on the Raudine plain in Italy. They wanted fertile land. Now they have it. My *tabula*,' he said, stretching his arm out towards Armin, who handed it over without a hint of resistance.

'Hey, Blondie,' he continued, turning to Wulf, 'you and your rebel brother will walk. You'll shoulder your baggage. We'll use your horses to carry the supplies that we bought at the store.' His voice was as soft and level as if nothing had ever happened. Wulf realized that the name, 'Flavus', 'Blondie' in Latin, would now become his nickname.

'We'll get started on today's march now.'

Taurus took lead of the column, flanked by one of his legionaries. Wulf and Armin were at the centre with the Germanic auxiliaries and the other legionaries bringing up the tail. They started down the same road that they'd taken the day before when chasing the two boys, the one that ascended towards the pass. Wulf and Armin's baggage consisted of a travel sack that contained a blanket for the night, their clothing, some salted meat, bread and a wooden cup for water. Any and every move on their part ground the straps into their raw, aching shoulders and made them bleed.

As they continued upwards, the horses were at risk of losing their footing on the slabs which had become icy overnight. The weather looked more ominous still. Black storm clouds edged with whitish fringes advanced from the west. Sporadic flashes of lightning lit up the big dark masses from within.

Taurus ordered them to pick up the pace so they would not be surprised in the open by the storm. The legionaries pulled their cloaks tight over their shoulders but the wind that was gathering made them snap like sails in the tempest. An icy drizzle stiffened the moustaches and beards of the Germanic auxiliaries and weighed down the crest on Centurion Taurus's helmet.

To look at him, with his hair greying at the temples, you would say he was a man of about forty-five, but he showed extraordinary energy. His rank allowed him to carry neither baggage nor a shield, but he wore a complete suit of armour with a massive gladius slung over his shoulder and a dagger at his belt. His right hand unfailingly held the *vitis*, his switch, which reminded his men of his rank but also of the severity of his punishments.

After a few miles of ascent, the rain turned to snow, falling in big flakes into the rocky gorges. The horses and mules were slipping more and more, and they often fell to their knees amidst whinnies of pain. The attendants struggled to get them back up to their feet. By midday the snow was half a leg high and everyone's limbs were frozen to their bones.

The Germanic auxiliaries were inured to the climate and they advanced sure-footed, the snow sliding off the fur cloaks they wore so that little body heat was lost. Even though Wulf and Armin were of the same stock, they were struggling with the pain of their wounds and hadn't slept well the night before.

After a bend in the road, Taurus knelt to wipe off a milestone that marked the distance to the pass: *IV M.P. AD SALTVM.*

'Come on, men!' he shouted. 'Only four miles and we'll be at the pass. There's a fire waiting for us there, and a hot meal.'

His words gave the men a shot of energy and the whole convoy picked up speed. Just as it was getting dark they made out the dim light of a lamp casting a little yellow halo in the midst of the flurrying snow.

'There it is, the pass!' shouted Taurus, his arm held out stiffly as he pointed. 'Let's get moving!'

The station soon appeared. A low overhanging slate roof was bolstered on either side by walls made of bales of hay and straw for the animals. The main building was constructed of stone. There was a wood shed full of fir trunks as well as a storehouse and a guard post manned by twenty or so legionaries from the Twenty-first *Rapax*. Their commander was on loan from the Twelfth *Fulminata*.

Taurus went immediately to greet him and the two officers embraced, slapping each other on the shoulders, exchanging compliments and obscenities. They had fought together and survived under both Drusus and Tiberius. Meanwhile, the legionaries and auxiliaries had entered the stone building and were sitting at tables. In the centre of the room was a fireplace where three or four fir trunks full of resin were crackling and burning white hot. The entire room was filled with the fragrance. A spit with pieces of venison was being turned on the embers and big chunks of fresh bread were being toasted as well, the aroma redolent of pine and mountain herbs. The cook brought out a big pot of legumes, with chunks of mountain cheese and fried bread dough.

Armin and Wulf slowly took off their soaking clothes and lay them out to dry in front of the fire. One of the servants, an old Helvetian woman, noticed that the two boys' backs were covered with welts and cuts. She shook her head, grumbling, and led the two of them into a secluded corner of the room, where she melted an unguent in a copper pot over the fire and began to spread it over their wounds. They had to grit their teeth to stop from crying out.

'That burns so bad!' growled Armin.

'But maybe it's good for us,' replied Wulf. 'The old woman seems to know what she's doing.'

'It's the same stuff they use to grease the roast!'

'So what? If it's good for the roast, it'll be good for us too.'

After feeling more dead than alive that whole day, the warmth seeping into their limbs and the smell of roasting meat put them in a good mood.

The old woman, who had left the room, returned with

pieces of cloth cut from a hemp sheet and she bandaged them carefully.

'See?' said Wulf. 'The ointment keeps the bandages from sticking.'

The old woman gestured for them to wait. When she came back, it was with a big bowl full of meat, bread, cheese and legumes and she set it on the floor in front of them. She added a jug of freezing cold melted snow.

They ate and drank and they were so tired that in the end they curled up right there in front of the fire on their cloaks. They fell deeply asleep in a matter of moments.

Halfway through the night, Wulf felt someone shaking him hard. 'Wake up!'

He opened his eyes and recognized his brother's face reddened by the glow of the flames.

'What do you want? Let me sleep.'

'They're all drunk, Wulf, and they're sleeping like stones. Let's go. We know the way down. We'll be home in a couple of days.'

'What?'

'We're leaving.'

'No way.'

'Then I'll go alone.'

'There are dogs outside, can't you hear them? Two steps and they'll catch you. Do you think Taurus would have let us fall asleep without tying us up if it were so easy to get away?'

The innkeeper showed up in his nightgown to add a couple of logs to the fire which soon started crackling again. The big Hermundur who had almost split Armin's head in two with his sword turned onto his side and burped.

'See? People coming and going all night. Give it up. We'll try again in better times. I don't want to freeze to death.'

Armin seemed convinced. 'Maybe you're right, but we're not finished with this.'

'We can talk again when we're awake and it's not so cold.'

'If we cross these mountains, you know we'll never get back,' said Armin. 'Is that what you want?'

'No. I'm sure we will return once we've learned Latin and they've trained us in their fighting ways . . .'

'We don't need to learn their fighting ways.'

'Yes we do. That's exactly what we have to learn.'

Armin smiled. 'I'm beginning to understand your strategy.'

'Then go to sleep. We'll talk another time.'

The big hall was filled with sounds of the fire sizzling and the resin popping inside the fir logs and with the deep snoring of the Germanic auxiliaries. The floor and the walls were warm. From outside came the shriek of a nocturnal bird and the howling of distant wolves.

THE NEXT MORNING light rained into the room from the same hole in the ceiling that let out the fireplace smoke.

The boys checked each other's bandages. Sure enough, the old lady's ointment had done its work.

'The important thing is that we're starting to feel better,' said Armin. 'But we can't let ourselves fall in love with this foreign country they're taking us to. We must never forget our land and our people. If we do that, the gods won't recognize us when we die, and they won't let us into their world of light.'

Wulf nodded his head as if to say that he understood or that he would think about it.

The old servant woman brought them two cups of warm goat's milk and a piece of toasted bread. She was so ugly that surely no one had ever wanted to marry her or do anything else with her, but she had the instincts of a mother.

Taurus went to say goodbye to his fellow commander at the guard station and gave orders that everyone prepare for departure. Resuming their march, they descended the mountainside on a route that had been cut into the stone.

The clouds of the night-time blizzard began to clear and a ray of sunlight beamed from a scrap of blue sky, rendering the snow blinding. They soon arrived at a point where a landslide had damaged the road, and the passage was very narrow. The cavalrymen and the baggage handlers had to blindfold the horses and mules and lead them by the reins. Taurus went first himself, on foot, pulling his horse behind him. Before crossing the bottleneck he tested it with his foot to make sure it was solid enough to allow their passage. He held one hand on the rock wall to steady himself and with the other, his right, he held the horse's reins without wrapping them around his wrist. It was no more than four steps forward, but the others watched with great apprehension. A single stone came free of the slide and bounced off the rock wall below, setting off further slides of gravel each time it hit and picking up mass as it fell until it crashed and clattered down to the valley. The soldiers were terrified.

'It's nothing,' exclaimed Taurus. 'Just a few stones. Stay close to the wall.' He took several more steps and was safely on the other side.

'See? It's nothing. One at a time!' he shouted again. 'The legionaries first, because they're lighter.'

The legionaries went first without incident, and then it was the turn of the auxiliaries. The first was a Hermundur, leading his horse. The warrior made his way forward slowly. When he had nearly reached solid ground, he tested a crumbly patch in the road with the haft of his spear. Just at that moment, a rock ptarmigan suddenly left its perch and took flight, squawking and squalling. The horse startled and reared up with a loud whinny, lost its balance and plunged down into the scarp, dragging his horseman with him. The others watched as he was smashed against the rocks, leaving a long trail of blood behind him.

At that point no one was willing to cross the treacherous passage, despite the centurion's imprecations.

Wulf volunteered himself and his brother. 'We'll go, leading one horse apiece. We're lighter. The others will follow on foot. But there's one condition.'

'Condition?' repeated the centurion.

'That we'll be able to use the horses afterwards to hang our baggage. It's cutting into our shoulders.'

Taurus hesitated and then said, 'All right.'

'Are there any more birds?' asked Wulf.

'How should I know?' replied Taurus. 'Move. It'll be dark before long.'

Wulf crossed first, with a horse, and then Armin followed his lead.

'There you go,' said Wulf. 'We can keep them now, can't we?'

Taurus considered him with a scoff. 'While you're at it, take the mules across as well.'

'Can we keep them too?' asked Wulf.

'No.'

The boys nodded, but one look at the mules told them that they were too overburdened.

'The crumbly part won't bear up under all that weight,' said Armin to his brother.

Wulf nodded. 'We can't refuse now, but I have an idea.'

'You do?'

'The Hermunduri are as strong as bears. We'll have them carry the mules' loads. Then you and I can lead the animals across.'

'You're right. It's the only way.'

The Hermunduri agreed to divide the load among them and they succeeded in crossing the bottleneck, one after another. Then it was Wulf and Armin's turn, leading the mules by their ropes.

Taurus turned towards the men who had refused to comply earlier. 'These boys have shown you that they've got harder balls than you do; you should be ashamed of yourselves. You'll have no dinner tonight and sleep outdoors.'

Wulf whispered in his brother's ear, 'This is Roman discipline too, I guess.'

'Shut up,' growled Armin.

Taurus turned the horses over to them. The boys hung their bags and leapt onto the horses' backs.

They continued their descent for many days, without ever leaving the road that never ends. They crossed a valley flanked by high snow-topped peaks and travelled alongside a rapidly flowing torrent.

The countryside around them was continuously changing as the air became warmer, the vegetation more luxuriant. Along the river were small villages that were similar to the ones that Armin and Wulf knew in Germania, with big pens which held flocks of sheep and goats. Stockades contained herds of cows and gigantic white-hided bulls. The changing stations were bigger and offered more facilities.

One of them even had a thermal bath, which consisted of a series of rooms with tubs of hot, tepid and cold water, latrines with continuously running water and a furnace that heated the air inside hollow cavities that surrounded the tubs on every side and ran under them as well. The baths had separate entrances for the men and women who came to bathe, to be massaged and to swim. The walls were adorned with figures painted in vivid colours or made of bright little stones that, when placed alongside each other, formed patterns and scenes of great beauty.

There were also women that the brothers were not allowed to have anything to do with, although they'd already heard them spoken about in the stone city of the Romans on the Rhine. Centurion Taurus called them 'prostitutes' and he used their services. One need only pay the price listed on a wooden tablet hanging in the upstairs hall and they would give themselves to anyone. The price depended on several things: how beautiful they were and how skilled in the game of love, and also how clean their sheets were. Wulf would have liked to play with one of them called Iole and he tried to give her a gift of a little silver bracelet, but she only took Roman coins, and Armin kept all of those in a case on his belt.

They remained at the *mansio* for several days because Taurus was expecting a letter from a messenger who would be passing through on his way up to Germania. One evening Wulf met Iole on the stairs leading up to the thermal baths. He tried to start a conversation with the twenty or so Latin words he had learned. She smiled, and answered him in the language of the Chatti. 'Are you Taurus's prisoner?'

'Something like that. You?'

'I'm a slave of this place. I'm one of the people who work here.'

'But who is your master?'

'Caesar.'

'I thought he'd been killed off a long time ago!'

'Anyone who commands over the Empire is Caesar. But they have another name for it, *Res publica*. It means every person and every thing: slaves and free men, soldiers and their camps, priests and temples, the elders and the laws they make, judges and courts and then most of the land, the roads and those who build and repair them, the water even, and those who work to see that everyone gets their share. Even the sky above their land is called *Res publica*.'

Wulf looked at her admiringly and pretended to have understood. 'How do you know all these things?'

'Men like to talk after they fuck.'

'Don't say that word.'

She laughed. 'Fuck? That's all I do, day and night. Should I speak like a fair maiden who thinks she'll find a beloved who'll become her husband and then have children with him? That's never going to happen. The Romans took me away from my village, me and lots of girls like me, and they sold us at an auction. I was bought by a tax collector on behalf of Caesar. Or of the *Res publica*, if you prefer.'

Wulf took off the little silver bracelet. 'Take this, please. You don't owe me anything. I just want you to have it.'

'Why?'

'Because it makes me happy to give you something, something that will remind you of me. My name is Wulf but the Romans call me Flavus. It means "Blondie".'

'You really don't want to fuck?'

Wulf dropped his head, then lifted it and stared into her eyes, as green as the lake that mirrored the sky between the village and the woods at home.

'Don't say that word,' he repeated, and he touched her lips with his fingers.

'Blondie,' she said, giving him back the bracelet, 'pretend I took it. They search me every night. They'd take it off me instantly.'

She turned around and walked away.

5

THOUGHTS OF IOLE ACCOMPANIED Wulf for many days and his distracted expression was noticed by Armin, who never let his brother out of his sight. Similar thoughts were going through his mind too. One day, not too long ago, he had gone with his father to the land of the Chatti – a four-day journey south of his village. Many such encounters took place between Germanic chiefs and served to establish friendships or alliances or to consolidate those that already existed. On these occasions religious rites were celebrated, with dancing and singing. Bards entertained the guests at banquets with tales of their gods and heroes.

That time there was a procession to welcome the beginning of spring. Everyone came out for it: the most important families, the priests, the warriors wearing their proudest armour. The ceremony was celebrated in a rock sanctuary in the middle of a dense forest.

A group of young girls, the daughters of the noblemen of the Chatti nation, wearing long gowns embroidered in red and blue, danced and sang hymns to Freya, the goddess of love. Their hair was gathered into braids or worn loose over their shoulders and they wore crowns made of field flowers.

'The finest young men from the noblest stock,' Armin was telling his brother as they rode along, 'were all invited so they could see the girls and ask for their hands in marriage.'

'I wasn't invited,' grumbled Wulf.

'It wasn't your time yet . . . At the end of the ceremony, the girls assembled at the entrance to a cavern and they all closed their eyes. At that moment – this is what Father told me – Freya would appear to one of the girls, from behind her closed eyelids, and would give her the gift of second sight. The chosen girl would have to keep the goddess's gift a secret until the high priest of the sanctuary called upon her to proclaim an oracle, on the eve of a great battle. The Chatti have a tradition: one boy among all those present catches the eye of the girl, who is the first one to open her eyes again, and he remains joined to her in an indissoluble bond.'

'Hmm,' said Wulf. 'I think I know where this story ends. Go on.'

'The colours of dusk were lighting up the sky. In those lands it was always a magical event when the rays of the dying sun pierced the clouds like swords and made them bleed.'

'Go on, I said,' repeated Wulf.

'One of the girls, in between two others and flanked by two huge Hermunduri, opened her eyes. I think she was the first. She turned to me and I met her gaze, so her eyes were staring into mine. Just for an instant, no more. Ever since then, all I do is think of her. I am certain that our destinies are joined. I know I'll see her again and that no one will ever be able to separate us.'

'Just what I thought,' mused Wulf. 'That's why you think you've got to get back at any cost. You nearly got the both of us killed.'

Armin smiled. 'I don't know how, but Father noticed right away. Do you know what he said? He told me, "Don't even think about it. Do you know who she is?" "It doesn't matter," I said. "She's mine." "She is the daughter of Seghest, a chieftain of our people, and she has been promised," Father replied. "To whom?" I demanded. "Tell me who it is. I'll challenge him to a duel and kill him." Father got really angry then. He said, "A prince and a princess do not marry for love. They marry the person chosen by their fathers, without any further discussion. Their marriage seals alliances, joins territory, and guarantees that pacts will be maintained. These marriages allow us to avoid war and to save lives. Or, if war is necessary, to win that war. Do you think that you getting all excited about that girl makes any difference to me at all? What's more," he said, "Seghest is related to us. Don't you realize what a disaster it would be if the promise were broken? So, son, you will obey me. Listen well," he told me. "You will never see her again, not even from a distance, not even at a religious festivity. If you are invited by her family for any reason, you will find an excuse not to go." "I'm sure that she loves me," I told him.'

'What did he say to that?' asked Wulf.

'He slapped me as hard as he could.'

'Of course he did. What did you expect?'

Armin took his eyes off the road for a moment, looking off to the right, where there was a lake bigger than any he had ever seen in his own land. It was surrounded by towering white-peaked summits that mirrored themselves in the water. Groups of wooden huts, but sometimes even houses of stone with tile roofs, formed villages and small cities that could be reached by a branch of the road that never ended. On the hilltops here and there small sanctuaries or images of divinities could be seen.

Right at that moment, Taurus got off his mount and the cavalrymen in his escort stopped as well, leaving the animals free to graze. A changing station came into sight at a short distance. Its lamps were being lit as people in the fields all around them hurried to bring hay home for the horses and cows, and bags of coal to light the fire in their kitchens and baths.

'What about your little whore?' asked Armin when they stopped. 'Do you still think about her?'

Wulf kicked his brother in the shin.

'Ahh! You really do care about her, then!' replied Armin. 'I didn't mean to offend you. She just does what she has to do. Sooner or later she'll get used to it.'

Wulf kicked his other shin. 'It's not like she has any choice,' he said. 'And anyway, let it go, as our father would say. It's not like you have better hopes than I do. Anyway, I know how it'll turn out for her. Sooner or later girls like her get sick. Lots of them die because of the abortions they're forced to have. They're not allowed to have children.'

'There's a lot you know about these things!' whistled Armin. 'How is that, at your age?'

Wulf tried to change the subject. 'The soldiers. Sometimes they talk. About lots of things, actually.'

'Listen. Neither you nor I can make any plans for our futures. We're just boys, after all. But no one can take my dream away from me.'

'The girl who was first to open her eyes.'

'Why not . . .' replied Armin. 'Don't you believe in oracles?'

'I believe what I see. What I'm seeing down there, for instance.'

He pointed at Marcus Caelius Taurus with his *vitis* at his waist, unrolling his *tabula* on a little bench.

Wulf approached him. 'Do we have much further to go?'

'See what you think,' replied the centurion, pointing his finger at the parchment. 'We're here. This green is the lake we have just behind us. This is our road, and this is Rome. That's where we're going.'

Rome, thought Wulf and it seemed like his head wasn't big enough to contain the word.

'Who made this?' he asked again. 'How did they do it?'

Taurus rolled up the *tabula* and placed it inside a cylindrical case. 'You're fortunate so see this. This is only the second one ever made. It's for our emperor, who wants a reproduction of our road system and all of the changing stations. I'm working on it myself. I measure all the distances on the Via Aemilia. Many other centurions in Gaul, in Spain, in Africa and in Asia are working with their instruments to make more measurements like these. We measure time as well: how much distance a legion can cover in one day's march, how fast a message can travel if it's carried day and night without stopping.'

'Great Thor!' exclaimed Wulf. 'The road that never ends . . .'

'We use a different name for it. *Cursus publicus*. But it means the same thing.'

'It's in Germania as well. That's where you found us. Do you think that the road will reach every single village in Germania as well?'

'No, the cost would be enormous. First you need cities, and then you build roads. All you have now is villages, and the paths that have been trodden by herds and flocks. Or by people's feet.'

'But why cities?'

'In a city there are a multitude of people who need clothing, food to eat, water to drink, stones to build houses and temples and porticoes. All this can't be transported on pathways; you need roads. When there are a number of cities and they're all connected, other connections can be formed. One city produces and crafts metals, while another produces mainly fabrics, conserved foods, jars and bricks. Another city might produce beer, or sour milk, the kind that you like to drink. Or the wine that we like. In this way, one city sells their things and another city buys them. People who earn money by practising trade of this sort can then afford a bigger house and more comfortable clothing, and so on. Every city gets rich in the end and the important families want to spend more to build monuments, stadiums and theatres, temples and thermal baths. Everyone lives better. The roads are like the veins in my body and yours. Do you understand?'

Wulf listened attentively and looked at the fields around him. He saw carts carrying barrels full of new wine that spread its aroma along the way. He could smell the fragrance of dried hay. He had watched as the leaves of the field maples and the grapevines had changed colour from one day to the next, from sulphur yellow to bright red.

Armin seemed to see nothing; he was too absorbed in his own thoughts.

Towards evening, as they neared the changing station, the sky began to darken and storm clouds gathered on the horizon. Big raindrops soon started to fall while lightning bathed the countryside in cold light.

They entered the *mansio* courtyard and ran for shelter under the stable roof. A rivulet of water descended between each double pair of roof tiles and poured onto the floor outside. The horses tore off mouthfuls of hay from the stacked bales and shook off their wet manes.

The building's windows were lit up and the voices of the guests inside wafted out. As soon as the downpour had let up a bit, they all made a run for the door and entered. They could smell meat roasting on the embers and freshly baked bread. The hungry patrons were making a din as they demanded to be fed. Wulf and Armin, Centurion Taurus and the others were given the regulation servings for military personnel.

Every now and then, Taurus would turn his head towards Armin because he wasn't talking or laughing; the old centurion would gladly have given a month's salary in order to read the boy's mind. That surly young man disturbed him. He was afraid that no discipline could tame him, that none of the marvels of the Empire would ever fascinate him. He'd known others like Armin over his long career as a soldier and in the end he'd had to suppress them. That's what shepherds did with those dogs that just wouldn't be trained and never stopped snarling and snapping, even after a beating with the strap had left them more dead than alive.

Flavus, as Taurus liked to call Armin's brother, was, on the other hand, curious and even-natured, interested in everything he saw or heard about. He understood, he asked questions. Not that he took punishment easily – on the contrary – and he had his moments of melancholy, but it was easy enough to get him out of a low mood by engaging him in conversation. A sudden sparkle of sunlight, a tasty morsel or a good jug of foamy beer would always make him smile.

THEY RESUMED THEIR march the next day although the weather hadn't changed much for the better. A light but incessant rain continued to fall the whole day. The legionaries and horsemen donned waxcloth so the rain would slide off their shoulders and they pushed on at a steady rate. To the right of the road ran a wide river brimming with clear water in which they could see schools of trout and silvery pikes swimming. Willows, plane trees and dark, shiny-leafed alders lined the banks. The river was called Ticinum and after three days' marching they arrived near a settlement that bore the same name. Beyond that flowed another, even bigger, river. Not quite as immense as the Rhine, but almost. They entered the city and the honour guard at the decumanus gate presented arms to the *labarum* of the Eighteenth Legion.

Taurus stopped to exchange a few words with the officer in command, who had pointed at the two boys as if he needed to know who they were. The centurion then gestured for his men to follow him to the city centre, to the intersection of the *decumanus* and the *cardo*, the two axes which defined the city; he bought supplies at the market there.

They left the city and set up camp in a wood that was sacred to a local divinity and each one of the soldiers received his ration of food and wine, distributed by the centurion himself.

After dinner the two brothers lay down and they looked up at the sky. The moon was mirrored in the large river that resembled the Rhine. They could hear her voice nearby, in the swishing of the water along the banks. Flavus was thinking of how long it would take him to learn the language of the Romans, which was so different from his own. Some of its sounds were sharp and difficult, but others musical.

'Don't you think so, Armin?'

'Think what?'

'That we should learn their language. Taurus speaks ours pretty well.'

'Haven't you ever asked yourself why?'

'He listens to the way we talk?'

'No. He's part like us. Half, I'd say. Haven't you noticed his accent? And what about his blue eyes?'

'On his mother's or his father's side?'

'What difference does it make? Probably his mother's. He certainly bears his father's name. Think about it: the way he looks at you with such intensity, the cruelty of his punishments, his own resistance to fatigue . . . he could only have learned that at the hands of a Roman soldier. Maybe his father was an officer.'

'One day I'll meet him in battle and I'll kill him.'

'Or he'll kill you.'

'I don't know about that. I know a lot of things about him. He doesn't know so much about me.'

'I'm not so sure about that either. Let's sleep, now,' said Armin.

They slept until they were awakened by a kick to the bottoms of their feet.

It was Primus Pilus Centurion Marcus Caelius Taurus giving the wake-up call at the first light of dawn. He personally handed out each ration of freshly baked wheat flatbread. They then set off marching to the bank of the larger river. There was a rope which stretched from one bank to the other and a ferry big enough to transport nearly all of them at once. At the embarkation they were joined by four archers and two slings-men. They all sailed together downstream, heading east, for two days until they landed at a city called Placentia. There the men and horses were put ashore and Taurus entered the city with two legionaries to consult with the commander of the garrison and inform him about the situation in Germania. The meeting took quite a long time, so long that the sun had time to rise high above the circle of the walls.

When the centurion returned, the whole column set off once again on its journey. They soon found themselves back on the road that never ends but at that point it had a name, and it was called Aemilia.

'Because a consul named Aemilius built it,' explained Taurus.

Neither Armin nor Flavus dared to ask what a consul was.

Had they done so, Taurus would have been pleased to answer, although he was more interested in demonstrating the work that was being done to double the width of the road, and the bridges as well. When they stopped for lunch, he showed the boys how the road was built and Flavus drew close, eager not to miss a single word. He took everything in: the excavations for the road bed, the foundations in stone and gravel, the layer of coarse river sand and the slabs which covered them. At either side of the road, dirt tracks allowed shepherds to pass with their flocks and herdsmen with their oxen.

'In a thousand years' time, or even more, this road will still exist,' said Taurus.

Even Armin, who did not demonstrate any particular interest, was in reality observing everything. He was beginning to understand what made Rome so great and so powerful: her roads, bridges, changing stations, the bathrooms and latrines with running water that kept disease from taking root. The way that a message could reach the most remote destination, travelling by day and by night, and an answer could be swiftly had in the greatest city of the world. He'd also noticed that each city had a name and that they were built along roads, at a distance of about one day's march from one another.

Travelling down the Via Aemilia gave Taurus the opportunity to stop now and then and meet the men who were overseeing the work. Sometimes they shouted but many other times they spoke softly, referring to a sheet they had spread on a table, on which their own bit of road was drawn out, mirroring the *tabula* that the centurion so jealously guarded. The same one Armin had managed to steal from him, a feat that had left its mark on his back and his brother's.

They continued their march for ten days, with the mountains looming ever closer on their right. They finally came within sight of the sea, the internal sea they had heard so much about. They pushed on until they reached the shore because everyone wanted to see it. The temperature was mild, the wind had dropped to a breeze and the waves came to die on the beach with a whisper. One of the Hermundur threw himself into the water, but his big body hit sand. The shallow water meant you could walk towards the horizon for two hundred steps with it only lapping at your ankles.

Further south they glimpsed a ship lying on its side, full of sand.

'It looks like it's still in good shape; why hasn't anyone come to get it free?' asked Flavus.

Taurus approached, climbed aboard and took a look around. 'Because the goods are marked with the brand of their owner: he's the second most powerful man in the Empire. No one would even dare to touch a clay vase on that ship. If her owner doesn't find her, she'll stay here and rot until she's completely covered with sand.'

Armin and Flavus could barely believe that the mere name of a man could keep looters and thieves at a distance.

They made their way along the shore until late afternoon. Taurus was headed to a city called Ravenna and it was there that they stopped. They could never have imagined such a place. It included a number of smaller and bigger islands connected to one another with wooden bridges. Some of the houses were brick, others were made of wood, and on the main island there was a fish market. Everyone moved by boat, it seemed, either to go out fishing or to transport the fish to and from the market.

However, it wasn't the city that Taurus was headed for, but the port. The group continued south until they reached a protected lagoon that communicated with the sea by means of an artificial canal. Taurus climbed to the top of a sand dune that overlooked the port of the imperial fleet that had authority over the entire eastern sea. Armin and Flavus were struck speechless at the spectacle of over three hundred ships at anchor: liburnian galleys, triremes, quadriremes and quinqueremes.

The sun had almost set behind them and the sky had begun to darken in the east. As the first stars dotted the sky, lights went on along the piers and on the ships. Right at that moment, the flagship appeared from behind the wharf, her fore and aft railings proudly lit. The immense vessel had her side turned to them and was just veering towards the entrance to the port. The two boys were still, stunned at the sight. Upon seeing their amazement, Taurus said, 'That is the biggest ship anyone has ever seen on this earth. Her dimensions are incredible. She is called the *Aquila Maris*. If you read Latin, you'd know that immediately from the wording on the stern sail and by the eagle painted on the mainsail. She's five hundred and fifty feet long and twenty-three feet wide. There are over four hundred men in her crew, between the galley slaves, rowers, sailors, officers and war machine operators. Look, at the prow and along the sides you can see the artillery pieces lined up: catapults, onagers and ballistas. Some are used to hurl fiery balls of pitch, others shoot off heavy steel darts capable of penetrating oak planks eight inches thick. The ram consists of a single bronze casting and weighs three talents. It is bolted onto a twelve-foot-long oak-wood framework.'

Armin and Flavus could not understand the import of those measurements, but they could perceive them with their eyes. They watched as the heavy pinewood oars were raised dripping from the water and immersed again as if a single mind were operating them. At the stern, the helmsmen were steering the rudders which stood more than ten feet higher than the ship's side. On the yard fluttered the standard with the name and symbol of the ship and of her commander. The ship passed majestically at a short distance from the shore and the dune where the soldiers and horsemen under Taurus's command had gathered. By the time the centurion had finished describing the wondrous vessel as she sailed before them, she had been directed to her anchorage, so they could distinctly hear the roll of drums and the voice of the oar-master setting the pace for the men.

A trumpet sounded at the bow and the crew lowered the mainsail, leaving only the foresail up. The helmsman paid out two enormous anchors at the stern that were dropped into the sea with a loud splash. The oar-master gave the signal to sink oars and block them in the rowlocks. The *Aquila Maris* immediately lost speed. Then the anchor lines snapped taut and the gigantic hull came to a complete stop, accompanied by a loud groaning of the planks. Two crewmen threw another couple of lines out to secure the bow to the moorings. A couple of gangways were lowered at the ship's side and the crew went to shore. Only a naval infantry squad remained on board to guard the *Aquila Maris* overnight.

More ships – four triremes and six liburnian galleys – queued one after another, heading to the mooring piers. Taurus ordered his men to move to the quarters which had been readied for them in the district of the port.

That night, a thin fog began to rise from the lagoon. It soon became thicker, blotting out shapes and deadening sounds. Only the calls of the guards on duty could be heard sporadically. More lights were lit on the piers; the last to be illuminated was the lamp of the lighthouse. Towards the east, a thin red line was still vaguely visible, delineating the mountain crests.

Much closer to the port district rose a round wooden building, not very tall, that was flanked by single-storey houses.

Flavus walked up to one of the Germanic auxiliaries. 'What is that?' he asked, pointing to the building.

'It's a school for gladiators,' replied the warrior.

'What are gladiators?'

'Slaves or prisoners of war who fight each other in an arena for the amusement of the people who come to watch them. The loser is killed by the winner, unless the public decides otherwise. If they don't like the way he has fought, they shout out, "Kill him!" If on the other hand they feel he fought well, they can shout out, "Let him go!" and he is spared.'

'Have you ever been to one of these fights?' asked Flavus.

'Once. When Taurus is in a good mood and the opportunity presents itself, he gives us passes to get in.'

'Did you like it?'

'No,' answered the warrior.

Flavus asked no more. He was lingering there, looking at the wooden ring, when he suddenly heard the sound of a gallop and then almost instantly saw the figure of a horseman emerging from the fog. The rider was mounted upon a black stallion and had the regulation armour of a Roman officer, but he wore no helmet and his hair was blond. He raced past the boy and in just a few moments the sound of his galloping had faded into the distance.

6

FLAVUS AND ARMIN were the first up the next morning. They began preparing their baggage, the horses and the pack animals so that everything would be in order when the centurion came to review them before departure. When they spotted Taurus, however, he was going aboard a liburnian galley.

'What is he going to do on that ship?' wondered Flavus. 'Taurus isn't in the navy. Not any more, anyway. He told me so himself.'

'That's a fast ship,' said Armin. 'The kind they take out to the open sea. He'll be giving the commander a message to take to someone very important on the other side of the sea.'

'Why doesn't he use the road that never ends?'

'Because even the road has to stop when it gets to the sea. Only a ship can travel the paths of the water that are marked by the stars.'

'Well, I'd like to know what message he's sending to the other side,' said Flavus.

'Something to do with us, for sure. And he wouldn't be doing it if it weren't important.'

In the meantime, Taurus was already descending from the gangway and walking to the camp to wake those of his men who were still sleeping. After breakfast, they made their way back to the road heading south, until they reached the Via

Aemilia, on which they would travel from one city to the next, crossing fields planted with fruit trees. There were many farms, where servants with ladders and baskets were gathering ripe apples and pears, loading them onto oxen-pulled carts and transporting them to storehouses. The servants sang and the animals under their yoke grazed on green grass. The fields without fruit trees were covered by expanses of gold-coloured stubble that the oxen were turning over at the plough. The earth was so damp that it let off a thin fog. It was a magical spectacle that left the boys almost as admiring as when they had seen the majestic *Aquila Maris* ploughing the waters at the port of Ravenna.

'Does this help to create the power of Rome?' said Flavus.

Taurus heard him because he was riding close by and he didn't give Armin the chance to answer his brother. 'Not any longer, I'm sorry to say. It used to be that nearly all Romans cultivated the land. They were proud of being self-sufficient and not having to ask anyone for anything. But, as new places were conquered, throngs of slaves have been brought in, and they've taken away the jobs of free men, many of whom have been reduced to poverty. Some have joined the army to earn a living. Others still have gone to live in the cities, where they sell their votes to the wealthy and the noblemen who want to be elected as magistrates. And both parties lose their dignity, in a single act.'

Armin and Flavus had begun to forget the smarting pain of Taurus's *vitis* and every day they increasingly appreciated his wisdom and even temperament.

Taurus noticed that the two boys were contemplating the golden strips of stubble lit up by the sun. They seemed enchanted.

He turned to Armin: 'Is it the gold or the dark you like?'

'The gold,' replied Armin.

'That's what I would have expected. You are a prince, after all. You know, the ploughed earth and the golden stubble remind me of something that happened long ago. I was serving with my legion in Germania, under the orders of General Drusus, who sometimes granted me the extreme honour of exchanging a few words. Three days earlier we had fought a terrible battle on the banks of the Weser and we were exhausted.'

'What did General Drusus say to you?' asked Flavus.

'He said, "We've won, Centurion, and yet I can't wait for all of this to be over. The Germanics are the only ones who can bear comparison to us, and that's why our fighting can only get bloodier. But the Empire of Rome has to be both blond and dark." Blond and dark,' concluded Taurus, 'like the field you see before you.'

They all resumed their march, the boys still stealing glances at the countryside as the sun slowly set behind the mountains.

They stopped for the night in the village of Caesena, where Taurus had arranged for the dinner and quartering of his men and where he hoped to meet up with his brother, Publius Caelius. His brother owned a couple of inns in Bononia, the city they came from, and in a number of towns between Placentia and Ariminum.

Marcus Caelius had a massive build and on special occasions he was wont to wear a complete suit of armour with all of his decorations, but this was only the informal meeting of two brothers and he showed up wearing Germanic-style trousers with a tunic and cloak and armed only with his regulation gladius.

Publius rushed towards him as soon as he stepped over the threshold of his inn and the two brothers embraced each other with exclamations of joy, obscenities and pounding on one another's shoulders. Then they sat together, waiting to be served.

'What are you doing here anyway?' asked Publius. 'It was a huge surprise for me when I heard you'd be stopping for dinner. I cancelled all of my appointments!'

'I'm glad you did. It's been too long since we've seen each other.'

Publius Caelius's expression abruptly changed. 'How are things going in Germania?'

Taurus furrowed his brow. 'Like usual. You can never trust them, not even the ones fighting for us. See those two wolf cubs down there?' he asked, nodding at Armin and Flavus.

'Of course I do. Why?'

'They are the sons of Sigmer, prince of the Cherusci.'

'I remember him well. I saw him on board General Drusus's ship as we were sailing down the Rhine towards the ocean; I hadn't been discharged yet and I was serving in the naval infantry. Back then people were saying that they'd become friends and that they kept seeing each other in secret.'

'Well,' added Taurus, 'those boys have become our hostages and I've been tasked with a very sensitive mission: I'm to transfer a Roman mind into the bodies of those young Germanics.'

'I wouldn't like to be in your shoes,' replied Publius Caelius.

'It is political strategy,' said Taurus. 'And you know well who the master of this art was.' He lowered his voice and spoke close to Publius's ear. 'Augustus. Gaius Julius Caesar Octavian Augustus himself. His house was like an orphanage, full of young boys and girls. They were the orphans of his enemies, and those of Julius Caesar. He instructed them personally, fed them, clothed them and prepared brilliant careers for them.

The children were certainly grateful, and yet they couldn't help but be aware that the benevolent man dressed in white was actually the murderer of their parents.

'You tell me: how could they ever grow up whole in spirit? Yet in many cases it seems to have worked. Think of young Juba, who now reigns serenely on behalf of Rome over Mauretania, along with the queen, his wife, daughter of Marc Antony and Cleopatra.'

'So all's well that ends well, no?' smiled Publius.

Taurus sighed. 'That's true, but I don't feel up to such a challenge myself. I think they should have turned the boys over to a politician – a senator, for example, or a magistrate. A philosopher, even. Why a centurion, whose very nature makes him the most unyielding of soldiers? My place, dear brother, is on the battlefield, not in a classroom.'

Publius Caelius nodded.

'Pretend I've said nothing,' Taurus continued. 'My mission is a state secret, and it is surely part of Augustus's plan for the future of Germania. You know something? This feigning makes me feel like a hypocrite; I'm just not convinced it's the right way. The fact is that General Drusus should not have died. He was quite a soldier, and even his enemies respected him! You know that yourself. You fought for him when you were in the navy.'

'I did.' Publius nodded. He shot a look at the boys every now and then.

'But I've received an order from our legate and I must obey it,' Taurus went on. 'I can't wait to get to Rome. Maybe I'll be able to turn the boys over to someone more suitable and get back to Germania, where I know what I'm doing. Anyway, brother, what about you? Business is going well, isn't it? You don't miss the military life, do you?'

Publius Caelius gave him a half-smile. 'To tell you the truth, I never really liked it. The reason I enrolled was to keep an eye on you and make sure you stayed away from danger, believe it or not. You were all I had left of our family, after all. I've just bought a new tavern in Bononia, not far from the theatre. It's a beautiful place, and I have plenty of clients. When you're travelling back to Germania, you'll surely be passing that way. If you let me know, I'll make sure I can be there too.'

It was now late and for Taurus it was time to retire. They said their farewells with an embrace; there was no need to add anything else. They both knew that nothing was ever sure in a soldier's life.

Taurus and his men left the next day for Ariminum, where there was a way station at the point where the Via Aemilia ended and the Via Flaminia began. Ariminum was also a flourishing fishing port. They watched as boats unloaded crates and crates of silvery-skinned fish at the wharfs.

Further out at sea, a fleet of warships passed, sailing south. Taurus said that they might all be arriving at their next stop, Fanum Fortunae, at the same time.

As they marched south, the mountains began to get closer and closer to the sea until the rocky cliffs were pushing up amidst the waves. Flavus watched the sea foam frothing at the foot of the craggy rocks and breathed in the air scented by the sea and the low flowering bushes along the shore. It made him feel intoxicated. It was a sensation of lightness and of deep happiness that was really inexpressible, so much that he didn't dare tell his brother, who was riding at his side, about it. Armin, lost in his own thoughts, was remembering the melancholy wind that rustled through the boughs of the black and blue firs in Germania.

Flavus noticed distant shadows out of the corner of his right eye. It wasn't the first time, but he'd never told his brother about it.

Armin felt his tension. 'So you've seen them too?'

'Yes,' admitted Flavus. 'They've been following the mountain ridges for days. But if we've seen them, so has Taurus.'

'Of course. But what difference does it make?' Armin seemed to give no importance to what they'd seen, but Flavus could tell that wasn't quite true. There was a quiver in his voice and a pang in his look.

'Do you recognize them?' asked Flavus softly.

'How could I? They're just dark shadows on the mountainside.'

'Are you sure? Is it you who summoned them?'

'Me? I've lost all hope. But maybe Father hasn't.'

'Father's not mad. He knows that trying something so reckless could only end up with us dying. Anyway, how long do you think a squad of intruders could survive in the heart of the Empire?'

'Longer than you think. They don't need much food or a place to stay; they don't need shelter from the night or the rain. They live like ghosts,' replied Armin.

'The other night in Ravenna,' broke in Flavus, 'I saw one of them galloping out of the fog on a black stallion. But he vanished as quickly as he'd appeared. Did you see him too?'

'I saw nothing.'

After a great deal of marching, they set up camp in the middle of a pine wood and Marcus Caelius Taurus passed out bread to his soldiers, as a father might do to his sons. The men pitched their tents, as did the two brothers. They spread a blanket over the pine needles and went to sleep.

'Father . . .' whispered Armin before closing his eyes. 'Where are you?'

THEY WERE AWAKENED by a pale sun and they resumed their march, reaching Fanum Fortunae before evening. It was a beautiful city with a temple to the goddess Fortuna. In a construction yard nearby an amphitheatre was being built.

'Gladiators will fight here,' Taurus offered briefly.

The horsemen on the mountains had disappeared. Flavus seemed relieved. 'It's better they're gone,' he said to his brother. 'What were they doing there anyway? They must have been soldiers making their rounds, or merchants transporting their wares.'

'They'll be back,' said Armin.

They spent the night in the courtyard of the way station and started off again early the next morning on the Via Flaminia, which they knew led directly to Rome. Two days after their departure they passed the city of Forum Sempronii but they did not stop there. Towards evening, the brothers caught another glimpse of the horsemen on the mountain ridge, at a distance of about a mile from the road. It was evident that they were observing the situation from above, or they would have been travelling on the road itself. Maybe they wanted a quick escape route.

Taurus seemed not to see them, and neither of the boys dared to ask him what he thought.

Armin and Flavus were fairly certain by now that the horsemen of the ridge were following them. Each was worried, not only about the consequences of any possible action on their part and how the other brother would react, but also about what might happen to the two of them.

Armin imagined that his brother wanted to get to Rome

and to settle there, rather than attempt a return to Germania. He saw how fascinated Flavus was by the spectacle of Roman power, by how her forces were always present, both on the sea and on land, on the warships and in the army. Armin couldn't stop thinking about the secret friendship that his father had had with General Drusus; Taurus seemed to know a lot about it, too much perhaps. The idea of an empire of two colours. The field half gold and half dark. Could his father and Drusus actually have talked about such a thing before the Roman general died?

The horsemen got smaller and smaller and then disappeared completely.

And with them, the boys' bitter thoughts.

Taurus himself seemed more relaxed, in a better mood. One night he let them set up camp in a place that was eight miles short of the nearest changing station. The archers had downed a roe deer that day. They flayed it and cut it into pieces and roasted it over an open fire. The moon was full and the air was mild. After they had pitched the tents, they all sat down to eat together, and Taurus handed out the wine that he'd been keeping in reserve. When the men retired to their tents for the night, Taurus ordered two of them to stand guard, with replacements every three hours.

Halfway through the second guard shift, the camp found itself under attack: a group of horsemen fell upon the guards and stormed the camp. One of them sent a hook flying into the boys' tent and dragged it away, while the others seized the boys, hoisting them easily onto their mounts. They disappeared into the woods which they'd emerged from, skirting the camp in a wide semi-circle. Taurus flew out of his tent with sword in hand and saw his two legionaries on the ground, wounded. He cursed.

'We can follow them, Centurion,' said the chief of the Germanic auxiliaries. 'We're used to riding in the dark.'

'Go, now. But take archers with you, and four of our horsemen. Bring back those boys unharmed – it's a question of life or death.'

The group rode off at a gallop.

As soon as they were out of sight, Taurus ordered his men to add wood to the fire, so that the blaze would be visible at a great distance. Then he had them bring him a polished shield with which to send signals. He directed the ray of reflected light towards the pass.

'Now we wait.'

'Wait, Centurion? Wait for what?' asked one of the legionaries.

'Wait until the guard corps posted at the pass see our fire. If we move out of here too quickly, the two wounded men will die. I know what I'm doing. Do you think I haven't seen that group on the mountain ridge following us? I've taken my precautions. Add all the wood you can find to the fire and continue to send signals with the shield.' The soldiers obeyed. The light of the flames focused on the rounded inner surface of the shield and was relayed again and again to the pass.

It wasn't long before an answering beam of light appeared to the north, just under the pass, and then one more towards the west. There was another in between these two as well as an intermittent flashing to the south-east.

'The circle is closed,' said Taurus. 'We can move on. Three men will stay behind with the wounded.' He indicated two legionaries and a Germanic auxiliary. 'Don't change their bandages; it would put them in danger of bleeding out. Prepare a couple of pallets on the baggage cart and get these men up to the pass. There's a surgeon up there who will be able to take care of them. I hope. If they seem better, turn back and try to catch up with us. The others with me, now.'

They lit torches and headed off on foot down a trail which took them in the direction marked by the second and third signals. These two red beams, shining distinctly on two rises, guided them on whenever the vegetation was thin enough to see clearly. Two Germanic auxiliaries rode ahead on horseback, slowing at times to pick up on the tracks of their quarry. They crossed a stream on a wooden bridge and soon after that saw horse droppings. A satisfied grin crossed Taurus's face.

'We're on to them,' he said.

He ordered his men to slow down and to replace the spent torches with fresh ones. A roll of drums echoed through the valley, and the long blare of the trumpets and horns was guiding them to their destination. Finally Taurus and his Germanic horsemen found themselves in a valley crossed by the same stream, with a number of small waterfalls that mirrored the full moon. At its northernmost edge the squad of raiders were just about to reach the pass, when a numerous cavalry squad, the auxiliaries who had ridden ahead, blocked their way.

The raiders tried to turn back, but any other way out had already been occupied. They found themselves surrounded by Roman troops on all sides, by all of the units which had been alerted, closing off every escape route. They closed into a circle, ready to fight to the bitter end. The Roman commanders were ready to sound the attack, but Taurus raised his hand to stop them.

'No one makes a move!' he shouted. 'I'll go to negotiate. I don't want the boys to be hit. They are my responsibility.'

The legionaries, who had already begun to approach the enemy formation, lowered their weapons and Taurus rode alone towards the warrior who seemed to be the commander of the raiders who had seized Armin and Flavus: a giant of a man wearing *lorica squamata*, scale armour of Roman construction.

'Who are you?' asked Taurus in the Germanic language. 'Who sent you here?'

The horseman did not answer and the valley became silent. The torch flames exposed the warrior's glassy eyes. Taurus had seen that fixed grey stare many times on the battlefield: it was the look that came just before death.

'Do you understand what I'm asking you?'

The warrior shook his head.

'Hand over the boys and I will leave you free to return to wherever it is you've come from.'

The warrior shook his head again. Taurus realized that another question would meet with the same response and he turned his horse to go back to his men but at that very moment the raiders' war cry rang out; it cleaved the night air and the pounding of horses' hooves shook the earth.

Archers let fly from the left and right, from the positions where Taurus's silent commands had sent them, while the legionaries hurled their spears and the auxiliaries flung their long pikes. In the torchlight and the soft light of the moon, no one failed their target. One after another, the Germanic warriors plummeted to the ground.

Flavus and Armin, stock-still and uninjured, watched the slaughter wordlessly. Once his orders had been executed, Taurus approached them. 'Come, we'll go back to camp. All is well.'

Armin whispered to his brother, 'Do you understand what happened?'

'The centurion saw them. He knew they were following us.'

'And?'

'So as soon as they made a move, he had his legionaries and auxiliaries ready to counter,' answered Flavus.

'No, you're wrong. Taurus planned this all out. It was he who lured them here, to this specific place. He deliberately took no action; he let them follow us for days and days while he was setting his trap here in the valley. He let them grab us, let them get away, but he knew the whole time that there was only one way out. He forced them into a funnel from which there was a single route of escape. Which he'd already blocked.'

Back at the camp, the brothers repitched their sorry-looking tent and slept all night. Armin dreamed of that mountain valley and of the lethal trap that the Romans had laid. He would never forget it.

THE NEXT MORNING, the convoy set off, sinking once again into the Apennine countryside in its continuously changing features. Mountains and hills, rivers and streams, rainbow-hued waterfalls, the cyclopic walls of ancient cities perched on rocky cliffs, temples of incredible beauty mirrored in crystalline pools, majestic bridges stretching over steep valleys, sweeps of silvery-leaved olive groves with enormous twisted trunks, gigantic fallen trees corroded by the elements over time; herds of bulls, buffalo and horses, flocks of sheep which whitened the green flanks of the valleys, lakes as round as volcanic lagoons, little islands barely surfacing, huge solitary oaks on the tops of hills where the asphodels were still blossoming. Images that couldn't be ignored or erased from their minds. Every scene was a sublime expression of nature and of the labour of man, of different men from different ages, of civilizations that had once flourished and then dissolved over the centuries.

They reached the destination of their long journey one dusky afternoon in October. Taurus halted his horse and the entire group drew up in a semi-circle behind him. The light breeze blowing from the west smelled of the sea. Flights of swallows dove towards the surface of a small lake to wet their chest feathers, then shot straight up to the heavens, disappearing into the deep blue. Flocks of cranes crossed the skies of the *Urbs* in their journey southwards, trumpeting loudly in their long lines. The Tiber River snaked between the houses, temples, colonnades and colossal bronze statues, reflecting the gold and red of the sky. Rome's seven hills rose in that timeless atmosphere, crowned with light and clouds, with towers and walls, with arches and with age-old red-barked pine trees. The boys spied an island in the middle of the river, connected to its banks by two marble bridges. The island was shaped like a giant ship of stone, beached on the blond sands. A temple rose at its centre, with a sparkling golden statue. To the left was a craggy hill and at its top another temple, grandiose, adorned by a myriad of red and ochre statues and covered with gilded roof tiles which glittered under the setting sun.

A star appeared in the sky.

Rome.

There was a long, dazed silence, and then Flavus's voice rang out: 'How long has this place existed?'

'Forever,' replied Taurus.

7

Night had already fallen by the time Flavus and Armin settled into their new accommodation on the Aventine Hill, in a house which quartered other children who'd come from far away: from Africa and Mauretania, from Britannia, Cantabrica and Cappadocia, Pannonia and Mesia, words pronounced by Taurus that had no meaning for the two brothers. A freedman named Diodorus, under the centurion's watchful eye, showed them to their room. There were two beds, a basin of water for washing, a jug filled with water as well and two glass cups. There was also a chest where they could store their clothing.

'Well folded and placed with care!' warned Diodorus. 'When you dress tomorrow, there must not be a wrinkle.'

Then, lamp in hand, he showed them the latrines and the water tap for cleansing. 'Wash every time you use the latrines, and keep your hair nicely combed. I won't abide any barbarian habits like long hair,' he said as he looked the boys up and down. 'As far as your garments are concerned, you'll be given something suitable as soon as the tailor gets your measurements.'

They walked out onto a colonnaded corridor that led to the rear garden. 'Clean your teeth at least once a day, and be careful to rinse your mouth well. Wash your hands after eating so you won't stain your clothing. You'll find something to eat for tonight in your room. Soup is eaten with a spoon, not by slurping it up noisily from the bowl like animals do.' He led them back to their room. 'Those,' he said, pointing to the cups, 'are made of glass and they cost more than you do. Try not to break them. No one is allowed to leave here unless accompanied by his tutor. No one is allowed to return later than sunset. What you see there on the northern wall is called a clock. You will learn to read it so you can tell the time. Anyone who violates the rules will receive an exemplary punishment, in the presence of all the other guests of this house. Have you understood well everything I've told you?' Flavus and Armin looked at each other, each trying to gauge how much the other had understood.

'It doesn't matter,' said Diodorus, noting the look in their eyes. 'I'll explain everything to you, and I'll teach you to speak in Latin instead of barking like the barbarians do.'

'Why does he always look at us when he says "barbarians"?' asked Flavus in a low voice.

'You know full well why,' replied Armin. 'The moment will come when he stops looking at us that way, but that won't be until after we learn Latin and start dressing and wearing our hair as he wants it.'

Taurus spoke up: 'These boys have been travelling for many days, sleeping just a few hours a night, and tomorrow they have to get up early. They need to rest now.'

Diodorus said nothing else and allowed the two boys to retire. Taurus stopped a moment to speak with him. 'Tomorrow I'll be turning them over to their tutor. Who is he?'

'You. Primus Pilus Centurion Marcus Caelius Taurus,' replied the freedman.

'Me? That's not possible. I have no desire and even less time to care for these snotty-nosed children.'

'That's what I was told,' insisted Diodorus. 'But tomorrow morning you'll receive word yourself and that will erase any doubts. A servant will take you to your room, where you'll find your dinner waiting with a jug of red wine. If you'd like something different, you need only ask. I wish you a good night, Centurion.'

Diodorus took his leave and a servant accompanied Taurus to his bedroom. There was some roasted lamb, stewed lentils and a piece of bread. The servant helped him remove his leather corset, then unlaced his sandals and took his travelling cloak off his shoulders. He set the lit lamp on the table and left.

Taurus bit into the lamb, had a few spoonfuls of lentils with the bread and drank the wine. He went to the latrine to urinate, washed, returned to his room and lay down. Although the hallway outside his door was silent, he heard a watchman pass by a couple of times with two dogs on a lead – Epirote mastiffs, from the sound of their growl. The house's guests were well guarded; intruders were not welcome.

In their own room, Armin and Flavus had finished their soup and drunk the water in their precious glass cups. They undressed and lay down. The beds were hard but comfortable, the walls had been freshly whitewashed and the intense, sweet fruity odour that wafted in reminded them of beer before it had fermented. They would have liked to talk, to exchange their impressions on what they had seen, on what they felt at the sight of Rome, the place they would be living in for a long time to come, but they were so tired that their conversation soon drifted into sleep.

They were shocked awake in the middle of the night by a screeching cry that made them jump.

'What was that?' asked Flavus, his heart in his throat. 'If it's one of the guests of this house, it must be some rule he broke. What are they doing to him?'

'It's an animal, can't you tell?' said Armin. But the dogs were barking; they were frightened too. 'Go back to sleep.'

BEFORE THEY KNEW IT, it was dawn and Centurion Taurus was knocking at their door. He took them to a training ring behind the building, gave each one a sword-shaped stick and a round wooden shield and then stood watching them for a while, his hands on his hips. The *vitis* switch was in his right hand. His leather corset protected his chest.

'Are you awake?' he asked in their Germanic language.

'Yes, Primus Pilus Centurion Caelius Taurus!' the two boys shouted in unison.

'Then attack me. Now!'

Armin shot a look at his brother and moved his head slightly to the left twice. It was a code they used when they'd started to follow their father Sigmer on his hunting expeditions. A glance was sufficient to decide on tactics. In this case, he signalled contact with a bear, given the adversary they found facing them. They'd never done it on their own before; they'd always just watched the adult warriors and imitated their moves and blows. But this time the only adult warrior was their adversary. Armin lowered his head imperceptibly and Flavus rushed forward with his sword held out before him, but just as he got close enough to strike, he twisted swiftly to the side. His approach was supposed to throw Taurus off balance in his direction, while the real attack came from Armin on the right – he shoved his shield towards the centurion's face and tried to thrust his gladius into the man's unprotected side.

Taurus intuited the move and flicked his *vitis* between Armin's legs, causing him to trip and fall. He wheeled around to face Flavus, who was now attacking him from behind. Taurus threw his cloak over the boy. Caught like a fish in a net, Flavus tried unsuccessfully to disentangle himself from the fabric, and ended up dragged to the floor by the centurion.

'Pick up your weapons again and do as I tell you. You have to learn how to strike without revealing your intent. You tried to surprise me, but you failed. If you were a bit bigger and I was older and slower, you would have managed to scratch me, but nothing more.' His lecture was interrupted by the arrival of Diodorus's servant, who handed the centurion a letter with the imperial seal. He opened it, read it, folded it again and tucked it under his corset. Then he turned to the boys with a peeved expression. 'It's as I feared. Augustus Caesar has written me a letter of his own hand, asking me to take responsibility for your military training and instruction. He is the most powerful man in the world and you can be proud of the fact that he has taken a personal interest in your upbringing. I too feel honoured at being selected by him to accomplish a mission that he evidently cares very much about. I will do as he asks because he is the supreme commander of all the forces of the Empire; my sense of duty requires it. I would have gladly shirked such a burdensome task; my place is on the battlefield, fighting. Not pretending to fight in a training ring . . .'

Armin had helped his brother to his feet and opened his mouth to say something, but Taurus stopped him with a gesture. 'From this moment on, you owe me total obedience. I will decide what you do every day, every hour and every instant of your lives. For the first three months you will speak only if I ask you to, because you are not capable of expressing yourselves. But in three months' time you will speak Latin, thanks to the experience and ability of Diodorus, your educator. Respect him, for he has known slavery and he has suffered

greatly. He was not born a slave. He became one due to misfortune.'

Armin walked up to Taurus and stared straight into his eyes,
in the manner of the Germanic warriors. A single glance told
Taurus more than a thousand words.

The brothers continued to mount one attack after another,
failing again and again, until the sun projected the shadow of
the meridian on the second bar. 'That's enough for today,' the
centurion said then. 'Go and get washed and dress in a decor-
ous manner. The barber will come to take care of your hair. I
don't want a wild mane nor do I want to see any poofy curls
on your forehead. A servant will take you to the room in which
Diodorus will see to your education.' Armin and Flavus were
beginning to understand almost everything, although neither
of them had any idea of what 'poofy' was.

As Taurus was still talking, a handsome lad who seemed to
be about the same age as Armin approached the ring. He was
wearing an elegant white gown trimmed in purple, with red
leather boots. He stripped at the edge of the field, showing off
well-developed muscles that belied his young age. He put on
a leather helmet, slung on the shield that was handed to him
by a servant and hung a belt on his left shoulder that held a
gladius, a real one. The ring was soon reverberating with the
clangour of two swords clashing: that of the handsome young
man and that of Taurus.

'Listen . . .' said Armin to his brother.

'To what?'

'The sword strokes. You can hear the difference between his
and the boy's.'

'Sword against sword. I wouldn't like to be in his shoes.
Who do you think he is?'

'He's someone like me and you. A prince. The son of a great man. Maybe one day we'll meet up with him.'

'But why do they use such short swords?'

'Do you know what carding is?'

'No, I've never heard of it.'

'Before you can make cloth out of wool, the fibres have to be separated. They use two curved wooden boards: one is convex, and it moves. The other is concave and is full of thistle needles, or sometimes iron nails. Between them you put the tangled-up bundle of fibres. The top part moves up and down and every time it goes down it crushes and tears at them until there is no longer any one fibre attached to another; all you have is filaments.

'Well, that's how the legion is: thousands of short, sharp swords instead of needles. Any formation that comes into contact with a front line, rife with those blades, gets gored, torn up, mutilated. They're bleeding from every surface, they're screaming with pain. Haven't you ever seen them carry a warrior back to our village from the battlefield and he's completely covered with blood? Haven't you ever looked closely at Father's chest? All of those scars . . . can only mean one thing. A close encounter with the legion.'

'Are you trying to scare me?'

'No. You asked me a question and I answered you.'

'THAT WAS A short lesson,' observed Flavus as the boys were walking back to their residence, after the training duel.

'It was long enough,' replied Armin. 'That's the way Taurus is. Remember? He whipped us until we bled, but only once. He's never punished us again, not even when we have maybe deserved it.'

'Are you saying he thinks well of us? He has a strange way of showing it. A drastic way. I'm covered in bruises.'

'Actually, I would say he does. But you know that he never repeats himself. Never, not with anybody. And he never gives you a second chance.'

'First he warns you. Then he kills you.'

'No,' said Armin. 'Not us.'

They reached the villa, which stood at the top of a hill and was surrounded by a big park.

'Look!' exclaimed Flavus.

Armin turned in the direction Flavus was pointing. 'Great Wotan, what is that?'

'A peacock,' said a thin voice behind them. Diodorus.

He'd appeared suddenly from behind a thick cane-apple shrub.

'He was pissing and we disturbed him,' hissed Flavus to his brother.

'Nothing of the sort,' replied Diodorus in an annoyed tone. 'I was checking to see whether the female of that stunning peacock had laid any eggs.'

'I've never seen anything that amazing,' said Flavus as the bird fanned out his iridescent tail. Just then the peacock let out a bone-chilling shriek.

'No one on this earth is perfect,' observed Diodorus. 'This animal expresses total harmony and utter perfection, but nature has given him a voice as shrill and piercing as a man being tortured to death.' He changed the subject; it was not his habit to waste time on banal chatter. 'The plants and animals in this garden have been brought here from every part of the world,' he concluded. 'And your lessons begin right after breakfast.'

The lesson was torture. Armin and Flavus had never been

forced to sit on chairs for such a long time without moving, attending to something that for them was meaningless and boring. They couldn't help but think back to long nights around the fire when they would listen enraptured to a bard telling of the endeavours of great warriors. Then they'd never wanted the story to end. The starry skies overhead looking like they were being held up by the oak and beech fronds, the night breezes ruffling the needles of green and blue firs and stirring up the smells wafting from the forest . . . Now they sat tracing out incomprehensible marks on a wax tablet. Diodorus's voice was drab and monotonous, but he was quick to scold them if they became distracted.

If that torture had lasted too long, they would have ended up strangling him like a turkey and Taurus realized that. He intensified practice with sword and shield, starting with wooden arms and going on to iron ones. He wore them out so thoroughly that sitting in a classroom with their teacher began to seem like a gift from the gods.

Then as the winter started, so did boar hunting with javelins in the oak forests of northern Latium. They would leave while it was still dark, wearing Germanic breeches and leather corsets, caps and boots, a supply of javelins strapped to their horses' sides. Sometimes it was just the three of them, but on other occasions as many as ten, including Hermunduri auxiliaries, Balearic archers and beaters with their dogs. Neither of the boys had ever hunted with dogs before. They were the same animals who prowled around the villa every night, growling on the leads of the watchmen making their rounds.

The hunt was always arduous and took place on rugged terrain. As soon as the dogs caught a whiff of the excrement and the acrid stench of a wild boar, they would go crazy and tear off at an incredible speed, no matter how dense the forest was. Once the boar was surrounded, the raging beast had to be brought down, and that was the boys' job. It wasn't rare for the boar to gore his way out of the circle by sinking his tusks into a dog's underbelly. He would rush off then, crashing through the forest, until a javelin from one of his pursuers ran him through.

It was a defeat for the two boys if someone else downed the boar. With Taurus's help, they worked on refining their skills and their aim. At times, the centurion would find a vantage point from which to watch them from above and, although it was hard to admit it even to himself, he was becoming quite attached to them. The cut of their hair and, even more so, the soldierly way they handled themselves was making them seem increasingly Roman, and closer to Taurus's own way of thinking and living.

When the hunt was over, any of the dogs who had been wounded were turned over to the veterinarian who washed out the lesions and sewed them up if internal organs had not been damaged, often saving the animals' lives. This stoked the boys' admiration too; they were not at all accustomed to the idea that doctors for dogs and horses existed. The task of flaying the downed prey also went to the boys. They would open the boar's belly and give the guts to the waiting dogs.

After every endeavour, whether it was a duel in the training ring or a hunt in the Sabina forests, Taurus had something to teach the boys.

'What did you learn from this hunt?' he asked Flavus after a successful run.

'That a hunting expedition is the best way to get rid of an adversary by feigning an accident.'

'Interesting observation. Maybe that's the reason I always try to find a high place to watch you two from. You might be tempted to take the opportunity to make me pay for my strictness! And what about you, Armin?'

'Nothing special. Only . . . I saw a man fall from his horse, one of the archers. It made me remember that a long time ago, when I was little, my father told us that General Drusus died after falling off his horse.'

Taurus scowled. 'How would he know such a thing?'

'Oh, it was a very famous event. Everyone was talking about it, all the way to the shores of the ocean. It was a piece of luck for us. A misfortune for you, I guess.'

'General Drusus was the finest combatant I have ever seen . . .' said Taurus, without acknowledging the boy's tone of provocation. 'There were rumours that there was a relationship of sorts between him and your father. Did you know anything about that?'

Armin shot his brother a look. 'We heard the same rumour,' he admitted to Taurus, 'but that's all it was. Maybe it was because they respected each other, even though they were enemies.'

Taurus and the two boys let the rest of the group move on with most of the slain animal while they took a different route, ending the evening up near the deserted city of Veio. The boys lit a fire, while Taurus macerated a good-sized piece of boar haunch in vinegar and onion to tame its gaminess. While the meat was roasting, he told them about the Roman siege of Veio, which lasted ten years like the besiegement of Troy. But before long, he returned to what they'd begun to talk about earlier. 'I was at Magontiacum when General Drusus was carried there. He was feverish and pale; close to death. When his brother Tiberius in Rome learned how badly he'd been hurt, he jumped on a horse and headed north, accompanied by a small escort. He raced day and night, stopping only to change horses.

He covered two hundred miles in four days, across the Alps, leaving most of his men lagging behind him. Drusus was close to death when he heard that his brother was on his way; he sent out a squad of horsemen to meet him and guide him over the remaining territory. When the news came that he was arriving, Drusus gave orders from his death bed that the legions be drawn up to greet him with the highest military honours. Tiberius made it in time to hear his brother's last words and dying breath.'

Taurus stopped his narration and fell silent. The crackling of the fire was the only sound to be heard.

'Go on, Centurion,' said Flavus. 'If you will.'

'I was given the task,' began Taurus again, 'the high honour, of preparing and directing his funeral. General Drusus's body was borne on the shoulders of six military tribunes in their dress uniforms, preceded by four legates, and escorted by the entire legion of the garrison. Six thousand men in battle armour, with the imperial standard and the eagle. As the procession advanced, the trumpets sounded, joined by bugles and the deep rolling of drums. Last of all, General Drusus's riderless horse, a magnificent Pannonian stallion.

'I'd ordered a pyre to be raised with oak and fir trunks. It was as tall as a tower. A ramp was built starting at a distance of two hundred steps and reaching all the way to the top. When the legion arrived at the base of the ramp they divided into two columns and marched in step until they completed a formation that stretched all the way around the pyre, in a square measuring half a jugerum. The coffin was carried on the tribunes' shoulders all the way up to the top of the pyre, where it was placed on the bier and then, at the blare of one hundred bronze trumpets, forty legionaries, ten on each side, set fire to the pyre. The entire legion presented arms, the steel-clad infantrymen stiffened in salute and shouted out his name. No one was left with a dry eye at that sight. Not even the most battle-hardened veteran. Not even me.'

Taurus's head dropped to his chest.

'His brother, Tiberius Claudius, took the urn with his ashes to Rome on foot, and laid them in the mausoleum that Augustus had had built for the members of his family. The emperor received the ashes with the highest honours; he wore a long black tunic and a cloak of the same colour, trimmed in gold. No Roman worthy of this name, from the emperor to the last foot soldier, has ever resigned himself to this loss.'

Flavus and Armin listened in silence to Marcus Taurus's heartfelt commemoration. Both were astonished at the way in which he narrated these events: it was as if he were speaking to young Romans; to young men whose job one day would be to defend the Empire. Their reactions were quite different, however. Armin, seemingly untouched, stared into the distance. He couldn't ignore the emotion he felt flowing from his brother but he certainly didn't share it.

The air all around them quivered with cold chills and burned bright with oaken fire. Marcus Taurus handed out the meat, cutting off a piece for himself with his regulation knife.

'Eat,' he said. 'You must be starving.'

After having their fill, the two brothers hobbled the horses and laid out their blankets, but they still weren't tired enough to sleep, despite the long day.

Taurus was browning his piece of meat over the embers. He raised his eyes and looked across at the boys. 'I've heard your tales of warriors who have fallen in battle – the spirits of death who receive them, the Valkyrie virgins who ride at their sides to lead them to the fields of perpetual glory. They're beautiful stories. We don't have anything like that. Our heroes are accompanied to the underworld by their own soldiers, no one else . . .'

He turned to Armin. 'Could you tell me what the difference between a soldier and a warrior is?'

Armin hesitated.

'I'll tell you. You are a warrior, your brother is a soldier.'

Neither of the two boys answered. It was as if they had heard an oracle.

'Centurion Taurus . . .' said Flavus.

'What is it?' grumbled the officer.

'Can I ask you a question?'

'If you must . . .'

'Who is the boy with the white tunic edged in purple that we meet up with at the training ring now and then?'

'You'll know when it's time. Do not speak to him and don't ask anyone else this question, not even when you're capable of speaking Latin. Go to sleep now.'

The boys stretched out on their blankets. They were awakened during the night by noises coming from the forest nearby and they saw the figure of Taurus, on his feet with his sword in hand, on top of a large mound of earth. The red moon was setting in the fog.

8

THEY SET OFF AGAIN before dawn. A grey dawn, that released from the darkness only the tall burial mounds of the ancient heroes of a city that, Taurus explained, was older than Rome and had once dared to defy her. Flavus and Armin had long understood that under the tough demeanour of their master at arms was a philosopher who asked himself questions about the destiny of men and nations, about the chaotic forces that can storm through history with blind violence, bringing about drastic changes and casting off – in the blink of an eye – what man has taken great time and trouble to build.

Armin and Flavus wanted to know who was there, under those mounds. What their names were, who their ancestors were. And why their weed-infested tombs were in such a state of abandon, showing signs of profanation and pillaging.

'No monument can survive, intact, without the civilization that has created it,' replied Marcus Taurus. 'Look at what remains of these walls. There was a time when no one would have dared to try to take them by force, but Rome did just that. And now they serve only to shelter wild animals. What was once a proud, powerful city has been reduced to a heap of ruins. Our own soldiers even took cover here four centuries ago when they were defeated by the Gauls at the Allia River. Now it is nothing more than a wretched village, destined to disappear from the face of this earth. Its inhabitants have even forgotten their native language and now they use ours.

'And yet the flame of their ancestral memory still burns, I'm told, in many of them. They were called, and still call themselves, Etruscans. One of them is among the emperor's first councillors and others are poets. Some have proved to be formidable fighters. Rome never wanted to destroy them or wipe out their race. All we want is peace under the same sky. We wanted them to fight on our side against common enemies, to mix their blood with ours in marriage.

'When this city was defeated, everyone was fighting each other for this land, but only one of those peoples was victorious: the Romans. Fate meant for this to happen. But, even when Rome remained alone and triumphant, more conflicts arose,' he sighed. 'I'm talking about Romans against Romans, citizens of the same republic. Some claimed to be fighting for freedom against the absolute power of an autocrat. In part, this was true, but it was also a lie. If they had won, they would just have claimed those powers for themselves.

'In the end, a single man put a stop to these fratricidal wars. Our emperor, Augustus. He succeeded in breaking the chain of revenge and bloodletting. And since then there has been peace. Peace, prosperity and all the freedom possible under such circumstances. Every city, every community, stands on its own, administering its own laws, organizing its own ceremonies to propitiate its own gods . . .'

Both Armin and Flavus had lots of things to say and ask but they knew well that it wasn't permitted. One of the strictest precepts in their house on the Aventine was to stay clear of politics, and that prohibition alone told them much more than any amount of talk about lost liberties.

By this time, the City – as everyone called her – was coming within view. They still hadn't become accustomed to that spectacle: the triumph of the sun on the temples and columns, the arches and bridges, the green and red pine trees, the twisted, silvery olive trees, the rearing horses and the winged victories in gold and bronze, the iridescent fountains. Taurus signalled for them to follow him. The roads were thronging with people. The notables, who refused to mix with the rabble, were carried on swaying litters while a steady stream of slaves, workers, craftsmen, washerwomen and bakers swirled below. Here and there, groups of pantomimes improvised comical shows, applauded by casual passers-by and intentional spectators alike. Thus flowed life at the feet of towering metal statues and of gleaming victory columns and triumphal arches, beneath the shaded porticoes, around the divine fountains, the altars smoking with incense, the meridians that marked time for the Empire.

In front of the palaces of government and the gates to the military quarter stood the magnificent praetorians, the guards of Rome and of Italy in their polished muscle cuirasses, blue uniforms and red-crested helmets. Their cloaks flapped like banners in the west wind.

Time passed rapidly, as if the red at dawn and the red at dusk had mixed into a single golden cloud. Taurus was headed towards the Campus Martius, where he stopped in front of a sculpted, painted monument that stood alone in a wide, open area. It seemed to the two boys as if the centurion had finally reached the site of some mysterious appointment.

'This is the *Ara Pacis*,' he said. 'Augustus's Altar of Peace. You should try to understand what it means. Each one of the figures you see sculpted here holds a message for the people and the Senate, but also for visitors like you who are coming here for the first time. It is here that you'll find the answer to a question that you have asked me many times.'

Neither Armin nor Flavus had a clue to what he was talking about, ignorant as they were of mythology, the imperial family and the symbols of state and religion. They tried in vain to remember what question he could be referring to. They were prompted by the sudden echo of a voice that was as clear as the water that flowed in the City's fountains. It was coming from inside the monument and the notes it sang made the marble walls vibrate like the sound box of a musical instrument. It was a subtle, melancholy air, like some sad lament. There were no religious celebrations going on, nor were there any priests or acolytes making votive offerings to the gods. That song seemed to be sounding out for a single reason: that the singer could not help but express those notes with heartfelt intensity in that sacred, sublime space.

Armin was startled, and moved to go up the stairs to see whose voice it was. He thought for a moment that Taurus was trying to stop him, but he was wrong. Taurus had not moved. He simply said, 'You won't find anyone in there. Only ghosts rendered in cold, lifeless marble.' Armin paused for a moment in surprise, but then continued up the steps and entered the monument. He was determined to see what was inside.

There was no one.

Not even the shadow of a person. Armin walked out the other side, still looking for an explanation. He could still hear the voice but it had faded, and seemed far away. Just when it seemed about to dissolve into the dusk, it rose into a shrill sharp scream of pain and then vanished into the gathering darkness.

Taurus was standing in front of him now and it looked for a moment like tears were shining in his dark eyes. Perhaps a trick of the light? Was it possible that such a tough, hardy soldier was feeling such emotion? The voice of a woman, so intense it could cause marble walls to vibrate . . . could it move even this stony warrior?

'No one can manage to explain this phenomenon,' he admitted. 'But one thing is certain. Every day at this time Antonia, the widow of General Drusus, descends into the imperial mausoleum. Look, it's over there, you can see it from here. Her tears honour the memory of her greatly beloved husband, the man she can never forget. The sad song you heard was the cry of a soul in pain, a lament strong enough, perhaps, to cross the threshold between the living and the dead. Follow me now. There's something I want to show you.'

He went to the southern side of the huge altar, where the inaugural procession of the Empire was represented. Every member of the imperial family was sculpted in bas relief on the wide marble surface. Taurus pointed to a standing male figure, his shoulders covered by a cloak; in front of him was a woman of extraordinary beauty depicted in profile as she turned to look at him. She was holding a child, dressed in a tiny tunic and toga, by the hand. Around his neck hung a pendant, a good-luck charm that protected little ones from the evil eye.

'The man with the cloak is General Drusus and she is Antonia, his wife. They were greatly in love and she would travel to the ends of the world just to be able to lie in his arms. The little boy whose hand she's holding is Germanicus, so named for his father's victories in the Germanic campaigns.'

Flavus and Armin exchanged a glance that meant 'not a word!'

'The lad that you've sometimes seen in the ring training against me with sword and shield is Germanicus. He was just a little boy when this image was sculpted.'

Armin shot another look at Flavus, filled with the memories of so many stories that their father Sigmer had told them. They'd long known about the reciprocal esteem that had persisted between their father and Drusus, despite the fact that they had often faced each other as enemies on the battlefield. And the boys were also well aware of how much truth there was to the legend that the two men had shared a deep, secret friendship.

Armin pointed to another figure further on in the procession. He was a young man, tall, dressed exactly like Drusus, with a tunic and military cape.

'Who's that?' he asked.

'That is Tiberius, the older brother of General Drusus,' replied Taurus. 'The last time I saw Tiberius, he was sitting on his brother's bed, holding his hand as he lay dying,' he added. 'He clasped him to his breast at the moment of his passing.'

'Where is he now?' asked Armin.

Taurus let his head drop forward and remained silent. Flavus shot his brother a look of warning that Armin picked up on instantly. 'I'm sorry,' he said quickly. 'I imagine that doesn't concern me.'

The centurion did not add another word.

THE BOY ARRIVED on time that day and Taurus went to help him on with his training armour.

Flavus and Armin had got to the ring earlier and were sitting at the side of the arena. Flavus turned to his brother and whispered in his ear, using their native tongue, 'What kind of a question was that for Taurus?'

'I said I was sorry, didn't I?'

'It's not a question of saying you're sorry. There's much more to it.'

'What, then?'

Flavus watched as the boy, who they now knew was Germanicus, engaged in hand-to-hand fighting with his instructor. Germanicus was sweaty and panting, Taurus was as solid as a boulder. Although he didn't need to worry about Taurus overhearing him, he spoke quietly nonetheless. 'It's a story that everyone knows about, but no one admits it and no one talks about it. Emperor Augustus, the supreme head of the State, and that means the most powerful man in the world, has only one daughter, Julia, who was born to his first wife. He arranged for Julia's first marriage to be with his sister's son. Marcellus was a good lad, but he died before he turned twenty. Poisoned, they say,' he added, lowering his voice even further.

At that point, he had to cut his story short, because the lesson with Taurus had finished. Master and apprentice were quenching their thirst with a pitcher of cool water. The centurion looked over at the edge of the arena and seemed to be noticing Armin and Flavus for the first time. He beckoned for them to come over. The two brothers obeyed and Taurus said, turning to Germanicus, 'Are you feeling up to defending your family name? Can you see how tall they are? And do you see the colour of their eyes?'

'Like the colour of your own,' said the boy. And then, scowling, he nodded. His proposed adversaries were fresh and rested, while he was exhausted after engaging in a bout with a man twice his weight without a libra of fat. But Germanicus, son of General Drusus, could not reject the challenge.

'You should be able to fight both of them at once and knock them both out, given the name you bear, but considering that you did a decent job of grappling with me, I'll let you, just this once, chose one of them. Whichever you prefer.'

Germanicus walked towards the two boys who looked at

him calmly, without locking eyes. He stopped for a moment at an equal distance from one and the other, then trained his glance on Armin. 'This one,' he said. Then, turning to Taurus, he asked, 'What kind of weapons? Training or real?'

'Metal helmet, leather corsets, wooden swords and shields,' replied the centurion. 'You must fight fairly. No going for your opponent's eyes, or his testicles. You might be needing those for continuing the dynasty,' he said, smiling, looking at Germanicus. 'I will signal the end to the fight by cutting through the air in a downward motion, using my hand as a knife. Combat will begin when I clap my hands.'

The duellists collected their arms and as Armin was putting on his corset, Flavus helped by lacing up his boots, taking the opportunity to make a suggestion in their native language: 'Defend yourself but don't hurt him. He's the son of General Drusus and the adopted grandson of the emperor. You'd be a dead man.'

'I know,' replied Armin curtly as he settled into a defensive stance.

The two opponents studied each other at length, each looking for an in to throw the other off guard. Taurus kept his eyes on both of them; he knew that if he could foresee their manoeuvres he could also prevent any unpleasant consequences. He was well aware of how much these boys were worth and he could see his own teachings in their every move.

The first lunge was Germanicus's, the tip of his sword directed at Armin's left side. Armin was quick to deflect it with his shield and attack his adversary's left side tip-on. A high parry followed, and then a low, edgewise crossing of blades. Germanicus tried to immobilize Armin's sword on the ground so he could strike at the base of his neck with the edge of his shield. Armin barely dodged the blow, which could have been fatal. They faced each other again and squared off, before letting loose with a violent exchange of blows and a series of boisterous collisions, shield against shield. Germanicus faltered. Armin did not let up, landing a surprise blow with the top of his foot on the back of his opponent's knee. Germanicus fell to the ground and Armin was about to point the tip of his sword at his throat to declare victory, but Germanicus twisted around, leapt back up to his feet and delivered a downward blow behind his back with the edge of his shield. A grimace on Taurus's face revealed the tension that was consuming him, but the centurion did not stop the fight. The two boys were dripping with sweat, tunics soaked through and hair pasted to their foreheads. Both showed bruises on their sides, their thighs, their shoulders and arms. Both were bleeding from multiple cuts.

The springtime sun was high and quite hot. Both boys were panting and looked exhausted, but they were still gritting their teeth and striking out with unflagging vehemence. Blow after blow, shields crashing, using up all the strength left in their weary limbs. When Taurus noticed that fatigue had set in hard and that their strikes were swinging wide, he finally decided to slash his hand downwards and declare the duel ended.

Armin returned to his brother's side as Germanicus went to the fountain to wash away his sweat. Taurus spoke: 'Neither of you managed to prevail over the other so I shall call this match a draw. There are two things, however, that I must take into account: Armin is taller and heavier than Germanicus, but he did perhaps hold back so as not to endanger his opponent and suffer the consequences. If he did so, he did it well, because the fight seemed completely authentic. I would say that it was somewhat similar to a fight between gladiators. I know that Germanicus has witnessed this type of spectacle, whereas

Flavus and Armin are barely acquainted with it. You are dismissed.'

Flavus helped his brother off with his armour so that Armin could wash at the fountain as well and then the two boys set off for their lodgings. Germanicus, accompanied by Taurus at a certain distance, was limping.

'What was he like?' asked Flavus.

'Strong. Often vicious.'

'Yes, but you fought as if your hands were tied!'

'That's not true. When you're in the middle of a fight you just strike out. And that's that.'

They went on without speaking for some time, each curious about what was on the other's mind.

'What are you thinking?' asked Flavus in the end.

'What you're thinking. If we ever meet up on a real battlefield . . .'

'The Cherusci are allies of the Romans.'

'And we're prisoners,' replied Armin.

'Guests,' corrected Flavus. 'Prisoners don't live like we do. Look at the clothes you're wearing, think of the foods you eat. Don't you remember that millet meal that Mother used to make?'

Armin looked down because he didn't feel like talking.

'Did he say anything to you when you were hand-to-hand?'

'Yeah, he was muttering something in Latin but it was more like growling than talking. Maybe he was swearing, maybe something else. Maybe one day everything will be clearer. Tell me where General Drusus's brother is.'

'You're still thinking about that? How should I know anyway?'

'I don't know. You always know more than I do about the Romans.'

'Because my Latin is better than yours and because I listen. And lots of people talk openly when we're around because they think we can't understand them, that's why I learn a lot more than you do.'

'Well then?'

'If you care so much, I'll tell you what I know. But we should go back to the marble altar. Everyone we need to talk about is sculpted there.'

'And how can we do that?'

'I can ask Taurus. He trusts us. You do realize that whatever we do, we're being watched day and night by people that we can't even see, right?'

Armin nodded. His mind had already returned to those figures carved in the marble, the incredible beauty they expressed, and he seemed to barely notice when Flavus commented, 'It would take centuries before we were capable of making something that magnificent.'

Nonetheless, he answered, 'We're warriors.'

'What, they're not?' replied Flavus with a sarcastic smile.

THE BOYS COULD scarcely believe it when they were given permission the next day to move freely around the City, which was crawling with people who'd come for one of the many religious or political celebrations. They took advantage of the opportunity to see parts of the City they were unfamiliar with. What impressed them the most was the Circus Maximus. They could never have imagined a structure of those proportions: how many people could fit onto those seating tiers? As many as there were in an entire Germanic tribe, for sure. They were even able to watch as a dozen or more chariots, each drawn by four horses, practised for the races. It was the most exciting thing they'd ever witnessed and their hearts beat quicker at the sight. After each lap, a large bronze dolphin-shaped counter was lowered by manoeuvring a hook. Every dolphin was in reality a fountain that directed its spray either upwards or downwards. Trumpets blared out from inside the enormous space, echoing on both sides. The track was covered with crushed stone that increased the traction of the chariot wheels; they watched the drivers gripping hard at the reins as the four steeds tore off at great speed. Once they reached the end of the long side of the track and began the turn, they had to vie for the innermost lane which would shorten the course and give them the best chance at winning.

Since what they were watching was only practice, the charioteers abstained from the most extreme racing strategies so they wouldn't risk damaging the chariots or laming the horses before the actual competition, when the winning driver would be crowned in front of an immense, delirious crowd.

'I'm sure that it won't be long before they bring us here to watch a real race and that's when we'll see what they're genuinely capable of. A race in the great circus of Rome! After that it'll be the gladiators. They say it's the most cruel, terrible show in the whole world, where men fight each other to the death for the sole reason of entertaining the spectators,' mused Flavus.

'Just thinking about it disgusts me,' replied Armin. 'I hope they don't force us. But nowadays there's not a big city anywhere that doesn't have an amphitheatre of its own, unfortunately. Even in Germania.'

'Yes,' repeated Flavus, without letting any emotion into his voice, 'even in Germania.'

They finally reached their destination: the monumental altar ordered by Emperor Augustus to celebrate the peace he had restored by ending the civil wars, the *Ara Pacis*. Flavus pointed out the images of both Tiberius and his wife. 'This is Julia. She's the only daughter of the emperor and, as you can see, she's beautiful, even in marble. Tiberius, General Drusus's brother, is the son of Livia, who had him with her first husband.'

Armin asked again, 'And where is Tiberius now?'

'On an island, between Greece and Asia. He leads a secluded life and rarely sees anyone; he writes letters to maintain his relationships. They say that he has long solitary walks on the island beaches, but that he still spends time training. He's always been very strong; a formidable soldier. But he's a strange man anyway. When the Romans want to punish someone they send them to a little island in the middle of the sea. He went there of his own free will.'

'Why?'

Flavus brushed Julia's marble face. 'Because of her. Because of Julia. Now that we're alone I can tell you the whole story. When she was widowed of her second husband, Agrippa, a very powerful man, her father Augustus decided to give her to Tiberius Claudius as his wife. Remember what I told you? Tiberius is the son of Livia, who is Augustus's wife.

'When Julia was still married to Agrippa, she had children with him, including two beautiful sons who are their grandfather's pride and joy. They're his own flesh and blood, you see, born of his daughter and of his best friend, Agrippa. See, here they are: this is Lucius and this is Gaius, and the figure with his head covered by his toga is their father, Agrippa.'

From outside they could hear the cries of the boatmen sailing up the Tiber with the day's catch, mixed with the din of the carts transporting every sort of ware and provisions for the capital of the known world. But the unnatural silence which reigned inside the great altar room contrasted with the life-like quality of the figures sculpted in marble. They were so convincing that it felt like you could hear the steady hum of their conversations. Army commanders, priests, the great ladies of the imperial house, babes and children who one day would become powerful like their fathers and uncles, and like their grandfather, who held the world in his hands.

Flavus roused himself from his thoughts for a moment, and then went on: 'So Tiberius – that is, Julia's third husband – had always enjoyed great fame for his military prowess. He is always at the forefront of any fight, has won countless battles in a great number of places . . . Everyone knew that he was the true defender of the Empire after Agrippa's death but he was repeatedly seeing inexperienced, incapable younger men being favoured for succession in his place. Meanwhile Julia, his wife, had become exasperated at having to comply with reasons of state: at being married off to men chosen by her father and continuously having their children. She wanted to live her own life, spend her time with the high society – poets, artists, philosophers, actors – and to have love affairs with them if it struck her fancy. Above all, to play out her passion for the only true love of her life—'

Armin interrupted him. 'Come on. It's not possible that you know all these things.'

'I told you, your Latin is terrible. I'm getting better and better at it, and Diodorus has even taken me under his wing; he's the one who repeats all the whispers and rumours of what's going on among the high-powered here in Rome. I think he gets more of a kick telling me this stuff than I do listening.'

'So is that why Tiberius Claudius is in some kind of exile on an island in the southern sea?'

'Wouldn't that be enough for you? He's the greatest soldier of the Empire, the commander of the armies of the north, and his wife's behaviour has turned him into everybody's fool.'

'Maybe he deserved it.'

'I would say the opposite,' shot back Flavus. 'I think he's a good man. He was forced to marry Julia. He was in love with his own wife. I've heard that if he sees her, even at a distance, he can't hold back his tears.'

'I can't believe that such a powerful man has any real feelings, apart from the desire for more power. And you heard that from Diodorus?'

'Well, it's not like he told me all of this at once. It's only every now and then, when he's in the mood to gossip. Actually, it's funny, when he talks about Julia – and he always calls her "beautiful Julia" – it's like he doesn't dare to say what he knows. When he stops talking, it's not because he's run out of information, it's because he's reluctant to talk about it. Who am I in his eyes anyway? Just one more boy he's responsible for tutoring, and a "barbarian" to boot. I'm convinced that his silences are hiding some big secret. So big he can't even admit it to himself. But we really need to get going now; it's time to get back to the Aventine.'

They walked back just as the sun was setting behind the hills and the shadows began to spread through the City. When they crossed the gardens, it was almost dark, but they were not afraid. They kept talking as they walked: Flavus in Latin, Armin in Germanic.

'Why won't you speak our language with me?' asked Armin.

'You know it's forbidden. And that's the real reason I know Latin better than you: I respect the rules. It's better all round. Latin is our language now. It lets me express ideas and feelings for which there aren't any words in our language. We'll never forget our own language, so let's save it to use it when we need it; when we don't want them to understand us. But let's live as though we've forgotten it.'

A rustling interrupted them. In a heartbeat, both had their hands on their daggers and had stepped apart to face the threat. It was a huge Hermundur, emerging from a laurel bush like a bear from the woods. His grey wolf's eyes were framed by tattoos. They recognized him as one of the auxiliaries who had escorted them to Rome from Germania.

'What are you doing here?' demanded Armin in his native language.

'I have a message for you from your father, powerful Sigmer.'

'Our father!' repeated the boys in a sigh as they resheathed their knives. The giant bared his white teeth, shook his head slightly and brought a finger to his lips. The first part of the message was made up of seven words, pronounced in his own dialect. The look the brothers shot one another was full of confusion – who could understand his guttural mumbling? The Hermundur must have noticed their dismay, for when he spoke again it was in Germanic: ' "The first who understands is authorized to reveal it, but if he prefers to keep silence, so be it." These are the words of your father.'

He slipped away at once, leaving no time for the boys to recover from their shock. They made their way in silence, walking slowly down the gravel path that led to the atrium of the house. The only sound to be heard was that of a drop of water slowly falling into a basin, marking the flow of time.

'What's that?' asked Flavus, taking a step back.

'A hydraulic clock. This morning it wasn't there.'

'So what time is it?' asked Flavus again.

'The first hour of the first guard shift. You can tell from those notches on the inside of the basin. See? You can even feel them with your fingers in the dark.'

They reached the peristyle and Armin spoke up again: 'Did you get what he said first?'

'You can understand the Hermundur if you watch the movement of his lips. Did you?'

'No, it was too dark.'

'Me neither.'

In truth, each suspected that the other had understood just fine, but was not ready to share what he'd heard, not yet.

'If the horseman that you saw galloping out of the fog in Ravenna were to ride by in front of us right now, would you recognize him?' asked Armin.

'No.'

'I think you'd be able to recognize him even in the dark, but that you don't want to say so.'

'I don't know,' said Flavus. 'Everyone has their own ghosts.'

9

'THREE HEADS BETWEEN two bodies. She at centre of all, of life or death.' The phrase was the result of Armin and Flavus consulting each other the next morning. Both boys had had a bad night, disturbed by receiving a message from their father and upset at not being able to interpret what seemed to be a silly riddle. In the meantime, all the memories of their childhood and youth had come flooding back, plunging them straight back into the forests of Germania.

In order to be certain of not influencing one another, each had written his own interpretation of what the Hermundur had muttered at first in his own dialect. They compared the tablets: the words were identical. If the message came from their father, was it referring to Germania? But no, both brothers felt that the phrase had to refer more to their current situation than to their past.

But how were they to get at the meaning of such a message? Was it something that concerned them personally? Was it something that their father had heard from General Drusus? But, since the commander hadn't been alive for a long time now, except in the minds of his wife, his brother Tiberius and Primus Pilus Centurion Marcus Taurus, it was evident that they needed to look *hic et nunc*, said Flavus in the end, flaunting his Latin with the expression for 'here and now'.

'*Hic et nunc*,' replied Armin, without missing a beat.

They were sitting on the edge of a fountain of water burbling from the mouth of a bronze dolphin held in the hands of a young Triton inside a round basin made of red marble. Cornelius, the gardener, was raking up fallen twigs just a few steps away.

'Three heads between two bodies, she at the centre. We have to figure out what "she" refers to, first of all,' continued Armin.

'You mean *who*. "She" has to be a person, not just a head,' Flavus observed. 'She's between two bodies and she's the centre of everything, of life or death.'

'Fine. But heads between two bodies? That doesn't make any sense at all.'

'You know, maybe the Hermundur misunderstood and what we're thinking is all wrong,' mused Flavus, trying to break the spell that the apparently meaningless phrase had cast on them. 'Or maybe we have to wait and we'll be given more messages as time goes on that will complete the puzzle.'

'No, you can't start thinking that way. This phrase is all we've got to work with. Listen, each of us interpreted the Hermundur's words on his own and we wrote them down separately, so we didn't influence one another. Yet they matched perfectly. The words are clear, even though their meaning is not. But I have a hard time believing that they come from our father. I've never heard him say anything close to that.'

'But we haven't made a mistake. We both understood exactly the same thing.'

The western breeze carried with it the scent of lilies and jasmine, of grass just cut. Inside the villa, the servants were busy with spring cleaning. Marcus Taurus was away for a few days and Diodorus had claimed the extra hours as his own.

They were studying Greek history, but also the recent history of the Republic. In order to help his pupils understand, their tutor had shown them a long strip of papyrus that reproduced the entire frieze of the Altar of Peace in which the members of the imperial family were sculpted. He'd taught them to recognize each one of them. It was evident that all students in Rome were meant to learn about the events of the last thirty years according to the version that had been laid down by her supreme ruler. It had occurred to both Armin and Flavus that nothing of this sort existed in their native land, details of which were becoming foggier in their minds as time passed. There were the songs of the bards, but that was entirely different.

What the Romans called 'history' was a narration that had all the semblance of truth, because it was based on the reports of people who had witnessed the events, or who had spoken with those who had. Most of the time, it was great men who wrote down the story of the events of which they themselves had been the protagonists, and no one would ever take it upon himself to contradict them, mostly because of the enormous esteem they enjoyed. That's what Julius Caesar had done when he wrote about the Gallic Wars. If there were other versions of the facts that didn't please those in power, they would slowly fade away and people ended up forgetting about them. So only one so-called truth remained.

Diodorus was very careful at explaining his way around history. He was only a freedman and he had no intention of saying anything that could be used against him, nor were the boys at liberty to question anything he taught them. One day he began to list the events that, according to his own interpretation, had led to the end of civil strife among the Romans. It had taken a war: the war of the man who everyone now called Caesar

Augustus and who then was called Octavian, against his great-est adversary – Marcus Antonius – who had married an Egyptian queen called Cleopatra. Antony and Cleopatra were now dead, and Augustus remained the sole master of the entire world, although he had never expressly declared it. So, the con-flict that had put an end to the civil wars was in itself a civil war – that is, Romans fighting against Romans. It certainly wasn't easy to find the truth behind this 'history'. But Diodorus also enlightened them as to why there was a good reason to study those facts: because a public commemoration of those very events was soon to take place, replete with parades, fes-tivities and athletic competitions.

One evening as the two brothers were strolling along the river, admiring how the sinking sun was setting aflame the water and the statues on the temple of Asclepius on the Tiber Island, Armin suddenly said, 'It's not the meaning of those words that we have to figure out first. We have to find out who gave the message to the Hermundur so he could give it to us.'

'Not our father?' asked Flavus.

'It may have been him, but I'm not so sure. Try to think backwards. Do you remember the phrase?'

'Of course: three heads between two bodies, she at the centre of everything, of life or death.'

'All right. Then forget about the Hermundur and think about the group of people with whom we have or have had a relationship. Besides our father, that would be Taurus, Dio-dorus, Germanicus . . . and the gardener, I guess, Cornelius. Am I forgetting anyone?'

'Taurus's two freedmen, Thiaminus and Privatus. But we've hardly even spoken to them,' said Flavus.

'Then let's play another game. Take this tablet and write the name of the person who you think may have thought up such a phrase. Turn it over and pass it to me and I'll do the same on the other side.'

It took just a few moments for the boys to write a name in the wax. Armin compared them. They'd both written the same name. Diodorus.

Curious about all the events that were being readied for the upcoming celebrations, and with that name in mind, Armin and Flavus crossed the river and the Campus Martius and set off on foot towards the Vatican Hill. Every now and then they would take off at a run, like that day when they'd been caught in the forest in Germania and taken into Marcus Taurus's custody. They finally drew up short, as they had then, in front of a grandiose spectacle. There were thousands of labourers on the hill and they were digging an enormous reservoir one thousand eight hundred feet long and one thousand two hundred feet wide. It was later explained to them that when the festivities were scheduled to start, it would be filled with water from an aqueduct and used to simulate the Battle of Actium, in which Antony and Cleopatra had engaged Octavian in naval combat and had lost.

The emperor would be present on the north stand, at the centre of the long side of the pool, to watch the ships re-enact the naval battle that had changed the destiny of the world.

It would be a memorable show, although many of those present among the public would have no trouble actually remembering that day. Among the children who were adopted into the House of Augustus after their parents had been killed in battle were the sons of Marc Antony. Their whole lives had been marked by this painful contradiction: the gentleman dressed in white who hosted them, who gave them food and clothing and the instruction necessary for them to take up careers in politics or the army or to marry into the highest ranks, was also the person responsible for the deaths of their parents, or at least one of them. Armin watched the carpenters working hard to build the stand where the supreme ruler would sit to admire the spectacle of that momentous battle, and he was struck by a certain thought. Was the emperor putting himself at risk by presiding publicly over the re-enactment of an event so close and still so painful to many? He stopped to wonder whether his brother Wulf, who the Romans called Flavus, could be thinking the same thing. His own name had been Latinized as well; just about everyone now called him Arminius. As they stood and watched, however, the two boys spoke in their native tongue so as not to let on that they understood Latin.

And in fact a small group of men, who had fallen silent when the boys showed up, went back to talking among themselves again, in lower voices but loud enough to be heard. The scene that Arminius had seen in his imagination began to take on a realistic shape. Flavus could see his agitation and motioned with his head that it was time for the two of them to leave. They retraced their steps, walking towards the Tiber. Evening was falling.

'Why did you choose Diodorus?' Flavus spoke up.

'Because he's the only one who could have an image like that in his head,' replied his brother. 'And you?'

'Well, I was thinking of that first time that Taurus took us into the City and showed us that monument with those figures sculpted in the marble. The same ones that Diodorus taught us about in his lessons. You remember, the ones on the papyrus that he said would help us better understand . . .'

'You're right. It's there we have to look.'

'When?'

'Now.'

'Taurus will have us whipped if we get back too late.'

'Yes, but it's worth the risk.'

They crossed the river again and found themselves at the big marble altar of the *Ara Pacis*. They took a couple of lanterns from their hooks and went inside.

'Let's split up,' proposed Arminius. 'You go north, and I'll go south.'

Flavus advanced slowly down the eastern side and then the northern one, coming back along the western side to end up at the southern side where they'd started. Arminius had already made his rounds in the opposite direction twice, analyzing the carvings figure by figure – the priests, the magistrates, the commanders of the great units of the army, the ladies of the Empire, the youngsters and the children – and then he stopped. He held his lantern high to illuminate a group of figures. The quivering light animated the faces and the draping of their robes, giving them a soul and a changing expression that no artist would be capable of rendering.

Two of the guards of the sacred area had entered, without making the slightest sound; they must have been alerted by the moving lights. 'Who are you?' one demanded. 'What are you doing here at this hour?'

'Nothing,' replied Flavus promptly. 'We'd never seen this magnificent monument up close because it's always so crowded during the day. So we thought we'd take advantage of no one being around. We're guests of the public house on the Aventine and our tutor is Primus Pilus Centurion Marcus Caelius Taurus of the Eighteenth Legion.'

'All right,' the guard growled. 'We'll be waiting for you at the entrance. Don't touch anything.'

Arminius nodded and as soon as the two guards had made

their way to the bottom of the stairs he turned to his brother, eyes bright. 'I've found her. I don't know how I didn't realize it before now. Come here, look! Here are the three heads. This female figure in the middle is complete, but you can only see the heads of the figures on both sides of her. Then there are two whole bodies, one on either side, who are Agrippa and Tiberius. Look, here they are. And the one between them, the one in the middle, is she who stands between life and death.'

He fell silent and stood looking at the full female figure.

'It's Julia,' he whispered. 'Beautiful Julia. It's the emperor's daughter. She's flanked by two men: her husband Agrippa is on her right and the tall male figure on her left is Tiberius . . .'

'The one she's married to now, who's living on the Greek island . . .'

'Yes, him.'

'Now all we need to do is interpret the last part of the phrase.'

'"At the centre of everything, of life or death." Maybe the answer to that can be found here as well. But we can't stay any longer. We'd only attract unwanted attention.'

They walked out under the watchful eyes of the two guards and made their way towards the Aventine. In front of the entrance to the gardens they found Marcus Taurus waiting for them. He was rhythmically flicking the *vitis* that he held in his right hand against his left palm.

Flavus turned to his brother. 'What did I tell you?' Arminius nodded with an indifferent air and shrugged.

DESPITE THE MENACING POSE, Centurion Taurus kept his punishment to a couple of lashes, which the leather of the boys' corsets pretty effectively neutralized. Once in bed, Arminius and Flavus turned on their sides so they were facing each other and started to talk through what they'd seen and heard in that emotion-filled day. That enormous gouge in the side of the Vatican Hill, the phrases muttered by the workmen . . . they were terse, cut short, but there was an urgency there, talk of a great day and of *libertas*. And then the reflection of their lanterns on the marble draping, the rush of the Tiber that ran just behind the altar, so close that its waters could almost lap at the walls. The perfection of Julia's features and the fixity of her gaze. Germanicus, still a little boy, looking cocky beyond his years in his miniscule toga. Would they wear a toga one day? Perhaps, without even fully realizing it, they'd begun to crave that symbol of dignity and self-worth. The noble bearing it required, the way it spoke of austere elegance and centuries-old tradition. Of course it was absurd to think that that could ever happen.

The noises of the night were drifting into the room from outside. The pacing of the guardians and their dogs, the rustle of leaves caressed by the west wind, the passwords called out by the soldiers changing shifts. That was another thing they admired: the Roman State – the *Res Publica* – was present everywhere. The words the soldiers used as they went on sentry duty, their synchronized gestures, their peremptory voices and the sharp clang of their weapons all embodied the authority of Rome and her jealous control of the Empire.

The two boys wondered aloud why the enigmatic message had been relayed to them by the Hermundur. Could it be because Diodorus (if he was responsible for the riddle, as they now assumed) wanted to stay in the shadows? That would make sense; the iron rule of staying away from politics surely applied to him, a mere freedman. But why on earth would Diodorus, of all people, expect the two of them, mere boys, to unravel the mystery and choose whether to act on it? A fine mess he'd put them in!

THE NEXT DAY, the governess of their small community, an old woman of about sixty, showed up with breakfast and an unguent for their backs. Centurion Marcus Taurus had sent her.

'He never changes,' observed Flavus. 'A whipping to show us that discipline must always be maintained, no matter what. And then the old lady with some ointment to let us know it's nothing personal. Or perhaps the opposite; maybe it's benevolence on his part, and even respect.'

'Wait, maybe he's our man,' said Arminius suddenly. 'He surely knows all the secrets of Roman politics. He has his informers and maybe even the ear of highly ranked officials.'

'If she is at the centre of life or death . . .' replied Flavus, 'and by she I mean the lady who's carved in marble on the Altar of Peace, then we're really looking at a vipers' nest. I don't know if he's the right person to go to. He's a lion on the battlefield but I suspect he'd rather keep a mile away from anything that reeks of intrigue like this does.'

'Well, let's say that if he is willing to get to the bottom of this, we're willing to help. If he's not, we shouldn't pursue it. Who can we trust if not him? Diodorus? That doesn't seem wise to me. We're not even sure that he's the person behind the message; that's just a guess on our part.'

They waited a couple of days and then asked for the centurion to receive them, going through Diodorus himself. They got more than they bargained for: an invitation to dinner in his quarters.

He met them dressed in a dark floor-length tunic with long, wide sleeves trimmed in a light blue fabric and deerskin breeches in the Germanic style. In a corner of the room hung his parade armour: the helmet with its transverse horsehair crest, the cuirass studded with decorations, the baldric and greaves, his *gladius* and dagger. They ate together sitting at a table as they would have done at camp. The table setting was simple, with ceramic cups. A silver-plated bronze pitcher for pouring wine was the only concession to luxury. They were served by a Syrian servant dressed in the robes of his native country.

After greeting them with great cordiality, Taurus informed them that he had always maintained contact with their parents in Germania, using public service messengers. He reported that both their father Sigmer and mother Siglinde were well, and that political relations with the Cherusci were good. He poured wine for his guests and asked about the reason for their visit. The two boys exchanged a glance and Arminius began to speak.

He told Taurus that they'd been given a message, delivered personally by a man who claimed to be speaking on behalf of their father. It contained an enigma that seemed very difficult to work out, but their recent visit to the Altar of Peace had suggested a possible answer.

After Arminius had provided details regarding the message and the messenger, Flavus took over, rolling out a long papyrus scroll on which the inaugural procession of the *Ara Pacis* was represented. He pointed at the figures that they believed were referred to in the message. In the middle was Julia, at the centre of life and death.

Taurus frowned and took a long look at both boys, to see if they were telling him the truth.

'How can you be sure it was a message from your father?' he asked.

'We're not, in fact,' replied Flavus. 'Thinking about it, we felt that the message was too complex to be from our father, especially because he would have had to be completely familiar with these sculptures and to know all about the people they represent.'

'We've come to you for advice,' said Arminius.

'Have you considered investigating the Hermundur?' asked Taurus.

They had thought of everyone but him.

'No,' admitted Flavus. 'If it's hard to believe that our father composed this puzzle, it's impossible to imagine that the Hermundur did.'

Taurus dropped his head and sighed, then began to speak again. 'Julia has many admirers and suitors, as well as a number of very powerful enemies. Many have tried to slander her name but I know that in truth she has had a single, great love in her life . . . an impossible love.'

So Taurus harbours thoughts of love under that tough shell! Incredible . . . thought Flavus.

'You see, a woman in her position is never allowed to follow her inclinations. Her political weight is too great; her womb gives life to those destined to rise to the top ranks of power and so others decide who will put his seed there. Not others, exactly . . . one other. Her father, the supreme Augustus, has always tolerated her adventures, as long as she obeyed when it came time to accept a marriage of state.'

As Flavus listened to his words, he thought of the young girl crowned with flowers who had fascinated his brother in the Germanic forest. A single glance, and he was lost forever. He thought of Iole the prostitute who was just a girl herself; she could never even hope to entertain certain thoughts. All that awaited her was disgust, sperm, blood and vomit. Until the brutal, never-ending violence killed her. She would die without ever having lived a single day of sun and happiness. Or maybe he had offered her a ray of light when he had looked at her with longing and given her a gift. Maybe sweet little Iole was dreaming that one day he would be back at that way station, a powerful man wearing shining armour, and that he would carry her away from all that misery.

A dream like that was poison. Better no dream at all.

Taurus's voice called him back. 'Even the son of Mark Antony and his first wife is depicted on the wall of the great Altar of Peace. Iullus Antonius is his name. He's the last figure of the inaugural procession.'

Taurus paused, and then went on.

'This man is Julia's great love. They met when they were just children, living together with the other orphans of the civil wars in the house of Augustus. A boy and a girl who fell in love in that odd orphanage. But can either of you imagine that such feelings between the offspring of the fiercest adversaries of the last civil war could be allowed to have a future? Julia always kept that great love of hers secret, but in reality anyone who needed to know did so. She has always been kept under strict surveillance. Everything about her is reported directly to her father, the supreme ruler of the Roman State.'

Arminius was astonished that Taurus was revealing such important, delicate matters to two young Germanic princes, but he didn't realize how intimately Roman he himself had become in those years of living in the capital of the known world. He didn't realize how his Germanic accent was disappearing, how he had learned the military tactics of the army and the rudiments of Roman law, how he had absorbed their elegance and sense of aesthetics, the custom of tending to his body in the gymnasia and stadiums, the habit of bathing and being massaged daily.

'When Julia's mother, Scribonia, became pregnant,' Taurus continued, 'her husband Octavian – Augustus's name at the time, before he became emperor – dearly desired a boy. As soon as Julia was born, he tore her from the arms of her mother and he immediately repudiated her, his own wife, deaf to her cries of despair. Years later, as soon as Julia had her first monthly cycle, she was engaged and then married to her cousin Marcus Claudius, who died before he turned nineteen. She was married again. This time to a man twenty-five years her elder, Marcus Agrippa, her father's right arm. He impregnated her five times but died eight years ago before he could grow old. Julia is now married to Prince Tiberius, who is said to spend all his time pacing the beaches of the deserted island where he has chosen to live alone in a kind of voluntary exile. The supreme ruler was Tiberius's adoptive father and he actually forced his son to repudiate his own wife who he loved dearly in order to marry Julia. They say that every time Tiberius sees Vipsania, even from afar, he is unable to hold back tears. He went on to have a child with Julia, but it died while only a baby.

'So with Tiberius gone, Julia is free to encounter her beloved, who is a poet. They are said to meet in the hidden corners of the secret city, but also at the gatherings of a literary circle. But for long years they never saw each other. Their souls were close only in the marble figures sculpted on the wall of the great altar.'

10

For a long time, Arminius and Flavus put the phrase pronounced by the Hermunduri warrior out of their minds, along with the enigma hidden there. They were always busy with Taurus, who had been put in charge of arranging a parade, with various military exercises which the Auxilia corps were to perform in the presence of Roman notables and army chiefs, including the commander of Taurus's Eighteenth Legion, Legate Sextus Varinius. There were to be other visitors in the afternoon as well, but no one knew who they might be. Taurus had been ordered to keep all plans secret so as not to lessen the effect when the moment came.

The audience had assembled, and Flavus was first to set out at the head of a squad of Chatti and Suebi, simulating a cavalry charge. The target they were tasked to assail was formed of mannequins made of straw and fresh clay equipped with wooden shields and corsets made of hemp. The two young princes wore leather helmets and a *lorica* of iron mail which was heavy but easy to move in, and carried two spears and two swords, the long swords favoured by the cavalry.

Arminius was second in leading the charge. Halfway into the exercise, his men all hurled their spears. He let fly the first and then the second, hitting both targets, then unsheathed his swords and decapitated two of the mannequins. He wheeled around, took another couple of spears from the arms bearers and led a second assault, once again hitting his mark perfectly with both spears and swords. More exercises with other groups followed, and then it was Flavus's turn again. He performed daring manoeuvres of great speed and skill. The exercises became increasingly more difficult and dangerous and cries of wonder came from the finest ladies in the audience. Flavus rode an extraordinarily beautiful stallion, as black and shiny as the wings of a crow, with tufts of horsehair hanging from his ankles to cover his lustrous tallow-coated hoofs. Arminius mounted a white steed with a long mane that Taurus himself had chosen for him, a horse worthy of a great warrior. The sun had risen high over the Campus Martius, and the only creatures not dripping with sweat were the guests positioned to take full advantage of the western breeze, sitting on shaded stands under a white linen canopy, drinking cold water out of silver cups.

At the tenth hour, Taurus called the two princes to him and a murmur of admiration passed along the rows of spectators as they watched the two handsome young men advancing on their magnificent stallions. Their muscles were gleaming, their hair flaming in the sun.

They vaulted to the ground with agile, elegant leaps. Taurus took them by the arms and pulled them close. 'Don't turn around,' he said. 'The emperor's on his way here.'

Both boys started.

'What does that mean, Centurion?' asked Flavus.

'Nothing in itself. He's heard about these exercises and he wanted to see them for himself. For the two of you it means a great deal. Show him what you can do.'

'And what must we do?' asked Arminius.

'I have a test in store for you. The toughest. If you feel ready?'

They stared into his eyes. 'We're afraid of nothing and no one,' replied Flavus.

'You'll need all your energy and all your courage. You will lead your united squads. You, Arminius, on the right and you, Flavus, on the left. The colour of your horses will make you visible to one another. Neither of you has ever shed blood. That will happen today. It's inevitable, because you'll be facing men who've known nothing but combat their whole lives and who have survived many a bloody conflict. Their bodies are full of scars, their spirits torn . . . they don't know what a heart is. A dog from hell sank his fangs into it when they were born. They are, and will be, until death . . . gladiators.

'They too will be mounted on horseback. You two can choose your weapons. If you should fall, get to your feet immediately. Back each other up.' He stopped for a moment to whisper something in the boys' ears, then continued in a normal tone of voice: 'If an adversary falls, kill him immediately or he will kill you. Good luck.'

Flavus chose the arms that felt best to him and then helped Arminius to put on his battle armour, saying something to his brother under his breath. They shook both hands and Flavus lined up on the left wing with three lines of horsemen behind him, seven across. When he turned right to memorize his brother's position in the formation he found alongside him the huge Hermundur who had travelled with them from Germania to Italy and who had brought them that cryptic message. He smiled, showing all his teeth under a blond moustache.

'What are you doing here, Hermundur?'

'I'm covering your side, son.'

The horses were snorting by now and biting at their bits. Arminius assumed the strategic command and passed through the ranks, giving orders in his native language: a great advantage in that situation. The words were referred to Flavus by one of Arminius's horsemen, who approached him, repeated a few terse phrases and returned to his place in line, while Flavus passed the word on to his own men until everyone in the formation had been advised.

The emperor had arrived. He was dressed in white and escorted by eight praetorians in full dress uniform, but without lictors, since he was making an unofficial appearance. When the two squads were ready, the *lanista* proclaimed that one trumpet call would signal the start of combat and another would signal the end. The trumpet blared and the two fronts, the Germanic Auxilia and the gladiators, set off at a gallop towards each other, weapons leading. The last two rows of auxiliary horsemen were advancing at a slightly slower pace, and remained a bit detached from those in front. The field had been sprinkled with enough water to prevent dust from being stirred up.

When the two opposing fronts found themselves at a distance of fifty paces, Arminius let out a battle cry and his men shouted after him: a syncopated uproar that cut through the air until the moment of collision. Many warriors fell, on both sides, and furious fighting ensued on the ground; Centurion Taurus suspected that many of the gladiators had slipped off their horses so they could exploit their superiority in the type of battle they were accustomed to.

Before the two front lines had crashed into one another, the last two rows of Germanic auxiliaries – one on Flavus's side and one on Arminius's – had set off at a wild gallop towards the flanks of the gladiator formation, circumventing and encircling them, then re-forming frontally to engage their adversaries from behind. The gladiators tried to fight back and found themselves crushed by the onslaught of the Auxilia charge. But they had a surprise of their own in store. From the wings emerged a score of slingers who thinned out the rows of attackers with a hail of shots which the Germanics were able to ward off only in part with their shields. Some were struck right in the forehead and tumbled to the ground, others at knee height, and others still in the shoulder, leg or groin.

There was no room for charging and even just manoeuvring the horses in the restricted space of the fray was nearly impossible. In the end, what was meant to be a battle on horseback had turned into a myriad of duels on foot, in which the experience of the gladiators was becoming more of a threat to the Germanics. At that point Arminius shouted to his brother, who managed to make his way through the skirmish on his black steed. Flavus dismounted and stood alongside his brother. The two of them advanced with their remaining forces until they got close to the chief of the gladiators, recognizable by his magnificently embossed bronze helmet with its scarlet crest. He spotted them and instantly realized what they were attempting. The clash became even more violent because even the greater experience of the gladiators could not match the inexhaustible vigour of their much younger adversaries. The number of wounded was increasing by the moment. To such an extent that the *lanista* became worried and raised his eyes towards the podium. The emperor saw this but he turned to his adopted grandson Germanicus, wearing his laticlave toga, as if to turn the decision over to him. Germanicus nodded and the *lanista* had the trumpet sounded. All weapons were dropped. Friends looked around for fellow friends, each man checked the one beside him. Brother sought out brother – in the thick of fighting, anyone could have disappeared. Arminius and Flavus found each other still side by side, each still holding his horse's halter.

It was up to the commander of the Eighteenth, Varinius, to proclaim the verdict and name the winners. He sent a couple of his men to tally the wounded and count the dead, if there were any, in order to have sufficient evidence to judge the two opposing sides. In the end, he felt it was advisable to call the match a draw, although he chose to point out the courage and valour of the two young Germanic commanders: Arminius and Flavus.

Shortly thereafter one of the praetorians approached Taurus. 'Caesar wants to meet those two young men before dinner in his house. At dusk. Get them cleaned up, they're not fit to be seen like that . . . Oh, I was forgetting, Caesar said to give you his compliments. You've transformed those barbarians into strong, disciplined soldiers.'

Taurus asked the praetorian to give Caesar his regards and best wishes for his health as well.

Once back at the house on the Aventine, Arminius and Flavus bathed and changed, putting on clean tunics, cloaks and boots. They reported to Taurus in his quarters. They were greeted by his two freedmen, Privatus and Thiaminus, carrying basins and linen towels for them to wash and dry their hands. They were the centurion's faithful assistants, ready at his slightest nod. Thiaminus was an excellent masseur and he took care of his master whenever he returned from a tough day of military duties. Privatus was his secretary. He kept his correspondence, wrote his notes for him and his private diary, which he read to Taurus every night after dinner, before he retired. Taurus had bought Privatus in Africa from a landowner whose shipload of wheat had sunk at sea and who needed to make up for his losses. Thiaminus, on the other hand, he'd obtained from a soldier in the East who'd simply wanted to get rid of him. He had emancipated them both after three years of service, but neither had wanted to leave his house.

Arminius and Flavus were received with a glass of wine and a couple of boiled eggs with salt.

'Eat something. You'll be received by Caesar later today, but certainly not for dinner.'

The two brothers looked each other in the eye, incredulous at what they'd heard.

'Caesar?' they repeated, one after another.

'Yes, that's right,' replied the centurion. 'It's an enormous privilege that very few people have enjoyed. Even more so because you are foreigners, although you are the sons of an allied chief. He has complimented me on how you've been educated and trained.'

You could see that he was bursting with pride for the commendation he'd received. He gave his pupils precise instructions on how to behave and converse with their host. 'Don't sit down unless he asks you to do so: you'll be able to tell if there are chairs in the room turned towards his table. Otherwise, stand facing him with your backs straight and heads up but without ever looking him in the eye. If he asks you questions, give brief, careful answers. One word less is always better than one more. Think before you open your mouths. He has no time for prattle or boasting, and he can't stand flattery. Avoid accompanying your words with gestures – that's what slaves do. Keep your voices low. He can hear well and he doesn't like people to be loud. If he offers you something to eat, give a bow with your heads to thank him but don't make any other move. Accept only if he insists by saying something like, "It's good, have a taste," or "I've grown them myself in my own garden." I know your father brought you up well and I'm sure you will conduct yourselves properly.'

Flavus regarded him with admiration; Taurus was the kind of man who always knew what to do and how to do it in any situation. 'Do you know all this because you've heard it said, or because you've spent time with him yourself?' he asked.

Taurus seemed to think that over for a few moments.

'I was with him at the time of the civil wars,' he replied. 'I was much younger than I am now; he was only a boy. No one could have imagined what he would have done. Over the years, we have met up now and then and he's always assigned me tasks of a certain importance.'

The sun was beginning to set and its oblique rays entered from the window that opened to the west, lighting up the objects that Taurus had gathered during his life. His armour, obviously. The suit he wore only for the most important occasions. There were many trophies of war: weapons, precious fabrics, jars of glass and of glazed ceramic, ethnic art pieces, images of foreign gods, rolls of papyrus, decorations, and coins from the eastern kingdoms with the effigy of Alexander the Great. Relics of past glory. None of those kingdoms even existed any more. Now the whole world obeyed Rome and Rome obeyed a single man. Two boys, who used to play in the forest of the Cherusci, at the limits of the Empire, were about to meet him.

'You are warriors, and so you'll go on horseback to his house on the Palatine, but unarmed. I'll send Privatus with you; he knows the way well.'

They took their leave and the boys returned to their own quarters to wait for the guide who would take them to their destination.

WHEN THEY ARRIVED, they could tell they had been expected. A servant took the horses by their reins and led them to the stables. Privatus followed them, chatting as they went along, and then went to sit on a bench in the shade of a fig tree to wait. The door-keeper accompanied the boys to the base of a stone staircase that led to a kind of tower. They saw nothing of what they'd imagined: no alabaster-floored rooms, no brightly coloured mosaics, no carpets or statues. Nothing like that at all. They were approaching an austere setting of rather small dimensions.

When they were just about ten steps away from the terrace in front of the entrance, the door-keeper turned to them and said, 'When he receives guests up here it means that he considers it an important meeting and that he doesn't want to be disturbed unless something very urgent comes up. I have to ask myself who you are to receive such a treatment. I've never seen you before. But I've seen kings and queens kept waiting for months before he received them . . .'

As the man was muttering to himself, Arminius spoke to Flavus using their native tongue. 'Hear that? Do you really think he summoned us here because we fought well? He could have had someone write a note and had it delivered by a servant.'

'No, you're right, of course,' replied Flavus. 'But why, then?'

'There's something that no one knows but us. There's no other explanation.'

'So you're saying that . . . he knows about the Hermundur's message?'

'He clearly does.'

'Wait, there's something else . . .'

'What?'

'The Hermundur was next to me during the battle. And at the end of it, he didn't have a single scratch.'

They'd arrived at the last step and their hearts were racing, certainly not because of the climb.

The servant opened the door. Flavus glanced downwards and saw Privatus watching them.

It was the look of someone who knew, but who wanted to know a lot more.

The servant motioned for the two young men to enter. There was a moment of hesitation, then Arminius walked in first and Flavus followed. They found themselves in the study of Gaius Julius Caesar Octavian Augustus, consul, pontifex maximus, father of the State, the most powerful man in the world.

He didn't look much like the statues that they were used to seeing in public. He was of medium height, slim, with long, thin fingers. He was seated on the folding chair that magistrates used, behind his working desk. Two cases held papyrus scrolls, one made of light-coloured wood and the other of ebony, the first evidently for blank rolls and the second for written ones. Next to the ebony case was a small terracotta statue that represented a god – Apollo, perhaps, thought Arminius – and within reach of his right hand was a Greek red-figure cup heaped with peeled figs and a cup of water with a folded linen napkin for drying one's hands.

On a small chair near the table were several wax tablets with a couple of styluses; Caesar must have been interrupted as he was dictating a letter that a scribe would have made a fair copy of using a virgin sheet of papyrus. A chest standing against the right hand wall probably held important documents; a key hanging from Caesar's belt must have served to keep it locked.

They greeted their host with a slight bow.

'Please, sit,' said the emperor. 'You are welcome in this house.' His voice was clear, resonant and strong. A voice used to giving orders. Arminius and Flavus both nodded their thanks and sat down.

The emperor took the cup full of figs and extended it towards them. 'Fruit?'

'Caesar, we're not—' began Arminius, but the emperor insisted.

'They're good. Just picked. I grow them in my own garden.'

Taurus had been clear. If he were to say that, they were to accept. First Arminius and then Flavus took a fig and brought them to their mouths; they were delicious. The emperor himself offered them the bowl of water and the napkin for cleaning their fingers. Then he began to speak: 'I know who you are and where you come from. I know how you got to Rome, where you are living; in fact, I chose your residence and your teachers myself. Taurus in particular. He is an extraordinary man, strong and sincere and a formidable combatant. Today, seeing you fight, I realized that I'd made the right decision in entrusting your training to him. You fought magnificently . . . bravely, but with intelligence. And this will be held in consideration when the time comes to give you an assignment.'

The two boys remained silent, as Taurus had advised them.

'But the reason for this meeting,' continued Caesar Augustus, enunciating the words well to make sure they were understood, 'is another. You were seen, and listened to, as you were conducting a late-night examination of the *Ara Pacis*. A visit that can be explained, perhaps, with another one: I know that a Hermunduri warrior brought you a message that induced you to return to that place, perhaps to find an explanation for what you were told or asked to do. I'm asking you now: did you find the explanation you were looking for? And what was it?'

Arminius spoke first: 'Caesar, we will tell you all we know. What you say is true. We studied the Altar of Peace thoroughly with our tutor Diodorus. But we'd already seen it, for the first time and by chance, with Centurion Marcus Caelius. And we returned there after the Hermundur came to us with that message.

'The message was: "Three heads between two bodies. She is at the centre of everything, of life and of death." It reminded me of an image on that altar that struck me the first time I saw it. We've thought about this for a long time and I think we've figured it out.'

The supreme ruler of the State was listening intently but without letting out a whisper of emotion; not a muscle of his face moved and his expression was like that of a statue. The folds of laticlave toga hanging behind him seemed somehow to be a part of his pale figure. You could see that his legs were crossed under his tunic and his slender left hand lay lightly on the solid walnut table, displaying the pale glow of a gold ring with his family seal. Flavus, whose sight had been honed by the gloom of the Germanic forests, could see on it the figure of a warrior holding a child by the hand and bearing an old man on his back.

'Continue,' said the emperor in a tone of voice raised barely above silence.

It was Flavus who did so. 'Diodorus, our tutor of letters and art, has a papyrus scroll that represents the figures carved onto the walls of the marble altar; he taught us to recognize each one. He showed us Germanicus – who is today a young and valiant combatant – as a child, then Agrippa, then Commander Drusus in his military cape and then you, Caesar. And there she was too, one of three heads between two bodies. The middle one, at the centre of everything, of life and of death . . . Your daughter, Caesar.'

11

WHEN ARMINIUS AND FLAVUS got back it was almost dark. Privatus rode ahead of them on muleback. Along the way, they'd spoken ceaselessly in their native language, although they knew that if Privatus recognized the sounds of a foreign tongue and reported that to Taurus, they would be in great trouble. The prohibition against the young princes speaking any language but Latin was strictly enforced.

Caesar Augustus had asked them to continue their investigations. Although they had solved the enigma contained in the message by relating it to the Altar of Peace, they still had to understand what the last part, about being 'the centre of everything, of life and of death' meant. The main thing was, whose life and whose death? The Hermundur had made it clear that they were free to decide how to handle the significance of what they managed to decipher; to act or not. Could that directive be coming straight from their father Sigmer?

Flavus attempted to tease apart the intricate puzzle.

Taurus clearly had direct access to the emperor; that's why they'd been summoned to meet with him in the first place. The emperor knew that it was the Hermundur who had brought them the message. Had he got that information from Taurus? That was logical; they themselves had told Taurus about it. It was also quite evident to the two boys that it was Caesar who had put the Hermundur in charge of protecting them as they battled the gladiators.

'So, the Hermundur was part of the group who escorted us to Italy,' mused Flavus. 'Taurus enlisted him then, surely, and is probably responsible for placing him in Caesar's service as a member of his bodyguard. As such, the Hermundur can easily maintain contact with our father, through the auxiliaries who have contact with the Germanic chieftains. I'm thinking that means that the message may have actually been given to him directly by our father. But how could Father have imagined that we would be able to identify the figure who stands at the centre of life and of death?'

'You're right,' nodded Arminius. 'He couldn't.'

'Well then?'

'For now we don't have an answer to that question. And if we're saying that Caesar learned about the message through Taurus, why didn't he just have the Hermundur tortured to get him to talk?'

'Of course. So why didn't he do it?'

'If I were him, I wouldn't have done so either. It's evident that if you entrust someone with a message to pass on by word of mouth, you're going to pick a person who's capable of memorizing it but who can't understand what it means. No sense in torturing the messenger.'

TAURUS INVITED THEM to dinner and the two youths were quite gratified by the invitation. Their relationship with the centurion was changing day by day, becoming more direct and confidential. Although it was clear that the veteran of so many battles had his favourite: he preferred Flavus's spontaneity to Arminius's more reserved, introverted personality.

They told him of the encounter with Caesar which had impressed them greatly.

'What struck you most about him?' asked the centurion.

'His simplicity,' replied Flavus. 'I was expecting a man wrapped in precious fabrics and flaunting jewels, crowns and bracelets, sitting on a throne in a room gleaming with marble and mosaics. A man in his position can afford whatever he likes. And instead we found ourselves talking to a man dressed only in a white hand-woven tunic, with a belt of plain leather and a pair of sandals that were sturdy-looking but not fancy. The only jewellery he was wearing was his family ring. And the room we met him in was elegant, but very simple as well. It could have belonged to anyone. Your own reception room, Centurion, is bigger and, may I say, even more ornate.'

'He who holds true power doesn't need jewellery or fancy clothing to demonstrate his worth. If someone feels this need, it's only a sign of his weakness . . . What do you think, Arminius?'

'I was struck by his hands. They're not the hands of a warrior. The only time they've touched a sword is in a parade.'

'He has the hands of a politician. He doesn't need to be strong. He has men who do that for him. The Battle of Actium was won by Agrippa, his right-hand man, while he was below deck vomiting his guts out. What he does need to be is intelligent, shrewd, wise, but also sceptical and even hypocritical, if necessary. You see, appearance can be more meaningful than truth, at times. It is thus that Caesar creates an image of himself and communicates that image to his people.

'More than one room in his palace,' Taurus continued, 'is decorated with theatrical masks. You could say it's an obsession. Did you notice? Did you ask yourselves why?' He didn't wait for an answer. 'Because power means wearing a mask. He wears that simple hand-sewn tunic because he wants people to think that he's not much different from an ordinary citizen who lives on a modest salary. I can tell you that he's a man capable of real emotion when he can afford to express it.

'Peace and prosperity reign within the confines of the Empire. It's certainly not the golden age that was announced by the procession sculpted in the Altar of Peace. But that man dressed in white has put an end to the civil wars and built roads, ports, aqueducts, bridges, thermal baths and libraries. He's reorganized the army and state administration. He's distributed land to those who owned no property. He's even asked a great poet to compose a national poem consecrating Italy as the heart of the Empire.

'What is he asking of you?'

It was Arminius who answered first: 'He wants us to keep probing, in order to understand what it could mean that Julia is at the centre of life and of death, but we're not spies, we're warriors! Although I'm afraid we won't be able to avoid finishing what we've started.'

'I fear you're right,' replied Taurus.

'But we're just not capable of getting at what he wants to know. We don't even know how to start. Julia's the most powerful woman in the City; it's pretty much impossible for someone like us to even approach her.'

'The most powerful woman in the City? Perhaps . . . but also the most fragile. As far as the two of you are concerned, show your faith in Rome and in the emperor. He will know how to repay you. As far as Julia is concerned, you're right to think you shouldn't approach her. You wouldn't stay alive long. I'll tell you what you need to know, and then you'll have to decide how to go forward from there.'

Both Arminius and Flavus were feeling rather dizzy: they

had just met with the most powerful man in the world and now Taurus was suggesting that they could remain within the circle of the great and powerful men of the Empire. Their childhood and youth were far away in their minds and insignificant when compared with where they found themselves now. The sensation was very strong and was growing by the day. Even Arminius had had his leonine tresses cut off and wore his hair in a flowing style that framed his face but didn't reach his shoulders. He expressed an original kind of elegance that made him even more interesting. Flavus instead had had his blond hair cut short in the military manner and had grown a short beard.

As the two boys sat down at the table across from their host, the first guard shift was going on duty and in the silence that followed Taurus's words, they could hear the commanders exchanging passwords.

'The night is still long,' said Taurus. 'When you leave here you'll know everything you need to know in order to tease the sense out of the message you've been given.'

He began to tell his story: 'Julia was Caesar Augustus's only child. Now, although the supreme ruler did not intend to formally announce that the Republic was finished and that a dynastic monarchy had arisen in its place, he wanted a direct heir. So he destined his daughter to a series of state marriages. The first was to her cousin, Marcus Claudius Marcellus, but he died very young after a year of marriage without generating a son. Poisoning was suspected. Julia was then joined in marriage with Marcus Vipsanius Agrippa, who was twenty-five years older than she. They had two daughters and three sons: Gaius and Lucius Caesar and Agrippa Postumus, born after his father's death. Agrippa died ten years ago, while you were still children and I was at the height of my own career. But Julia's womb was too precious to let her go, and so Augustus forced

Tiberius to divorce his own wife Vipsania, whom he loved dearly and with whom he'd had two children, and to marry Julia.

'For Tiberius, the loss of his wife has remained an open wound. I've heard that whenever he catches sight of her in public, tears come to his eyes.'

'But if he loved her, why did he repudiate her?' asked Arminius. 'I'd never . . .' he stopped, sorry that he'd spoken.

But it was Taurus who continued: 'You'd never what? You'd never do such a thing, would you? This leads me to understand that you still don't know what makes Rome great. Something that you barbarians . . .' Arminius's face flushed and Flavus's lips twisted into an ironic smile, 'can't even begin to imagine. The State. That's what makes Rome great. That is, the people, the Senate, the army and the magistrates, the gods and priests and temples. Rome's sacred borders. The vestal virgins who cultivate the sacred fire of our ancestors in their sanctuary. Our seas and our lands. For all this, we are willing to sacrifice anything and any person: our home or our fields, our wives or our sisters, our sons and daughters, all of our worldly goods and those of our forebears.

'I know what you're thinking. That there aren't many of us that uphold these ideals. That a great number of us have been corrupted by money and our greed for more, by excess and decadence, by the ultimate, extreme conceit of owning other human beings as if they were objects or hardly more than animals. But the few of us who remain faithful, raised by our fathers to respect hard rules of discipline, are more than sufficient to keep our ideals alive for those who have lost them. Tiberius's tears, if what they say is true, show how painful giving her up was. But they also show his firm intention to place obedience to the State and its supreme ruler before private sentiments, no matter how deep and intense those may be.

'Tiberius was with Julia long enough to conceive a child who was born at camp in Aquileia, the city of the legionary eagles, but who died soon thereafter. Generated against the will of his parents in that far corner of Italy. After that Tiberius left at the head of his army, heading east to extend our domain all the way to the Danube.

'Julia, on the other hand, tired of the political marriages she'd had to submit to starting from the age of fourteen and found freedom. Her body was slim and desirable again after giving birth, her husband far away in savage lands. She finally gave herself over to the high life of Rome that she'd always dreamed of. Parties, elegant gowns, perfume and jewels, admirers who would cut their veins to enjoy her favours. She happily gave herself to some and denied others if only for the pleasure of seeing them consumed with jealousy and maddened by desire . . .'

Arminius and Flavus both had the same thought at that moment: that Taurus himself had tortured himself over her or had perhaps even enjoyed her favours.

The centurion picked up where he had left off, while fingering a little bracelet of silver and Nordic amber: 'Her intemperance was always overlooked. Her father knew well that he owed her for having provided him with heirs. If it became hard to ignore her excesses, he preferred to write to her: "I'm told your behaviour at so-and-so's house left something to be desired . . . remember your position and your responsibilities . . . that dress was rather low-necked . . ." But she always knew how to retaliate.'

Arminius and Flavus found themselves thinking the same thing once again: how could he know the content of such letters? Maybe he was just imagining those phrases. It could be that he was simply dropping names to show how high up he was, or even that such things were common knowledge in certain circles. In any case, Taurus's words made it clear that these kinds of matters were always resolved within the family. And that Julia was in fact untouchable, because her father loved her sincerely and she knew that.

'But it might well be this attitude of hers that ends up betraying her in the end.'

Taurus paused and Arminius thought he had finished his talk, but that wasn't the case. Privatus entered the room along with a servant carrying two small trays with their simple supper. A third was immediately brought out for the host, who ate a bit and then continued.

'Gaius and Lucius,' he said, 'are their grandfather's pride and joy. Augustus adopted both of them as his own children. They're just a few years younger than you are and they'll soon be sent to the legions to start their training to become great leaders of armies.'

'Like General Drusus?' asked Flavus.

'Exactly,' Taurus said. 'Agrippa Postumus is much younger than they are, and for now he's a bit timid and doesn't seem particularly clever. But that doesn't mean that when his time comes, he won't be treated like his brothers, as is fitting for his rank.'

Everything that the centurion had told them was clear, but he hadn't finished. 'Julia is also very fond of her children, but lately she's become distracted by a new group of . . . acquaintances. I fear they may lead to her ruin.'

Taurus stopped and ate a few spoons of stewed lentils with some bread toasted on the embers. Arminius and Flavus asked no questions, but waited for him to continue with his story.

'The people she frequents purport to be a kind of literary circle but they are suspected of spreading insinuations and even harsh criticism of Augustus's government. The emperor doesn't seem alarmed, but I'm sure that nothing escapes him. He has informers everywhere and I believe that one of his people may even have infiltrated the group. He obviously knew about the message that you received from the Hermundur because the man is one of his bodyguards. And you, Arminius, discovered that Julia is the central figure of this situation. You don't know why yet, but I'm almost certain you've hit the mark. She is at the centre of everything.

'I'm quite fond of her myself and I would do anything to save her from her own carelessness and from frequenting the wrong kind of people, but I'm afraid there's nothing I can do here. There's a simple reason: the soul of that "literary" circle is the man that she's been in love with since she was a child – Iullus Antonius, son of Marc Antony and his first wife Fulvia. The people he associates with are a suspicious bunch. There are others who have been orphaned, like himself, by the *Dictator perpetuo*, and they are fierce, angry and out for his blood. There are veterans from the civil wars who have never resigned themselves to peace and who dream about uprisings, reprisals and more blood. Then there are the scions of the Republican nobility, frustrated and impotent, who don't want to believe that the world has changed. I'm sure she feels it's all an exciting game. She's fascinated by them because she was robbed of her own youth and she's still looking for thrills. She doesn't realize she's playing with fire.

'Augustus himself doesn't dare strike out against them because he's terrified by the mere thought of another civil war. He's dedicated his life, you see, to making sure it will never happen again.'

He chewed on some bitter greens with a bit of toasted bread in silence, allowing the voices of the night to penetrate the walls of his house.

'Well, what can we do?' asked Flavus.

Taurus seemed startled. As he motioned for the freedmen to remove their tables, he had red wine poured into three cups. He handed two of them to his guests. 'Drink up. The wine may excite your minds and give you an idea that could prove useful.'

Arminius drank. There was so much to think about: had the emperor heard about the cryptic message from his bodyguard, the Hermundur, or could he have actually thought it up himself? No one knew the sculptures on the Altar of Peace in their every detail better than Augustus did, but that particular image must have been always present in his mind.

But there was another image that kept pushing itself to the forefront of Arminius's mind: the ceremony of the festival of spring in the Germanic forest so many years ago. He was standing next to his father when he saw the girl crowned with flowers who glanced at him for a moment. She was flanked by two other girls and by two gigantic Hermunduri; again, there it was: three heads between two bodies. Sigmer had seen that as well as he had, and it may have remained impressed on his mind too.

A possible explanation was beginning to take shape. Sigmer may have learned from the Hermundur that Julia was part of a dangerous plot, and he had thought of associating two images – similar yet different – to a moment that he knew Arminius would remember well. The procession in the forest and the procession of marble. Arminius was also suddenly struck by the realization that Sigmer may have seen the altar with his own eyes; when the monument was inaugurated, the allied sovereigns had certainly been invited to the ceremony.

So it might truly have been his father who had sent the message, leaving Arminius free to choose whether to reveal its meaning . . . or to keep it hidden and allow the events to play themselves out. Might Julia be thinking of taking a leading role in some plot? She was certainly protected by her high social position and by the love of her father, who would never believe she would do anything to harm him. So just where exactly might this all be leading? Certainly to something that would deal a harsh blow to the emperor and to the Empire.

If, on the other hand, Arminius chose to speak up, he could put a halt to the events which seemed to be coming to a head, and he would thus earn the unconditioned trust of the emperor, along with all the rewards that would result from such a situation.

Taurus unrolled the parchment depicting the procession of the Altar of Peace on his work table and gestured for the two boys to join him. He pointed to one figure in particular, the first on the left on the northern side. 'The next time you visit the altar, look at this man well and fix his features in your minds. He is Iullus Antonius, the love of Julia's life. He's most likely the one who has pulled her into this mad adventure that could destroy her in the end. And now tell me whether you are willing to help me.'

Arminius and Flavus rapidly exchanged a glance and then turned to the centurion and nodded.

'Then we've understood each other,' said Taurus. 'It's time to move. I've reflected upon this at length and I believe I can introduce you into a setting which should prove to be an excellent observatory and where you may be able to make some very interesting encounters. The work site of the *naumachia* on the Vatican Hill.

'The enormous artificial lake which is being dug there will

be used to stage a commemoration of the naval battle of Actium, the thirtieth anniversary of which is coming up. For me, and those like me, that battle meant the end of the civil wars that bloodied our lands for more than half a century, whereas for others it signifies the beginning of tyranny. The latter is the kind of person that Julia has lately been frequenting.

'Don't expect rapid results. It might take you months, or even years. You must be patient and very careful indeed, but your role may prove crucial. You may still be outsiders now, but you are certainly ready to enter Roman society.'

The boys didn't leave until late, at the end of the second guard shift.

As they walked down the path that led to their quarters they were talking quietly, as they did whenever they had experienced something unusual. Both felt very uneasy about having been tasked to act as informers, simply because they had recognized an image on the frieze of the Altar of Peace, but Flavus pointed out that Taurus would never put them in a position that was less than honorable. He had trained and instructed them for years, dedicating a great deal of sweat and even blood to this purpose: to make them ready for anything. They decided to continue in this new role, if nothing else for curiosity's sake, and to make their way up in the society which they found themselves part of and which, thanks to their new assignment, they would learn about in every last gritty detail.

THEY ENTERED THE worksite as directors of security. Thousands of men from every corner of the world were working there, both slaves and free men, depending on their duties. They spoke many different languages and tended to form groups based on their ethnicity, language and habits. Given the situation, there was no end to the brawls and fistfights which would explode, greatly slowing down the rate of work. The building contractors could in no way afford this. There were already foremen and supervisors in charge of taking care of any fracas using a cane or a whip, so Arminius's and Flavus's main job was to appear threatening enough to put rebellion, escape or clashes of any sort out of anyone's mind. They were both very tall and powerfully built, and they wore the muscle cuirasses and crested Attic helmets of the superior officers of the Roman army. They carried spears instead of javelins and wore long swords of Germanic style but Roman crafting on their shoulders. Extremely fast to act whenever needed, they made themselves feared to the point that it became rarely necessary for them to intervene and they began to look more like ornamental statues perched on the embankments than members of the armed forces on duty.

As the operations proceeded, the site became crowded with noble men and ladies of the Roman aristocracy and the two young warriors were greatly admired as masterpieces of nature. It wasn't long before they began to be invited to the thermal baths, both those in private villas as well as in public facilities, so that the ladies of the highest society of the capital of the world, as well as the rich eunuchs who rented out the baths, could stave off boredom by admiring the breathtaking nudity of the young Germanic warriors. They were soon invited to parties and banquets as well. They embarked on friendships and on more intimate relationships, first with young freedwomen and then with women from illustrious families, whose husbands were away being governors of some far-flung province.

These kinds of relations – being accepted or even sought after by powerful men and by beautiful, sophisticated women –

both gratified and flattered them, making them feel part of a world they'd long lived at the margins of. Their fluency and pronunciation were greatly improving, so that they could appreciate nuances and irony, underlying messages and double meanings. And they expressed themselves spontaneously with equal ease.

They were well aware that those who invited them never stopped considering them barbarians, the sons of wild, untamable nations. And although they knew that was where a great deal of their fascination lay, they were also becoming a bit tired of the game. For the first time, they were finding it was possible to conceal certain aspects of their past, when they wanted to do so.

They began to pick up on the thoughts and the inclinations of the powerful, even in a political sense. They could confront the marble statues in which these figures appeared majestic and solemn, thoughtful and amiable, with the actual everyday reality around them – the intrigues, the resentments, the small-mindedness.

They were thus put, little by little, in a position to learn what the supreme leader wanted to know and to report on what they'd found to Taurus, but they stopped short at spying or informing on people, refusing to betray confidences. Treasonous behaviour was unworthy of the education they'd received as warriors, both in Germania and in Rome, and of the future officers – it was as such they imagined themselves – of the greatest and most powerful army existing in the world.

WITH THE PASSING of time, Arminius and Flavus were employed in more important tasks than managing security on the Vatican Hill worksite, and they were often housed in the camps of the Germanic Auxilia rather than in their residence on the Aventine. Then, one day, they were summoned to the port of Ravenna, where they found Primus Pilus Centurion Marcus Caelius Taurus waiting for them.

They warmly shook hands and gripped one another's arms in the military manner, and then Taurus spoke: 'She truly is at the centre of everything, of life and of death. Someone has to save her from herself. I've thought of a plan, but I'll need the two of you. Will you help me?'

'We will, Centurion,' Flavus replied. 'What must we do?'

'You'll have to agree to some hard training . . .'

'Training? For what?' asked Flavus.

'For a naval battle.'

12

Both Arminius and Flavus repeated what Taurus had just said as a question: 'A naval battle?'

'Exactly. It's only a few months until the great celebrations are due to begin. The huge body of water on the Vatican Hill will be inaugurated with a staging of the Battle of Actium. It will be a memorable spectacle. I've heard that the emperor is quite undecided as to whether the flagship of Marc Antony and Cleopatra should be reconstructed with their ensigns; he doesn't want the public to have a return of nostalgic love for the triumvirate. I don't think I'm wrong in predicting that he'll choose not to do so; he's too wise a politician to make such an error. He knows that the enthusiasm of the people must be regulated and guided in the right direction.'

Arminius felt that he'd grown enough in Taurus's estimation to hazard a challenging question. He would never have dared to make such a request just a year earlier.

'Let's hear,' replied the centurion.

'Since the last time we spoke, I've been wanting to ask you this question, because I know that you'll tell us the truth regardless of your political beliefs: if you had to choose between peace and freedom, which would it be?'

Taurus shook his head with an expression that might have been interpreted as condescension. Arminius realized that

Taurus probably considered him quite callous and probably overly ambitious.

He answered nonetheless. 'I'm a soldier. I've seen death thousands of times on the battlefield. I've seen men who had been bursting with strength and with life vomiting blood as they take their last breath, others enduring agony and calling out for death to take them, others throwing themselves on their own swords. Thousands of them, tens of thousands. I've seen the earth soaked with blood too many times not to understand what life is worth. Life, my boy, is absolutely our most precious treasure and there's only one thing worth sacrificing it for: saving other people's lives.

'Freedom is an abstract concept. Whose freedom are we talking about? Is a poor man, who doesn't have enough to support himself and his family, free? During the times of the Republic I saw droves of people lined up in front of the houses of the rich and powerful to sell their votes in exchange for bread. And I'd led many of those very men onto the battlefield, led them to victory. What they conquered made the aristocrats commanding those armies rich beyond measure, while they returned even poorer than when they'd left. They found their neglected fields sold off, their wives prostituting themselves to whoever had the money to buy them.

'One of our greatest commanders, eight times consul at the time when only the best men were given that title, was a defender of the proletariat. In a speech for his candidacy he turned towards the Senate curia and, pointing at the people who supported him, shouted, "These men who have conquered an empire for you do not have enough ground to bury themselves in." '

Taurus and Arminius were walking side by side while Flavus was just a step or so behind them, and he could hear every word of what the centurion was saying. As they reached the gladiators' stadium, he thought of the horseman he'd once seen, mounted on a black stallion galloping swiftly through the thick fog, and of how he'd disappeared into the night, leaving only the sound of pounding hoofs behind him. And he remembered the gigantic quinquereme as it entered the port, its dripping oars being raised in unison.

'I've seen civil war as well,' continued Taurus as he approached the horses who waited tied to the crib outside the *mansio*. 'The most obscene and most cruel of events, the curse of this people who were born from the fratricide of Romulus and Remus. Can you imagine how it feels to leave your house in the morning without knowing whether you will return at nightfall? Living day after day in the chaos of blood, revenge, savagery, torture, all of it meaningless, without honour and without end? How it feels to hear a footfall behind you, in the dark, with the fear that a blade is about to be plunged between your shoulder blades just because someone has written your name on a wooden board in the forum? Someone who has promised all of your goods, your wife as a concubine and your children as slaves to anyone who offers to kill you? Nothing but disgust, horror, shame.

'What does peace mean? In most cases it means a serene life, having what you need, the dignity of not having to go out begging. But peace can also mean freedom, if it is wisely managed. I'm going to stop here. I've already said too much. I know what a young man thinks: that freedom is the arena of glory, while peace is for the old men who are afraid to die because they don't have the strength to defend themselves any more.

'Tomorrow you'll begin training on board the ships.'

'But why are we even doing this training? Will we be

participating in the *naumachia*?' It was Flavus asking the questions now.

'First of all, because the Empire's forces include both the army and the navy, so you must be capable of fighting on both land and sea. Secondly, yes. This has to do with the re-enactment of the sea battle of Actium, but I don't know whether you will be playing a role, or what it might be. I'll let you know when the time comes.'

THUS ARMINIUS AND Flavus began to learn how to move agilely on a warship and how to handle the weapons on board, like onagers, ballistae and scorpions, as well as the sheets and lines for letting out and taking in the sails. Taurus guided them in the exploration of the swift, agile liburnian galley, which could be powered by oars or sails. They walked between the benches where the oarsmen sat and observed how their synchronized movements combined with those of the helmsmen at the stern. They climbed up the masts and yards to spread the sails and they practised arming and aiming the various artillery pieces. On the shore at a short distance from the ship, a wooden plank had been propped up as a target. The two brothers competed fiercely to see who could better centre the target with a five-libra arrow, vying to be considered the best shot. One of the veterans on board the ship told them that when he was still in service in the legion, he had fought in Africa and that they had used arrows of that weight on the battlefield to down elephants.

Both brothers became passionately interested in those devices and became more and more precise at hitting their mark. They also practised swimming, something they'd always done in the rivers and lakes of their childhood home, but also now in Rome, in the pools of the public baths. Completing their training took a couple of months, during which they were taken to the amphitheatre where they witnessed gladiators fighting. Neither of the two could understand the Roman passion for such exhibitions. In their minds, a man fought only if he had a fundamental reason to do so, like defending his land from an invader or taking revenge for an insult or a betrayal. Fighting and losing one's life for the enjoyment of spectators seemed completely atrocious and meaningless.

Nonetheless, the amphitheatre itself was an impressive structure. The two curves on the short sides were perfect, as were the long sides. The entrance gates were located so as to permit the crowd to flow in and out easily, and there was a grandstand reserved for the most important spectator of all.

After all of their training was over, Taurus and the two young men travelled back to Rome on horseback, down the Via Flaminia, the same road they'd taken when they had first come to Italy. They chatted as they rode, remembering the old times, the beatings and the punishments suffered at the hands of the strict centurion, their uncertainty and homesickness, their first encounters with love. Flavus's enchantment with little Iole. But by now their Germanic origins seemed remote and practically forgotten. Only the thought of their parents, especially their father, was still vivid, as they continued to receive news of him. The memories of their mother Siglinde had faded, tied as they were to when they were children; they remembered her voice, sometimes, and the old ballads she would sing to them, and even her face framed by long hair.

Back in the capital, Arminius and Flavus came to appreciate the excellent qualities of Thiaminus, Taurus's servant. He was an extraordinary massager and his services were sought after at the baths by the most fashionable and influential people of the City, both men and women. The ladies had to pass him off as a eunuch in order to bypass the rigid rules of the female baths, and no one had ever bothered to check whether that was true. Thiaminus was very discreet, and so his clients tended to relax with him and opened up by speaking their minds freely or by allusion. He'd grown quite used to this over the years and he'd learned how to interpret such confidences.

The day of the Ides of May marked the forty-sixth anniversary of Taurus's birth. That morning Privatus had gone out with the cart to shop for food at the Forum Holitorium market, where he bought legumes and lamb to roast. The guests arrived in the late afternoon, bringing with them meats, cheeses, spices and amphorae of fine wines. His friends from the Eighteenth and the Ninth Legions, Quintus Silvanus and Titus Macrus, who had fought at his side for years, had been invited, along with Publius, his beloved brother from Bononia.

As he walked in, Publius recognized the two boys. 'I'd always hoped to see you in Ravenna or Bononia, hopefully with that bear of my brother, but we never met again after that time at the inn.'

'Centurion Taurus is always very busy,' spoke up Flavus, 'and he keeps us that way too, if you want to know the truth. It seems like he's always got some new torture in mind for us. We never stop training, while I thought we'd come to Rome to have some fun!'

'Ah, no complaints from you, young man,' replied Publius Caelius. 'The two of you are young, handsome and you have your whole lives in front of you. What I would give to be your age again! I'd trade anything, even my inns, believe me.'

As usual, Thiaminus and Privatus were greeting the guests. They had organized the dinner with the help of some servants hired out for the occasion by an impresario who ran such solemn events for the senators. Arminius and Flavus were not invited to the dinner, but they made themselves comfortable in the garden, where they were served the various courses and wines at a pretty little table made of Lunense marble.

Between one course and the next, Flavus noticed Thiaminus handing something to Privatus as they crossed paths at the kitchen door. Privatus came their way with a tray of roasted lamb and a jug of red wine. He greeted them, set the tray in front of them and said quietly, with the hint of a smile, 'Under the plate.'

Arminius and Flavus gave a nod and began to eat. Only when they'd finished the food and drunk the wine did they lift the empty plate. Beneath it was a little roll of parchment; Flavus scanned it then passed it to his brother, who read:

Tomorrow, at the second guard shift, come to the grain warehouse at the port on the Tiber and look into the opening you'll find on the roof.

'Do you understand it?' asked Flavus.

'I think so,' replied Arminius, 'but what I can't figure out is why everyone here in Rome likes these riddles so much.'

'So you know where the port is?'

'Sure, we've gone past it many times.'

'So what's to see there?'

'Something dangerous, otherwise Taurus would have gone himself.'

'He's not afraid of anyone.'

'Yes, but he never risks anything unwisely, least of all himself.'

'When do we go?'

'Tomorrow, at the second guard shift. Right? Just like the note says. We'll go light. Just a dagger and a couple of throwing knives. Barefoot so we won't make any noise.'

Macrus, Publius Caelius and Quintus Silvanus spent the night at Taurus's house, talking until very late. The artificial lake that was being completed on the Vatican Hill took up much of their discussion. A grand parade was to take place, with seven legions represented, and Taurus would take part in his dress uniform, wearing all the decorations he'd earned on the field. Publius sat listening to him with great admiration, as though it were the first time he'd ever had that pleasure. Then Taurus and his brother retired to a smaller room where they could continue their conversation in private.

THE NEXT DAY after dark, without breathing a word to Taurus, Arminius and Flavus found their way to the spot described in Privatus's missive. They crossed the Tiber at the Pons Aemilius and continued downstream for about three hundred paces until they spotted the warehouse. It was connected to a pier where cargo ships moored. The whole area was pitch-black, except for a few lamps that let a prostitute's clients know where to find her. A glimmer of light was visible coming from a crack just above the warehouse door, indicating that someone was inside. Strange, given the time of night. But Arminius and Flavus had learned that the dark nights of Rome were much more animated than one could be led to believe. Illicit lovers meeting on the sly, fortune tellers ransacking the cemeteries for body parts to use in their spells or as charms to ward off the evil eye, thieves and hired killers lying in wait . . . a little light was no reason for particular alarm.

Although they'd never attempted anything of the sort, they were eager to get started, and their curiosity drove them to explore the area with no regard for any of the dangers that such a mission might have involved.

Arminius climbed up on his brother's shoulders and hoisted

himself onto the top of the building, trying not to make any noise. The roof was practically flat, smoothed over with a mix of lime and cement, and he couldn't make out any opening. It was so dark that he couldn't see anything on the terrace.

A halo of light rather suddenly appeared on one side of the rooftop. He approached and spied an opening under some wooden boards – perhaps meant to allow the smoke from a fireplace inside to escape. He moved the boards aside and looked down. Inside there were a couple of men working at a revolving platform. On it was a ballista that Arminius was well familiar with, having used them with his brother on the warship in Ravenna. To one side, sitting on a table, were several five-libra darts made of tempered iron.

Arminius kept going back to check on his brother, who was posted below at the back of the building. Once, just as he was turning back to his observation point, he heard a soft whistle. It was Flavus, trying to get his attention.

He peered over the edge of the terrace and saw his brother nodding at something on his right: a small group of people walking behind a couple of lamp-carriers who were lighting the way down the dark road.

Arminius nodded back and, as Flavus flattened his body against the wall, he slowly backed up towards the middle of the terrace as the group was approaching the building. Someone, maybe one of the servants holding the lamps, called out a few words and the door to the warehouse creaked open. The night was so dark that even the dimmest light cast their faces in clear relief, and Arminius recognized one of them, a figure he'd seen sculpted in the frieze of the Altar of Peace: it was Iullus Antonius. Poet and magistrate, Julia's great love, son of triumvirate Marc Antony.

Arminius positioned himself back over the opening so he

could have a full view of what was going on inside. The men were speaking in low voices, but he could see the two of them who had been standing near the weapon clearly. They removed a cloth which had been covering an object: it was a model of a liburnian galley, with two ballistae on each side, one fore and the other aft.

Arminius thought that he'd seen enough for one night. He covered the opening with the wooden boards and moved back towards the edge of the terrace. Flavus, staying as close to the wall as he could, raised his arms to help him descend and they moved swiftly away.

They waited on the side of the road, in an area where the vegetation gave them good cover, until the group who'd entered the building came out again. The two brothers followed surreptitiously as they started to walk towards the Forum Boarium. Just then, a carriage pulled by a couple of horses passed in front of the Theatre of Marcellus and stopped at a point halfway between the Temple of Portunus and that of Hercules, as if that were an assigned meeting point. Just past the Altar of Hercules, the group split up and Iullus Antonius walked away on his own. As he approached the Temple of Portunus, the door of the vehicle opened and a woman wrapped in a white stole appeared in the reflection of the two braziers in front of the temple, which lit her face. Arminius could not believe his eyes: it was the face between two heads and two bodies, at the centre of the Altar of Peace frieze.

It was Julia.

Arminius turned to his brother and whispered, 'Do you see who that is?'

'Barely, I couldn't make out—'

'Julia,' replied Arminius, raising the tone of his voice just slightly.

Flavus put his finger to his lips and hissed, 'Are you crazy? Don't even say that name. You're putting your life in danger, and mine, and numerous others. Let's get out of here, now . . .'

Arminius shook his head and moved into a shady area, well out of sight. 'No, let's wait just a little longer.'

'If you won't come with me, I'm leaving on my own.'

Iullus got into the carriage next to Julia and the door closed, then the servant holding the reins called out to the horses and drove off towards the Tiber Island.

Arminius and Flavus exchanged glances, but Flavus shook his head hard. 'Don't even think about it. We've done what we were asked to do and even that was too much. It could have been a trap, with someone luring us into that dark, out-of-the-way spot. We're going home now.'

In the brief silence that followed Flavus's words they could hear the river rushing between the banks and through the archways of the bridges, but they heard another sound as well: the snorting of a couple of horses and the shuffling of their hoofs on the pavement. Arminius cautiously approached, following the sounds, and found himself standing in front of two horses covered with black wool blankets and tied to a wooden bar. He leaned forward to get a better look, and saw two guards who'd stopped on the riverbank to urinate; they were just about to turn back. In a few moments they would reach their horses. But Arminius grabbed a blanket, wrapped it around his body and head, then jumped onto the back of one of the horses and set off at a gallop in the direction that Julia's carriage had taken.

He waited at the head of the Fabricius Bridge which connected the Tiber Island to the Judaean quarter that Julius Caesar had established in the capital. He walked his horse across the bridge and then crossed the island and the other bridge as well, keeping his pace slow, until he found himself in a residential area populated by a mix of people, including poor Romans and numerous immigrants from the East.

The carriage had stopped.

Swathed in black in the dead of night, Arminius was nearly invisible to see. He tied the horse to a post and stole behind the corner of an old house to watch what was going on. The woman and her companion were getting out of the carriage and knocking at a door. Someone opened it and let them in. The woman had covered her head and her face.

Arminius slid along the wall, trying to find an opening that would let him in, so he could see and hear what was going on inside. He found no door, nor a passage of any sort. A light breeze was picking up, smelling like seawater and rustling tree branches . . . rustling the leaves of a plane tree, a giant that rose up in front of him right behind the northern corner of the house. It was enormous, its roots certainly soaking up water from the river nearby. A branch as thick as a tree on its own stretched towards the house's roof and Arminius scrambled up its trunk, using the stumps of cut branches as footholds until he reached the limb he needed. He crossed it on foot, holding his hands out for balance, until he could lightly press his bare feet on the roof tiles. He reached the top and went down the other side until he found the gutter, going onto the atrium and the impluvium. He knotted the black blanket to a drain pipe and lowered himself to the ground.

He was inside.

Sounds were coming from the study and the reception hall, animated voices, people arguing. A woman's voice, but only one.

Could it be her?

The centre of life and death.

Maybe he could finally understand. Maybe somewhere in that dark house was the key.

The house gave him the impression of being usually uninhabited. There were no servants to be seen, nor was there any smell of food. There was very little furniture and just a couple of lamps that let off a dim light. Just enough so that he could avoid falling into the impluvium pool and not bang into its sharp edges. He followed the voices, although he was sometimes led astray by sharp echoes that ended blindly.

He found himself in front of the hall. It was separated from the rest of the house by a curtain of embroidered wool that absorbed most of the sound within. Arminius thought it must have been very hot in there, but that keeping this evidently secret meeting quiet was worth their discomfort.

As they spoke they kept the tone of their voices low. Everything about their discussion was muted. The lighting was very low and Arminius could barely tell their shadows apart. He was hearing words more than phrases but they were enough to give away what was being discussed. The circle was closing, as the beautiful woman carved in marble found herself at the centre of that gathering of ghosts.

It was time for Arminius to leave and find Flavus; he felt the need to speak with his brother, to consult with him so they could decide together what to do. And he felt fear as well; it wasn't in his nature to sneak around in the shadows of an abandoned house. The wide wool curtain was full of dust and all at once a sharp, dry cough burst from his chest.

All talking stopped as those on the other side of the curtain looked at each other in shock. Their movements became panicked; they turned to the curtain that isolated them from the rest of the house and rushed forward with their daggers drawn. Arminius had already fled, raced to the impluvium, grabbed the cloth that hung from the drainpipe and was climbing up the roof quickly.

He reached the top, scrambled down the other side and jumped onto the huge tree bough, even as he could hear the tumult of his pursuers behind and beneath him. He rapidly made his way along the branch, risking a plunge below at every reckless step. He reached the fork and began to slide down the tree. The foliage was so thick he was effectively hidden from the ground but then he saw flashes of white appear, and he knew that they had realized that this was his only escape route. They were posted all around the tree, trying to hide from him as best they could. As he slid down the tree trunk he saw that the white patches that he'd spotted were the cloaks of some of the men who'd been inside the house. They'd been left on the ground, behind some bushes, but were easily visible from above. They'd taken them off to move more swiftly and handle their weapons with greater ease. Like a hunted animal, his senses were keen and his mouth dry, but his heart kept beating at a slow, steady rate. Could he strike first? But he would be turned over to the authorities. A barbarian who had wounded or killed a Roman citizen would get no mercy. From the tree he couldn't even see where he'd left the horse. He finally let go of the trunk and leapt to the ground but the circle of his stalkers was tight and daggers were coming at him from every direction, trying to slash through the black blanket that he'd wound around his arm and that loosely protected his body.

Arminius pitched forward, but four men blocked his way and pushed him back. They were aiming to kill, trying to stab at a vital organ. Arminius fought back furiously, a dagger in each hand, but his attackers were closing in.

A hoarse voice said, 'Let them kill you, boy, it'll be best for you. A clean blow and it's over. If you're taken alive, your death will be excruciating . . .'

He was still talking when the earth shook with wild galloping. A black figure on horseback broke into the circle and knocked the men to the ground, trampling them. A yell in Germanic: 'Jump!' Arminius leapt onto the steed. By the time the men on the ground could react the brothers were far away. On the opposite side of the road, a carriage sped away with the woman aboard.

Arminius gripped Flavus's belt as he continued to spur on the horse in the direction of the Aventine.

They rode swiftly past the half-asleep guardsman who didn't even have time to guess at who the two horsemen draped in black might be.

As soon as they were safe, they slipped to the ground. Arminius stripped off the black wool blanket and hid it in the attic, in an old chest. The horse was dried off and left with the others in the stable.

'Was it the other guard's?' asked Arminius.

'The one you left for me. But it wasn't so easy for me. I had to throw his owner into the Tiber.'

When the patrol made their rounds of the gates and the enclosure wall, everything was quiet and in order. Arminius and Flavus were in bed and appeared to be sleeping. They didn't move or breathe as long as the sounds of the inspection were going on: doors slamming, dogs barking.

'Why did you follow me?' asked Arminius in a whisper.

'Because I realized you really were stupid enough to get yourself into such a nasty mess. Who knows what our father would have said to me in front of your stupid ashes: that I didn't keep you out of trouble.'

'Thank you,' said Arminius.

'What did you find out?'

'She's part of the plot.'

'Julia?'

'There in person.'

'What kind of plot are you talking about? She can't be plotting against her father.'

'Why not?'

'Because that's monstrous.'

'Julia is the only daughter of the emperor. She doesn't need anything: not freedom, not elegance or luxury. She already has all of that. It's boredom that she has to vanquish. She was never allowed to be young; her youth was robbed from her, her only true love sacrificed to reasons of state. She's found him again now, and she's found that treachery is the most exciting game there is. Maybe she doesn't even realize the seriousness of what she's doing.'

'What now?' asked Flavus.

'I don't know. Some things we know, but others we don't.'

'Maybe Taurus would know how to interpret the pieces and put them together. He knows a lot of things and we know very little.'

'I don't think we have another choice.'

'We don't. He'll be summoning us. All we have to do is wait.'

THE INVITATION CAME SOON, through Privatus.

'He's expecting you for dinner tomorrow,' he told them. 'You will be his only guests.'

Arminius and Flavus understood well what that meant. Taurus didn't want to be distracted or bothered by social niceties. He'd waited two days to extend this invitation, days which he needed to mull through the situation and the boys needed as well.

'Please let Centurion Taurus know we thank him for his invitation,' replied Flavus.

The two brothers decided quickly on what their moves would be, what information they would give him and what they wouldn't.

They showed up the next evening at the time of the first guard shift, dressed as befitted an important encounter. Taurus seemed calm and confident, and spoke to them as though he were completely in the dark about everything. As though it hadn't been him who had penned the message on that slip of paper.

They spoke of many things. The calendar of the coming amphitheatre games and the circus races, the new management of the public baths and the situation in the East, including the problem of the Judaeans continuously disturbing the public peace. Nothing of what was on their minds. When it seemed that the evening was drawing to a close, Taurus considered them with an ironic expression and said, 'Speaking of disturbances, I heard that the two of you went out the other night. I was told that there was a rather wild chase on the other side of the Tiber, and that someone even risked getting killed. And that guards were searching for a couple of individuals dressed in black who had disappeared . . . Know anything about any of that?'

Arminius spoke, in the most discreet terms possible: he talked about a warehouse and a couple of craftsmen at work, about a big, dark house on the other side of the Tiber, about things half said, gestures cut short. About a plane tree, a chase and . . .

A beautiful woman.

13

THE SILENCES THAT FELL as they spoke that evening gave them time to pause and reflect. Arminius and Flavus often exchanged looks and gestures, to remind each other of what they had decided. They were ready to put all the pieces together and to hazard a hypothesis. Taurus on the other hand was more cautious, unwilling as yet to admit out loud the conclusions he'd come to.

Dinner went on until late, and when Privatus had finished clearing the table, Taurus spoke up again. 'The work going on up on the Vatican Hill is nearly completed and the day of the great commemoration is drawing near. The convoy carrying the parts of the ships to be assembled for the naval battle will arrive soon, sailing up the Tiber. They will dock and unload at the artificial lake, where a branch of the aqueduct that's just been built is already active and filling it with water. It's been calculated that getting it to level will take about two months.'

'Two months?' repeated Flavus.

'At least that long. The quantity of water needed is as much as all the aqueducts of Rome carry to the City over ten days' time. It reminds me of when General Drusus dug the canal that would let our ships enter the ocean without having to sail all the way west and then all the way north on the Rhine. Ten thousand men worked on it for two years. I can still see that moment when we opened the canal onto the Rhine. We'd left a stretch of solid ground extending five hundred feet to the north. We built a series of retaining dams and sunk them deep into the virgin land across the entire width of the canal, going down fifty feet; all this at one hundred feet from the southern bank of the river.' He was getting more animated as he described the amazing feat achieved by his commander. 'So, when the canal was ready, we were able to dig the last section, all the way to the Rhine, without letting the river's water flood through, because each of those retainers was designed to resist the water pressure for five or six hours. When the time came, they all collapsed at once and the Rhine burst into the canal. It was such a spectacle; I'll never be able to forget it . . .'

'I think that our father was there too, if I remember well,' commented Flavus. Arminius didn't think this was strictly true, but Flavus took pride in saying that his father had witnessed the final phase of General Drusus's extraordinary enterprise.

Taurus continued his tale: 'The river hit the canal like a battering ram. It rushed in at such speed that it was dragging all kinds of detritus and sediment with it. It was thick and foamy, and it plunged through the plain so fast that when it hit the water of the ocean it raised a wave so high that it flowed over the surface of the canal all the way back to the old bank of the Rhine, while the deepest part of the current continued in its race towards the ocean. It was a titanic clash that left us all gasping, but when the flow finally slowed, a yell burst out of the mouths of thousands of workers and legionaries who had witnessed that miracle. Three days later, General Drusus's flagship sailed triumphantly down the canal and her prow finally ploughed through the waves of the ocean.'

He stopped, realizing that he'd let himself be carried away by his memories instead of guiding his two young charges in the completion of their task. He returned to the purpose of their meeting: 'I still don't know everything I'd like to know. But it's enough to understand that something big, and terrible, is about to take place. The Battle of Actium is going to be re-enacted, the battle in which Antony was defeated, and you've just seen his son, who is an adult now, in the intimate company of the daughter of the victor. There's certainly something behind all this and I can't exclude that whatever is being plotted could attempt to tip the balance of history. What I don't know is how.'

How what? thought Flavus to himself.

'I don't think what I've mentioned will come to pass so soon. I think it depends on the level of the water inside the lake on the Vatican Hill. A measuring rod has been installed on the part opposite the aqueduct inlet. Check it every three days and write down how fast it's increasing.'

'Of course, Centurion,' replied Flavus.

AS THEY WERE accustomed, on their walk home Arminius and Flavus sized up what had been said during their dinner with Taurus.

'Can't he just say things more clearly?' said Flavus.

'Obviously not. This whole affair is too dangerous. Not even he can take certain risks.'

'So what should we expect at this point? And what's with this measuring rod?'

Arminius smiled. 'They couldn't live in Rome without their clocks, their meridians and their measuring rods. They count the hours and the half-hours. But here, it's a tool that will let us count how much time we have before a very dangerous event might occur. I saw those men at the warehouse working with a model ship, so it's reasonable to think that the artificial lake will be involved, and the lake is in the process of being filled. We have to try to figure out what may happen and be ready for it.'

They had reached the door and, as Flavus was turning the key in the lock, Arminius wheeled suddenly as if he'd sensed a presence. The instinct of the young Germanic wolf had been kindled, and indeed, in the darkness loomed a gigantic warrior. The Hermundur. He was watching them without making a sound. Either the dogs hadn't heard him or his presence hadn't alarmed them.

He walked slowly towards them and the two youths gripped their daggers under their cloaks with sweaty hands.

'I have a message from your father,' he said in a raspy voice.

'Talk,' replied Arminius.

'The message is: "The time is now. She who is at the centre of life and death will let death strike. It is your task to establish whether he who is the target will live or die."'

'Did our father tell you this or was it someone else?'

The Hermundur did not answer. He bared his white teeth in a mocking smile, then turned around and left. The key turned in the lock, the door opened with a click. The two boys went in and lay down to sleep, but Flavus was still in the mood for asking questions: 'If it should happen, what will you do?'

'What would you do?' replied Arminius.

'I don't know. It depends who the target is . . .'

'Don't ask me any more questions. I don't know how to answer.'

'I know what I'd answer,' added Flavus. 'And I hope you do too. I can't imagine that the two of us would ever be apart.'

'I can't either.'

'Promise?' asked Flavus.

'I promise.'
They then fell asleep.

IN THE FOLLOWING weeks Arminius and Flavus checked the measuring rod every three or four days to see how fast the water level was growing and to calculate when the lake would be full. In the meanwhile long carts drawn by oxen lumbered up from the Tiber one by one, carrying the planks and beams for building the ships. When one pontoon had been unloaded, it was turned in the direction of the current and left to drift towards Ostia while others, still laden with goods, continued upriver until they reached the building yard.

One day at mid-morning Arminius saw Germanicus arriving at the yard on horseback. He stopped to watch the phases of ship assembly. You could see that he was particularly interested in what the shipwrights were working on. He was asking the naval architects so many questions that it made Arminius curious and he started paying more attention. Germanicus suddenly sensed his presence, as he raised his head to wipe the sweat from his forehead, and the two boys locked eyes for a moment. Germanicus seemed to be trying to recall where he'd seen Arminius before. Arminius looked away and started walking towards the opposite end of the artificial lake.

After that first time, he would see Germanicus returning to the worksite almost every day. This went on for the whole period that the first ship was being prepared for its launch, which would take place using a slide because the water level was not high enough yet.

Time passed and the water rose to the level necessary for re-enacting the events of the Battle of Actium in a spectacular *naumachia*. From those who had actually been the protagonists of this battle, only Augustus would be attending.

Marcus Vipsanius Agrippa, who held the supreme command at that time and who had been the engineer of that victory, was ten years dead. And so were the defeated Marc Antony and his Egyptian wife, Cleopatra. The emperor had always been careful never to refer to his enemies by name, and many Romans were wondering whether re-evoking the battle might not be an opportunity for remembering them and even re-kindling their popularity, which seemed extinct but still flared up occasionally. Even Virgil, the poet who had written the *Aeneid*, was dead. His national poem celebrated the battle that had opened a new golden era for Rome, putting an end to the civil wars.

But certainly one person would not miss the show: the lovely lady who had been immortalized by a great artist on the frieze of the Altar of Peace. Along with many of the others represented in that procession. A thought occurred to Arminius, something that he'd thought of more than once in recent times: would he ever be immortalized in marble or bronze? This thought led to another. If he should one day deserve that honour, it would surely be in Rome. His ancestral people didn't practise any form of art or literature, nor did they know how to work metal or raise crops. He was reminded of the flaxseed meal that he had eaten practically every day as a child. And then there was no comparison between the wine the Romans drank and the dense beer of his homeland, nor between the liquid gold olive oil and the melted fat of urus or boar. And yet, those distant roots that he seemed to have severed still emerged now and then in his mind and heart, while Flavus, who was his own flesh and blood, appeared completely immune to any feelings of that kind.

Flavus . . . they were united by a promise, an oath. And there he was, in flesh and blood, standing in front of him.

'Where did you come from?' he asked him.

'I've been standing here in front of you for a while,' said Flavus. 'You've just noticed me? You must be thinking some deep thoughts . . . Is it that girl with the crown of flowers who's on your mind?'

'No, I just got distracted thinking about old stuff. What's happening?'

'Come with me.'

Arminius followed him along the bank of the basin until he stopped about one hundred steps away from a separate work yard where the final parts of a second ship were being mounted.

'Take a careful look,' said Flavus. 'I remember that you talked about seeing a machine being assembled in that warehouse at the river port. Did you hear any words being spoken?'

'No, I couldn't understand anything. Their voices were too low.'

'Do you see anything that catches your attention on that ship?'

'If a life-size version of the model ballistae I saw were on that ship, it would be covered by that taut sail three-quarters of the way towards the stern.'

'You're right. But I don't think they'll let us have a closer look.'

'I think you may be right about that. In any case, make sure that I'm put on that ship the day it's launched, posted on the right side if possible.'

'I'll go look for him right now,' Flavus replied, and it was understood that 'him' was Primus Pilus Centurion Marcus Caelius Taurus.

Taurus scowled as Flavus told him of the suspicions that he

and his brother had, as they had pieced together all of the fragments and feared that danger was at hand.

'Danger for whom? And who is behind it?' The centurion's voice was peremptory as he asked the first question, but quavered with the second.

Flavus did not dare make the final conclusion plain. He was sure that Taurus would do so himself, but there was something stopping him; something that almost seemed to be blinding him. But what on earth could be clouding the mind of the stony centurion? Was it a memory, perhaps? A mistake? A mistake that he himself had made?

'Don't say a word to anyone. I have to leave this instant . . .'

Before it's too late, Flavus thought to himself, completing Taurus's speech. He then added out loud, 'The ship I've told you about is practically finished. They're just taking care of the final touches. Arminius wants to be on that ship the day it touches the water.'

Taurus nodded and had Thiaminus bring his horse. He rode off at a gallop.

The next day, Flavus noticed that planks were being unloaded to serve as seating, along with frames to support them; the workers were using them to build a small stand to accommodate about twenty spectators. He imagined that a number of important people would be invited to witness the launch of the ship that was surely ready by now. They would be previewing how the ship could be manoeuvred around the lake that was being prepared for the *naumachia*. Since most of the battleships had not yet been built, there would still be time to make changes, especially as far as size was concerned.

ON THE DAY of the launch, only the workmen were present on the Vatican Hill, in small groups of ten or so, scattered around the perimeter of the lake. There were boats at each work station that would allow them, if needed, to cross the lake much more rapidly than if they had to cover the distance on foot.

Arminius went aboard the ship when the oarsmen were already sitting on the benches and the two helmsmen had taken their place at the tiller. He carried a big bag, like the ones the assembly foremen used for their tools, and had a tablet in hand on which to take notes. The captain stopped him. 'Who are you? I've never seen you before.'

'I'm in charge of analyzing the manoeuvrability of this type of ship in a closed space.' He showed him the badge he wore around his neck impressed with the code of the Ravenna war fleet. The captain let him stay aboard without protest and Arminius went to sit on a coiled-up rope on the right side, close to the stern. The captain ordered the men to lower their oars and the foreman began beating out the rhythm for rowing.

Arminius turned to look at the opposite shore, and saw that the guests were taking their places on the small stand. The ship was gliding east, over the lake's still waters, heading towards the stand. As they approached he could begin to see its occupants more clearly. Four of the men were wearing togas, and the others were praetorian guards, at least thirty of them. Evidently the personages in their togas had wanted to see how the ship would handle itself on the water, in view of the historical commemoration soon to take place. Who were they? They must have been of very high status to warrant the presence of so many guards.

Now he was getting close enough to make out the features of each individual. He recognized one of them by the cut of his hair, another by the way he let his left hand dangle and tucked the thumb of that left hand into the belt of his tunic.

He'd seen this man much closer up and had been able to study him at length.

Augustus. The emperor.

Arminius started, and suddenly realized what might be about to happen in the time of a couple of oar strokes. He opened his tool case, extracted the interlocking segments of a spear shaft and he gripped the iron tip tightly. The Hermundur's message was ringing in his ears. The destiny of the world, of Rome and of his ancestral people, was in the palm of his hand. But where was the threat coming from?

It had to be behind the furled sail; it was the only area hidden from view. He crawled over the planks of the aft deck to get a closer look.

There was a man bent over, behind the sail, who was uncovering an object hidden under a piece of canvas. A ballista. He was turning an iron bar to make it taut. He was loading a three-libra bolt.

They were just in front of the stand.

The man moved the sail aside and reached out his hand to remove the safety catch.

He aimed. The commander of the guards saw him and yelled something.

Arminius had already mounted the tip. He hurled his spear and it nailed the man's hand onto the ballista's wooden frame.

What on earth had he done? He felt confused. Screams all around him. He dived into the lake, sank deep into the murky water and swam as far away as he could, then lifted his head just enough to see what was going on: the emperor was completely surrounded by praetorians, cargo boats had encircled the ship and armed men were climbing aboard to seize control. He heard the shrieks of the man as they tore out of his nailed hand the spear Arminius had thrown with such precision. He watched as they dragged him onto a boat and transported him to land.

Arminius reached a pontoon at anchor, climbed onto it and hid behind some bales of rags and construction materials until nightfall. When the site was completely deserted and silent he heard the hoot of an owl, repeated three times.

'I'm here,' he said. 'On the pontoon.'

'Come ashore,' rang out a voice. It was Flavus. He'd brought him clothing, food and a little wine. A carriage drawn by two horses was waiting nearby, with a man at the reins. They drove off.

Back at their house on the Aventine, they talked as they had so many times before, until very late.

'I realized that he was about to kill the emperor. I had to decide in an instant whether I would stop it from happening or let events take their course,' said Arminius. 'That's when I understood what the Hermundur's message meant, but I reacted out of pure instinct. I mounted the pieces of the shaft that I had in my bag and I hurled my spear at the killer just as he was about to let that bolt fly. I nailed his hand to the ballista frame and threw myself straight into the water. I didn't want to be seized and interrogated. I'd done enough.'

'You did the right thing,' said Flavus. 'They captured the perpetrator alive. They'll torture him until he spits out the names of everyone who's involved in this plot. I wonder what will happen to the lady.'

'She's the one who stands to lose the most. She got into something that was much bigger than she was, maybe even without realizing it, but this is going to crush her.'

'Taurus will inform us tomorrow. We're not going to get much sleep, wondering about that, but there will be a lot of people in Rome who won't close an eye tonight. They're already wandering the streets looking for a place to hide, but they're finding out that such a place doesn't exist.'

DAWN.

The sun rose on a city immersed in silence. But the two brothers, who rose at the first cock's crow, could imagine the screams of a man being tortured to death so he would say what he knew. Above all, the names of those who had armed his hand. Arminius knew some of those names himself and, given the chance, could recognize the others who he had seen inside a workshop at the river port and in a house on the other side of the Tiber.

By the time the sun was high above the horizon, terror had taken over the City. Many people had been arrested and the word was that Julia herself had been summoned by her father to his private study. She had remained there at length and was seen sobbing as she left. Her house was being guarded by two praetorians.

Taurus, who had gone out very early on his horse, came back at the fifth hour and sent for Flavus and Arminius. He was waiting for them, a scowl on his face, at the threshold to his house.

'You were right,' he started out, as soon as they had entered. 'There was a conspiracy, like the one that forty-two years ago took the life of the divine Caesar on the Ides of March. The commemoration of the Battle of Actium has been cancelled. The Battle of Salamina will be re-enacted instead; it won't make any difference to the populace. A great number of people were arrested last night. The would-be killer was tortured and he revealed the names of a couple of people, who in turn named others.

'Even Julia's freedwoman, Phoebe, was questioned under

torture, but she did not say a single word. This morning they found her hanging from her breast band. She knew she couldn't stand another day of torture, so she killed herself to protect her mistress. The emperor visited the dungeons at dawn; it seems that, when he saw Phoebe's body hanging from a ceiling beam, he said, "I would have preferred her as my daughter."

'Augustus is preparing a document to be delivered to the Senate. Its contents are a secret for now. But what seems certain is that for Julia, being the emperor's daughter will do her no good this time around.'

Taurus turned out to be right. That document sent to the Senate was an act of public accusation of his daughter. But strangely, Augustus did not charge her with conspiracy but with crimes of sexual misconduct, adultery and participation in orgies. The trial proceedings were not, however, those used for sexual crimes but rather for high treason. Many of the accused were sentenced to death, including Iullus Antonius. Others were exiled and their assets confiscated. Julia's life was spared but she was banished to the isle of Pandataria. Her mother, Scribonia, from whom she had been taken shortly after she was born, refused to abandon her and chose to share her fate on that black, lonely rock.

PART TWO

14

SEVERAL DAYS AFTER THE document that Augustus had sent to the Senate was made public, Arminius was summoned again by Taurus, along with his brother.

The two of them walked to the centurion's house early in the morning and were accommodated in his private study, where Thiaminus served them bowls of broth and toasted bread for breakfast.

They ate with relish. Taurus dried his lips with a napkin, nodded to his freedman, who cleared the tables, and turned to Arminius: 'What you did was noticed by everybody, including the emperor, but no one has really understood why you fled. Some even imagined that you'd fallen into the water and drowned. Caesar, however, had no doubts, and he summoned me last night.'

Arminius did not say a word and Taurus continued: '"I owe my life to that young man," he told me, "and I regret enormously that I cannot give him the public recognition he so amply deserves. You see, I can't publically celebrate the young foreigner who saved me from the plot where my own daughter was a conspirator . . ."'

As he spoke, using the emperor's words, Taurus was reliving the scene of that dramatic dialogue: '"Caesar . . . pardon my impudence, but perhaps it's too soon to condemn her with such certainty. I'd invite you to—"

' "That's enough, Centurion. You know how much I respect you and I've often had the pleasure of decorating you with the highest honours, but do not say another word now." '

Arminius examined him and saw the eyes of the soldier hardened by infinite battles grow damp, and he heard his voice tremble. It had to be love. A secret, tormented love, unutterable, never confessed, not even to himself. Perhaps he had always loved that beautiful woman, the daughter of the most powerful man in the world. And perhaps he loved her still, as did her father, even now that she had been publicly disgraced. That phrase pronounced in front of the lifeless body of Phoebe, the humble, heroic maidservant who had chosen to take her life rather than betray her mistress – who knew with what pain Augustus had uttered such a thing.

'What will become of her?' asked Flavus.

Taurus shook his head slowly, looking at the floor. 'She'll never be able to come back to Rome, unless a miracle occurs. A woman accustomed to her freedom, open-minded, as bold in love as she was in life, banished to that bleak island, with the company of no one but her mother. She'll never be able to reconcile the splendour of her previous life with the miserable existence she has been condemned to. But you're not here to listen to such words; this is a very important day for you, Arminius.'

The boy didn't dare ask what he meant by that and Taurus continued: 'Enough of this sad talk! You are both here because I've been asked to give you a message from Caesar in person. Arminius, considering your merits, and despite your young age, you will henceforth command the entire corps of the Germanic Auxilia, with the cavalry rank of *Praefectus*. This might be the first step for you to one day becoming a Roman citizen, despite your foreign birth.

'You'll soon be assigned responsibilities in keeping with your rank, but for now the emperor has nothing on his mind apart from the drama that's playing out in his home. He's decreed Julia's divorce without even notifying her husband; no one knows when Tiberius will be returning from his self-imposed exile.'

He then turned towards Flavus: 'Your help and support have also been recognized, and you too will be entrusted with an important position.'

Arminius replied for both: 'Please let Caesar know how grateful we are. We are both greatly honoured.'

FOR MANY MONTHS, the situation in Rome remained difficult. Many important families had been accused of involvement, and Julia's punishment seemed too severe to a great many citizens. The people were on her side and even considered her the victim of a cruel and self-serving manoeuvre of state. Livia, who was Augustus's wife and Tiberius's mother, was especially vehement in condemning her stepdaughter and everyone could be certain that for as long as she was alive, she would do everything in her power to prevent Julia's return. Julia had a single hope: her own sons Gaius and Lucius, who had been adopted by Augustus and were being prepared to succeed him. They were the only ones who could perhaps, some day, liberate her.

Some time passed before Arminius was summoned for an assignment: he was ordered to go to Brindisi, an important port from which many vessels sailed eastwards. His final destination was unknown to him and he was not told who he would be travelling with. Flavus would be staying in Rome with Taurus for the time being, but they had hopes of departing together for another mission, perhaps in Germania.

The two brothers said goodbye with an embrace.

'Be careful where you put your feet, wherever you end up,' said Flavus.

'You too. If they should send you to Germania, see if you can meet up with Father. Let him know that we haven't forgotten him.'

'I will,' replied Flavus, 'but he's always known that.'

Arminius mounted his horse and, with a group of soldiers, headed off towards the Via Appia, the oldest paved road in Rome, which crossed over the swamps, traversed the Apennines, and ended at the port of Brindisi. The journey would only take one week, because they were carrying little baggage and they'd be able to change their horses at every station along the road. They slept no more than five hours at a stretch, just what was strictly necessary, travelling from first light to last.

The group was made up of ten Germanic auxiliaries, ten Roman soldiers and two officers: Sergius Vetilius, military tribune of the Twelfth Legion, and Rufius Corvus, prefect from a cavalry branch of the same legion. As they rode, Arminius tried to make conversation with his travel companions. 'Seeing that we have a long journey ahead of us, it's best if we introduce ourselves, if that's all right with you.'

'Of course it is,' replied Vetilius and he introduced himself with all three of his names, Sergius Vetilius Celer, his rank, his cohort and the legion he belonged to. As did Rufius Corvus Afer.

'What about you?' asked Rufius.

'I'm the commander of this unit,' replied Arminius.

'What?' said Sergius Vetilius.

'The commander of this unit,' repeated Arminius. He

showed them his credentials, signed by Centurion Taurus on behalf of the imperial house.

'But who are you?' insisted Rufius. 'You can't be higher in rank than I am.'

'You're right, I'm not,' replied Arminius. 'I've been given this commission by order of Caesar. If that's a problem for you, once we've arrived you can consult the commander of the port. He's already been informed.'

'I think I understand,' said Sergius Vetilius. 'You must be the one everyone's talking about.' And the matter did not come up again.

During their journey, they always had their meals together. This gave them the opportunity to get to know one another, to exchange ideas and to talk about the mission that awaited them.

'Where do you come from?' asked Rufius at a certain point.

'Why, is it important?' asked Arminius.

'It's not,' replied Rufius. 'Just simple curiosity.'

'There's no hurry then, is there?' observed Arminius.

The ship waiting for them was a navy vessel; the group boarded early one morning. Seeing a huge battleship weigh anchor and cast off was always an emotional experience, especially for Arminius, who had never even seen the sea before coming to Italy. His men made themselves comfortable, since there was an entire crew managing the ship. They stretched out on the folded spare sails or on the cots they'd been given to sleep at night. Only the two officers stayed in motion, walking back and forth on the ship's sides or positioning themselves aft at the helm or forward to watch the horizon or the crew's man-oeuvring, or simply to listen to the beat of the drums that set the pace for the one hundred and seventy oarsmen rowing in unison.

As soon as the wind was in their favour, the rowers pulled in the oars and the crew raised the mainsail and the foresail. A monster was depicted on the huge sail: it had the body of a lion, the tail of a snake and a second head, a ram's head, on its back. Underneath was the name of the vessel: *CHIMAERA*.

What most impressed Arminius during the ship's transit was that the machine was a kind of extension of the men; the men were the energy that moved the machine and made it work. He thought he remembered his father saying something similar regarding the experience he'd had on board General Drusus's flagship on the Rhine, but no story could get close to the reality that he was seeing with his own eyes. Even the force of the wind itself was tamed by the helmsmen who gathered it into the sail and set the ship going in the right direction. The speed that the vessel could pick up using the full force of the wind was very high, but the ship couldn't travel as fast as it could if the sea wouldn't tolerate it. If the waves were too high, they acted as obstacles for the prow and the hull, which made horrible creaking noises, alerting the crew that they had to take in the sails before the ship was damaged. And so there was this incredible balance of wind, hull, sea and men. It also occurred to Arminius that the ships used by General Drusus, made to sail down a river, had little in common with the *Chimaera*, designed to ride the waves of the sea.

They rounded Cape Maleas and set course east and south, passing from one island to the next. Some were barren and craggy, others were covered with pines and palm trees, like little solitary paradises. Arminius had never seen an island before and he was amazed at those tiny lands made of rock and water, with their little bays and towering cliffs that rose up like dragon's scales from the waves. But the light was the thing that filled him with awe: the way that the sky and the water reflected it in such a myriad of nuances. Every wave was a mirror with thousands of fragments and the moon at night left a long silvery wake that stretched all the way to the horizon. He understood how that sea had given birth to so many kingdoms and civilizations and he realized what an abyss separated his ancestral land, so dark and swampy, from these dazzling places. How could he ever think of returning to the long, frosty winters of the north and abandoning that world of light and infinite colour?

After seven days of navigation the ship set ashore in Rhodos. Before the passengers disembarked, the ship's commander gave Arminius a small leather-encased coffer that he was to give to the man who would be waiting for him at the port. The same man would accompany him to his destination, to ensure that he reached the house of the illustrious person who it was his mission to meet with.

The person that the captain had spoken of was waiting at the port. He was a Greek freedman named Antemius who appeared to be a servant from a very distinguished household. Arminius handed him the coffer which the man opened at once; there were only letters inside. He had the house seal impressed on a wax tablet to acknowledge receipt. Communication was difficult: Antemius's Latin was weak and Arminius only knew a few words of Greek. Four of his men, including Rufius Corvus and Sergius Vetilius, followed them, serving as an escort although there was no need to assume a particular formation. They were also useful as interpreters.

They made their way up a winding road and after they had circled around a large temple, they found themselves staring at a spectacular sight that left Arminius speechless. A bronze giant, whose legs up to his knees were the only parts remaining erect, lay in bits and pieces scattered over the surrounding area; the crowned head had rolled on its side, and the hollow inside of the torso looked like a cavern and was vast enough to hold thirty men. The arms were enormous, the hands alone so big that no man, no matter how well he was built, would be able to encircle the thumb with his arms. This must be the *Colossus of Rhodos* that his teacher Diodorus had told him about, but seeing it with his own eyes filled him with amazement. How had they ever managed to raise such a giant?

Sergius Vetilius broke into his thoughts: 'He was built in an age when anything seemed possible. But they say that the sculptor made a fatal error in designing him, and that he killed himself in despair.' In fact, it was an earthquake that felled the giant.

There were many things that Arminius would have liked to ask, but he didn't want to appear ignorant. He was fascinated by such a marvel and continued to ponder it as they walked. There had to be some kind of mysterious reason behind the fact that all the peoples and nations living around that sea had finally joined, whether willingly or not, the single Empire of Rome, which kept them linked to a common destiny. That Empire must surely last for centuries. Only a cataclysm or the hammer of Thor could possibly bring her down, like the giant of bronze scattered in chunks that recalled his original greatness. If Rome were to collapse, the world would be plunged into a long era of darkness.

He thought back to the moment in which he'd decided to throw the spear that stayed the hand of the man who was preparing to strike Caesar with the deadly bolt of his ballista. And he thought that he'd done the right thing, even if no one had ever discovered that it was him.

When they reached their destination – a beautiful villa surrounded by a garden of palm, myrtle, pine, fig and pomegranate trees – he was led into the atrium by Antemius and he waited there until a man walked in. He had an imposing build and a serious expression on his face. Antemius whispered to him, 'This is Tiberius Claudius, son of Livia Augusta, brother of Drusus, commander of the imperial armies.'

Arminius observed this sad prince closely. He had been exiled for years in a golden prison, far from Rome, unwelcome in the capital of the Empire. Perhaps the coffer that Antemius was handing him now contained a letter from his mother with the latest news. Tiberius opened it at once and rapidly scanned one of the scrolls, his face darkening as he read. 'So you are the man who saved Caesar's life,' he said coldly.

Arminius merely gave a nod.

'You're very young . . . perhaps in time you'll regret what you've done.'

Arminius did not know what to answer and he chose silence.

'You'll wait here for me to give you the replies to those who have written to me.'

Arminius remained there for nearly two hours. He was served drinks and fresh fruit as he waited.

Tiberius finally returned, followed by a servant who carried the coffer with the answers for his correspondents.

'The man who has you at his side in combat is a fortunate man,' Tiberius said. 'Antemius knows who these should be delivered to, before you set course again for your destination. I wish you a safe voyage.'

'Thank you, Commander,' said Arminius. He left with Antemius and rejoined his men. Once at the port, the freedman led Arminius on board a swift open-sea vessel which would soon set sail for Ostia, with a number of deliveries for the imperial house. Arminius handed over the letters and then asked to return to the trireme on which he had been travelling.

He was rather shaken from his encounter with Tiberius, an experience that had left him feeling light-headed. He had arrived this close to the highest levels of powers in such a short time, making acquaintances that he had never dreamed of. He'd also learned how to behave around such people: speak as little as possible and only if requested to do so. Men of Tiberius's ilk were always surrounded by a flock of adulators, spies and courtiers, whose company they usually couldn't stand. Especially a serious, reserved person like Tiberius, a man with an old-fashioned upbringing, a keen soldier, a reluctant expert in the matters of family politics and in the hypocrisy that reigned sovereign. The latest events, which he certainly had been informed of, must have surely disgusted him even further. He did not let on how much he knew about what had happened, but certain aspects must have left him feeling troubled indeed.

It was before dawn the next morning when Arminius's men, under the command of Tribune Sergius Vetilius, went off to fetch a person who was to join them, while Arminius stayed aboard the ship, waiting to receive this mysterious passenger. He watched them as they made their way back, a little procession of shadows coming from one of the twisting roads that descended the hillside overlooking the port. He let down the gangway when they were close and he assembled the men remaining on board, both Romans and Germanic auxiliaries, to welcome the newcomer and render honours.

Arminius maintained his position within the honour guard as the guest was escorted to the stern where he'd been assigned quarters. Dawn was just breaking, so the light was still too low for Arminius to make out the man's features.

On his feet at the prow, Arminius scanned the horizon, veiled by a light mist which would dissipate as the sun rose. The wind was east and north, promising good sailing. A voice rang out at his side: 'You must be the man in charge of my escort.' Arminius startled; he hadn't heard the slightest noise, not a single footfall. In fact, the person standing next to him was barefoot, and wore only a long-sleeved tunic.

'I am Publius Quinctilius Varus,' he said. 'I governed Syria until the new governor was installed a year ago.'

'Hail, Legate,' replied Arminius. 'I am indeed in charge of your escort and will be assisted by Tribune Sergius Vetilius and Cavalry Prefect Rufius Corvus. We are at your disposition. We're expecting fine weather and the crossing should be smooth. We will land in Laodicea in six or seven days, depending on the wind.'

'You seem like a born sailor,' replied Varus. 'How many times have you been to sea?'

'This is my first time, Legate, in a position of command, although I was instructed for several months at the base in Ravenna.'

'Very good,' replied Varus. 'On the other hand, if what they say of you is true, there's little to be surprised at. You are a young man of great intelligence and you have a strong spirit of initiative. Is it true that you brought letters to Tiberius Claudius?'

'That is true, Legate.'

'And you can tell me nothing about what they contained?'

'Nothing, Legate.'

'Obviously,' replied Varus without further insistence.

They met again the next day, after the crew had been mustered to deal with worsening weather conditions. The captain ordered them, as the wind picked up, to first shorten sail and then to truss it up. At that point, the oarsmen and helmsmen would take over. 'Let's hope that the gales hit while there is still daylight. In the meantime, we'll try to get closer to the coast; the rocks are less of a threat to us than the open sea in a storm. We'll try to find shelter. We'll use the sails for as long as possible to gain time.'

Neither Arminius nor Publius Quinctilius Varus seemed worried and they continued their conversation. Evidently the legate knew much more about the young man than he was letting on. It was well known that Varus had ties with the emperor. Arminius would later discover why in speaking to Sergius Vetilius and Rufius Corvus, loyal men and fine officers who were clearly called upon for the most sensitive missions. Such as this one.

In the meantime the sky was getting dark and the wind was strengthening, but the coast was coming into sight at the north and with it the Gulf of Antalya, with the eastern Taurus range towering behind it. The captain ordered the helmsman to turn the rudder to port and to keep the plumb line in the water. The sea was swelling up much faster than they'd expected. The sail was immediately trussed up and the foreman picked up the rowing beat to get them to the western coast of the gulf as quickly as possible. But the north wind was pushing the ship out to sea, causing her to drift leeward over the grey-foamed waves. A sudden burst of very strong wind tilted the ship onto her right side and tore the yard from the mast, causing it to fall on the deck. Rufius, who had been trying to give the crew a hand, was trapped underneath.

Arminius rushed over to help him, grabbing the shaft of an oar to use as a lever. The prefect managed to slide out from under and free his leg, which was bruised and bloody but not broken. He was taken straight to the sterncastle where he could be treated by the doctor. Then Arminius returned on deck to help the crew in their struggle to attach the yard somehow to the base of the mast and the sail to the yard so it wouldn't do any further damage. Publius Quinctilius Varus observed him from his cabin, finding himself impressed by the strength and the ready reflexes of the young officer who was commanding his guard.

The foreman accelerated the rowing rhythm in an attempt to beat the force of the wind, and the ship's prow slowly began to move into the shelter of the mountain and then the promontory. The foreman slowed the drumbeat to let the oarsmen catch their breath and the ship continued to advance towards the end of the gulf, where the sea was almost calm.

The sun pierced the cloud cover and shot out towards the horizon, sending bloody flashes through the sky and sea. The ship was finally able to drop the fore and aft anchors and it stopped for the night in the harbour.

The crew lit the on-board lamps to signal the *Chimaera*'s presence to other ships seeking haven there during the night. The captain had a very frugal dinner distributed to the crew and oarsmen, with just one cup of water a head. Arminius sat with Rufius and Sergius; he was pleased to share a meal with them after such a long, tiring day. They spoke about their passenger and it was thus that Arminius learned about how close that man was to the emperor, since he had married Vipsania, who was the daughter of Agrippa and his first wife. He had acted as judge and arbiter in a trial between King Herod of Judea and his children and heirs, and he had subdued a revolt in Jerusalem by crucifying two thousand rebels.

15

THE NEXT MORNING, after breakfast, Varus made a point of congratulating Arminius for the way he'd helped cavalry officer Rufius Corvus when the yard had fallen from the mast to the deck, pinning him underneath. He wanted to see Rufius as well, who approached them with a limp. His leg was still hurting him because the surgeon had had to stitch up a gash that bared his shin bone. The wound had been rinsed with strong vinegar and straight wine so it wouldn't become infected, and bandaged carefully.

The sea was not as rough as it had been the day before and they were able to set sail again, once the yard had been returned to its place, its sail half clewed so that it would not offer too much resistance to the wind, which was still rather high. They sailed along the coast of Pamphylia. Every now and then, when the captain veered south to pick up the wind, some of the mountains of Cyprus could be seen ahead. On the fourth day of their voyage they sighted Cilicia, a land ruled by an elderly sovereign without heirs. It wasn't difficult to foresee what the future of that tiny kingdom might hold.

The wind had turned and was now blowing from the southwest. The sea was calm enough and that put an end to their worries; it was consoling to realize that peace had been brought to that pirate-ridden stretch of sea half a century earlier by

Pompey. He had rounded up all the pirates in the Gulf of Alexandria of Cilicia and given them a choice: would they rather be relocated inland and become farmers, or crucified from the first to the last? They had chosen the former.

Varus laughed recounting those long-past events.

They had begun to sail by night and each dawn was more beautiful than the day before. Every now and then they would pass close to the small islands that were scattered around and Arminius wished he could have gone ashore to see what they were like. He often wondered what the island that Julia had been banished to was like; he imagined her wandering the confined spaces of an unfriendly landscape, or sitting on a lonely rock, scanning the horizon like the survivor of a shipwreck waiting for a ship to spy her and save her.

They finally reached Laodicea, where they were welcomed by a squad of cavalrymen. After spending the night there, they continued on to Antioch.

Arminius was very excited at what he was seeing and experiencing. The East was coming alive before his eyes in one astonishing place after another. Ancient cities, which had been founded before his ancestral people had given themselves a name, such as Aleppo and Jerusalem, Babylonia, Damascus, Tyrus and Sidon, Byblos and Thapsus. Others had become centres of blinding splendour over the past three hundred years: Antioch, Gaza, Seleucia, Alexandria and Palmyra. He'd heard all about their greatness and their past and present splendours from Diodorus. He remembered his tutor's lessons on Alexander the Great, who had reunited all the nations from the Danube to the Indus and the Nile in a single vast empire. But that empire had instantly dissolved upon his death. Arminius often thought about this and wondered whether it was inevitable that every empire should collapse sooner or later. Maybe even Rome. The thought almost frightened him.

When they would stop in the way stations or cities, Varus would attempt to strike up a conversation with the young man who commanded his guard and who showed such acumen and desire to learn. And Varus had plenty to teach him. 'Our world today is divided up between two empires: ours and the Parthian Empire which extends east all the way to India and represents a continuous threat to our borders and to our allies. Some say that Julius Caesar, before he was assassinated, was organizing the invasion of the Parthian Empire in order to extend our borders to the very heart of Asia, where only Alexander had succeeded in arriving three centuries ago. However, the project ended with his death.'

The journey continued until they reached Antioch. It was a city of marvels, the third largest in the Empire, after Rome and Alexandria. Her streets were flanked by columned porticoes and majestic temples. The statues within had been sculpted or cast by the greatest artists of the day and of times past. Some of them were even animated; they could move their arms, tilt their heads and turn their eyes to the left and right. There were hippodromes and baths with hot and cold waters, and even pools more than one hundred feet long, where one could swim and play ball.

Antioch was the point of arrival for all the caravans coming from Persia, India and Bactriana laden with precious stones, silken fabrics, pearls and spices. The city was the seat of the Roman governor, who represented the power of Rome and had four legions at his command, but it was also the land of every pleasure, from the most refined arts of love to the most scandalous perversions. It was a paradise for revellers and hedonists, the land of one thousand temptations – the ideal place for a young man eager to experience every sensation of body and soul.

Arminius had left his ancestral land when he was barely an adolescent. His only thought of love so far had been born that spring day that he saw a girl with a crown of flowers, and their eyes had locked. How long ago had that been? It seemed like an eternity, even though many years had not really passed. But each of those years had been dense with events, thoughts, fears and enthusiasm, hopes and dreams. Each one of those years had been worth at least three or four, and Arminius felt like a man, an adult; he was responsible and aware, and knew much about the complex, intricate ways of the world.

He never remembered his dreams; it was as if they were snatched away before morning. But he was sure that in some of them he was living wild adventures with his brother, riding horses at breakneck speed, flying even, over the peaks of mountains, skimming the tops of forest trees, gliding over rivers as silvery fish splashed in the water. Not because he could remember images, colours or sounds, but because the feelings and emotions he felt in his dreams survived for just a few moments in the mornings before he opened his eyes.

That evening he had escorted Proconsul Quinctilius Varus to the residence of Governor Calpurnius. He had been dismissed on arrival and had no further duties, so he met up with his friends Rufius Corvus and Sergius Vetilius, who'd offered to give him a guided tour through the labyrinths of pleasure.

Quinctilius Varus, guest of the highest Roman authority in Syria, spent a tranquil night talking about business and politics with his colleague and then sleeping in a comfortable room at the centre of the garrison headquarters.

For Arminius that same night was a descent into hell,

teeming with sensations he'd never experienced. He'd never be able to forget it, not for his whole life.

Prostitutes were everywhere in Antioch. The finest ones called themselves '*hetairai*', using the Greek term for 'companions'. They lived in private apartments and they were free, not slaves. The ones who were best known for their skill in the erotic arts commanded a very high fee and managed to amass fortunes. The dream of each and every one was to find a steady, wealthy companion willing to pay for her exclusive services. In that way, he could have sex without protection and avoid promiscuity with other clients. She would be ensured a life of luxury in an elegant residence with a garden, servants, pets, refined food and costly wines. The more ordinary prostitutes, who were nearly always slaves managed by a procurer, lived in quarters where no man or woman of high social ranking would ever dream of being seen. But Antioch was the capital of the province, and there were at least two legions camped near the city, with thousands of young men who wanted their needs met.

As they neared the entrance to that quarter, Rufius Corvus offered his young companion an object that would protect him from some very disagreeable and even disfiguring diseases, and he taught him how to use it. They set off together in their discovery of Eros and pleasure. The first thing they did was to watch a play in which the scenes of love were acted out live by actors and actresses, with women coupling with men, men with other men and women other women. His friends told him that sometimes actual orgies were acted out in simulated banquets. In certain theatres, mythological scenes were played out; for instance Leda, completely naked, would offer herself to an actor dressed like a swan. At the moment of ecstasy, he would let out the sharp, raucous squawk of a bird. Other theatre companies acted out the union of Pasiphaë with a bull. The sham queen of Crete would crawl inside a wooden cow, to be mounted by an actor disguised as a bull, re-enacting the monstrous coupling that would generate the no less monstrous Minotaur.

Last of all, Arminius and his two companions watched the pederastic union of Zeus with Ganymede, where a large, hairy man took off his eagle's feathers and deflowered a passive and resigned young hero, an actor so bony and wrinkled that he bore no resemblance at all to the plump statuary models that Diodorus had shown them. The public's reaction was more hilarity than arousal, because the staging was so shabby and the actors and their costumes were so rough that no one could be fooled by them.

Every now and then, Arminius stole a look at his companions and they seemed to be just as amused as the other spectators. He was about to suggest that they return to their quarters and forget about the rest of the evening, but Rufius Corvus and Sergius Vetilius had prepared a sexual initiation for their young friend, who they imagined to be inexpert in the ways of Eros. He may have attracted Roman matrons with his statuary build and his blue eyes, but they were certainly no match for the refined lovemaking games of the Antiochian *hetairai* who had honed their skills for thousands of years, winning the favour of the highest-ranking lords of the Euphrates and the Nile with the only weapon they had at hand.

Arminius realized instantly that his friends were well known in the district. They handled themselves with ease and were greeted warmly by the girls who lived there. It was a different world from the theatre here; no improvization. There were girls from every corner of the earth: Phrygians, Egyptians, Persians and Babylonians, Phoenicians and Greeks,

Ethiopians with limbs the colour of bronze and dewy eyes, Armenians with green eyes and raven-black hair, and even Jewesses. Each wearing the costumes and the jewellery of her native land.

Rufius Corvus and Sergius Vetilius entrusted their friend to the attentions of two Phoenician girls with amber skin, paying in advance for their services. His companions in pleasure offered him wine, undressed him and, in appreciation for how young and handsome he was, dedicated their utmost expertise to bringing him to the brink of delirium time and time again. They stretched him out in a state of semi-consciousness, in a light, quivering tension, only to awaken him again and again, one, then the other, and then together, to give him a taste of extreme ecstasy.

It lasted all night.

Just before dawn they prepared a bath of thermal water scented with aloe oil, and they immersed themselves with him, passing a sea sponge over his back and his chest. They dried him off, wrapped him in a sheet of Egyptian linen and they clung to him with their smooth bodies until he closed his eyes.

THE THREE SOLDIERS arrived at headquarters just in time to report to the legion, their faces showing the signs of their sleepless night. After they rendered honour to the standard and the silver eagle, they retired to their rooms to catch up on a little sleep.

In the days that followed, Arminius returned to the city of pleasure, mainly to observe that strange, alien place where he had lived for a few hours without really comprehending it and without seeing many of its hidden corners. He thought often of Iole, the girl prostitute who Flavus had fallen in love with; maybe she was already dead by now. He imagined that situations like hers, horrible as they were, were the price to be paid in order for civilization to go on existing.

He returned to the life of every day and every night. For a month, work went smoothly as they prepared another journey towards the East. Arminius had plenty of time to explore Antioch and the cults of Baal, Mithras and Astarte, or Ishtar, with her sacred prostitutes. It was said that the goddess of love herself – called Aphrodite by the Greeks and Venus by the Romans – would appear to the faithful who experienced sacred sleep inside the Sanctuary of Astarte. When Rufius and Sergius noticed that Arminius was curious about that place, they arranged for his curiosity to be satisfied. The feat he'd carried out in Rome certainly merited the embrace of a goddess.

And so one evening, as he was wandering in the temple district, Arminius was approached by a little boy selling water. He took a cup and began to sip from it. From that moment, his conscious mind abandoned him and he was immersed in a sort of dream where the goddess herself appeared to him in a lush, sweetly scented garden of roses and pomegranates. Her beauty was as intense and inebriating as the perfume of that garden. She was encircled by a lunar aura, a glassy light that exalted her face and features. She wore a gown of an unfamiliar fabric, open from her belt to her feet. Her divinity was clear by the absence of a navel on her belly. There was just a slight hollow there, more an ornament than a scar. She had lain down beside him and he could not believe in such a miracle. The dream was so real that the caresses of the goddess made him tremble, shiver, vibrate like a reed in the path of the wind.

And there was a song. In an unknown, remote language, its melody subtle and unnerving. His heart and his thoughts were burning with desire. He was ablaze with a fever he'd never felt before; sweat beaded his forehead and he could feel it dripping onto his face like tears.

Then, without seeing and without speaking, he slipped into her and he fell prey to a wild delirium, an uncontrollable shaking. The tension was so strong he could have died of it. When he withdrew from her the dream vanished, and he sank into a darkness that was blacker than night. A hot breath blew at him: the mountain wind? The sea? Then, a light scented rain, drops of mist, washed his body softly, purifying him.

For a moment he was sure that he would slip from dream to death without feeling pain.

And that he would never wake up again.

THEY LEFT FOR THEIR eastward journey very early one morning.

Proconsul Varus travelled in his carriage, but also every now and then on horseback, and they followed the road that went from Syria to Anatolia. The Taurus range remained on their left, its peaks still snow-covered. To their right was a wide plain, green at first, with grapevines and fields of wheat as well as small groves of date palms, becoming arid and flat as their journey went on. The villages were made up of a few houses of raw clay bricks and straw where farmers lived. It took about fifteen days to arrive at Nisibis. They then turned south towards Carrhae.

Carrhae. Arminius had heard that name but he couldn't place it.

'It was here that, half a century ago, a tremendous battle took place,' Sergius Vetilius began to tell the story. 'A magnificent Roman army with a full seven legions was annihilated by the Parthians. It was commanded by triumvir Marcus Licinius Crassus. He had ventured into this territory deceived by information provided by local tribal chieftains, who urged him to attack with all his soldiers. As incompetent as he was greedy, Crassus wanted to reach Seleucia, where he hoped to find the legendary treasures of the Parthians, and he trusted the advice and instructions of an Arab sovereign who ruled over a small kingdom. It was a trap. Crassus drove his men at a forced march into a flat, arid territory under the burning sun. The Roman heavy infantry was exhausted before they ever met the enemy. The commander of the Parthians, who was young and astute, masterfully manoeuvred his armoured cavalry and his fearsome mounted archers. They are such experts with their bows that they can hit their target facing backwards, while fleeing on their horses or pretending to flee . . .'

The landscape all around them seemed to make those distant events real and dreadful. Varus and his companions on horseback regarded the sun-scorched plain; on their left still rose the walls of Carrhae, an ancient and oft fought-over city. The only sound to be heard was the thin hiss of the wind that raised a slight haze from the vast, flat, barren ground. Varus seemed to be listening to only the wind, absorbed in his own thoughts.

Sergius Vetilius continued: 'Crassus drew up his men in a compact block that made it even easier for the enemy to encircle them. The Parthians never engage in hand-to-hand combat; they always strike from afar and disengage. All around the Roman block, the Parthians beat gigantic drums that struck terror and despair into the legionaries. The Roman commander was desperate; his only hope was that the Parthians would run out of arrows . . . but he hoped in vain. They had camels, hundreds of them, laden with what seemed an infinite supply of their deadly weapons. The rain of arrows was incessant. Nothing could protect his men from that deluge. The darts pierced their shields, and then their arms, and their hands. Many of them tried to fight on by wrenching the arrows out of their bodies, but that only served to lacerate their flesh even more, and then the bleeding couldn't be stopped . . .'

Sergius Vetilius seemed to be in a hallucinatory state, as if he were seeing the scene play out in front of his eyes. More than once, Arminius found himself turning around to check for an imminent attacker, as if those demonic steel-covered horsemen might appear from one moment to the next.

Vetilius seemed to be scanning the area all around as well, and he took a few steps back. He was like an actor in a tragedy, moving around on stage, his face covered by a mask from which his laments could be heard. 'The Roman commander attempted a risky manoeuvre: he had his own son Publius lead a charge of the Celtic cavalry against the enemy horsemen. The enemy rode off as if they were fleeing and his men gave chase, giving Crassus the illusion that the charge had been victorious; once again he was wrong. When Publius and his Gallic horsemen were far enough away from the heart of the battle, the Parthians surrounded them. In the end, Publius was suffering from so many wounds that he asked his attendant to kill him because he didn't have the strength to wield his own sword. The Parthians chopped off his head. One of them stuck it onto a pike, rode over to the Roman formation and galloped by, his trophy raised high, so close that Crassus and all his men could see the end his son had come to.'

The narrator's voice trembled as he pronounced those words. Rufius Corvus said something into Arminius's ear: 'The young attendant who plunged his sword into Publius Crassus's side and helped him to die was his grandfather. I don't know how many times I've heard this story.'

Arminius could not understand how they had ended up in

that place, at that time, listening to that tragic reenactment and why Varus had wanted to come all this way, since he seemed completely disinterested. He had not said a word, and his back was turned to the huge deserted stretch of land.

'The massacre went on until nightfall, because the Parthians, like the Persians, never fight after darkness falls. Crassus abandoned his wounded and tried to reach Carrhae to save himself. The next day, the wounded were all killed, one by one, four thousand men. All told, the battle lasted three days. In the end Crassus died as well. His head was taken to Seleucia and was later used, I've heard say, in a play: *The Bacchae*, by Euripides, in a scene where King Pentheus is torn to pieces by women in a Dionysian orgy.'

Sergius Vetilius fell silent as the sky began to cloud over to the north. Varus roused himself from his torpor and said, 'Let's go on. I want to see where the battle took place.'

'Proconsul,' objected Rufius Corvus, 'perhaps we should go another day, when the weather is better.'

'I want to go now,' replied Quinctilius Varus. 'The storm is far off, over the mountains.'

The two officers and Arminius thus put themselves at the head of the squad and proceeded south. Varus joined them on horseback as well.

Both Rufius and Sergius seemed familiar with the road and Arminius thought that was why Quinctilius Varus had wanted them with him.

Their route was not free of perils. Borders were very unclear in that area, because the desert extended for hundreds of miles in every direction and marauders from the nomadic tribes came and went as they pleased, often travelling with groups of Parthian horsemen, still swift and deadly half a century after the battle.

It was nearly mid-afternoon when the first signs of the massacre began to appear: rusty weapons corroded by the wind and sand, Roman helmets and swords, broken fragments of armour which were hard to even identify, arrowheads stuck in the ground in such numbers that Arminius and the others chose to proceed on foot so they could pick out a clear path and their horses wouldn't be injured or lamed.

As they went on, the landscape became increasingly horrifying.

Bones.

Tens of thousands of bones.

There were so many of them. The remains of the four thousand wounded men abandoned by Crassus and butchered by the Parthians. Chopped to pieces. Beheaded. Varus had become increasingly withdrawn. He didn't say a word as he let his gaze wander over the endless field of death. Now and then his face would contract suddenly, or he would jump slightly, as if he were hearing the screams of the dying and the thunder of the enemy's drums.

Then they saw the bones of horses mixed with human remains: the huge skeletons of Publius Crassus's Celtic warriors. You could still see the marks left by the teeth of the jackals and hyenas that had stripped them bare half a century earlier. There were Gallic horsemen among the Germanic auxiliaries accompanying them, and their faces turned as grey as the soot at their feet at seeing the wretched remains of their ancient comrades.

'Let's turn back, Proconsul, please,' said Sergius Vetilius, incapable of staring for another instant at the remnants of the worst defeat Rome had suffered, after the Battle of Cannae. 'The weather is getting worse. If a dust storm picks up, we'll risk getting lost and ending up like these poor souls here.'

Varus seemed to suddenly become aware of the situation, as thunder rumbled in the distance. 'Yes,' he said, 'we'll go back to Carrhae.'

The wind picked up, raising a cloud of dust, and the sky darkened. The parched tamarisks in the dry riverbeds were blown through by the wind, which had turned into a hiss and then a lament. The horsemen rode bent over in the fog like ghosts. The first raindrops fell and the air was filled with the scent of quenched earth. The haze cleared and a bolt of lightning flooded the plain with blinding light, as a crack of thunder exploded over their heads. The rain began to fall thick and heavy. The soil could not absorb all the water and rivulets soon formed, gathering in cracks in the rocks and then pouring into the riverbeds. Arminius thought of the skulls of the fallen soldiers being bathed by the rain, the water slaking the thirst of their disjointed jaws. He asked himself again why they had come in the first place. He couldn't ask the proconsul the reason for their journey, but perhaps Sergius and Rufius could help him understand.

Arminius missed his brother, who he would always turn to when he had a question on his mind. He had no idea at all where he was.

The rain stopped late that night and the full moon showed through the tattered clouds, spreading its glow over the chalky plain. Arminius saw Rufius and Sergius sitting near a campfire, where they were drying their wet clothes. He got off his horse and joined them.

'Why have we come all this way if there's nothing here but bones? Why did we come to see that battle ground?'

Sergius Vetilius spoke first: 'It's been the dream of many commanders to defeat the Parthians and avenge this massacre. Varus was the governor of this province, and he may be considering doing just that. His ambition is enormous. He put down a huge revolt in Judaea and crucified two thousand people. Not a glorious endeavour. The work of a butcher.'

'I don't understand,' said Arminius.

'I think that maybe this gruesome reconnaissance mission is his way of putting the temptation out of his mind. It would be suicide, and Varus is no fool. The debacle of Carrhae would be enough to dissuade anyone of the notion. It's the only thing I can think of.'

Rufius stepped in: 'Your interpretation is just not plausible. It's highly improbable that he would be re-assigned to this region. But he is also very aware that his career has room for advancement and the fact that he's close to the house of Augustus just feeds into his ambitions. He is here simply to look at the errors of the past so that he will not repeat them in his future military career. After dinner, when I read him my report based on the diary I've been keeping, that was the impression he gave me.'

'So what conclusions has he come to?' asked Arminius.

'There's no way he would tell me, nor would I dare to ask. But I told him the conclusions that I came to myself,' Rufius continued, counting on the fingers of his hand.

'The Roman army, as battle-ready as it may be, can be defeated.

'Never trust a foreigner, even when he is an ally.

'And lastly, never let yourself be lured into a territory that you don't know but that the enemy knows like the palm of his hand.'

The three officers regarded each other in silence. The call of a jackal, sounding like a long lament, echoed through the desert of Carrhae.

16

ARMINIUS THOUGHT LONG and hard about Quinctilius Varus's strange quest. What struck him most was his comrade's assertion that the Roman army could be defeated. Although this remained with him, he would have many occasions in the following years to convince himself of the opposite. He spent nearly four years in the East, travelling almost always with the same people who had seen Carrhae with him. In that long stretch of time, he learned much about the Empire of Rome and became good friends with Rufius Corvus and Sergius Vetilius.

In these long years, he also learned how the postal system worked. One merely went to the nearest port and got information about the ships that were setting sail, on what day of what month, and the name of the captain, with whom you could discuss price. If you were lucky, you'd find a direct ship to Ostia, which then went to Rome, sailing up the Tiber. In Rome, you got someone to go to the harbour to pick up the parcel or letter. He would then consign it to the *cursus publicus* office, and from there it would continue by road until it reached its destination.

He wrote to Diodorus first, at the house on the Aventine, certain that he would still be there. He was much less certain of where to find Taurus, who as a man of arms was certainly sought after because of his experience and his many virtues; he would never be left at home for long. He asked his one-time tutor to forward a letter to his brother Flavus, including it in the same sealed case. If he received a reply, Arminius asked him to send it to Antioch, to the headquarters of the Twelfth Legion *Fulminata*. In less than two months he received, to his great surprise, an answer.

'Winds are favourable on the sea,' explained Rufius Corvus, handing him the message. 'And the weather on the continent is good. Here's your letter.'

Arminius's heart was pounding as he opened it. The case showed all the signs of its long travels; it was scratched and scraped, the least you could expect from a journey many thousands of miles long. He carefully unrolled the parchment. The letter was written in clumsy, ill-formed Latin, surely the work of a camp scribe, but Arminius felt a strong jolt of emotion at reading those words:

> *Flavus, to his brother, hail!*
>
> *Yesterday I received with great joy your letter in which you tell me about the wonders of the East and its cities. Instead, I find myself in Germania on the Rhine front, in the army of Marcus Vinicius where we combat continuously, making very little progress.*
>
> *I have been named prefect of one of the cavalry alae and I have been assigned special quarters here in camp. I have an Illyrian slave who serves me at table and a woman who washes my clothes and consoles me during the long nights.*
>
> *It is still very cold here. I miss the climate in Rome greatly. I have no doubt about where I'd rather live. I hope that destiny will join us again soon.*
>
> *Stay well.*

It wasn't much, and yet Arminius was happy to receive a letter from his brother from the edge of the world and the ocean shore. It seemed like a miracle to him. He read it again and again. He was really glad to hear that Flavus was hoping they'd be together again. He went to his room and prepared his reply:

> *Arminius to Flavus, dearest brother, hail!*
>
> *It was with great pleasure that I received your letter this morning. Congratulations for your promotion in Vinicius's army.*
>
> *I hope to be in Rome next autumn and I count on seeing you there. I have so many things to tell you and I'll be bringing a gift. Let me know as soon as you can when you will be returning to Rome, and if you've had the fortune of seeing our father and finding him in good health. Be careful not to put yourself in harm's way and take care of yourself.*

The letter was sent off on a cargo ship heading first to Naples and then to Rome, from where it would be carried north.

Even if Flavus managed to answer him, his brother's letter would have to wait for him at the headquarters of the Twelfth for a long time. Arminius was preparing to escort Quinctilius Varus to a number of cities in Syro-Palestine, where he had work to carry out on behalf of the emperor. When King Herod was still alive, he had enjoyed Augustus's favour and the emperor had educated two of his sons in Rome. But when he died, a number of years earlier, tiny Judaea had been divided among his sons, who fought over succession in both lawful and unlawful ways. Varus was thus acting incognito as the emperor's privileged informer on current happenings in Judaea.

And so Arminius had the opportunity to visit the most austere city of the East, the opposite of Antioch: Jerusalem. Here the people adored a single god, quick-tempered and invisible.

He was said to be present in the temple which was one of the largest constructions of the world. It had been built by King Herod and was frequented by millions of pilgrims who flocked in from the east and the west. In the beginning, Augustus did not pretend direct dominion over the Romans in Judaea, rebellious and uncontrollable as the region was. He preferred to let first his client-king Herod, his protégé, maintain order in those lands, and then to let the task fall to Herod's sons after his death. Their borders were protected from the Parthian Empire by the Roman legions stationed in Syria. Including the Twelfth.

Arminius visited the Antonia Fortress and from the top of its towers he beheld, amazed, the immense temple enclosure, the porticoes, the staircases and the Holy of Holies, the place where their invisible god dwelt. No one was allowed to go in there except for their high priest, who entered once a year and pronounced the name of their god.

Arminius had never seen another place like this one. So small and yet so crucial. The Parthian Empire was just one hundred and fifty miles from the coast and they must be prevented from reaching it, at any cost; if they did, that would split the Roman Empire in two. Arminius had never been so keenly aware of how the government of Rome succeeded in mixing wisdom and cynicism as in Judaea, in this tangle of small territories ruled by tiny kings, complicated by delicate and difficult dealings with the clergy of that temple and the high priest himself, who was not only the direct intermediary with god but also with the Roman emperor. Arminius realized that wielding power well was an extremely complex operation, which required intelligence and a great deal of experience. It occurred to him that in his ancestral land, this art was wholly absent. The only way that power was exercised was through force.

One night, when he got back to the fortress where Varus was being lodged, Arminius noticed that he was scowling.

'Is there a problem, Proconsul?' he asked.

Varus nodded. 'I've just received word that the grandson and adopted son of Augustus, Lucius Caesar, son of his daughter Julia and Marcus Vipsanius Agrippa, has died.'

Arminius was shocked. Had Julia heard as well, on her desert island?

'Augustus is heartbroken,' continued Varus. 'He adored that child and had certainly hoped he would be his successor. The letter recounts that the emperor immediately donned mourning robes; it says that his face seemed all the paler in contrast with his black tunic. And he escorted the body to Rome in tears, burying the boy's ashes in the family mausoleum.'

So the master of the world could cry. He had punished his daughter by ruthlessly banishing her but he bitterly wept over her son's body. The harshest reason of state could thus co-exist with human emotion.

'I've had my secretary write a letter of condolence for the emperor,' continued Varus, 'and I've ordered a statue portraying Lucius Caesar to be sculpted and installed in the Campus Martius.'

'If I may ask, Proconsul,' said Arminius, 'does this mean we'll be returning home?'

'No,' replied Varus resolutely. 'We'll stay here until the end of next spring, and then we'll set sail to Rhodos.'

'To visit Prince Tiberius?'

'Not only,' replied Varus. He dropped his forehead onto his left hand and Arminius took his leave. He still had to review his auxiliaries as well as the legionaries guarding the towers. Below them, the lit torches and still-burning braziers raised their smoke to the sky and their flames to the mute, invisible god of the Judaeans.

He went to bed after the first guard shift and thought of Flavus, who at that same hour was also lying down after a hard day of battle. Each of them at opposite sides of the world. With, perhaps, their father Sigmer in the middle.

He could hear the psalmodizing of the priests in the night, mixed with the guards' calls coming from the towers, and he thought of his father's message and of how he'd interpreted it, hurling his spear at the would-be murderer. Is that what Sigmer had wanted him to do? Or something else? Perhaps one day he would know.

THAT AUTUMN AND winter they visited Galilee, then crossed the Jordan River and the regions of Gaulanitis and Iturea, travelling alongside Lake Tiberias, and reached Damascus in Syria, a splendid city fragrant with roses and jasmine, harbouring blood-red pomegranates in its secret gardens. A gigantic temple to Jupiter Dolichenus stood in the great square, built on the foundations of a previous Canaanite temple to Baal. Those sublime sights taught Arminius how civilizations were born and grew and then decayed and perished, and he understood how the great empire of Alexander first and Rome later had gathered them into a single immense system, drawing on their power and strength to create new marvels. Small systems like a little village on its own could produce only modest structures: huts made of wood and animal dung or humble dwellings built of dried mud mixed with straw.

What Rome had achieved cost blood. But not even the smallest communities were immune from civil wars, killing, poisoning, massacres, without ever achieving anything great and admirable.

The place that he dreamed of seeing was Egypt. He had heard it spoken about as the most extraordinary land on earth: wealthy, astonishing, magical. Pyramids built as high as the sky, the purest of geometrical shapes. They were covered with white stone and tipped in gold, and like diamonds they mirrored the sun. The temples of Thebes, rich with forests of hundreds of stone pillars so thick and so tall that they seemed millenary oak trees, decorated with thousands of mysterious symbols that would take a man's entire lifetime to understand. Colossal statues standing on pedestals or sculpted into the walls of mountains. The Nile, the greatest of all the earth's rivers, which nourished dragons whose jaws were bristling with sharp teeth and whose bodies were covered by impenetrable shields, as well as other huge snorting monsters that blew water and steam out of their noses; 'river horses', they were called. A kingdom that for thirty centuries had never been subjugated in the end had to submit to Rome.

One thing was true: a Roman army could be defeated, but not Rome. Arminius was absolutely sure of this. In comparison his ancestral land seemed very distant, dark and cold, full of bogs.

He asked Quinctilius Varus if they would be going to Egypt and he answered, 'No, that's not possible. Egypt is the private property of the emperor. No one of senatorial rank can enter without his explicit permission and I have not been tasked with entering Egypt. One day, however, that might happen and when it does you will be at my side. You are a young man of great sagacity and good sense. You are brave and, when necessary, you can be hard, aggressive and implacable.'

'When necessary, Proconsul,' replied Arminius, and his eyes shone with a cold light, like frozen lakes in winter.

*

WHEN HE RETURNED to Antioch, Arminius found Flavus's reply. His brother had written from Germania:

Flavus to Armin, dearest brother, hail!

I received your letter with delight. I've calculated that it took only two and a half months to reach me at our winter headquarters where we have settled to allow the winter to pass. I don't know when you'll receive this or if the winds will be favourable, but I am nearly certain that we will see each other again in Rome, with the help of the gods.

The Cherusci have rebelled and Consul Vinicius has had to intervene. He did not ask me to follow him at the head of my unit. I wasn't told why but I can imagine. But he's wrong. Wulf no longer exists.

I am Flavus.

I'm sending you this letter from Magontiacum and I've been ordered not to leave the fort. You'll understand why I have not been able to see our father, nor will I be able to do so.

Stay in good health.

The *Chimaera* weighed anchor one morning in March and sailed along the southern coast of Anatolia, heading west, until she reached a vast bay where they stopped to wait for the northern wind to abate. The captain decided that they would stay three days at anchor before continuing their voyage to Rhodos and leaving the coast of Lycia behind them. The crossing took place without too much difficulty, although the crew often had to man the oars and helm to counter the sea currents and stay on route. During the voyage, Arminius read and reread his brother's letter and tried to understand how he was feeling. Had he cut every tie with their people, and even with their father? He thought back once again to the significance of the message that the Hermunduri warrior had given them on the Aventine. Sigmer had left them the choice of whether to act or not, once they worked out the puzzle that it was Julia at the centre of everything and that the life being threatened was that of her father, Emperor Augustus.

Arminius had made his choice. But evidently, for his father it was the wrong one, if he had decided to sever his alliance with Rome and lead the Cherusci in rebellion against the Romans.

When the outline of the island of Rhodos appeared, everyone on board breathed a sigh of relief. Arminius thought of what a ship's view of the island must have been like when the bronze giant made by the Rhodians to celebrate the sun god's help in resisting a siege was still standing. The colossus had remained on its feet for only seventy years, and yet the entire world would remember that superb, daring work for centuries.

Quinctilius Varus found hospitality on the island in a beautiful house overlooking the port, while Arminius, Sergius Vetilius and Rufius Corvus, along with the men of the escort, were quartered in a house used by the port workers.

The next day, Varus decided to venture out with only Arminius and the other two officers, leaving the men in their quarters. They accompanied him to Tiberius's villa but remained outside in the garden talking with the servants. Hours passed, and it was time for lunch. Varus was nowhere to be seen; most probably the prince had invited him to join him in a meal.

Servants brought some food for the three of them, and it wasn't until afternoon, close to the tenth hour, when Quinctilius Varus exited the villa accompanied by a freedman.

Rufius Corvus, after having accompanied the proconsul and his comrades the entire way back to the port, went off on his own.

'Where is he going?' Arminius asked Sergius Vetilius.

'Why are you asking such questions?' replied Vetilius. 'You're used to commanding men, aren't you?'

'Of course. But I have the impression it's not a woman he's after.'

'No, I don't think so either. Even though it was a long voyage and Rufius is a vigorous man.'

Rufius got back late that night. Arminius recognized the gait of his horse and walked outside to meet him, as if he'd been awakened by pure chance.

'Can't sleep?' asked Rufius.

'No, I heard a noise. You know I'm a light sleeper. News?'

'Yes, actually. Young Gaius Caesar, the brother of poor Lucius, will be coming this way. The boy is the only one remaining of Augustus's direct successors, and he's being sent to the Eastern army to cut his teeth. He'll be passing through Samos in a few days' time, heading to Armenia. Tiberius will have to lower himself in front of this spoiled, presumptuous youngster, to ask permission to return to Rome. Can you believe that? Tiberius is the Empire's greatest soldier, and I know what I'm talking about. I fought for him. He conquered the Alpine border with Drusus, creating an impenetrable belt for Italy, and he subjugated the Illyrian regions all the way to the Danube. And now he has to prostrate himself in front of an inexperienced child who's spent more time playing dice with his grandfather than learning how to use a weapon. It's hard to explain why he has to be humiliated this way. It feels like a punishment.'

Arminius didn't say anything else, apart from asking about a practical matter: 'Will there be anyone with him? Are we needed in some way?'

'I don't think so,' replied Rufius. 'I think that Varus is here to observe him and report back to Rome. Tiberius's position is very difficult. Right now the only person he can count on is his mother, Livia. Well, good night, then.'

Arminius wished him a good night as well and turned to go back to his room.

'Can I ask you a question?' said Rufius.

'Of course.'

'What's in that letter that you're always carrying around with you? Why has it put you in such a bad mood?'

'It's a letter from my brother, Flavus. It's just the answer to a letter I wrote him. Nothing important. We'll see each other in Rome, it seems, and he's really eager. I'm not in a bad mood at all, I don't know why you got that impression.'

'Maybe,' replied Rufius, and walked up the stairs towards his own bedroom.

NEITHER QUINCTILIUS VARUS nor any of the three officers of his guard were asked to accompany Tiberius to Samos where Gaius Caesar had put ashore in the meantime with his escort. But Rufius Corvus and certainly Quinctilius Varus himself had eyes and ears on the island. Tiberius did not even remain overnight – a sign that he had not been invited. It was learned later that Gaius Caesar had behaved horribly with him, as did his comrades from the ship, who turned out to be his companions at home as well. Varus later heard that during a banquet one of the young men, already half drunk, announced loudly that he was ready to set sail on the first ship for Rhodos so he could kill Tiberius.

When Varus told the story, Arminius imagined the scene in his head: that little braggart would show up with an intent to kill Tiberius, take one look at the man and then run away, terrified at the mere sight of the greatest soldier of the Empire.

Being young, he thought, *is neither a merit nor a virtue. It's simply a time of life.*

He could not put the thought of Tiberius out of his head. That man, one of the most important and, in theory, most powerful people in the world, lived in a state of constant humiliation, was forced to put up with non-stop criticism and had to calculate every step he took. Who he should receive and who he should ignore or refuse. What he wore. What he did and what he avoided doing. Every single step he took, every act, was spied upon, interpreted, judged. And yet he was on the list of the possible successors to Augustus.

'It's not an easy thing,' said Sergius Vetilius. 'The first designated heir, Claudius Marcellus, died very young and the second in line, Lucius Caesar, died under suspicious circumstances in Massilia, Gaul. Another son of Julia and Marcus Vipsanius Agrippa, Agrippa Postumus, has been confined to an inhospitable island, without having been charged of any crime. The official reason is that it is said that he is mentally disturbed, violent and aggressive, but that's never been demonstrated, nor has he ever attacked or wounded anyone.'

'So, the only possible successor,' concluded Arminius, 'is Gaius Caesar.'

'That's not said. Gaius Caesar is still very young and he's being sent off to war in Armenia. Tiberius remains in the line of succession. And there's another player in this very complex game: Livia, wife of Augustus and mother of Tiberius. Have you ever wondered why Livia has never given Augustus a child in so many years? He fathered a daughter, Julia, with his first wife, and Livia had two sons, Drusus and Tiberius, by her first husband. How is it that since they've been together, Livia has never borne a child, neither male nor female, to Augustus?'

Arminius didn't know what to answer.

'Because she takes drugs that prevent her from getting pregnant. She wanted the Empire to go to the sons of her first marriage. Drusus is dead. Tiberius is safe in Rhodos. Gaius Caesar is at the Armenian front. So many things can happen at war . . .'

'So they are the only two contending succession?' asked Arminius. 'There's no one else?'

'There is, but it would mean jumping a generation.'

'And who would that be?'

'Germanicus,' he answered.

17

They stayed in Rhodos for quite a long time, and Arminius even had the opportunity to sail to other nearby islands. Those little territories surrounded by the sea fascinated him and he also began to take great pleasure in swimming, especially underwater. Not only did it develop his muscles, but it allowed him to explore a dreamlike expanse of various colours and shapes, although some of the creatures were nearly invisible because they took on the colour of the rocks or sea bottom. He started to eat seafood as well, roasting fish with his friends on the shore over a little campfire, sprinkling olive oil over molluscs and enjoying shellfish, whose delicious white flesh he had never tasted before. And he had discovered the celebrated Rhodian wine which was exported in entire shiploads from the port for sale in all the cities around the inland sea.

The evening breeze, the flaming colours of sunset, the singing of the fishermen and the women who waited for them with children clinging to their necks, the fish spilling out of the nets on shore: all this was new and magical for him; he had only ever seen the Adriatic coast and the banks of the dark Rhine in which forests of black fir trees were mirrored.

Arminius had little official business to take care of because Varus already had informers on the island. Direct contact wasn't lacking either, since Tiberius, who was aware of Varus's presence in Rhodos, could not avoid inviting him with a certain frequency. After all, they had been colleagues in the consulate only a few years earlier. This left Arminius mostly free to enjoy the company of a pretty Greek freedwoman whom he'd met at a reception to which he had accompanied Varus.

Nearly two years had passed since they had left Syria and the pleasures of Antioch, when a fast ship arrived at full sail, flying a black drape at the stern and from the top of the mast. Something very serious must have happened. Arminius, accompanied by Rufius Corvus, Sergius Vetilius and his men, rushed to the harbour. Varus arrived shortly thereafter, followed after a brief time by Tiberius himself, escorted by twenty legionaries and two lictors. He wore his laticlave toga instead of his usual Greek pallium, and his military boots instead of his soft leather Rhodian slippers.

A gangway was lowered from the ship to allow the captain to come ashore with a military tribune and a naval infantry squad who rendered honours to Augustus's stepson.

Tiberius stepped forward and the tribune spoke to him directly: 'Hail, Tiberius Claudius, I bring you lamentable news. Proconsul Gaius Caesar fell victim to an ambush in Armenia, in which he was gravely wounded. It was a miracle that his men managed to save him from the jaws of death and get him to a doctor who attempted to treat his wounds. Heedless of the pain and the fever that was devouring him, he continued to carry out the tasks he'd been entrusted with, but in the end death came to him at Limyra, in Lycia, not far from here. His ashes were taken to Rome where they will be buried alongside those of his brother in the emperor's family mausoleum.'

Tiberius showed no emotion at those words. He remained impassive; not a muscle in his face twitched. Two young men in the prime of their lives, Augustus's favourites and idolized by the youth of the capital, were gone. In truth, they had always detested Tiberius for his silence, his discretion, his reserved ways, but mainly for achieving military glory that no one else could possibly hope to match.

Arminius thought of beautiful Julia, prisoner on that barren island, and of when she would hear of the death of her second son, torn from her by a ruthless fate. He may have been her last hope of liberation from exile.

Tiberius thanked the ship's captain and the military tribune in a few dry words. Not a single detail of that scene escaped Varus, not a gesture or a breath, and many thoughts flooded through his mind. In two years' time, Augustus had been divested of the two grandsons that he adored and had adopted, in the hope of a direct succession of his own bloodline. What would he do now? What would be the next move from the most expert of players?

When Tiberius and his retinue had left, Varus turned to his officers: 'Be ready to set sail tomorrow. We are returning to Rome.'

THE VOYAGE LASTED eight days, with a crosswind at first. After their passage through the Strait of Messina, the south-west wind was more favourable but also difficult to harness. They set ashore without incident at Ostia and then travelled up the Tiber until they reached their landing dock in the City. Arminius took his leave from Sergius Vetilius and Rufius Corvus. 'I hope to see you again soon. I've enjoyed your company these past years.'

'See you soon then, friend.'

'Yes, soon,' replied Arminius and he headed off towards the house he had lived in on the Aventine. The dogs seemed not to recognize him at first and started to growl, but as soon as they heard his voice they calmed down, wagging their tails and coming close to be petted by him.

'Well, look who's here!' echoed a voice behind him.

Arminius turned and found himself face to face with his brother. They hugged each other hard and long then just stood looking at each other, both hands on the other's shoulders. In their eyes danced images of their childhood and youth.

'It feels like a century since we've seen each other,' exclaimed Arminius. His brother looked worn and quite thin, but his arms were as strong as ever.

'You look good!' said Flavus. 'You've been living the good life in the East, haven't you?'

'You're right, I've had my fun. The women are magical, divine; they're enchantresses, like nothing you've ever had or could even imagine. I saw incredible places, extraordinary things. It's a pity we didn't make it to Egypt. Varus tells me it's an unforgettable place.'

'Maybe we'll go together one day,' said Flavus.

'I'd like that!' replied Arminius. 'Shall we have dinner together?'

'It will be a joy after all this time. I think it's just about ready.'

'Do you know how many times in Syria I found myself thinking, *If only my brother were here* . . ., especially when there was a decision to be made. And what of Taurus?'

'I've lost track of him. My commander, Vinicius, kept me busy. The missions have always been demanding. But I'm certain we'll meet him again, sooner or later.'

They dined in the garden near the small lily pond; their voices were accompanied by the gurgling of the fountain. Arminius talked about Antioch, Laodicea, Jerusalem and Damascus and Flavus listened to him spellbound.

In the end it was Arminius who raised what had been on their minds from the start: 'I'm sorry you never saw Father. You weren't so far from him.'

'Discipline is the heart of the Roman army,' said Flavus. 'Everything else comes later, even family. Disobeying an order is not conceivable. I myself, as the commander of an *Ala* of the auxiliary cavalry, often had to punish my men if they took liberties outside the regulations. Discipline is what has made Rome great. Remember Taurus?'

Arminius nodded. He certainly remembered his lashings. Neither one of them went on to talk about the past, or the future. They'd forgotten the first, or so they thought. The second was unfathomable. The only thing that was untouchable was their relationship.

When they finished eating, Flavus said, 'I have a girlfriend.'

'The slave?'

'No, she was just for camp. The girl I'm engaged to is the daughter of the Magistrate of Roads in Magontiacum.'

Arminius wanted to protest, 'You are a prince of noble lineage . . .' but he chose not to risk a nasty retort. He said instead, 'What's she like? It would be nice to meet her.'

'She's pretty. She has beautiful eyes, a nice body and she's really sweet-natured. I'll soon be assigned a more prestigious house and we'll begin our life together.'

'Iole? Do you ever think of her?'

'I knew her for such a short time . . . I do think of her, though. She's surely dead by now. So young, in that place . . . she can't have lasted long.'

They spoke for hours like they used to do as boys, lying in their old beds, which had been prepared for them. 'Thiaminus, maybe, or Privatus? Are they still around?' asked Arminius.

'Yes, they're still here,' said Flavus, 'and that means that Taurus will be back too, sooner or later.'

THE CITY WAS still draped with all the recent signs of mourning for the death of Gaius Caesar. The altars were adorned with cypress fronds and black curtains hung on the temple facades. The altar of the family mausoleum offered up smoke.

Taurus returned twenty days after Arminius's arrival. Tiberius returned from Rhodos at almost the same time.

The centurion settled into his house on the Aventine and invited Flavus and Arminius to dinner, to inform them about the situation. 'The emperor was devastated by the deaths of Lucius and Gaius Caesar, his grandchildren and adopted sons, but he has to guarantee succession nonetheless. Tiberius's recall from his long exile can mean only one thing. What's more, operations in Germania are stagnant; there's been no progress on that front. It's probable that the emperor wants to turn around this Germanic campaign, which has lasted too long without giving definitive results. To do that he'll need the greatest soldier of the Empire, the idol of all the armies of the Rhine to the Danube: Tiberius Claudius Nero.'

'A soldier who has not taken up his sword for many years . . .' observed Flavus.

'A soldier is always a soldier,' replied Taurus. 'But there's more . . .'

Neither Flavus nor Arminius had imagined that there wouldn't be.

'A single heir remains of his bloodline, the youngest son of Julia and Marcus Vipsanius Agrippa. Agrippa Postumus is supposedly a violent, menacing lad; at least that is how he is described in the rumours artfully spread by people I know well. He lives like Philoctetes on an island full of snakes.

'But then there is another young man whom the emperor is very fond of. A splendid lad who you met once; you even fought against him in my training ring. The build of a statue with two formidable arms.'

Germanicus! thought Arminius. *The son of General Drusus.* Many memories came unprompted to the minds of both Flavus and Arminius, memories their father had planted.

Rarely was Marcus Caelius Taurus wrong. No more than three months went by before the supreme ruler of the State adopted Agrippa Postumus and Tiberius Claudius, who in turn was ordered to adopt his nephew, Drusus Claudius Nero Julius Caesar Germanicus, as his son.

Arminius thought of the day in which that 'splendid lad' had appeared in the ring, when Taurus had ordered the boys to face off against him. They were brow to brow, they had breathed in each other's breath, and yet there was a chasm between them. So many of the heirs to the Empire had been dying lately. Would Germanicus survive long enough to become the next emperor of the Romans? He thought of the little boy wearing a toga and a pendant at his neck, portrayed on the marble frieze of the Altar of Peace – how much he had grown, in every way.

Arminius was soon summoned to resume his military duties as commander and instructor of the army's Germanic Auxilia. His days became increasingly full with appointments and training activities. He never made it back to the house on the Aventine before evening, but he and Flavus were often invited to dinner by Taurus. That gave Arminius the opportunity to ask for advice on how to lead and instruct his men. With them he used his ancestral language, because he wanted his commands to be instantly understood and executed. Using their language meant that the men often confided in him. He was curious to learn about their thoughts, their aspirations and hopes. One evening when he had gone to Taurus's on his own because his brother was occupied elsewhere, he asked Taurus about something that had been on his mind for some time. 'My father's people have fought and are still fighting against the Roman armies of Ahenobarbus and Vinicius. You're aware of that, of course?'

'Yes,' confirmed Taurus. 'That is so.'

'And why have no retaliatory measures been taken against us? Flavus and me?'

'Because you are no longer young hostages; you are fully qualified officers of the Roman army.'

'Is there news of my father?'

Taurus fell silent for a few moments, then replied with another question: 'Is it important to you?'

'He is my father,' said Arminius.

'I know nothing. Honestly. He may have fallen in battle. I knew him; he was a brave combatant. I can say that if he had been forced to choose between saving his sons and achieving independence for his people, he would have chosen the latter.'

'That's true,' replied Arminius.

'If I manage to find out something about him, I'll tell you. But don't count on it. I haven't heard anything for a long time.'

Arminius dropped the subject of his father. He asked Taurus only about what he and his brother could expect.

'Well,' Taurus began, 'Augustus has never given up on the idea of extending the northern border of the Empire from the Rhine to the Elbe. This would mean annexing, educating and assimilating the Germanic peoples. It's a big dream that all started with General Drusus . . .'

'Yes, I've heard about it,' said Arminius.

'That the Empire should include Germania, with all her strengths and her indomitable attachment to independence and freedom. One day there will be emperors who are Illyrian and Celtic, Iberian and Dalmatian and . . . Germanic.'

'Do you think that's truly possible, Centurion?'

'Certainly. There are already Gallic senators in our curia. General Drusus wanted the Germanics inside the Empire because he had faced them in many battles and he knew their merits well. This is what makes Rome great: a single home-land for a number of different nations. My own mother was Germanic.'

'With your blue eyes, Centurion . . . I'd always thought so.'

Arminius turned his gaze to Taurus's armour displayed on a hanger like a trophy, topped with his cross-crested helmet, covered with decorations. 'It must be something that you believe in deeply.'

'Certainly,' Taurus replied. 'With all my heart. The Empire of Rome is the only place in the world worth living in.'

'I've heard myself that a big offensive is being prepared in Germania. I'm expecting to get a call at any moment. May I ask if my brother will be coming with me?'

Taurus seemed to reflect for a few moments. 'As far as I know, Flavus will be the first to leave for Germania, to the area bordering Batavian territory, in preparation for Tiberius's arrival. The commander will be leaving shortly.'

'What about me?' asked Arminius.

'You'll be leaving as well.'

'For where?'

'You'll know when it's time. Rest now.'

'Should we be saying goodbye?'

'I don't think that's necessary. Two Roman soldiers always end up meeting again. Farewell for now.'

'Farewell, Centurion.'

Arminius went back to his room. When he awoke the next morning he walked out onto the terrace that overlooked the City and noticed a little convoy coming down the hill in the direction of the Tiber, perhaps going to board a ship. He recognized Taurus on his horse, followed by his freedmen on a cart which held the centurion's armour and his personal belongings. He asked himself, in the silence of the early morning, whether he would ever see him again.

Barefoot and unheard, Flavus walked out behind him and touched his shoulder. 'Did you say goodbye for me?'

'You know what he's like. He doesn't like goodbyes. He said he'd see us again, before long.'

'You and I can say goodbye, though. No tears, promise.'

'Of course not. When are you leaving?'

'It's a question of days. I've received notice.'

Five days later, Flavus got his orders to go to the Campus Martius where he would assume command of his Germanic cavalry unit and move north with the legion.

He began to gather his things and put them into his saddlebags and Arminius watched.

'I'm leaving,' said Flavus.

'I can see that,' replied his brother.

'No tears?'

'No tears.'

They clasped each other tight. Arminius watched as Flavus left the room. Ten days later it was his turn. When he had collected everything he was going to take with him and turned to close the door behind him, he had the clear sensation that he was also ending the most important time of his life, and that he would never return to it.

★

DURING THE VARIOUS stages of his journey, Arminius had more opportunity than ever before to witness the Empire's power first-hand: armies coming from every direction to converge on the Alpine passes, endless columns of soldiers, slingers, archers, cavalry, the heavy infantry of the legionaries; hundreds of carts carrying food, supplies, spare parts for the weapons, camp equipment, tents; triple-spiked implements of defence which could be hidden in the soil to cripple horses and enemy foot soldiers, artillery pieces such as ballistae, catapults, scorpions and onagers, all of which were transported disassembled for mounting at the moment of use. For each combatant there were at least two men in logistics, in the rear lines and in the workshops. What's more, the camp hospital counted hundreds of surgeons and nurses.

And when they arrived, after marching for two months, at the ports of northern Gaul, they saw the fleets: hundreds of cargo ships armed for amphibious operations. Thousands of shipwrights and blacksmiths were at work day and night, with the shipyards constantly receiving new stocks of planks, beams for building the hull frames, piles of oars, winches, anchors, coils of rope, stacks of hemp cloth to be used for the sails and the masts to which to mount them. He could only imagine how many people were still at work behind the lines in order to supply the building yards with fir and ash wood, oak and beech, planing and shaping the beams, constructing the cranes to lift them and the carts for transporting them.

At the peak of that vast pyramid was one man: General Tiberius Caesar Claudius Nero, never defeated in his whole life. A nod from him sufficed to move hundreds of thousands of men, horses and pack animals, ships, crews, oarsmen, naval infantrymen, legionaries, artillerymen . . .

Arminius understood as he never had before what the power of command really entailed.

One day, as he observed a column travelling down the road that never ends, he thought he recognized his brother Flavus at the head of a cavalry squad. He called out, but his voice was drowned out by the noise of crashing and clanking, of shouts and whinnies, of trumpet blasts – the voice of the greatest army the world had ever known.

Arminius also had the fortune of witnessing the arrival of the supreme commander. Tiberius passed on horseback between the legions drawn up three deep so that everyone could catch a glimpse. He wore the scarlet *paludamentum* which was the symbol of his rank, and his muscle cuirass but not his helmet, which he held under his left arm so the men could see his face.

The centurions shouted out the order to present arms and the legions thrust forth their *pila* in perfect alignment, as the standards, *labara* and eagles were dipped at his passage.

But this iron discipline soon gave way to wild enthusiasm. The legionaries were almost all veterans of Tiberius's campaigns on the Alps and on the Danubian front. One voice echoed powerfully, 'Commander, we meet again!'

Tiberius turned towards the legionary who had shouted out and pointed his finger at him as if to say, 'I see you and hear you!' At that point, many others joined in.

'Commander, how are you? In top form?' And Tiberius flexed his muscles for them.

'Commander, I was with you in Armenia!' Tiberius nodded and smiled.

'I was in Rhaetia, Commander!'

'You decorated me in Vindelicia!'

'Me too, in Pannonia!'

'I in Germania!'

The drawn-up legions were delirious. A roar broke out, and then the clanging of their *pila* against their shields, a rhythmic pounding that went on and on. The commander who had always led them to victory was passing between their ranks without an escort because the whole Army of the North was his escort! Arminius, in formation with his auxiliary cavalry, felt a chill run down his spine. After Tiberius paraded a young man wearing the insignia of legion commander, surrounded by at least fifty praetorians in full dress uniform. He was quite close, and Arminius could see him clearly. Germanicus.

For a moment their glances met.

Germanicus blinked. Had he recognized him?

Towards evening the legions withdrew to their camps and their tents. Shouting and carousing were echoing everywhere. The campfires blazed until very late. The centurions and tribunes closed an eye, or both of them, to the prolonged revelry.

The next day the war started.

18

THE SIGHT OF THE boundless power of the Roman Empire, of the glory of its supreme commander and the astonishing organization of its structures, had completely dazzled Arminius, who came to understand why Flavus no longer had any doubts about where he belonged. Living among the units of the Army of the North, he realized that the legionaries and cavalrymen, the archers and slingers, belonged to every ethnicity – Hispanics, Italians, Gauls, Germanics, Rhaetians, Dalmatians, Greeks, Numidians, Syrians . . . – and they all saluted their commander with the same enthusiasm. Each and every one of them identified with the ensign of their cohort and legion and with the eagle of gold that represented the force of the legion and the honour of its soldiers.

He fell in with his combat unit and embraced its rigorous discipline with great earnestness and dedication.

Tiberius initiated operations with the determination and strategic intelligence that had always distinguished all of his military actions. It seemed as though he had spent the last ten years leading great expeditions and battles on the field, instead of studying and attending rhetoric lessons on the distant isle of Rhodos. He moved his troops with the swiftness of lightning. He was shrewd in using his reserves, in sending light units forward for reconnaissance, in gathering information about the conditions on the ground and about the populations they would meet with.

It quickly became clear to Arminius why so many ships were being readied on the northern coasts of Gaul and Germania. Tiberius was subjugating all the peoples who had settled along the main rivers: the Rhine, the Ems, the Weser and the Elbe. It was evident that those rivers would subsequently be used as waterways for the navigation of the fleet, both for getting supplies to the army rapidly as well as for providing reinforcements.

The first to be attacked were the Cananefates, a strange name for a nation because it meant 'leek masters', although there were, in fact, a great number of those vegetables growing on their territory. In this first campaign, Arminius found himself commanding the auxiliaries of a highly ranked officer, Velleius Paterculus. Velleius was a very well-educated man who kept a diary of everything that was happening. He told Arminius that his initial intention had been to write a very detailed account but that he had resigned himself to keeping much more succinct notes, perhaps because he was finding it difficult to keep up with Commander Tiberius Caesar's rapid advance.

Next it was the turn of the Chattuarii, a tribe settled between the Rhine and the Ems, and then the Bructeri.

At first, Arminius stayed behind with an army unit that was left as a garrison in Chattuarii territory, but he was soon recalled by Velleius in light of the manoeuvres that were to come. Arminius arrived at dusk with his unit and an orderly of the camp prefect showed them where they could pitch their tents. He also informed Arminius that Legate Velleius was expecting him in the praetorian tent at the centre of the castrum.

As soon as his tent was ready he put his baggage inside, but did not take off his armour, as he would be reporting to the legion commander shortly. He made his way on foot between the lit torches that illuminated the two main axes of the camp, at the intersection of which the commander's own quarters were located. He suddenly saw the Hermundur looming in front of him on his brown horse. He did not speak, but motioned for Arminius to follow.

In a darker area of the camp, he leapt off his horse and approached Arminius. Even on foot, he was a good head taller.

'Hail, warrior,' said Arminius.

'Hail to you, Armin,' replied the Hermundur.

'Whenever you suddenly appear there's a baffling message to be had. Baffling, but crucial. This time?'

'Noble Sigmer, your father, remained faithful to a pact for many years knowing you were in Rome and how you got there.'

'It's all ended well.'

'But the situation has changed recently. The chieftains of the lands between the Rhine and the Weser have decided to fight back, and he cannot refuse to join them. The Cherusci are at war. There has been no confrontation yet, but there's no time to lose. Speak with Legate Velleius and then return here. I'll take you to your father, tonight.'

The words he was hearing made him tremble.

He would see his father.

'Wait here,' said Arminius. 'I'll be back as soon as possible.' He strode off towards the praetorian tent.

Velleius greeted him with a cordial expression and had him sit on a folding chair next to his own. He had a map in front of him, drawn on oxhide.

'This shows our operations over the coming days. The Cherusci have abandoned their alliance with the Roman people and have united with other Germanic tribes between the Rhine and the Weser, but as you can see, we'll have them trapped. Our legions and our cavalry units will be advancing from three directions, leaving them no way out. Your unit will move along this red line,' he concluded, pointing his finger at the route already drawn on the map.

Arminius remained silent for a few moments.

'I know what you're thinking,' said Velleius. 'But this is the highest proof of your loyalty that you can give to your commander, Tiberius Caesar, who already knows what you've done for the emperor.'

'Legate, I'm here to propose a different solution that could resolve the problem without spilling blood. Commander Tiberius Caesar is the brother of General Drusus, who fell thirteen years ago during a campaign in Germania. You may not have been aware, Legate, that my father, noble Sigmer, had a privileged personal relationship with Drusus . . .'

'I thought that was just hearsay.'

'It's the truth. My father himself told me about it.'

'And what might your solution be?'

'I know that my father was forced to abandon his alliance with the people of Rome and I know that he is against war. Perhaps I could convince him to accept a new treaty of alliance that would also be acceptable to Commander Tiberius Caesar.'

'There's no time. We'll be attacking very soon.'

'I'm ready to leave now.'

Velleius sighed and put a hand in front of his weary eyes. 'Now? You mean tonight?'

'Yes. I'll be back before dawn.'

'Do I have your word?'

'You have my word.'

Velleius nodded. Arminius left the tent and walked south

down the *cardo*. He met a picket of legionaries on patrol who recognized him and saluted him. When he reached the point where he had met the Hermundur, he left the torch-lit road and walked into the dark.

The warrior emerged from the shadows, holding two horses by the reins. They mounted them at once and rode at a walk to the nearest gate. The Hermundur showed a pass to the guard on duty and then immediately spurred on his horse, followed by Arminius. They galloped down dark, hidden paths, crossed fords, splashing up clouds of water, thundered over a part of the *pontes longi* and pulled to a halt at the edge of a clearing. The moon was peering over the treetops.

'He's here,' said the Hermundur. Arminius sprang to the ground. He still wore the armour of the Germanic Auxilia of the Roman army and it made him uncomfortable, but he did not take it off. Just a short time later, a pounding of hooves could be heard and a snorting of horses. Powerful Sigmer, Lord of the Cherusci, appeared. Escorted by fifty warriors in full battle order. Sigmer advanced slowly on his mount, as if on parade. As night had fallen the temperature had dropped and the animal blew little clouds of steam from his nostrils.

Arminius went towards him on foot. 'Father.'

Sigmer dismounted and walked towards his son until they were facing each other. His grey hair was gathered at the nape of his neck. He wore rough wool trousers and an oxhide cuirass. A long sword hung at his side from a silver-studded baldric.

Arminius felt his heart pounding, as if he were still a child, standing before his father.

'Father,' he said again.

'You've grown,' said Sigmer, with a grimace.

'You look well.'

'You were seen fighting with great energy against our allies of the north.'

'The same allies of the north who fought against you many times. The Romans always stick to their pacts.'

'What should I do, then?' asked Sigmer.

'I want to show you the way out of a very dangerous situation. So dangerous that it might prove lethal for you and your people in just a matter of days.'

'Our people,' his father corrected him.

'There's no time to argue about words. Listen to me: Tiberius Caesar is the older brother of General Drusus, who you knew well. He is just as brave as his brother, and so strong that no one can stand against him, so powerful in battle that he's never lost a single one. Not one battle. If his brother brought the border to the Rhine, he brought it to the Danube. In a matter of years the two brothers established the confines of the Roman Empire.

'You have no way out, Father. I don't think you want to see your people massacred or enslaved, the women raped and sold to the highest bidder, the villages burned. I am in the position to negotiate a good treaty between the Cherusci and the Romans. Between you and Tiberius Caesar. You will keep your kingdom and continue to govern your people, and you will renew the pact of alliance with Rome at more or less the same conditions as before.'

'The same conditions? But that is impossible.'

'It is possible. It's already happened. Listen to me. Please. Think about it: it's because Tiberius knows war so well that he prefers peace, where possible.' Big clouds had begun gathering in the middle of the sky and were hiding the moon. Lightning slithered at the horizon and distant rumbling could be heard. 'Permit me to negotiate for you, Father, before the storm hits!'

Sigmer lowered his head. A flash of lightning carved deep furrows into a face hardened by many seasons and by many wars. 'You have my permission,' he said, as if throwing a boulder off his chest.

Arminius embraced him and after a moment's hesitation, Sigmer returned his embrace.

'Go,' he whispered. 'Ride as fast as you can.'

Arminius jumped onto his steed and raced off through the forest, with the Hermundur right behind him. The god of storm was riding the clouds at their back, swallowing the moon and the stars, one after another. Lightning enflamed the streams with blinding flashes and lit up the rugged landscape before them, the path twisting between colossal trees that cast their tragic shadows on the ground.

The storm exploded all at once, the rain pounding down from open gates, but Arminius knew that unless he arrived before Tiberius addressed the troops, all was lost. Nothing could hold back the eagles.

They risked their lives more than once snaking between the dripping rocks, slipping on the rain-drenched moss, but in the end the Hermundur led Arminius to the castrum, the encampment where the quarters of the high commander were watched over and defended by five hundred praetorians. They pulled on the reins and drew up to a halt at the tower which guarded the decumanus gate.

'Open up!' yelled the Hermundur.

'Who goes there?' demanded the sentry.

'Commander Tiberius Caesar will roast you over a slow fire if you don't let me in. I have a message of the utmost importance to give him. It's a question of life or death! Open!' shouted the warrior and a clap of thunder exploded above them so loudly that it seemed that the gods themselves were giving the order.

The gate opened, screeching and sighing, and the two Germanic warriors raced through the camp, not stopping until they came up short against the swords of the praetorian guard.

'Tell the commander that Sigmer sends a messenger who asks to negotiate!' exclaimed Arminius.

'Get out of here!' yelled the tribune who commanded the guard. Another burst of thunder was followed by silence, and then the voice of Commander Tiberius Caesar: 'Let him in.'

Arminius entered, soaking with rain and dripping with mud, and saluted the supreme commander.

'You've had a difficult journey,' said Tiberius, throwing him a distracted look.

'It was worth the trouble, Commander. I bear news of great importance.'

'Speak.'

'I know that you are an extraordinary soldier, and that you've never been defeated on the battlefield, but I've also heard that whenever the opportunity presents itself, you prefer negotiation to the use of force . . .'

'Go on,' said Tiberius, without committing himself.

Arminius decided to risk it nonetheless. 'I've met with my father, the lord of the Cherusci, Sigmer. It was I who asked to speak to him. I hadn't seen him since I was taken to Rome as an adolescent by Primus Pilus Centurion Marcus Caelius, known as Taurus.'

'I know him. Continue.'

'I told my father that he had no hope of saving his people and himself from your attack. I advised him to surrender . . .'
Tiberius did not say a word. Arminius had come to the most

difficult part, and couldn't back down now. 'He said he wouldn't hear of it and I, knowing that your troops will soon be crossing the border of the Cherusci territory, decided to make him a proposal that I was certain he would accept. I did that without knowing whether you would accept, Commander. I promised him that if he re-allied himself with Rome that you would accept him at the same terms as before.'

'You are mad,' replied Tiberius. 'I would never even consider it. Your father betrayed the trust of the Roman people and he will have to bear the consequences of such an act.'

'Commander,' Arminius continued, 'I beg you to accept my request. Not for me and not for my father, but for the memory of your brother, General Drusus, who died in your arms.'

'Do not name my brother!' exclaimed Tiberius.

'I am naming him,' insisted Arminius, 'in the name of the friendship that bound him to my father . . .'

'Nothing but a legend.'

'You're wrong, Commander. What they say is true. I was little more than a child when my father told me about his friendship with General Drusus. He wouldn't have lied to me. I can tell you about things that only the two of them knew. Like your brother's struggle with the Germanic oracle.'

Tiberius fell silent and lowered his head. Arminius's words had hit their mark.

'All right,' he said. 'At the same terms. I give you my word. But you make sure that I don't live to regret this. There won't be a second time.'

'That won't be necessary,' replied Arminius. 'I'll go back now to give him the news and to prevent anything unforeseen from happening.'

Tiberius did not try to stop him. The storm meanwhile had abated in intensity. Arminius reached the Hermundur.

'Well then?' the warrior asked him.

'He accepted renewal of the pact under the same conditions. It's a good solution that is advantageous for everyone. I want to go back now. I don't want anyone to convince my father to do something he'll later regret.'

The Hermundur did not utter a word. They mounted their horses and together they rode back on the path that had just brought them to Tiberius. They took the return of the moon between the wind-tattered clouds as a good sign for their journey. They were familiar by now with the obstacles and could proceed at a fast rate.

They arrived before dawn at the clearing where the meeting had taken place; several of the warriors were still there. They were the ones who led them to the place Sigmer had chosen to spend the night. Among them was Ingmar, brother of the Cherusci sovereign, who presented himself to his nephew. The two men embraced and then set off for their destination: a hunting cabin built of wooden planks, plastered over.

'I never imagined I'd see you again,' said Ingmar. 'I wouldn't even have recognized you. It makes me think of how young you and your brother Wulf were when you were taken from us. But there was a Hermundur who always kept us informed. Is it true that you fought Germanicus hand-to-hand?'

'Yes,' replied Arminius, 'but it was just training. We ended up even.'

Ingmar was greatly pleased with the news of a return to the old pact of alliance with Rome, which had ensured power and prosperity for their people. He showed no concern over the fact that they would have to fight against other Germanic peoples. That was nothing new, and it never had been.

'Once this war is over,' Ingmar said, 'no one will be able to compete with us. We will be the most powerful people on earth. Everyone will have to respect us and fear us.'

Sigmer was also greatly relieved by the news Arminius bore. The idea of leading his people in war against the Romans, who had been their allies for so long, had tormented him.

'And so, that which remains of the night,' he said to his son, 'you'll be spending in the house of your father. This is a great joy for me.'

'For me as well,' replied Arminius, embracing him once again.

The next morning, Velleius, back at camp, waited in vain for Arminius's return. He complained again and again with his officers about the duplicity of the Germanics, people you could never trust.

Arminius returned at the sixth hour and reported to Velleius as he had reported earlier to Tiberius Caesar. Velleius wrote it all down in his diary.

The campaign went on through that whole year, and only in December did the high commander allow his men to retreat to their winter quarters. Then Tiberius Caesar left with a reduced escort for Italy. He crossed the snow-covered Alps to reach his adoptive father and recount to him how the Germanic campaign was proceeding. But certain disparagers suggested that there was another reason for that journey: to meet with his mother and to make certain that no one, in his absence, had succeeded in undermining his political position and the line of succession.

Come spring, Tiberius hoped to achieve something that had never been attained by anyone.

The subjugation of Germania.

19

ARMINIUS REMAINED IN GERMANIA all winter. Under the orders of Legate Velleius at first, in the winter quarters of a legionary fort west of the Rhine. Later in the winter he requested permission to join his father at his home, and Velleius did not object, well aware that it was Arminius who had urged Sigmer to re-ally with Rome after breaking away and had then convinced Commander Tiberius Caesar himself to ratify the agreement. His precious mediation had avoided a long and bloody campaign against one of the most powerful Germanic nations beyond the Rhine.

Sigmer's home was the same one Arminius had lived in as a boy and adolescent. It was built of debarked tree trunks and had a roof with two slopes. Its long side faced south and it was big enough to house at least thirty people. In front of the entry door there was a canopy supported by two poles on which a capital and base were roughly carved. Inside there were several rooms separated by partitions made of reeds which had been plastered over; there was one large central room where visitors were received. Its walls were decorated with weapons and armour, shields with crossed spears, trophies from defeated enemies and hunted animals. There were also gifts brought by important visitors that were placed in the most brightly lit areas.

Arminius remembered the room that his parents slept in;

he and Wulf would sometimes manage to sneak in early in the morning and jump on the enormous bed covered with bear-skins. The rugs on the side of the bed were made of bison hide.

He had so many things to tell his father, and his mother too. He had never dreamed he would see her alive again. Not because of her age, but because she'd always had such a feeble constitution that made her slender and fragile-looking, but also gave her a soft, delicate air, especially in her face and her twinkling blue eyes. Arminius remembered his father's friends being so surprised that such a frail-looking woman could have given birth to such sturdily built sons.

When he had embraced her and offered a rather clumsy caress, she had dropped her eyes to hide any show of emotion, because Germanic women had to always be models of forti-tude. 'Mother, it's been so long . . .' he said.

'So long . . .' she sighed.

In the months he spent at home, Arminius often went hunt-ing with his father, his uncle Ingmar and sometimes with the bodyguards. It pleased him that he was becoming reaccus-tomed to the rigid climate and harsh conditions of an en-vironment that during his long stay in Rome and in the East he had almost forgotten. His father gave him a horse, a Pan-nonian steed used to racing through the endless plains of the land he came from; he had been a gift, in turn, from the chief-tain of a distant tribe. His name was Borr and he was a fine horse indeed.

The winter nights were long ones. At dusk the sun des-cended into the gloomy, foggy, hovering vapours and slowly drowned in the swamp.

The snows began, big flakes that danced in the wind and laid down a white blanket on the earth from horizon to hori-zon. In those lazy days Arminius spent his time by the fire, adding a piece of wood every now and then and listening to it crackle and sizzle. His father kept him company. His mother, sitting in the corner, spun wool with a spindle and distaff.

'What do the Romans do in the winter time?' Sigmer asked his son.

'You've never spent the cold season with them?'

'No.'

'They repair their weapons, their carts, their roads and bridges. They go through their warehouses and take inventory. The officers write letters to their friends, their girls or their wives, to complain about the cold, the damp, the food, the sour wine. In the evenings they bet their salaries on games of dice; sometimes they even lose the clothes off their backs. The smarter ones invest in wool underwear and trousers . . .'

Sigmer shook his head, perplexed. 'I've never understood what they're looking for here, with everything they have in Rome and in Italy.'

'A border. The safest and most dependable one possible. And barbarians to civilize. They feel that's their mission.'

'You?'

'You shouldn't need to ask. You had long conversations with General Drusus. I know the doubts in your mind: why should my people have to pay taxes and tributes to the Roman governor? It's true, maybe he's robbing you. But he's also building cities and roads, bridges and aqueducts, he's digging canals and draining swamps, and if he had the time he'd be raising libraries, thermal baths and theatres. Romans pay taxes and tributes to their own state as well. They complain about it, but they pay. And the citizens can see what their money is good for when they travel down a road or cross a river using a bridge meant to last for centuries. All we've done is worry about killing each other, and every new generation is fiercer than the one before it. You know? Since I've been here, with you, with Mother, with the things from my youth all around me, instead of mellowing I'm becoming fiercer and wilder every day.'

'It's our nature,' replied Sigmer. 'We live in a cruel, merciless place. You're not changing. You're what you've always been. You just forgot, living for years like you did in such an enchanting, luminous land.'

Arminius fell silent for a long time, as if he were listening to the voices of the forest as darkness overcame it. Then he said, 'Have you ever seen that girl again?'

Sigmer looked at him questioningly.

'The one that I saw at the spring festival.'

'She was a little girl. And I told you to forget it. You mean that girl?'

Arminius nodded.

'Her name is Thusnelda.'

'Is she married?'

'No, but as I told you then, she's betrothed.'

'So she's waited for me.'

'Because you looked at her?'

Arminius decided that the time had come to ask him the only question worth coming all this way for. 'Was it you who sent me a message through the Hermundur? The message that spoke of a woman between two heads, the centre of everything, of life and of death?'

Sigmer sighed. 'I didn't know much about how the two of you were faring, just what the Hermunduri warrior would tell me, but it was enough. I knew that your position, and the friendship of Centurion Taurus, would allow you to intervene and to bend the course of events in the way that the two of you – but you in particular – felt would be best.'

'Couldn't you have been more explicit?'

'No. A written message might have been intercepted and one that was any clearer might have put you in a dangerous position. The Hermundur himself could not be allowed to understand the meaning of the message. Only you and your brother. If you had found yourself in fortunate circumstances, you could have provided the crucial key; you might have made a decision that would put you in a position of great advantage. Either as far as the Roman emperor was concerned, or . . . on behalf of all of the Germanic nations that for more than three lustra have been fighting against him and his sons, Commanders Drusus and Tiberius.

'For me, it's always been an unsolvable dilemma: on one hand the destiny of our peoples, on the other the thinking of General Drusus, to whom, as you know, I was tied by a strong bond of friendship and an even stronger one of admiration.'

Arminius was not letting a single word of his father's escape him.

'In the end, you decided to stay the killer's hand, and thus you gained Augustus's trust. I don't want to ask you whether that was your final choice but I would say it was, and I'm beginning to believe myself that it was the right one. As far as I know, your brother Wulf has no doubts and he is considered one of the most valuable officers of the Roman army. I'm getting along in age and my temples have turned grey, while you, my son, still have many years ahead of you to come to a firm choice. I hope I've answered your question.'

At that moment Arminius caught his mother's glance and he had no doubts about what her thoughts were; you could see them in the cutting light of her eyes.

★

ONE EVENING, at twilight, as Arminius was returning from the hunt with a roe deer tied to the back of his horse, he found himself suddenly facing a wall of fog, seeping forward from the century-old trees. He stopped to find his bearings, glancing around to look for an alternate route. The fog would soon be swallowing him up as well. What would he do then? The odour of the deer's blood would attract the wolves. How could he have been so foolish? He moved his dagger in its sheathe onto his chest, in order to be ready. There were hills over to his left; he could try to reach the closest and find a place to spend the night there. He loosened the knots which bound the deer and let it slip to the ground as he turned towards the hill. In that instant he heard the sound of pounding hooves and saw a horseman burst out of the fog; he was racing dangerously fast for that kind of terrain.

Arminius reached down for the sword which hung at his side and prepared for combat. The horseman halted his steed and unsheathed his own sword.

'What language do you speak?' asked Arminius in his ancestral tongue.

'Yours,' replied a voice that Arminius knew well.

They jumped to the ground at the same moment and they hugged each other hard enough to crunch their bones.

'Wulf!'

'Armin!'

'What are you doing here?'

'What you're doing.'

'So why were you riding so fast in a place like this?'

'To get away from the fog, the dark and . . .' They heard a howl. '. . . them.' Yellow eyes emerged from the night and they could hear snarling, very close.

'A horseman storming out of the fog on a black stallion . . .'

mused Arminius. He'd already seen that. Was it in a dream? A night in Italy? In Germania?

They let the horses free and clambered to the top of the hill as the wolves fought over the deer carcass.

'And when they've finished?' asked Flavus.

'We can try to push on. But with this fog we'll risk getting lost and other packs could attack us. We'll stay here. They're only wild dogs, after all. These will do it,' said Arminius, lifting his sword in his right hand and his dagger in the left.

The siege started in the dead of night, the wolves encircling and then closing in on them. Neither of them was wearing armour and they planted themselves back to back to stand against their assailants. Their blades flashed in the dark, tracing perfect semi-circles. But the wolves were organized, following a precise strategy, attacking and retreating to find a breach, flesh into which they could sink their teeth.

'Where were you headed?' asked Arminius to lighten the tension.

'Home,' panted Flavus.

'Me too,' said Arminius. 'I've been home for a month. Where were you coming from?'

'The island of the Batavi.'

They fought to the point of exhaustion, wolf carcasses scattered all around them while new ones kept coming out of the woods.

Then all at once a flaming meteor flew across the sky and landed just a short distance away from them: a lit torch that sizzled on the snow, followed by another. Flavus picked one up. 'We're saved,' he said.

'Who on earth . . .' began Arminius, picking up the other.

'We'll worry about that later. Let's follow the horses' tracks while we can see.'

They set fire to dry twigs and branches at the foot of the oaks that had been hit by lightning. They burst into flame, crackling loudly, blazing with incandescent heat. The wolves backed off and fled.

Flavus and Arminius found their horses, who had managed to stay safe, and they headed towards Sigmer's house, illuminating their path with the torches. From a hilltop, they made out a vermillion light pulsating half a mile away in the middle of the wood.

'It's him. Whoever threw us the torches so we could defend ourselves from the wolves,' said Flavus.

'Who?' asked Arminius.

'I don't think we'll ever know. We owe him our lives, that we know.'

Sigmer couldn't hide his delight at seeing both of his sons together. He hoped they would remain with him for the rest of the winter season, but this was not to be. Both brothers set off one cold February morning, heading north. After only three days, they separated. Arminius was directed to Velleius's winter camp and Flavus would be crossing the Weser on a ferry.

'I hope we'll see each other again soon,' said Arminius.

'Maybe,' replied Flavus. 'Anyway, it's best we say goodbye.' They embraced, and Arminius watched as his brother and his black horse boarded the barge that would cross the river.

AT THE END of the winter, Tiberius Caesar returned as high commander of the Army of the North and military operations began again. In the meantime, the fleet, aided by winds blowing from the north and west, had already set sail up the Ems, the Weser and the Elbe, carrying supplies, equipment and the first troop contingents. The bulk of them would be arriving later. An enormous number of men would be deployed: tens of thousands of soldiers, including legionaries, cavalry and auxiliary troops, coming in on hundreds of ships. Velleius was promoted to general staff and became Tiberius Caesar's personal aide.

The high command intended for this operation to be the definitive push that would bring the subjugation of Germania. Tiberius had already conquered all of the Balkan populations and even before that he had fought alongside his brother Drusus to stabilize the Rhine-Danube border. He was the man who had never lost a battle, he was the idol of the army and he was not about to fail the most important mission of his life. The fleet landed the first contingents of troops along the rivers' banks, some on the left side of one river and others on the right side of the other river, so that the armies could converge on the territory from the east and from the west at the same time, including the interior regions, and gain control of everywhere at once. The land of the Cherusci was crossed but not devastated, as had been convened. Other peoples were given the opportunity to discuss terms of surrender.

At the beginning of this huge initiative, Arminius got himself assigned to garrison duty on the territory still governed by his father, so he could manage to avoid operations that would force him into front-line combat against his own blood.

Velleius seemed to approve of this line of conduct. 'I trust you,' he said, 'but the moment will soon come in which you'll have to fight at the front against other Germanics. There are bonds stronger than friendship that form in a war – a little like love, no? It puts a man to the test. And for soldiers that might mean a test of blood.' He looked straight into Arminius's eyes as if to search for an opening into his thoughts, but Arminius's gaze was as indecipherable as the sphinx's must have been when Oedipus was at the gates of Thebes. 'There's one thing you should remember: there's never any pity for the Germanic auxiliaries on the part of enemy kinsmen. That's why they have to fight to their last drop of sweat and their last breath.'

'I'll remember that,' replied Arminius, in a flat, toneless voice.

He met Sergius Vetilius and Rufius Corvus again in the Eighteenth Legion camp. Corvus commanded a front-line centuria of the third cohort, while Vetilius was the military tribune of the fifth.

They often joined up to drink a beer and play dice in the village of huts and tents put together by the merchants who were following the army. Their friendship strengthened as an effect of the military camaraderie, as they shared all of the toil and bravado that kind of life required.

In the second part of the campaign, Commander Tiberius Caesar personally ordered that Arminius be moved to the head of the auxiliary cavalry and that he assume authority, if needed, over the commander of the Germanic infantry fighting with the Romans. In all, about fifteen thousand men.

Arminius knew little about what was happening to his brother, apart from rare information offered every now and then by a stray messenger. He always appeared to be at the front, attached to various legions. It almost seemed to Arminius that someone was trying to keep them apart, if not actually far away from one another. In reality, both brothers acted in the same way: they fought with great valour against the enemies of Rome.

More than once, Arminius had intervened to save Roman forces from a dangerous situation and Tiberius's esteem of him continued to grow. It didn't take long for the army's supreme commander to realize that Arminius was a true combatant, a war machine. It was enough to toss him into the fray for all of his most ferocious instincts to come to the fore. Nothing else mattered, not even having to attack men who spoke his language or shared his blood. The high commander did nothing to spare him this type of encounter, first of all because that would be impossible and secondly because Arminius's actions were proof of his loyalty to the Empire and to the emperor. In his heart, Tiberius thought that if his commander of the Germanic Auxilia continued to fight in such a way, he would request that Arminius be honoured with the highest rewards.

The spring offensive had the Army of the North moving beyond the Weser in the direction of the Elbe where, according to Augustus's plan, the borderline between the east and north would be established. In order to achieve such a result, Tiberius Caesar could leave no pocket of resistance or rebellion behind him. Augustus had endured almost twenty years of war at huge expense, losing a great number of soldiers and some very fine commanders like Drusus, without ever having succeeded in his aim: to reduce Germania to a Roman province with a Roman governor, a Roman administration and the Roman rule of law.

One evening, after the general staff of the Eighteenth Legion had met in the praetorian tent, Legate Velleius invited a few of his most highly prized officers, including Rufius Corvus, Sergius Vetilius and Arminius himself, to dinner. At their meeting they spoke about the great operation that Tiberius was readying. The oceanic fleet was sailing up the Elbe, putting a number of contingents ashore in correspondence to the size of the enemy settlements to be occupied. Sometimes an entire legion would be transported this way, requiring at least two days for such a complex manoeuvre.

At dinner, conversation continued along the same lines. 'The fact is,' said a legate, 'that it's not like Gaul here. My uncle, who fought with Julius Caesar, always said that in that land, the settlements are very similar to our own cities in every way, and that each one was a centre around which a vast area revolved, including all the people living there. So it was enough to conquer one of these strongholds for the whole region to be conquered as well. The Gauls defended them strenuously, one by one, and in the end it's calculated that they paid for this heroic resistance with over one million dead . . .' Arminius couldn't help turning towards him. 'Here, instead, all we find are villages of huts, like the Romans had at their very origins, with maybe fifty to two hundred inhabitants, no more, scattered all through the forests and around the swamps. Dominating all of them is nearly impossible, unless you totally clear the entire territory.

'So that's what the commander intends to do: the army of the Rhine will move east, and the army of the Elbe will move west, flattening to the ground each and every village, and every people, who refuse to surrender. Do you remember Virgil's words? *Parcere subiectis et debellare superbos.* Spare the vanquished and subdue the arrogant. Am I right? They are being given a choice.'

'Will we succeed, Legate?' asked Sergius Vetilius. 'This war has lasted almost twenty years.'

'I say we will,' replied Velleius. 'Commander Tiberius has never lost a battle, let alone a war. It's true, this conflict has been dragging on for far too long, but if it ends up the way I think it will, it will have been worth it. There will finally be peace, for centuries to come. The grandchildren and great-grandchildren of the people we conquer will slowly forget about the blood shed by their forebears like the Gauls have. After all, Gallic leaders have seats in the Senate of Rome now and wear laticlave togas; they promulgate the same laws that Roman people have learned to comply with. In a few generations, it will be the same for the Germanics. They'll have become legionaries, curators of aqueducts and roads, merchants and contractors. They'll receive honours and awards, they'll live in houses with running water, they'll eat foods cooked according to elaborate recipes. Some of them will become poets, philosophers and musicians, others will govern as magistrates. They'll cut off those wild manes of hair and adopt our styles. But they'll also adopt the Latin language, and they'll do it of their own free accord.

'I know the commander well. He won't stop until he has achieved the job he has set out to do. And I know how this campaign will end, because he never puts his soldiers' lives at risk without a reason and he'll never join a battle he's not sure of winning.'

'The chaotic element of history does exist, Legate,' said Sergius Vetilius.

At that moment a voice, one that nearly all of the guests sitting under the great pavilion recognized, rang out: 'That is true. Events can be unpredictable. But there's one thing that Tribune Vetilius has forgotten!'

Taurus! Arminius thought to himself.

'Well, let lightning strike me,' whispered Corvus into Vetilius's ear. 'Where did that old bastard come from?'

'Come forward, Centurion!' ordered Velleius.

Taurus, gleaming in his regulation armour and wearing his cross-crested helmet, strode forward.

'What did I forget?' Vetilius asked him.

'You've forgotten General Drusus,' he replied. 'He was Tiberius's brother and he died in his arms, in front of his legions. No god or mortal man, in heaven or in hell, will ever stop Tiberius from exacting revenge. There exists no room for chance.'

20

EVERYONE WHO HAD HAD their back to the entrance of the tent turned towards Taurus. No one could imagine how he had managed to appear so suddenly, at that moment and in that place.

Velleius got up, walked towards him and raised a hand to the centurion's shoulder.

Taurus stiffened into a salute to the legate of the Eighteenth Legion. Velleius gestured towards the table and Taurus joined the others. 'Finish your thoughts, please, Taurus. What you were saying about General Drusus is important.'

Taurus spoke again: 'In any situation, many imponderables certainly exist. There are convulsions of nature, like storms and lightning bolts, but then there's human nature itself. Men cannot always control their feelings and their emotions. I was present at the funeral of General Drusus and I saw the cold tears on Tiberius Caesar's face.'

'Ah, the centurion is a philosopher!' Velleius smiled. 'Who would have guessed?'

'It's not philosophy so much as direct contact with our men. We give them an example of courage. Being first to put ourselves in death's way means that we can ask them to sacrifice everything. We learn to know our men. But we also know well how the unexpected can affect any situation. There's nothing predictable about war.'

VALERIO MASSIMO MANFREDI

'Of course you're right, Centurion. Nonetheless, we'll do everything in our power to ensure that our efforts will produce the results we all desire. Please, sit and listen to what movements are being planned for our legion so you can prepare yourself adequately. I asked for you to be sent here knowing that you have often been assigned special tasks. Have something to eat with us. The wine, at least, is good.'

VELLEIUS AND HIS LEGION followed Tiberius in the entire second Germanic campaign. First against the gigantic Chauci warriors, the mere sight of whom was terrifying. That feeling only worsened when they let out their bone-chilling war cries. In pitched battle against the most seasoned of the Roman legions, they soon realized that their towering height provided no advantage, either against the closed formation of the Romans, the *testudo*, which gave them a wall and roof of shields as protection, or against the rain of *pila* that poured from the sky like steel hail, and least of all against their machines which shot three-libra bolts and fiery spheres of hemp and pitch. As a result they resorted to ambushes, suddenly appearing in the thick of the woods, surfacing from swamps black as hell, wielding axes and big knives. But they could not prevail over the Romans.

In the end, after seeing so many of their warriors put on a funeral pyre to be welcomed into the heavens as heroes, the Chauci chieftains had no choice but to surrender. They went to the Roman camp and laid down their arms at Tiberius's feet. The supreme commander received them sitting on a throne set on top of a wooden stand. He was encircled by standards and ensigns, flanked by two uniformed legions drawn up in formation, armour shining. The mournful sounds of lutes and horns were joined by a rhythmic thundering of drums. Everything had been arranged so that the Chauci chiefs would be stunned at what they saw, so that the Roman commander enthroned on a high platform, decked in his red paludamentum and his muscle cuirass, would look exactly like an invincible god.

Then the legions of Tiberius faced off against the fierce, primitive Longobards who lived along both sides of the upper Elbe. It was the first time that a Roman army, with its eagles and its ensigns, had reached the banks of that river, more than four hundred miles from the Rhine. It was here that the fleet which had circumnavigated the shores of the northern ocean and then sailed up the Elbe, laden with reinforcement troops, met up with the Army of the North. More than one hundred warships dropped anchor on the eastern side of the great river. The naval infantry standing at the ships' sides saluted the legionaries who were going ashore to join their comrades-in-arms already on the ground. Trumpets blared in greeting for the soldiers who had come to assist their fellows in executing the greatest enterprise ever attempted by a Roman army in all of her history.

Arminius fought untiringly in all of the battles, and was at the side of his Hermunduri as they crossed his tribe's territory. By the end of the autumn, all of Germania had been cleared, from the Rhine to the Elbe, from the ocean to the mountains of Bohemia. Only one land was still to be conquered. It was inhabited by the Marcomanni and it was a powerful nation, a kingdom with borders that were always shifting because their sovereign was eager to constantly extend his territory. His native name was Marbod. He negotiated with foreign sovereigns as equals; he was shrewd and intelligent. His army was powerful and well-armed. Tiberius wasn't about to take risks with him; for one thing, if Rome were defeated, the barbarian would have a clear and open path for invading Italy. Tiberius knew that he had to hit so hard that Marbod would be knocked senseless, if he survived the blow, and he would never lift his head to challenge Rome again.

Tiberius convened a meeting of his general staff for early October. Present were Sergius Vetilius, Velleius Paterculus and Sentius Saturninus, the commander's right hand. The commanders of three of his legions were also summoned: Atilius Celer, Sestius Longinus and Aulus Priscus. The last to be admitted was Marcus Caelius Taurus, even though he was a simple centurion. None of the high officers present were surprised, so great were the fame and the merits of this man.

Tiberius was calm, as if he had the solutions to all of his problems already in mind. He was wearing a red wool floor-length tunic and a pair of oxhide boots, and he sat on a curule seat. One of his freedmen was pouring him red wine which came from his estate in Rhodos while another placed a sealed calfskin scroll on the table. Before Tiberius began to speak, he dismissed the two freedmen with a nod and they left the praetorian tent. He broke the seal on the scroll with a flick of his sword and spread out the calfskin. It turned out to be a beautifully painted map of the entire region between the Rhine, the Elbe and the Alps.

'I'll establish my base at Carnuntum, in Noricum,' began the supreme commander, using a cane to point to the locality. 'The city is at the centre of the two directions we will march. The first, from the north, will be led by those of you present here. You will leave contingents to garrison the strategic points,' he continued, using the cane to indicate them, 'to preserve what we've already accomplished. Each of you will receive an identical copy of this map. You will commit to memory what I am telling you now.

'In the meanwhile, there will be four or five legions moving to my base in Carnuntum from Illyricum and Dalmatia, and from there we will move north. At the same time, you will be moving south, with three or four legions, depending on necessity. You will send a messenger every day or two to inform me of your position. You will receive information from me through the same messenger. All information will be relayed by voice only. In the end, our two armies will arrive at the target on the same day.

'Marbod is a fox, but he will have no choice but to surrender unconditionally if he doesn't want to be crushed between our jaws. The king of the Marcomanni is not a stupid man; as soon as he gets wind of the avalanche of iron that's about to be unleashed on him, he'll come to my camp and ask for our friendship. We will make Bohemia a client state. They will absorb any provocation from the north, and that will give Rome time to prepare in case of any threat of invasion.

'Germania will thus become our latest and, I hope, our last province. The Roman Empire will become invincible, by adding Germanic fury to Roman discipline and experience. In no more than two generations, her peoples will understand that the Empire is the only place worth living in. And if necessary, worth dying for.'

The six officers present, as well as Centurion Taurus, were amazed: their high commander, Tiberius Caesar, was mobilizing one third of the armed forces of the entire Empire, to achieve in two years what nearly twenty years of uninterrupted war hadn't accomplished. They got to their feet, unsheathed their gladii and beat them rhythmically seven times against the cuirasses that covered their chests. Each man stiffened in salute.

Tiberius looked at them one by one with satisfaction. 'It seems that my plan meets with your unanimous approval.

Nonetheless, if you have anything to say, speak freely. You are the best officers of the Empire and I've summoned you here to have your advice; your loyalty I am already sure of.'

Velleius spoke: 'Commander, I believe I'm expressing the thoughts of all of my fellow officers in saying that your plan is impeccable. It couldn't be better. Only you, after Augustus, have the authority and the power to move such a force over such a vast territory.'

'I thank you,' replied Tiberius. 'And yet, Velleius has told me what Centurion Marcus Caelius Taurus said that evening in his tent. I think his words need to be pondered. So, Centurion, what were you thinking when you said what you did?'

'In reality, I wanted to say that your desire to avenge your brother Drusus's death, and to bring this venture to completion, will prevail over any unforeseen circumstance. This war has gone on for nearly twenty years but nothing can stop us if we are certain that we are doing the right thing. We are all with you, Commander.'

'Thank you, Centurion,' replied Tiberius. 'Is there anything else?'

'I have a request, which I hope you will be able to grant.'

'Speak,' said Tiberius.

'In this war, Arminius, commander of the Germanic Auxilia and son of Sigmer, the prince of the Cherusci, has given proof of his great loyalty to the Empire by fighting against tribes which are not his own yet are of Germanic stock. I believe that he deserves to become a Roman, like all of us who are present here today.'

Tiberius showed surprise, then answered: 'I've had in mind to do just what you've suggested, and I thank you for both your reply and your request. May the gods always preserve your friendship and your faith in me. Men like you are quite rare.'

At this point, Velleius asked to speak and Tiberius nodded his assent.

'Commander, pardon my boldness. When at the head of your Army of the North you were descending south after sweeping away all resistance, Arminius came to me asking with extraordinary courage to go to his father in the dead of night and in the middle of a furious storm in order to convince him to return to the long-standing alliance with the Roman people. A promise that you accepted and ratified with great wisdom and magnanimity. A number of our allies have been given the rank of *Eques* along with Roman citizenship. I believe that he deserves it, and that receiving this honour will create an even stronger bond with us.'

Tiberius nodded again, but then asked for the approval of his staff: 'What do you think?'

Taurus was the first to speak, and he said, 'I wouldn't have dared to ask so much, but I believe that Arminius merits this privilege. His intervention avoided the spilling of much blood and he recovered a powerful ally for us.'

The legates who commanded the legions confirmed their agreement, one by one.

'Very well,' concluded Tiberius. 'I also am in favour of Velleius's proposal. And now let us return to the main question of this assembly.

'We are well into the season, and for this reason my plan will be put into action next spring. In less than a month, our legions will be returning to their winter quarters. Velleius has gathered precise information regarding the size and quality of Marbod's army. I should add that his organization and structure resemble our own quite closely, and for this reason he is dangerous and should not be underestimated.'

When he had finished speaking, he left the floor to Velleius so his aide could report what he knew about the characteristics, the strength and the composition of Marbod's forces. When he had done so, they all retired to their individual quarters to rest.

Arminius was granted Roman citizenship and promoted to *Eques* as had been decided. He was surprised and somewhat shaken. He felt confused about receiving such an honour.

'In reality, you remain what you've always been,' said Taurus, when he brought word. 'Being Roman doesn't mean that you are part of an ethnicity. It's the way you conceive of life. You've lived as a Roman for most of your existence; all that's left is accepting recognition of that. Nothing will change for you, apart from the consideration of other people. You can look forward to a bright future once this war is finished. There will be a great need for men like you who understand both peoples. It's true of me as well. My mother, as you know, was Germanic.' He paused. 'I've brought you a present.'

Arminius was surprised again. 'A gift for me? Why?'

'It's customary,' replied Taurus, handing him a pinewood box.

Arminius opened it and saw that there was fabric inside. He unfolded it and spread it on the chest where he kept his personal things. 'A toga!'

'The distinctive sign of a Roman citizen and an *Eques*. If you are not both of those things, you can't wear this. You'll have to learn to put it on. It takes some doing.'

'Thank you,' said Arminius. 'This is a wonderful gift, but you shouldn't have. It must have cost you a fortune.'

'It was my father's. He's no longer with us and I don't have a family of my own. I hope this will help you to remember me with fondness, even though I've had to teach you discipline with a heavy hand at times.'

Arminius lifted it and draped it around his body. He had so

often longed to don that garment: solemn, majestic and yet cumbersome all at once.

'When you are wearing this, all of your movements must become measured and elegant,' Taurus said. 'You and I are combatants and we're used to wearing very different attire. Well, I'm about to leave again for a long journey. Perhaps to Rome, perhaps elsewhere.'

'In Rome you once told me that two Roman soldiers know they will always meet up again, sooner or later.'

'It's true. So we shall certainly meet again,' Taurus said with a nod.

The centurion walked out, leaving Arminius to listen to the sound of his footsteps on the pavement.

ARMINIUS SPENT SOME time at his father's house, hunting with his uncle Ingmar who had dogs, horses and arms for hunting boar and bear. When he returned to the Eighteenth Legion's winter camp, he found a letter from his brother Flavus:

> *Flavus to brother Armin, hail!*
>
> *I have heard about the great honours you have received, and I'm almost envious of you; make sure you live up to them.*
>
> *I'm marrying. You are invited the third day before the Kalends of November in Magontiacum.*
>
> Well, thank you, thought Arminius, *you could have at least told me where it's going to happen. Magontiacum is a big place.*

He set off nevertheless a day before the event, arrived in good time and quartered at the army's winter camp. He had brought the pinewood case with the toga that Taurus had given him, and he prepared to put it on with the help of a maidservant who worked at the prefecture. The girl, who was pale and rather slight, examined the fabric thoroughly to check for any stains, inspecting the stitching and hems as well, and then draped it around Arminius's shoulders and his left arm. She straightened the folds one by one as if she were working for the prefect himself. This all took place in front of a large mirror of polished bronze that reflected his image.

If Arminius had had any doubts, the vision of himself actually wearing the toga swept them away. With his tall stature, athletic build and wavy chestnut-coloured hair, he was striking and elegant. The girl regarded him with admiration.

'You look magnificent, master,' she said in broken Latin with a strong Germanic accent.

Arminius smiled. He also had her lace up the suede boots that he'd bought at the forum and which looked a great deal like those worn by the senators. He could have hired a litter, but he was ashamed at himself for even considering such a thing; he had always disapproved of men who had other men carry them when they could walk perfectly well on their own feet. The girl advised him of the practical side of that means of transport: 'If it rains this evening, master, you'll arrive at the celebration with the bottom hem of the toga all muddied.' Arminius thought that he would run that risk. The city roads were paved and there were gutters to drain off the rain water.

He learned almost instantly at the prefect's office in the winter quarters that weddings were celebrated in the forum at the twelfth hour. When the time came, he set off walking towards the ceremony site with his gift for the newlyweds in hand: an amphora of wine. On his way he crossed paths with two men who were perhaps returning home from the market, since one was carrying a bag filled with bread and a wheel of cheese.

'Look,' said one to the other in Latin. 'A barbarian in a toga!'

The other replied, 'We'll have to get used to such a sight. You see all kinds of things happening lately.'

Arminius would have liked to beat them to a pulp with his own fists, but he controlled himself. He didn't want to draw attention by acting violently, but those words had disgusted him and soured his mood.

Flavus's face lit up nonetheless when he saw his brother and he walked over at once to embrace him. He seemed surprised; maybe he hadn't expected Arminius to accept his invitation.

He pointed at the bride, who was standing to the side, her face covered by a veil that fell to her belt.

'Her name is Vatinia. She's Germanic, but she has a Latin name like I do. Pretty name, isn't it?'

'Yes. As long as you like it,' replied Arminius.

The ceremony was brief because other couples were waiting. Later there was a dinner at Flavus's house with some of his friends and fellow soldiers, both Roman and Germanic, along with the bride's parents. Arminius's amphora of wine warmed up the atmosphere quickly. After dinner a small choir of girls had been engaged for the occasion to sing nuptial songs that would bring luck to the couple. They then retired to the joking and ribaldry of the guests, who were all quite tipsy by then.

In a few months, the bride's pregnancy began to show and Arminius received news in the winter quarters. Flavus wrote using very simple Latin.

> *The day before the Ides of February*
> *Flavus to brother Armin, hail!*
> *Vatinia is expecting a child. With the help of the gods, you may become an uncle.*
> *I hope you'll share my happiness as I become a father.*

And so Arminius spent the winter in the Eighteenth Legion's

winter camp, in a situation suspended between boredom and waiting for something indefinable to happen, in a sort of interior discontent in which a certain phrase kept ringing in his ears: 'Look! A barbarian wearing a toga!'

So this was what being an *Eques* meant? The Roman citizenship his people aspired to? A barbarian in a toga?

That spring, Arminius returned to his parents' home to say goodbye before the departure of the army, which would begin when Tiberius Caesar came back from Italy. He found them preparing for the festival of spring. It was a very ancient celebration in which all of the village chieftains and their families participated, but he remembered it for one reason alone: the apparition of Thusnelda and the blue light in her eyes. An epiphany that had seared her features into his heart.

'Can I come with you?' he asked.

Sigmer looked at him with surprise at his unexpected request, until he realized the reason behind it.

'You're wrong,' said Arminius as if he could read his father's thoughts. 'That face and those eyes no longer exist, just as my adolescence no longer exists . . . except sometimes in my dreams.'

'Come with us, then. News travels fast; everyone's eyes will be on you.'

Arminius participated in the procession through the woods wearing his Germanic warrior's armour. His father lent him his own weapons and his silver-studded leather tunic and it was as Sigmer had predicted: all eyes were on Arminius.

He searched for Thusnelda among the girls who paraded with crowns of flowers in their hair, hoping to catch just a glimpse of the visage that had filled his dreams, fluctuating between the lights and shadows of the forest.

'There she is,' rang out Sigmer's voice. Arminius turned

towards where his father was pointing. A spring of water at the base of a cliff covered by dripping moss. The girl had dipped her hand in and was bringing it to her mouth to drink. A young woman at the peak of her splendour which encased the girl she had been, like a golden circle encases a gem. But her gaze was darker, the colour of her eyes like deep water now.

He wanted her. He would have her at any cost.

21

THEIR EYES MET AND it was just like it was on that distant spring day: a burst of fire.

Sigmer saw but said nothing. He remembered when he had sought out Antonia's gaze on General Drusus's flagship, without ever succeeding. All those times he had told himself, *She's not for you.* How many times in the years that followed had he thought of his secret friendship with Drusus in terms of an insane attempt to see her again? The vision of the two of them making love, projected by the lamp onto the walls of his tent, continued to torture him.

But here, in the sacred forest, everything was very different. Arminius was a prince of the Cherusci people and she was a young noblewoman, the daughter of Seghest. She must not have seemed so unreachable to his love-lost son. In truth, Thusnelda was betrothed but not yet taken, that's what his son must be thinking. And yet he intended to dissuade him now as he had then.

'Son, there's not a girl among our people who doesn't dream of becoming your wife and bearing your children. You're a prince and yet you're also a man of high rank in the empire of the Romans, and that's immensely attractive to all of our youth. Why that one? It can only lead to violent clashes and the letting of blood . . .'

'Father, if I give up, I would spend my whole life regretting it. Regretting not having fought to have her. There is no other woman for me. I'll come to blows with anyone who tries to stop me. Even you, Father.'

Sigmer said nothing else and Arminius went to say goodbye to his mother. He found her fretting over the fate of both her sons. She knew that combat was their everyday occupation. They weren't like the warriors of her people, who battled only when necessary or to defend themselves. But how could Arminius explain to his mother what the Roman Empire was?

For her, the Romans were the ones who had stolen her sons away when they were very young and carried them off to a land so distant that she never got news of them. The Roman warriors all looked just the same, with the same armour and the same arms, like ants. And only one of them commanded. How could he explain to his mother what Roman discipline was? What a public work was? How Rome brought land to where there was water and water to where there was land? How to explain the road that never ends?

He hugged her tightly and said, 'Mother, I'll be back soon to see you; I won't leave you alone again. If you knew how to read, I could send you my words even from a long way away.'

His mother gave a pale smile. 'Do you get along with your brother? I've heard that he's married.'

'We get along, Mother, but it's not always easy. Life is tougher here than when we were in Rome. I've seen his wife; she's the daughter of a very important man in the city that was built on the other side of the Rhine.'

She stood in front of the door to her house and watched as Arminius jumped onto his horse and rode off at a gallop, until he vanished into the distance.

★

ONCE HE GOT to Magontiacum, Arminius joined up with his unit and then with the Eighteenth, where he met with Velleius and awaited orders.

Tiberius's order to mobilize came at the end of February. His second in command, Legate Sentius Saturninus, assembled the entire Army of the North; four legions plus the cavalry *alae*, which also included the Germanic Auxilia, began their descent south, crossing a land that was apparently calm.

On the same day in which the Army of the North was to begin its march, four horsemen without insignia left Carnuntum and headed to Pannonia to take an order to the Pannonian-Dalmatian army corps, composed of four legions. They were to move towards Carnuntum and then proceed in the direction of the kingdom of Marbod, who had already tried to contact Tiberius in order to negotiate favourable conditions for his surrender.

The conquest of the last part of Germania that was still independent was at hand.

Arminius felt the excitement, not only of the legionaries, but also of his Cherusci and Hermunduri horsemen. Everyone was convinced that the Roman army was invincible and that the constitution of the province of Germania was imminent. It was clear that whoever contributed to the project could hope to attain privilege and a position of power and prestige within the vast new borders of the Empire. Emperor Augustus was growing old and would be sooner or later succeeded by Tiberius, who wouldn't forget his friends and his soldiers.

Arminius wondered where his brother Flavus might be; how could he be missing from such an event? He hadn't spotted Taurus either, although finding any single person in a sea of twenty thousand was very difficult indeed.

Tiberius's orders had been for all units to find themselves at five days from Marbod's kingdom at the end of March, and that moment was approaching. His messengers arrived almost daily, and Saturninus sent just as many in his direction. In this way the two corps were perfectly synchronized, their positions recorded every day on the great map.

On the evening before the last stage of their approach, Velleius invited Arminius to dinner in his praetorian tent along with other officers of the legion. He illustrated to them the itinerary they would be following. Their endeavour was practically completed: they were only five days' march away from Marbod's borders. The mere fact of coordinating the two army corps had been a strategic stroke of genius which would be talked about in manuals for many years to come. But just as the dinner was winding to a close, they heard scuffling and voices outside. A messenger had arrived at a gallop and asked to speak immediately with the commander of the Eighteenth. He was brought to Velleius's presence; he was dripping with sweat and unsteady on his feet.

'Legate,' he said, 'I'm afraid I have bad news.'

Velleius startled and Vetilius's words sprang to mind: 'the chaotic element of history does exist . . .'

'Speak,' he urged the messenger, motioning for the servants to bring him some water, which the man drank down in a few gulps.

'Pannonia, Illyricum and Dalmatia are in revolt.'

'That's impossible!' exclaimed Velleius.

'I'm sorry. It's true.'

'And so?'

'Commander Tiberius Caesar must turn back with the legions he has brought here.'

'No, that's a mistake. We have to finish what we've begun.'

Arminius started and his reaction did not escape Velleius.

The messenger continued: 'Commander Tiberius has sent another messenger like me to Marbod. He'll be told that if he so much as moves a finger against Rome, Tiberius will turn back and he will go to the ends of the earth to find him. And when he does, he will not leave a blade of grass or a human being or a sheep or a calf untouched anywhere in his kingdom. He knows that Tiberius always keeps his promises. Our supreme commander feels that Marbod will not move and that his inertia will be an example to all of those living between the Rhine and the Elbe.'

'But why don't we enter Marbod's kingdom now and show him we're not joking?' asked Velleius as if he were speaking directly to Tiberius.

The messenger must have been a person of a certain importance, capable of responding for his commander: 'Tiberius has already run a great risk by leaving the eastern provinces undefended. The road to Italy, and Rome, is open now and if the barbarians attempted an invasion there would be no one to stop them. The risk is too great. It must be seen to immediately.'

Velleius dropped his head. There was no alternative.

'Is that all?' he asked.

'If I may,' said the messenger as he approached Velleius more closely, to speak into his ear. 'Commander Tiberius Caesar asks you to start off as soon as you can, with the legions and the auxiliaries, towards Carnuntum. From there you will move on together to your destination.'

'I'll have some food prepared for you, and a room for you to sleep. You must be exhausted.'

'I'll have something to eat,' replied the messenger, 'but have me called at the third guard shift; I have to return as soon as possible to report back.'

Velleius dismissed his guests. Early the next morning he woke the messenger himself, having prepared a fresh horse, food, water and blankets for warmth if the weather worsened.

'Tell Commander Tiberius that I thank him for his trust, and that I will reach him as soon as I can.'

Two DAYS AFTER the arrival of the messenger, Arminius set off with his Cherusci and Hermunduri auxiliaries in support of the Eighteenth. He rode alongside the legionaries during the long march to Carnuntum, and then to the foot of the Alps and to the Danube, the other great river that marked the borders of the Empire.

Combat was harsher than anything they had ever seen in Germania. The peoples of Illyricum, Pannonia and Dalmatia were rebelling against the ill treatment received at the hands of the Roman governors. They were ready to die in battle rather than live as slaves.

After Tiberius had captured one of the rebel chieftains, he asked why they had revolted against the Roman State and received this reply: 'Because you did not send a sheepdog to govern us, but a wolf.'

They were proud peoples, fiercely attached to their native land, no matter how poor and barren it might be. Most were shepherds and livestock herders, while others cut wood, mostly oaks, to sell to the Romans for their shipyards on the coast or for the wooden frames of their stone houses, arches and aqueducts.

Arminius was long accustomed to showing no mercy, because there is only one rule in battle – kill or be killed – although one could add sow terror to avoid attack. There was another thing to keep in mind in warfare as well: learn all you can without giving away anything of what you know.

He never stopped thinking about Thusnelda. She was always on his mind, even when he had coupled with a terrified barbarian woman who'd been captured in one of the villages, taking her brutally and then turning her over to his men so they could satisfy themselves with her as well.

But when the time finally came to drop onto his camp bed at night, utterly exhausted, he would fall into a deep sleep and her gaze would rise from the gloom like the light of the moon in summer. He dreamed of riding with her along the bank of the river where Sigmer once took his two boys when they were children. He spoke to her with words that faded instantly, leaving only a melancholy whisper that echoed in his heart.

He sometimes heard her singing in a voice he had actually never heard, a voice clear and melodic, singing the songs of his people. He dreamed, only once, of a night of love with her, a dance of shadow and flame, her body completely naked like the statues he'd seen in the temples and squares of Rome.

He spent more than a year in the middle of the horrors of a war so ferocious it did not seem real. Rivers of blood that threatened to drown him. The heat of the battle, a vortex of screaming violence, burned into his heart. And all of that suffering ended up being acceptable, inescapable, a necessity. He realized that he had crossed the line, the limit beyond which there is no return.

ONE DAY, TIBERIUS Caesar's adjutant sent for Arminius to tell him that his father was dying. The supreme commander had therefore decided to deploy him to the headquarters of the Army of the North. He was given a couple of messages to take to Sentius Saturninus, Tiberius's right hand in Germania, and a small unit of brawny Hermunduri auxiliaries to serve as an escort.

Arminius left at once, his heart aching. He was eager to reach his father before he died. Maybe Flavus had got a call as well and was hurrying as he was to join their father before he went to the paradise of heroes. Arminius crossed Noricum and decided to cut through Marbod's kingdom to save time, knowing well what a risk he was taking. He entered the territory at night with his black-cloaked Hermunduri, gigantic and terrifying to look at, covered in tattoos, their weapons bristling with iron spikes. They rode for three days and most of the nights, only stopping for a few hours at a time to rest. On the fourth day they were stopped and surrounded by one of Marbod's cavalry squads.

'Who are you and where are you going?' demanded the man at their command.

'I am Prince Armin of the Cherusci, son of Sigmer, and commander of the auxiliaries under Tiberius Caesar. What do you want from me?'

'You're travelling through the territory of Marbod without being invited and you're asking me what I want?'

'I'm trying to reach my father before he dies,' replied Arminius. 'You can try to stop me if you want, but I wouldn't advise it. You'd be the first to die.'

'But then you would die too, you and your Hermunduri. Better if you follow me.'

'Where to?'

'You'll see soon.'

Arminius nodded to his men and they all followed the cavalry squad that had stopped them. The king was at his camp, which was close by, and this explained the presence of armed squads patrolling the surrounding territory.

Marbod was a heavily built man with a penetrating gaze. It was the first time that Arminius had met him face to face.

'So you are the son of Sigmer and the head of Tiberius's Germanic Auxilia. You're rushing to the bedside of your father, who you claim has fallen ill, and you're crossing my kingdom with these frightful warriors without even asking my permission. What manners are these?'

'I have no hostile intentions. I want to see my father before he dies. If I'd had time, I would have come to ask for permission. I must see him before he closes his eyes.'

Marbod was in no hurry; he was dragging out their conversation with sarcastic remarks and making Arminius very nervous. In the end, however, the intention of the Marcomanni king was sufficiently clear. 'I'll leave you free now to go wherever you like with those dreadful-looking bodyguards of yours, but remember one thing: given the situation, I've had to accept a pact with Tiberius. More than a pact, actually; more like a capitulation. You can even call it surrender if you like; I know my army is not strong enough to take on ten Roman legions, six *alea* of cavalry and ten thousand auxiliaries. Now Tiberius has his own troubles in Pannonia, but he could change direction at any time and reappear at my borders. Saturninus has withdrawn from my northern border but he hasn't gone away.

'Regardless of how things turn out, remember this: if the anti-Roman movement prevails, I let you free today and I treated you as a friend. If the Romans should win, remember that I helped a Roman citizen, commander of the Germanic Auxilia forces. Do we agree? Whenever you have anything important to tell me, remember that my door is always open.'

Arminius nodded and the two men shook hands.

He spent the night with his men undisturbed in Marbod's camp and very early the next day, they resumed their journey.

In seven days' time, Arminius had reached his father's

house. His mother Siglinde, Sigmer's first and only wife, greeted him with a tear-clouded gaze.

Her son looked deeply into her eyes with a question in his. She looked down. 'Your father is dying.'

'Where's Wulf?'

'I don't know where he is, but I've sent one of your father's men to Magontiacum, where many people know him.'

'I'll send one of my Hermunduri; they'll be sure to find him. Take me to my father.'

Siglinde led him into the dimly lit bedroom. Sweat was pouring down Sigmer's face; he was pale and emaciated.

'What's wrong with him?' Arminius asked his mother.

'No one knows. After you left to go off with the Romans, and your brother had disappeared as well, he departed on a long journey himself, accompanied by a group of warriors. When he returned, he was no longer himself. He seems to be living in a nightmare, day and night; it's as if he is seeing things that terrify him, or fill him with horror . . .'

Arminius wanted to tell his mother about the horrors he had experienced in the war he fought with the Romans in Illyricum and Pannonia, and that you can survive horrors, but he didn't do that. He drew close to his father and took his bony hand in his own. 'I'm here. It's me, Armin. Wulf has not disappeared. He's married and he'll have had children by now. You'll see them.'

Sigmer turned towards him but did not meet his eye. He was staring into an empty place, and yet he seemed to see and somehow understand. But it must have been other places that he was seeing, other times. At a certain moment, Arminius realized he was beckoning for him to come nearer and he did. He leaned his ear close to his father's parched mouth and he thought he heard a sound, and then another. A phrase, a jumble of phrases. His father seemed to be speaking in a language that he had never heard, but that was somehow comprehensible. And yet he couldn't make sense of the flow of words; too many of them escaped him.

He felt one thing clearly: a deep sense of horror and fear.

Then he knew.

'Great Thor, Father! Did you go to consult the Germanic oracle? What have you done, Father? Why? Why?'

More words spilled out of Sigmer's mouth in that strange language that was alien and familiar at the same time . . . Arminius tried hard to listen, to let himself understand.

All at once he realized what his father knew, what the oracle had revealed to him: it was what Arminius had been keeping hidden in his heart. It was the slow, painful labour that had given birth to the certainty that his wild roots remained. The truth was so terrible he could not share it with any human being, not even his brother. It was a secret. But the secret had been revealed to Sigmer.

Destiny had rung Sigmer's last hour at the very same moment that Arminius had come to a final decision. And here, on his death bed, Sigmer was imploring his son to give up what he was intending to do.

Arminius could not believe what he was hearing. He had always known that it was his father who had accompanied General Drusus to the oracle's cave where the Roman would hear his death sentence: 'You will die first.'

And now, through the voice of his father in agony, the oracle was telling him, 'You will die after.'

He felt an icy blade run through his heart. There was no turning back.

'It's too late now, Father,' he said. 'I've decided. I will liberate our peoples from the Roman yoke, for always. I've earned

Rome's trust. I've always obeyed blindly, even if I loathed what I was doing. I became one of them. But perhaps now I can convince Wulf to come over to our side. Together we will found a Germanic empire, stretching from the Rhine to the eastern plains. Even the Celts will unite with us when they see that we can win.'

Sigmer gazed at his son intensely, his eyes full of incredulity and despair. They stopped looking then, all at once, and took on the stunned fixity of death.

THE FUNERAL OF Sigmer, the lord of the Cherusci, lasted three days. The priests invoked Wotan at great length, chanting, beseeching him to welcome the great warrior rising towards his gilded palace. The bards sang of his deeds while the Cherusci warriors, carrying their finest weapons, rode three times around his pyre, shouting his name and letting out their war cry. The fire was lit at the four corners of the mound. Just then Flavus appeared on his horse in the middle of the clearing, wearing a simple grey tunic, his sword slung over his shoulder in a silver baldric. Arminius rode over to his brother and together they unsheathed their swords to salute their father, as one. That gesture warmed the hearts of many of those present but in reality the two brothers had never been further apart.

After the ceremony, Sigmer's ashes were buried at the foot of a huge, centuries-old oak tree and the women surrounded Siglinde to pour tears on the burial mound of the greatest of the Cherusci.

Arminius and Flavus rode in silence to the hill that over-looked the darkening lake and Arminius was tempted to tell his brother what he had said to their dying father, but he could not find the words. He asked a question instead: 'Did your wife give birth?'

'Yes,' replied Flavus. 'A boy.'

'Have you given him a name?'

'Yes, Italicus. Do you like it?'

'It's a nice name,' replied Arminius. Then he asked, 'Who does he look like?'

'He's blond, so me. His mother, you know, has brown hair.' Flavus fell silent for a spell, listening to the sound of their horses' hoofs clopping on the beaten path. When he began speaking again, he said, 'You know, yesterday there was a rumour going around at camp, just before I left. It seems that the emperor has chosen the man who's going to be the next governor of Germania. Until now Saturninus has covered both the governing duties and the military command, but they say that now Tiberius might need him in Pannonia and Illyricum, so he'll have to be replaced.'

'Who do they say the new governor will be?'

'The name I was hearing is Publius Quinctilius Varus. You know him well, if I'm not mistaken.'

'I do,' confirmed Arminius.

At that moment, Arminius saw his future play out clearly before his eyes. The Germanic oracle, consulted by his father, had spoken. It had indicated a destination for him, and his people, from which there was no turning back.

He was like a dog who suddenly remembers it is a wolf.

He understood that he could not speak to his brother in any way about his plan, and that their roads would soon separate forever. He thought that one day they might be fighting each other on the field of battle and the idea broke his heart.

22

IN THE MONTHS THAT followed, Arminius often withdrew to the woods deep inside the Germanic forest to think and to try to understand the path that had led him to abandon all the convictions that had been instilled in him during his long years in the Roman world.

When he became a citizen and an *Eques*, he felt sure that Rome would be his world. He'd tried in every way to forget his roots, those days when he and Flavus would run until they were out of breath, or would hunt game until it was too dark to see, or would simply stretch out in the luminous afternoons of spring and watch the falcons fly over the treetops.

For a time, a very long time, he had been fascinated and won over by the majesty of the Empire. By the power of her armies, but also by the music and poetry. The comedies and tragedies performed in her theatres, and the imposing monuments. He had dreamed of making that civilization his own, of making Rome a part of him and making himself a part of Rome.

Then slowly, secretly, his ancestral origins had come back to life, had trickled into his limbs, flowed through his blood again. His nature was that of the bear, the wolf, and the high-soaring falcon. Almost without realizing it, he had understood that Roman discipline – obedience to the norms of society at the cost of losing one's own freedom – was a sacrifice too great to ask of himself.

There hadn't been a real turning point, a single event that had broken him, that had liberated the wild beast within him. It had been imperceptible, so slow that it had never come to the fore. His ancestral people were wild, their customs and habits rough. Bloodthirsty, you could say, but innocently so, in the way that one animal that mangled and tore another to pieces was innocent. The peoples who the Romans called barbarians were simply more ancient and closer to the origins of creation, to the scattering of life from the hands of the gods.

He had come to conceive of an enormous plan, almost without realizing it: the defeat of the Roman Empire and the liberation of the Germanic peoples.

He knew all the secrets of the Roman armies, their strengths and their weaknesses. They called them their 'Achilles' heels' although he didn't really know what that meant nor who Achilles was exactly. He had won their complete trust: the trust of Centurion Taurus, of Velleius, of Corvus and Vetilius. The trust of Tiberius Caesar and perhaps even that of Augustus. At first he had been sincere, but then he became duplicitous. How or why that had happened, he wasn't sure.

There was only one key person missing from this list, but he might turn out to be the most dangerous of them all. The son of General Drusus and his beautiful Antonia. They too were carved into the Altar of Peace and that son of theirs was just a little boy, wearing a toga and a pendant around his neck. An amulet – who knew what it contained. Arminius had never fought alongside him. They'd exchanged glances on occasion but not more than that. Not enough to understand . . .

Germanicus.

And then there was one more person who surely would

never believe him, who would never trust him. The one he missed most, with his golden head of hair. Mocking, cynical, loyal to his masters like a Molosser with a collar of spikes. His brother, the person he loved most. Flavus. Which of the two of them might lose his life?

Arminius had sought out Thusnelda, time and time again. Only once did he succeed in speaking to her, but just from a certain distance. She had not let him get close. Maybe she was afraid of him, or afraid of herself, of giving in to him. What would it be like for them to finally look into each other's eyes, to talk? What was her voice like? Her scent? Her hands? He was sure he knew – his dreams had told him everything.

He also pondered long and hard over why his father had gone back to consult the Germanic oracle. As a young man, he had brought General Drusus to her and he had watched the Roman fight against the giantess, the very symbol of Germania. Why had his father wanted to consult the oracle again? And why did he have to die? What was the language his father had spoken in, so like his own and so different? What nightmares had sunk their claws into him? Maybe Arminius would never know. Maybe it was the same secret at the core of the relationship between Sigmer and Drusus.

In his heart he feared an encounter with Germanicus. Would the two sons replicate the destiny of their fathers?

He also feared meeting up with Taurus again. He would have liked to forget him. While he was not at all disturbed by the thought of seeing Publius Quinctilius Varus again; he was just waiting for the right moment.

In the meantime, Tiberius's Germanic campaign had left an uneasy calm between the Rhine and the Elbe, more like torpor than voluntary inactivity. And yet, the natives had learned much from his passage; it had taught them how a Roman army moves on the field, under the orders of a skilful commander. When they attacked and on what kind of terrain, and what kinds of situations they tried to avoid.

Arminius soon began to travel through tribal territory, with the pretext of scouting and of meeting with the most important Germanic chiefs in order to gauge their reactions and discover their intentions. He began with his own ancestral people: the Cherusci, who had accepted him as their head after the death of his father Sigmer. Flavus played no part in Arminius's plan. Knowing Flavus, it wasn't even conceivable to think of convincing him, even though he had promised his father he would try.

Some of the Germanic chieftains were opposed to Arminius's ideas: 'But weren't you at the service of the Romans? Aren't you still? How many Germanic warriors did you kill in battle, fighting under their orders? How can we listen to you? You want to drag us into war to satisfy your own ambitions, not because you love us and want us free!'

Arminius answered point by point. When he had the floor, his eyes gleamed and his voice thundered. He'd often listened to the great orators in the Roman forum haranguing the crowd from the rostra. He'd memorized their movements and gestures, their tone of voice, and mastered the way they paused to create expectation. He'd even trained in public speaking in the school on the Aventine. But it was all much more difficult here; he found himself having to give explanations where there were none to be had.

He spoke from his gut: 'I'm no different from you. How many times have you killed warriors from other Germanic tribes and how many of your fathers fought with the Romans? Mine did, for one. How many of your warriors fight at their sides as auxiliaries? Many of them are even part of the Praetorian Guard that protect the emperor. And I was no different.

But do you know why we do this? Because we don't know that we are stronger than they are! We continue to combat each other and to accept everything that the Romans impose upon us. But we can defeat them. We can unite and put together an army of one hundred thousand warriors! I know everything about the Roman army, and I know how to defeat them. Taken one by one, they're small men, weaker than any of us, less courageous, and less tough.

'The time has come to liberate Germania. I don't want to see their fasces or their axes any more! I don't want to see their togas! I've learned that my spirit cannot be bartered with anything and there is nothing in the world that is worth losing our freedom for.'

Thus he spoke, and little by little he convinced many of the chieftains to follow him and trust in him. He met with them in secret in the wood where they would never be seen. He made sure to know who he was talking to, and even surer to find out more about the ones who did not light up with enthusiasm at his words, but listened in silence.

Soon the new governor, Publius Quinctilius Varus, arrived and very shortly thereafter Arminius was summoned to Rome's headquarters on the Rhine.

He wore his toga.

Varus received him with joy as if he were an old comrade in arms. 'I can barely believe my eyes!' he said. 'It seems like yesterday that we were riding with Vetilius and Corvus through the desert of Carrhae.'

Arminius returned his greeting with warmth. 'Please allow me to congratulate you for the position the emperor has entrusted you with. I hope you will be able to exercise your authority in the most fruitful of ways. Consider me at your complete disposition.'

Varus had had dinner prepared and, with dinner, a surprise: Vetilius and Corvus appeared suddenly and embraced Arminius like an old friend.

'You look wonderful in that toga!' exclaimed Corvus. 'Whoever would have thought . . .'

'Remember that night in Antioch?' added Vetilius.

'Who could forget it,' replied Arminius, laughing. 'I learned more things that night than in all the years I'd lived until then!'

They continued with light talk, chuckling over the obscenities that the two legionary officers recounted non-stop, drinking the wine that was continuously replenished. It was the kind of evening that you could have expected Taurus to show up for, although he never did, nor was he ever brought up in conversation. Arminius breathed a sigh of relief; he would have been uncomfortable the whole evening had Taurus been there.

When they'd finished eating, Varus took Arminius's arm and walked outside with him. 'I'm glad to have found you here, my boy. I have a very important plan in mind for this land, and men like you will be indispensable. There have been too many wars here; I want peace. I want the people to understand what the law is and what enormous advantages can come for them with respecting the law. Not even the law of Rome, just the law, the natural order that protects the weak against the bullies, that ensures that what's right prevails over what is unlawful.'

Arminius thought of the two thousand Judaeans that Varus had crucified when he was governor of Syria.

'You understand our way of life and you know your people as well. With you by my side I can bring – after so many years of war – a period of peace in which arts and trade can thrive, along with craftsmanship, education . . . in which your people will understand that respect of the law is an advantage for everyone . . . Will you help me?'

'I'll certainly help you,' replied Arminius. 'Everyone will benefit.'

IT WOULD BE nearly a year before Varus assumed full authority, and Arminius spent the time perfecting his plan in every detail. The Cherusci were the first to fall in line with his vision, first of all because with Sigmer gone, Arminius was his only heir, seeing that Flavus had made his choice of irrevocable loyalty to the Empire, and secondly, because his words had won them over. Their conduct towards Rome continued to be impeccable, so that the governor would never have any reason to suspect them of untoward intentions. Arminius then turned to the Bructeri, who lived between Lipias and the Ems, and then to the Chatti, warriors accustomed to keeping disciplined battle lines and capable of forming strong infantry units. He was shown Thor's Oak, a thousand-year-old sacred tree with an immense trunk, populated by nocturnal birds of prey who by day found shelter in the deep shadows of the numerous trunk hollows and gaping scars. Arminius felt confused and quite moved by the sight. None of the naked statues in Rome could compare to the purity and power of that immense moss-covered tree.

Arminius turned to the Marsi as well, even though they were the smallest tribe in that part of Germania. Their allegiance would ensure continuity of territory, and moreover they were fantastically resistant to pain, hunger and the cold. Altogether, the Germanic peoples covered a vast area, many parts of which were impervious to anyone who did not have a profound knowledge of the territory.

When he reported back to Varus it was to speak of his patient mediation and extraordinary results in consolidating Rome's alliances. He was always at Varus's side as an intermediary when the governor had dealings with the tribesmen. He seemed a model Roman citizen and *Eques* to all intents and purposes. This served to increasingly convince Varus that the consequence of Tiberius's campaigns had been the tribes' willing capitulation to Rome, driven by their desire for peace.

The governor spent the next summer and autumn travelling from one community to another and administering justice personally wherever he went, as if he were a praetor in the Roman forum instead of the governor of a rebellious, hostile and never before tamed territory.

Germanic tribal justice was simple. Whenever there was a conflict between two warriors or notables, it was settled by a fight. The loser was wrong, the winner was right. The weaker party could choose to surrender and recognize the rights of his adversary. Bravery and boldness were at the heart of this non-written law, and problems were solved directly by the two parties involved. Varus instead implemented Roman law, ignoring Germanic customs. He applied the law inflexibly, humiliating those subject to judgement. Few of the tribesmen spoke of rebellion because the memory of Tiberius was still very fresh, but as time passed, greater numbers of warriors were attracted to Arminius's plan and the desire for revenge became stronger than their fear.

The winter was very harsh that year, and Varus ordered the army to take to their winter quarters earlier than usual. Arminius received permission to return to his father's house in the land of the Cherusci to look after his mother, who was a widow now and lived alone. Varus offered no objections. Velleius or Taurus might have seen things differently, but they had not been stationed to headquarters. Velleius had returned to Rome and Augustus had entrusted him with the task of conducting a legion to Illyria to reinforce Tiberius, who was still facing fierce resistance from the peoples of the regions in revolt. A great honour, which the legate did not fail to note on the tablets he still carried with him. One day he would write his memories. As far as Taurus was concerned, no one knew where he was, although rumour had it that he had returned to Italy to the bedside of his nearly eighty-year-old mother.

Alarming reports began to filter through to the command of the Army of the North regarding strange encounters and movements of the tribes along the Rhine. Several of the officers tried to learn more but with very little success. It did not go unnoticed that the moments in which the rumours were circulating happened to coincide with Arminius's absences from the winter quarters.

They would have been surprised to see him sitting next to the fire talking with his mother.

'Are you still in love with Thusnelda?'

'More than ever.'

'Stop hoping.'

'Where is she?'

'You're asking me?'

'You know everything, Mother. Everyone confides in you. So?'

'She's with her sister, who's about to give birth. At the village, on the little lake.'

The next day Arminius set off in the direction of the little lake, where his father had always kept a hunting shack. He settled in with Borr, his horse. Just so he might see her. Even from a distance.

She appeared two days later. She went to the spring, broke the ice with a little axe and took some into the house. The setting sun had just emerged from the clouds and its rays made the millions of miniscule ice crystals sparkle and set her golden hair aflame. Arminius wanted to leave his hiding place, but he didn't wish to frighten her. He thought of the day he'd first seen her and it brought to mind the prophecy of the Chatti: the one girl who sees Freya under her eyelids the day the rites of spring were celebrated would be given the gift of prophecy. And she would pronounce an oracle on the eve of a great battle. The sun had been setting on that long-ago day and the sun was setting now, over an expanse of snow. He reflected at length, then waited for night to fall and lay down to rest. He would depart early the next morning.

Dawn roused the lands of ice and although the sun was just a sliver of light on the horizon, it whitened the sky and lit up the snow on the ground. Arminius mounted his horse and retraced his tracks to return home. He had seen her, but he hadn't dared speak to her. After a short while, he urged his mount into a stream at the bottom of the valley so as not to leave a trail. He was thirsty, and several times he slid down the side of his horse, a white stallion that vanished in the snow like a pegasus disappears among the clouds. He travelled downstream for a while, then exited and climbed up the hill to his left. From there he could see a long valley that opened on the southern side of the little torrent; it was black with fir trees that left space here and there for gigantic skeletal oaks. He'd never gone that way before and he set off, although he was aware he might get lost.

The colossal oaks and the firs that pierced the sky filled him with an unfamiliar feeling halfway between wonder and fear. The wind whistled through the valley, hissing among the oak branches and bending the tips of the fir trees. He sensed that he should turn back, but there was something pushing him forward. He stopped for a moment on a high bit of land and looked as far into the distance as he could. All he could hear was the rush of the torrent and the snorting of his stallion puffing out little clouds of steam. He tried to move on, but the horse baulked as if something was wrong.

'Come on, Borr, forward! What is it? What are you afraid of?'

Borr scraped the ground with his hoof and dilated his nostrils. Arminius stroked his neck to calm him and as the wind seemed to abate, he suddenly sensed a presence behind him. He unsheathed his sword and spun around.

Thusnelda.

'What are you doing here?' he asked her. 'Why are you alone?'

'Because I like you. And because no one even dares to look at the daughter of Seghest.'

'I've dared. I've been watching for two days, freezing for days and nights, and you haven't noticed.'

'I didn't know it was you, but I felt it.'

'And I felt you, spirit of the dawn and of sunset. I fell in love with you without even knowing what love was. I've desired you without knowing what desire was since I was an adolescent. I dreamed of you in the perfumed nights of Rome and Damascus; you appeared to me light as air. I could smell the fragrance of your skin and of your hair even though I've never been close to you. Why did you follow me?'

'Because I saw you leaving. I recognized you and I wanted to see you, talk to you. I've dreamed of you too under the resin-scented beams of my bedroom.'

Arminius sprang to the ground and she let herself slip from the side of her horse as well.

They were facing each other.

'I remember the first time I saw you at the festival of spring. I was dazzled by your beauty, by the way you looked at me. Then you closed your eyes. They say that the girl who Freya appears to in the darkness of her closed eyelids receives the gift of prophecy. Were you that girl? Did Freya appear to you? Did she?' Arminius insisted.

Thusnelda looked into his eyes but did not answer.

They were very close. The wind picked up and blew their capes into a tangle. An eagle circled wide above them letting out a shrill cry that echoed between the smooth slabs of rock that covered the sides of the mountains.

'After I returned from Italy,' said Arminius, 'I was called to come home, to the bedside of my father who was dying. Sigmer, fearless warrior and my teacher. I have a brother, Wulf, who now bears the name of a slave, Flavus. He and I were captured by the Romans and deported to Italy, to Rome, to make us Romans. But I know now that it was fate that allowed me to be taken. Before he died, my father consulted the Germanic oracle, the same that once pronounced General Drusus's death sentence.'

'Armin . . .' murmured Thusnelda. He could feel the heat of her body so close that it warmed his chest. He took her right hand and put it on his heart so she could feel it pounding, his passion.

'My shining star,' he said. In the sky a single star remained, trembling in the clear winter blue. 'Now I know what he went to ask and what answer he got.'

Thusnelda shivered, not from the cold, and said, 'You will die first,' and she was speaking of Drusus.

'Do you know the second part of the prophecy too? What was revealed to my father, about me?' asked Arminius. His eyes filled with tears.

'You will die after,' she said.

'After what?' Arminius went on, his voice strong.

'After you have fought the great battle . . . and after your most relentless adversary has died.'

Arminius dropped his head. Thusnelda was silent for a while, then spoke again: 'You're still in time.'

'No. I've come all this way and I can't turn back. But tell me, my love: what did my father see for the future of our people and what did he dream of?'

'Blood,' the voice coming from the girl's lips trembled. 'A people drowning in blood.'

They were breathing in each other's mouths. Arminius felt suffocated by the horror of that vision, but his lips joined hers, open to welcome him. Perhaps he'd already done this in a dream. He embraced her and held her tightly to his chest. He had no more strength to speak.

Half of the sky turned dark while the other half was still blue, staining the snowy peaks of the mountains. The snow came from the north, a flurry of white flakes. The black fir valley was shrouded in white.

'I have to travel down this valley to the end,' said Arminius, 'but I'll take you back to your sister's house first. I'll come back for you when I've reached my destination.'

'I'm coming with you,' said the girl.

'You can't. We don't have provisions and you aren't dressed for this.'

She shook her head, jumped on her horse and flanked Arminius on his steed. They set off and Borr advanced obediently, urged on by the heels of his master.

THE VALLEY WAS completely covered by forests: huge oaks, white-hooded fir trees that stood out against the sky, age-old, twisted field maples, towering birches shaped like candlesticks, their silvery barks streaked black. Flakes of snow gathered on the autumn leaves still clinging to the tips of the smallest branches and formed sheets that slid downwards, making small thudding sounds as they fell to join the snow on the ground.

They advanced at a walk, hour after hour, until the sun which had maintained a small dominion over a strip of sky finally hid behind the dense fir forest, casting long shadows. Then the sun dropped below the horizon but the snow continued to reflect a glow that spread over the silent countryside.

Before it became pitch-dark and the cold became too bitter, Arminius dismounted to search for a shelter under one of the mountainside cliffs. He found a little cave and widened the entrance, removing the loose detritus with his sword and dagger. The tumbling of the gravel and sand were the only sounds to be heard in the immense valley that extended for many leagues downstream and towards west. Their shelter was finally ready and even comfortable, in its own way. Arminius had set aside some dry sand and had spread it evenly over the floor of the little cave, and had then lain the raw wool blankets he kept tied to Borr's back over the sand, leaving one to protect the horse from the cold of night. He laid a bearskin that he had taken from Sigmer's hunting shack over the blankets and he helped Thusnelda enter the cave. They still needed a fire. He made a heap of pine needles and on one side placed some very thin resinous branches. He struck a spark using the flint he always carried with him on his solitary journeys. He was used to the Roman army, where the fire was never allowed to go out and anyone could use a firebrand to start his own. As soon as the pine needles caught, he added the resinous twigs and then bigger and bigger pieces of wood until he had built a big crackling fire.

'It'll keep the wolves away,' he said. 'They can smell the horses, and they'll attack immediately unless we stave them off.'

'So fire keeps the wolves away?' asked Thusnelda.

'It's the smoke, more than the fire. When they smell smoke

they're afraid the forest is burning and they run off in the other direction. Bears will do the same.' He remembered the flaming torch that someone had thrown onto the hilltop, when he and his brother were surrounded by wolves.

Who could it have been? A god, perhaps? Or a mortal man?

'Just think,' he said aloud, 'if there were someone on that mountain top and he happened to turn this way . . . our fire would be the only light in all this darkness, in all the visible universe. The only presence, the only warmth. My father Sigmer told us that when the Frisii came running to help General Drusus when his ships had run aground in the low tide, each one of them held a torch, and it looked like a river of fire was flowing that night on the beach, between the forest and the ocean.'

Thusnelda looked into Arminius's eyes. 'A river of fire . . .'

Arminius undressed. The light of the flames flickered over his muscles and made his skin glow like polished bronze.

'I can't sleep with clothes on,' he said with a touch of embarrassment.

'Neither can I,' whispered Thusnelda. She loosened the laces on her red wool dress and let it fall like a rose that withered at her feet.

They sought each other under the bearskin, frenetically, with hands, lips, nails. Her face lost in a cloud of gold, his arms clasping her waist to pull her close, to feel the fire in her loins. When she guided him in, he saw her eyes widen and light up in ecstasy, mirroring the rising flames. He felt himself sinking into an ocean of fire and he lost every sense of time or place.

A wolf's howl echoed through the mountains and Thusnelda held on tighter to Arminius's chest. Borr kicked and neighed loudly. The two lovers let themselves fall back alongside each other, panting and exhausted, brows pearled with sweat.

*

IN THE MIDDLE of the night Thusnelda woke up suddenly with a scream. Arminius startled, then gathered her into his arms.

'What's wrong? Did you have a bad dream?'

'Yes. The torrent, flowing full of blood, dragging dead bodies stained red . . . What are you going to do, Armin? What is all that blood?'

'You must tell me. You who saw Freya smile at you behind your closed eyelids.'

'I don't know . . . I saw the torrent flooding over with blood,' she continued repeating.

'I'm going to unite all the Germanic peoples in a single nation. I want to build an invincible Germanic empire and to drive the Romans out. Out of our lands. Forever.'

'Whatever you do, whatever delirium, whatever carnage I'm witness to, I will always be with you. If I can, I will give you a son, so he can fulfil your legacy, when the time comes.'

The wolf let out another howl that echoed through the entire black forest valley. Borr pawed the ground and scraped the icy snow with his hooves. Just then the moon pierced through the wandering clouds and lit up the marshes and swamps at the end of the valley.

When they were almost asleep again, they heard thunder, although the sky had cleared and no clouds hovered above them. The sound was close, although it seemed distant and somehow stifled; it made the earth tremble and their hearts faltered.

'What is that?' asked Arminius, as if he were talking to himself.

Thusnelda looked at him with a dismayed expression. 'It's the hammer,' she replied, 'the hammer of Thor.'

'It will be here,' said Arminius. 'This dark valley will be their tomb.'

23

THE ARMY SPENT MOST of the summer in camp, while Varus travelled to different parts of north Germania with a robust escort, to administer justice. Arminius could not understand if someone had given him that apparently absurd order or if it was his own initiative. Many young men had begun to become enamoured with Roman civilization, but the veteran warriors who had experienced the force of Tiberius's armies and then the justice of the new governor were disgusted and repulsed by this new way of resolving problems between individuals or tribes that was completely foreign to them. They also could not bear to pay taxes: they saw them as a tribute that subjugated peoples had to pay to their victors, and they did not consider themselves anybody's servants.

Arminius often accompanied Varus, and at times they crossed through actual cities under construction, with roads, squares, basilicas, theatres and baths. Mountains of stone and of white Lunense marble, huge piles of wood to build the frames for archways and the vaults for house ceilings and other materials were continuously brought in from every corner of the Empire. This enormous movement of men and supplies involved the circulation of money, and with money came the possibility of buying goods and objects never seen before. In the Roman mentality, the city was the place where the barbarians would realize that up until that moment they'd been living more like animals than human beings. It was the place where the mentality and the customs of men and of peoples could change. For Romans, the *Urbs* – the city – and the *Orbis* – the world – were one and the same, and every city had to evoke the majesty of Rome.

MEANWHILE, ARMINIUS HAD persuaded an ever growing number of chieftains to unite with him. Even the Cherusci, who had accepted Roman terms, were anxious to take their independence back and couldn't wait to take up arms. But Arminius had fought with Tiberius. He had seen the devastating power of the Roman armies and he'd understood perfectly that his own warriors, even the very best of them, those with the soul of the wolf or the bear, would never be able to win on the field of battle against the Romans. He had convinced them that he alone knew how to crush those apparently invincible formations, but he needed total freedom of command to do so.

The only thing that made him anxious on his journeys with Varus was being separated from Thusnelda. Being away from her stopped him from thinking, even stopped him from speaking at times.

He had promised himself that he would have her and that moment had come. He sent a message through a slave girl who served in camp in exchange for a bracelet and an amber ring. She was to say this: they would meet in a secluded place, in the forest where he'd first seen her crowned with flowers for the festival of spring. She must come dressed in men's clothing so as to ride away in haste. At dusk.

'Will she come?' he asked the slave girl when she returned.

'It wasn't easy to talk to her, but I managed in the end. She will.'

Arminius added a few coins to the jewellery he'd promised her, so she could spend them at camp. He spent days planning for their meeting. As the moment drew closer, he felt more and more apprehensive: did he have the right to take her away with him, take her away from the future that her father, Seghest, had wanted for her? Would he be capable of giving her a happy life? The only thing he was sure about was the feelings they shared; everything else was in the hands of the gods. He showed up at the appointed place on foot, holding Borr by the reins. Such a long time passed that he feared she wasn't coming, but when he saw her arrive, at the time in which the shadows begin to lengthen, he realized that he had got there too early. Thusnelda leapt off her mount lightly and let him free to graze in the field.

'There's no escaping my father's watchful eye,' she said. 'I'm afraid he'll be out here any moment looking for me.'

'Then we don't have much time.'

Thusnelda threw her arms around him.

'For what?' she said. 'For this?'

She kissed him.

'No. I want us to go away together. I want you to come with me and to live with me, always.'

'My father won't give up. He'll get help from the Romans.'

'There aren't going to be any Romans any more. It's going to be only us. He'll have to accept what we are. I am yours and you are mine.'

Thusnelda pulled away. 'He'll consider it an abduction. I am promised.'

'I have the command of four Germanic nations and others will join us. I'm not afraid of anyone if you are with me.'

'He's my father.'

'Then you have to choose.'

'I already did when I spent the night with you in that cave and the hammer of Thor thundered through the valley.'

'Then come with me, now. I've had a house built for us, in a secret place.'

The two of them rode off at a gallop through the impenetrable forest, down a path flanked by a steep precipice, then raced through a hidden valley until it narrowed to snake between two wooded slopes placed so that the passage between couldn't be seen until one was quite close. On the other side was a thick wood of oak and beech trees, its floor covered with tangled undergrowth. In the middle of this wood, a clearing. On one side of the clearing rose a well-built house of wood and stone cut from the mountainside. Horses grazed all around.

'Here no one will find you. No one can approach without being seen, and stopped. There are fifty armed men in the forest. You can't see them but they're there. They are my most loyal men and the most courageous. We can spend the night here and, if you like, many more nights.'

Two days later, Seghest launched his men in a search for Thusnelda in every corner of the land, its woods and pastures. They returned empty-handed, but the last group to come back brought a herdsman with them. He claimed to have seen a beautiful girl in men's clothing and a strong-looking young warrior meeting at the well of spring. Seghest had no doubt that the girl was Thusnelda and that she had been abducted by Arminius, son of Sigmer.

DURING THE SECOND part of the summer, Publius Quinctilius Varus chose to stay in the entrenched camps near the Rhine and gave no indication he was planning to move from there. Arminius went to him with the auxiliaries he commanded, to join the army corps made up of three legions, the Seventeenth, the

Eighteenth and the Nineteenth, along with six cohorts of infantry and three cavalry squadrons. Such a force hadn't been seen on the march since the time of Tiberius and also General Drusus before him, but for the moment Varus seemed to be deploying them merely as a show of force, without any real intentions of drawing them up on the battlefield.

Arminius settled into the camp on a stable basis and he was often invited to dinner by the governor. He took the opportunity to reminisce about their journeys in the East, never forgetting to bring up his titillating encounters in the forbidden quarters of Antioch, giving rise to much laughter and many salacious remarks. He scrupulously avoided any mention of their excursion into the desert of Carrhae so that Varus wouldn't be prone to thinking about certain things, such as the danger of penetrating into little known territories peopled with untrustworthy natives.

It truly seemed that moving Varus out of his fortified quarters was impossible; the governor was tenaciously sticking to where he felt safe. Although he may have occasionally picked up on a little discontent here and there, he was mainly convinced that the lands he had travelled through remained untroubled. When moving around to the most important centres to administer justice, he had relied on Arminius to provide reconnaissance, a task that Arminius carried out with great skill and efficiency. He was always able to assure the governor that the territory was calm and that passage would be clear. Since Varus had found this to be true in every situation, Arminius's prestige had increased accordingly, as had his familiarity with the governor.

This was why Arminius was so often invited to join Varus for meals in the praetorian tent or at headquarters in the legionary forts. Arminius was always impeccably dressed in his toga, when the regular army officer uniform of field tunic, cape, *balteus* and sword was not required. Allowing him to dress as he saw fit was another demonstration of trust on the governor's part.

At the same time, and especially when he had been tasked with a reconnaissance mission, Arminius joined up with his men in the forests and other secluded places that effectively made them invisible. Meetings were arranged from time to time; he utilized his scouts to confirm or change them. The Empire's system of communication had taught him many things. What had impressed him in particular was the way the movements of two army units could be synchronized, even when they were hundreds of miles away. He'd seen the way Tiberius did it with the army of Illyria and the Army of the North.

Arminius's real problem was something else. The two army corps that Tiberius had concentrated on Marbod's kingdom were part of the same army: they marched under the same standards and obeyed the same commander. Arminius, on the other hand, would have to first lure Varus out of his quarters and convince him to penetrate into the interior, a task that was becoming increasingly complicated, and then coordinate the movements of not one, but two enemy armies, made up of tens of thousands of men: the Germanic army under his direct orders, and Varus's army, which must be induced to walk straight into the trap already waiting for them. Another huge problem was keeping his plan secret until it was time to strike. If Varus became suspicious, or was informed about what was being planned, Arminius was sure to meet an atrocious fate, even if he was a Roman citizen.

He decided to deal with one problem at a time. He began by urging Varus to move into the interior.

'If I may be so bold, Governor, given your close relationship with the emperor and the trust he has shown in you, don't you think he may fail to be impressed if you never move from the fortified castra? You've seen for yourself how calm the country has become. You've spent enough time in Rome to know that your worst enemies might not be here but there, in the capital. They surely have informers here who report on every move you make, or don't make. It could be taken as a form of inertia, or lack of initiative on your part.'

Varus shrugged. 'Let those informers fuck themselves. I've administered justice, as I was meant to do. I don't see why I should push my luck and provoke the Germanic tribes into reacting. There's a saying where I come from: "Let sleeping dogs lie." And what's more, it's getting close to winter.'

'True. I was just saying . . . because I know you consider me your friend. But you know, if you wanted to, there would be a way to win a great deal of credit without any risk.'

'Really? And just what would that entail?'

'A big parade, or an expedition if we want to call it that, from here to the Weser. The Elbe is too far. It would give you enormous prestige without putting a single man at risk.'

'Interesting. Just what do you mean by that?'

'You'd simply be passing through the territory of a big, bellicose nation, which will not lift a finger against you. People will line the way as your troops march by with their eagles and standards.'

'Which nation would that be?'

'My own. The Cherusci are my people now that my father is gone. Now they obey me. To make you feel even safer, I'll be watching your flanks and your back.'

'I will have to think about it,' replied Varus.

Arminius now felt more uneasy than he ever had; not only

had he not managed to convince him, but Varus would certainly consult others whose advice would be very different from his. He risked failing all the way down the line. A more concrete reason was needed to convince the governor to move his troops; a stroll to the Weser wouldn't do it.

That same evening, Arminius had the idea that could overcome Varus's reluctance: a request for help, or even several. He wouldn't be able to refuse. Arminius immediately sent for one of his most trustworthy men and gave him the job. He would depart at once, in secret, and return within three days' time at the most, asking to report directly to the governor. Arminius wouldn't move; he would wait to be summoned.

The horseman set off and the commander of the Germanic Auxilia returned to his normal life in the legionary fort. Three days later, his man arrived as they had planned, showing all the signs of an arduous journey: his horse was exhausted, his clothing was torn, his face was scratched and he was clearly suffering from hunger and thirst. He told the guards at the front gate that he had urgent messages for the governor.

It wasn't long before Arminius was called to the praetorian tent, where he found Varus intent on speaking with his man, who showed no sign at all of knowing Arminius.

'This brave horseman has brought me messages. In part orally and in part written in very poor Latin. Take a look and see what you think.'

Arminius scanned the document with attention and interest. He explained: 'It seems that the communities which are furthest away from here are asking for support and a stable garrison to defend them against the raids of enemy tribes, to re-establish order and to ensure the passage of provisions . . . foodstuffs and other supplies.'

Varus was silent for a short time.

'You could very well ignore these requests . . .' Arminius spoke up again, trying to elicit a clear response from Varus.

'I don't think that would be a good decision,' said Varus. 'If we don't respond to a call for help like this one, how can we call this place one of our provinces? Is your offer of passing through the territory of the Cherusci still valid?'

'Certainly, Governor. I'll just send a group of my horsemen ahead to alert everyone to our passage. In any case, I will ride at your side to ensure your safety. And now that you've made your decision, please allow me to tell you that you're doing the right thing. Right now, the emperor's attention is not focused on Palestine or Armenia or the border with the Parthians. His attention is focused here. Play your opportunities well while you're here. It is in Germania that the future of the world is being decided.'

Varus stared into his eyes as though he was trying to read his thoughts. 'You say so? And why would that be?'

'Germania is a poor country. There's no ivory here, nor gold, nor vast fields of wheat. No olive trees or grape vines grow here; all the land is good for is raising livestock.'

'Then why does Augustus care so much about it?'

'Augustus is looking at the future. He has founded a monarchic system destined to last for a long time, if not forever. But he needs the Empire to last forever too. The Germanics can pose a great danger and that's been abundantly clear. Twenty years of war have not tamed them. They are multiplying and they can deploy big armies without going to any great expense; they are warriors at heart. Meanwhile, the Empire's forces are spread over a vast area and the costs of running the army can only increase. Our greatest poet, Horace, has prophesized that one day the barbarians will take over Rome herself.'

'Poets are not prophets.'

'But Horace is close to the emperor and he is familiar with his worries. And that's why Germania must become Roman, at any cost.'

'Is that what you really think?' asked Varus.

'How could you doubt it?'

Varus peered at him again, intensely, but he saw only the icy bright blue of his gaze. Nothing filtered through.

'I don't,' he said in the end. 'I have no doubts.' He seemed lost in thought for a while, and then said, 'I have to check my mail before I lie down. A good night to you.'

Arminius asked to be dismissed and Varus retired to his private study.

THE CALL OF the second guard shift startled the governor as he was sealing the last parcel to send out with the first messenger the following morning. As he was preparing for bed, a freedman of about forty named Ausonius knocked on his door to announce an urgent, unexpected visit.

'Who is it?' asked Varus as Ausonius entered.

'His name is Seghest, he is a nobleman of the Cherusci nation. He has to see you immediately for a matter of the utmost importance.'

Varus nodded and Seghest practically burst into his study.

'I must speak to you about a very serious matter, Governor,' he began.

'Speak freely. I know that you and your tribe have always been faithful allies of Rome. This is your house and you are always welcome here.'

Seghest thanked him with a bow of his head and immediately began blurting out words with great agitation. Ausonius remained to translate.

'A revolt is being planned, an attack on you and your men. The person behind it all is your friend Arminius.'

Varus seemed lightning-struck. 'Arminius? But he's the best of my men.'

'He is a traitor. A man without integrity and without honour! Hear me out, Governor: he is gathering a huge force in order to strike at you and annihilate you. Have him arrested and put into chains at once. Arrest me too!'

'You too? Why should I arrest you?'

'Because I am an important chief of the Cherusci people and without me my men will feel abandoned. Arrest his friends as well and put them in irons. No one will dare move if you do as I say. The Germanics are lost without a leader.'

'I will do no such thing. What you're suggesting would be an act of hostility against an ally. What's more, against a Roman citizen. Just the thing for setting off rioting and revolts. I must investigate such an outlandish claim. He has offered to ride at my side, you see; how can he attack my army if he is at my side?'

'I know what I'm saying, Governor. I beseech you, arrest everyone. Arrest me! Torture them and they will talk.'

'You're tired, Seghest, and so am I. Let's go to sleep. We'll talk about this tomorrow, when our minds are fresh. Ausonius, have my guest accompanied to his quarters.'

Seghest followed a servant carrying a lantern, grumbling and cursing in his harsh language. Ausonius stayed behind.

'What do you make of this?' asked the governor.

'There's a reason why he's furious, master, and it's because Arminius has abducted his daughter, the splendid Thusnelda, who he had promised to another nobleman. He would do anything to see him in chains, whipped and tortured. It's just his personal honour he's concerned with. I would stay well clear of this if I were you.'

'I'm sure you're right,' replied the governor, and with Ausonius's help he undressed, baring the considerable girth at his middle, and then put on his dressing gown, covering it again.

WHEN THE GOVERNOR finally left his fort on the Rhine, he joined Arminius's auxiliaries who had preceded him to the other side of the river. They headed with the entire army towards Cherusci territory, where Varus was greeted with manifestations of friendship. He felt increasingly reassured that Seghest had been motivated by personal rancour. There could be nothing true in his accusations with such a reception. Arminius never left Varus's side; even if he had wanted to, there was no opportunity for him to bring harm upon the governor.

Varus arrived at the territory belonging to the tribes that had asked for his protection. He left several garrisons to protect them from enemy raids. Establishing a solid alliance also meant that they would provide support at his rear as he moved on and could ensure safe passage when he decided to return to his camp on the Rhine. In the meanwhile, a man sent by Seghest asked to be received and Varus rather reluctantly agreed to see him.

'You must listen,' the man told him, 'if you've decided not to arrest Arminius, at least turn back now before it's too late.'

Varus replied that he couldn't base his plans on gossip and that he would not show unjustified distrust, much less open hostility, towards the Germanics. The man gave up. There was simply no convincing him.

Having terminated his expedition in the direction of the Weser, Varus began thinking about manoeuvring his army for re-entry to base. He was quite satisfied that everything had gone so well.

That evening, Arminius approached him, saying that an urgent situation demanded his attention.

'Governor,' he said, 'I've just been informed that one of the tribes dwelling in the north-western territory has rebelled, killing Roman citizens who were attempting to establish contact and commercial dealings with them. Certainly it's not a good idea to leave this deed unpunished: their example could become contagious.

'We would have to take a different route, but it wouldn't rob us of too much time. They live in the stretch of land between the hills and the plain that extends all the way to the ocean shore. I could open the way with my cavalry; that way we'll be sure the situation is secure before you have to make your way in unfamiliar territory.'

Varus agreed. The legionaries grumbled when they heard about the detour; they were tired of long marches wearing their heavy armour and they couldn't wait to be dismissed so they could enter their winter quarters, much more comfortable than their camp.

Arminius seized on their discontent to introduce another topic with Varus: 'I know that you've been hearing some slanderous stories about me and I wanted to tell you how things really stand. It's untrue that I abducted Seghest's daughter. We fell in love the first time we saw each other, many years ago. I'd asked for her hand many times. Through my father at first, and then through a number of our noblemen. It was all in vain. Seghest has always been scornful and offensive towards me and he refused, making any number of unjust accusations against me. She and I were in love; we had no choice but to run off together. Thusnelda followed me of her own accord, listening to her heart instead of respecting propriety. I hope you believe me.'

Arminius's eyes shone and his words were so spontaneous they could not be false. Varus reassured him of his trust and the next day Arminius set off at the head of the column. The valley was wide and the ground was dry, the weather fresh and agreeable. At a certain point, he rode over to Varus's position. 'There's a difficult passage at about fifteen miles from here. I'll take a hundred of my men and move forward to reconnoitre. If you agree, we'll remain to secure the pass until we see you arriving. We can't be too careful.'

Varus was impressed by the sagacity of the commander of his Germanic auxiliaries and watched as Arminius galloped off down the valley.

For two days, all went well. No cause for worry or alarm. Only the skies were gradually becoming more threatening, but Arminius had foreseen that as well. When night fell on the second day Varus gave orders to halt the march. As usual, the tribunes and centurions instructed the sentries and guard patrols to take position. There was no room to pitch camp properly and this led to general disgruntlement and uneasiness. A blare of a trumpet warned that someone was arriving and thunderous galloping immediately reached their ears. Before Varus had the time to ask himself who it might be, he found himself facing a dozen horsemen. They were led by a man covered in dust and panting for breath: Primus Pilus Centurion Marcus Caelius Taurus.

'Commander,' he demanded, 'what are you doing here?'

Varus felt the earth shift under his feet. 'Arminius told me that there was a small tribe in rebellion along this route. I've come to restore order.'

Taurus's brow wrinkled. 'Arminius? Where is he now?'

'He went ahead with a hundred of his horsemen to occupy

the pass and ensure it stays clear until we arrive. But what are you doing here?'

'An attack is underway against all of our garrisons. They are thousands strong and they're massacring us. I'd come to ask you for reinforcements, but I see that's impossible. Your column is more than two miles long. There's no room for you to manoeuvre here, much less regroup. You can't even build a camp. How did you let yourself get dragged into this gully? All we can do is use the carts to set up a defensive perimeter.'

Varus gave the order to do so immediately, while the news Taurus had brought travelled up and down the column of soldiers and their blood ran cold.

A suffocated sound could be heard at the same time, like thunder, but different: deep, muffled but very, very powerful. It crashed into the mountainsides and made the ground tremble.

'What is that?' asked Varus,

'The hammer of Thor,' replied Taurus. 'It means "no mercy". Arminius won't be coming back.' As he said these words he saw panic flooding the eyes of Varus, who could not grasp what was happening. How had Arminius convinced him to put his neck under the Germanic axe?

PART THREE

24

ARMIN HAD PREPARED THE greatest war operation ever attempted on the field against the Roman forces occupying Germania. A large number of tribal chieftains and warriors of the noble class had approved and agreed to implement his plan. The one thing that joined them together was the conviction that the prince of the Cherusci was the only person capable of defeating the Romans because he knew their military system so well and where their weak spots were to be found. But not all of the combatants were so sure. The devastating attack conducted by Tiberius three years before was lodged firmly in their minds, and they feared the overwhelming strength of the imperial legions.

He needed a way of showing them that they could win by creating a situation where they could strike without ever facing the powerful Roman formations drawn up in all their glory, or Rome's best combat units, and they could attack from a secure and unassailable vantage point.

The place to which he had lured Quinctilius Varus, the Teutoburg Forest, was perfect in every way for this purpose. A mortal trap; a slaughterhouse rather than a field of battle.

Taurus had no doubts about what was about to happen. Sergius Vetilius and Rufius Corvus had already informed him of Seghest's mission; of how he had tried to convince Varus that Armin was betraying him, of how he had urged him to arrest Armin, and chain him up together with his friends. Anyone would have understood that Seghest was telling the truth. Except Varus.

'We'll turn back,' said Vetilius, who had been named the legate of the Eighteenth Legion, after Velleius had followed Tiberius to Pannonia. 'It's evident that bastard is waiting for us where the road gets most narrow.'

'I don't think that'll work,' replied Taurus. 'If we reverse our direction of march, we would simply be doing an about-face; it won't change where we are. The enemy is likely to be everywhere, all around us, and could attack from one moment to the next, especially while we are trying to manoeuvre in such a treacherous area with all the carts and the pack animals. We don't even know whether the return route is clear. Many of our garrisons have already been destroyed, the warehouses and armouries sacked. I saw a lot of suspicious movement as I was making my way up here; actually, it's a miracle I'm still alive.

'There's nothing we can do now. Night is falling. Give orders to set up all possible obstacles on the left flank of the column, send out forward sentries in every direction, get some fires started and get some food to these men. They have to stay strong.'

Corvus advised the commander and the order was passed down the entire length of the column.

At the second guard shift, the weather worsened. Lightning flashed in the distance and a clap of thunder tore through the silence of the night and then continued to echo between the mountain flanks. It was rattling down to a finish when another crash sounded, low-pitched and stifled but incredibly powerful. It roared from a distant gorge, shook the earth and the hearts in the men's chests.

'They want to sow panic,' said Sergius Vetilius.

'They're succeeding,' retorted Taurus. 'Look at our men; they're terrified. They're used to doing the menacing, not feeling imperilled themselves.'

The night passed without much damage, but no one managed to close an eye, hands cramping around the hilts of their swords. At the beginning of the third guard shift, a suffocated outcry burst out of the darkness, then another and then a third. Three sentries collapsed to the ground. One was hit in the belly and his guts spilled out onto the dirt; he couldn't stop screaming. Taurus swiftly put an end to his suffering: 'Farewell, my friend. We'll see each other in hell before long.' Trees rustled in the wood; the enemy had hit their targets and were melting back into the thick forest. Only they knew all its thickets and hollows.

The army began marching again at first light – a grey light that barely filtered through the black clouds. It wasn't a road they were travelling on at all, more of a trail that wasn't always practicable. The surface was made of boulders and loose stones and both sides were covered by thick vegetation that only increased the legionaries' fears. Nature was a dark, ominous force, the forest inhabited by disturbing creatures. And there was a storm coming.

The wind arrived first, bending over the tips of the oak and beech trees. All at once, a torrential rain began to batter the weary men. A lightning bolt struck a huge old oak and an enormous branch fell across the path, wounding a number of men, crippling others and blocking their march. The injured were loaded onto one of the carts, where perhaps they would be seen by a surgeon and saved. Forward movement was becoming increasingly difficult; the carts and animals continuously hindered the march, while the pouring rain had made the ground slippery and created a state of profound discouragement in the soldiers. It was almost as if they were resigned to defeat before the battle had even begun.

The steady stream of losses increased at nearly every step. The Germanic warriors were comfortable fighting in the thick wood. Their movements were light, easy, invisible; they struck swiftly and pulled back to seek out their next hiding place. With no chance of defending themselves, the Roman soldiers felt like the sitting targets of a deadly, ruthless hunter. The deep rumble of the hammer of Thor never let up, making air and earth shudder.

'Isn't there any way to make that stop?' shouted Corvus over the din of the storm.

'How?' shouted Taurus back, even more loudly. 'The sound comes from everywhere at once. For now, all we can do is go forward until we're out of this storm and until, gods willing, we find a widening in which we can deploy our force!'

The further they went, the more frequent the enemy raids became. Sometimes a flash of blinding lightning would suddenly reveal the face of a Germanic warrior streaked with black like a ghost from hell. Their attackers wanted to wear them down, to bleed the long snake as it slithered forward. A moment came when it seemed that not even the natives could resist the raging storm. Taurus was quick to set off with a group of scouts to explore the route going forward, but it was then that a horseman appeared glittering in the rain on a black steed, his face covered by a mask of bronze.

'Who are you?' demanded Taurus.

'A Roman cavalryman,' replied the man. His voice was young, and accented. Germanic.

'What do you want?'

'I wouldn't go on, if I were you. Let me go first, along the ridge.'

Taurus thought he'd already heard that voice, but he couldn't recall when. The horseman shouted, 'Don't move!' and rode off at a gallop under the drenching rain. He spurred the horse on and disappeared into the wood. Some time went by and then he reappeared one hundred paces beyond them, on a slight rise. He tossed something at the feet of Taurus and Sergius Vetilius. The heads of two Germanic warriors.

With a wave of his hand, he gestured that they could advance, and then he disappeared again. At that point, Taurus turned his horse and rode back to where the general commander, Governor Quinctilius Varus, was. Vetilius stayed where he was, at the head of the army, loathe to relinquish control of the riskiest position. He also thought that it was worth making sure that the masked horseman had liberated an observation post by taking out the enemy sentries.

Taurus informed the governor that he intended to advance with a few men beyond the head of the column to see if he could find a passage of adequate width. He rode off as fast as he could go; his path was full of holes and of jagged stones and other objects and the rain was turning it into a turbulent torrent. He skirted around a great number of damaged carts, others sunk up to their wheel hubs in mud. Many of the pack animals had been crippled by the sharp rocks underfoot. The hundreds of civilians that accompanied the army to sell food, wine, clothing and other wares were hindering the march, especially because they insisted on sticking as close as they could to the ranks in order not to fall prey to the attackers themselves. There were many women among them as well, including the camp prostitutes, and some were carrying or dragging children along as best they could, rain-soaked and sobbing with fear and fatigue.

In less than an hour, Taurus and his men had arrived at a point in which the path seemed to hold fewer obstacles to transit, although it was no less muddy and dangerous. The trail stretched along the base of a rocky hill standing about four hundred and fifty feet tall. The flatter part at the top was crossed by murky rivulets that ran down the slope of the hill and gathered in an enormous swamp towards the north. The top of the hill was completely covered with vegetation; as far as Taurus was concerned, anyone could be hiding there. But since he saw no one, he turned back to advise the rest of the army which was still stretched out into a column well beyond two miles long.

The attacks and ambushes had been intensifying and many soldiers had fallen, wounded by the arrows and javelins flung by invisible enemies. Taurus shuddered when he realized that these were Roman weapons, raided from the garrisons attacked by the Germanic forces. The legionaries could hardly fight back in the driving rain, caught between slippery slopes to their right and left and burdened by iron armour that weighed nearly a talent. The soldiers' shoes were disintegrating on the rough surface, and many were pushing on with bloodied feet.

All at once, the storm seemed to abate and even the wind died down. All that could be heard was the sound of an army on the march – fifteen thousand men covered in iron.

They were making progress and, as Taurus had reported, the road was becoming a little smoother. One part curved at the base of the rocky hill while another forked off towards the muddy swampland. For a short time even the hammer of Thor seemed to fall silent.

A savage war cry burst out, echoing loudly, and from the hillside a cloud of darts lifted. Thousands of Germanic javelins sailed towards the sky to then plunge headlong, whistling, into the marching legion. They crashed onto raised shields and helmets like steely hail.

Taurus, who had pushed on to the head of the column, took stock of what was happening and raced back, shouting, 'To your left! Ambush! Shields on your heads! *Testudo!* We'll scale the enemy rampart! Come to me, men, to me!'

A second volley and a third followed in quick succession and the deadly rain pierced thousands of men: in the neck, between their shoulder blades, in their arms, legs, stomachs. The soil was so slimy that the legionaries were sinking up to their calves.

Rufius Corvus arrived at a gallop, spotted Taurus and joined him, protecting himself as best he could with his shield. 'They've deliberately set us down this path! They've got us right where they want us. We have to get out of here, you have to get out of the range of their javelins! Out, out! Do not attack the enemy! Don't do it, Centurion! We have to get away from here. I'm going back to head off the soldiers who are still coming on.'

Taurus, who had been ordering his men into a *testudo vallaria* formation in order to attack what he had just realized was an enemy rampart built into the hillside, retreated instead, keeping his men united in close ranks under their shields.

The enemy had raised a wall, evidently made of clods of soil and grass applied over a framework created from reeds taken from the swamp, so perfectly camouflaged that it was indistinguishable from the green cover of the rocky hill. Taurus had failed to see it himself when he'd reconnoitred the spot. Now the ground was slick with blood and the air echoed with screams of pain. The wounded men attempted to yank the arrow and spearheads out of their chests and thighs, tearing the flesh off their bones. Others were floundering in the mud and had become easy targets for the darts hurled by their enemies.

Armin waited. When he was satisfied that Varus's army had been decimated by the Germanic javelins and were dispersing, incapable of moving forward or of counter attacking, he launched the men who were still behind the wall into the assault.

The Germanic warriors had never faced the legions at close quarters before, but the Romans were in the grip of panic and confusion. It hardly seemed possible to Armin's men that they could finally unleash their long pent-up rage on the soldiers they'd put to rout. Wielding double-bladed axes, they ripped, slashed, maimed relentlessly. Striking out with blind rage, they hacked at flesh and broke bones, decapitated men who had fallen to the ground without a means of defending themselves and stuck those heads on pikes as trophies.

Taurus's unit, which was small but tough and compact, was like a rock against the breaking waves of attackers. They continued to defend themselves. All around them was horror, blood, screams, and mutilated limbs.

Numonius Vala, cavalry prefect and Varus's second in command, found himself in the middle of the long column and therefore had no idea of what was happening up ahead. He had thought at first that they were being attacked by a small rebel tribe but as he took stock of the reports filtering back from the front, he realized that one of the greatest military disasters of all time was taking place. He ordered his men to accelerate their march in order to provide support. All this achieved in the moment was to worsen the situation, adding more troops to the massacre and generating even more panic and chaos.

Taurus managed to break through to Vala, the cavalry commander. He instructed him to move his men further up the column and to deploy as many troops as possible to where the standard-bearer guarded the eagle of the Eighteenth Legion, still staunchly planted into the ground. Taurus was determined to turn the fight around. He knew that if he could get his men to an area that was sufficiently clear and slightly elevated, a makeshift camp could be organized. He could get reinforcements. He would send some of Vala's best horsemen to reach Lucius Asprenas, Varus's nephew who was quartered on the Rhine. Asprenas would send them troops, and they could turn the battle around.

Meanwhile Armin, astride Borr, was raging against the impotent, mud-mired Roman soldiers. Something soon caught his eye: towards the east, a group of resistors was regrouping around Taurus. He realized how dangerous that could prove to be, and hurled towards them, sword in hand. He was upon them before Taurus even knew what was happening.

'Two Roman soldiers . . .' shouted Armin, 'always meet up again somewhere. Don't they, Centurion?'

Taurus narrowly avoided a sweeping blow from Armin that would have lopped off his head. He gathered himself into a close guard, shield low and gladius high. Armin whipped Borr around so fast it nearly broke the horse's back and he lunged forward again at the centurion.

'You tasted my whip once and you're going to taste it again, you bastard! Man of no honour!' shouted Taurus, but he found himself on the trajectory of a horse weighing a thousand libra spurred on by a horseman six feet tall. Taurus stood his ground, solid as a statue. As soon as Borr got close enough, he thrust his Balearic sling between the horse's legs, causing him to crash to the ground along, with his rider.

'If you've hurt him, I'm going to skin you alive!' growled Armin, springing back to his feet.

'Try it!' retorted Taurus, entrenched behind his shield, the legionary eagle at his back.

They pounced on one another, swords high, sending sparks flying, but Taurus was fifty-three and Armin twenty-six. The centurion was fighting on a long sleepless night, a grinding march, hours of incessant combat and an empty stomach. His fate seemed to be sealed, when a voice rang out on their left: 'Try that with someone your own size, fucker! Not an old man!'

Armin spun around and found himself facing a man on a black stallion whose face was hidden behind a mask of bronze. He wore a Roman uniform but brandished a Germanic sword.

'Bring it on!' howled Armin.

Who was he? His voice was deformed by the mask, which gave his words a metallic ring.

Taurus leaned back against a rock, exhausted and panting. He hadn't escaped the encounter with Armin unharmed; a stream of blood ran down his side.

All around them a delirium of shrieks and groans, the clatter of clashing arms, wheezing animals, the shrill whinny of horses whose bellies had been slashed open. But there was a slight rise at the head of the column, where many of the soldiers who had survived were making their way. They were readying for their last battle, even if that meant the death foretold by the dull roar of Thor's hammer.

The two horsemen were dragged apart by their galloping horses. The black stallion moved at a furious clip while Borr was slower, still hurting from his fall. They finally drew up at the edges of a sandy clearing near the Great Swamp. The two warriors faced off, on horseback at first and then on foot, with violent slashes and stabs of sword and dagger. Armin wielded an axe as well, whirling it with enormous strength, making it roar in the dense air of Teutoburg. The masked horseman bent sharply to dodge it and came up ready to smite with a Germanic sword in one hand and a Roman one in the other. There were no words left; all they could do was strike repeatedly with incredible violence, trying to maim each other, aiming at arms, legs and heads.

A strong swipe by Armin at his adversary's left shoulder was deflected from above by the steel plates of the segmented shoulder plate and his mask fell to the ground.

They stood facing one another, gasping and wheezing.

'You!' said Armin in shock.

The horseman jumped onto his black stallion and raced away, crossing the field of blood and death at a gallop.

25

THE MASSACRE RESUMED IN the afternoon, with a vengeance.

The Germanics, who had so often seen their best warriors, their youth, mowed down by the legions, couldn't believe that they were finally able to get revenge. They'd been let loose to vent their ferocity on a disjointed, pinned-down army. Many of the Roman army's commanders were gone; some had been killed, others had escaped in the hope of reaching Castra Vetera. A number of soldiers had sought to flee as well, heading north, but when they tried to circle the Great Swamp, many were sucked in by the slurry mud at its banks. Squads of Germanic warriors, crouching in the vegetation at the shore, had been waiting for just this chance and eagerly let their arrows and spears fly so they could watch their prey fall and then float away in the black waters of the huge bog.

All the Romans who were able to do so tried to regroup, with the horses and carts remaining to them. A small redoubt had been established on a little area of sandy high ground. Although it afforded them some shelter, they were still caught between the swamp and the rampart, from which swarms of sharp javelins continued to rise and then fall from the sky to cut, break, pierce.

Thiaminus and Privatus, who were part of the entourage of civilians, baggage wagons and pack animals still following

Taurus, tried in vain to convince the centurion to evacuate from the redoubt. They had hoped to bring Taurus to safety for the duration of the battle but there was no dislodging him from the heart of the fight.

Meanwhile, the Germanic warriors were trying to storm the circle of carts defending the Roman position. They knew their best chance would be before the sun set and the shadows of the night enveloped the pass and the bloody bog of Teutoburg, but their attack proved to be unsuccessful. A few portable ballistae fortuitously discovered in the bottoms of the carts provided the defenders with sufficient ammunition to discourage their most resolute assailants. Part of Numonius Vala's cavalry had also managed to enter the circle before it was closed off.

'You must leave,' Taurus was saying to his freedmen. 'It's an order. You are not legionaries, you don't owe it to anyone to die in this disgusting hole.' It was like speaking to rocks. They looked at him, smiled, and did not move a step.

The hammer of Thor began to let out its dark roar, to remind the surviving soldiers that they would soon be dead, down to the very last man.

The sky darkened and became black as pitch. The ear-splitting thunder was accompanied by bolts of lightning that lit up a desolate landscape: bloody mud trampled by thousands of feet, cadavers that were missing their heads. Their skin was grey and so were the once vital organs now on display, matching the hue of the mud they were mired in. The swollen clouds rolled and twisted, releasing a brief storm of huge hailstones, which covered the ground with a blanket of ice. Here and there stony faces took on sad expressions, pelted by the rain. Then a strong wind ripped through the clouds and let the pale moon shine through for a brief moment.

Publius Quinctilius Varus's guard had fought their way through the battle to lead the governor to the high ground, where he was safe, but to all intents and purposes he was a larva. His face was leaden and there was panic in his every gesture, in his trembling hands and flaccid belly, his sunken eyes rolling in bewilderment. He was not capable of giving orders, or of instilling a drop of courage into his exhausted soldiers. Rufius Corvus, practically unrecognizable because of the dried blood caked on his face, approached Varus. 'Governor, Centurion Taurus has a plan and he would like to explain it to you. I'd like to call together all the surviving officers.'

Varus nodded, and a glimmer of hope seemed to make his gaze less pathetic.

The meeting of the remaining men of the general staff took place inside a covered wagon at the centre of the camp, a sort of makeshift praetorian tent, the last homage to their commander on the part of his soldiers. It was completely dark. The centurion spoke first: 'The Germanics are quiet for the time being. They're tired too. They've killed so many of our men, it's too much even for them. The die is not cast. We can stop this vile fate from claiming us.'

'How?' asked Varus anxiously, as if Taurus could perform a miracle.

Rufius Corvus could barely believe what he was hearing: Varus was looking for salvation from one of his men, while he had had every opportunity to prevent the disaster from ever happening. He remembered when they had accompanied Varus to Carrhae, together with Armin. To what remained of the battlefield where Marcus Licinius Crassus's army had been completely annihilated. Bones bleached by the sun, thousands of them, covering the barren desert. He had thought then, and had even discussed these thoughts with Armin, that the governor who had been capable of crucifying two thousand Judaean rebels had at least learned a crucial and very simple lesson. He remembered his own words, and without meaning to he screamed them out, one by one, nearly spitting into Quinctilius Varus's face.

'Even the most battle-ready Roman army can be defeated!

'Never trust a foreigner, even when he is an ally!

'Never let yourself be lured into a territory that you don't know but that the enemy knows like the palm of his hand!'

Varus didn't dare respond and Rufius continued yelling: 'We were in Carrhae together! How can you have forgotten those lessons? Didn't you see all those bones? They were Romans, Romans like me and you, Governor, and like us they were sent to slaughter by an incapable commander! Armin was there with us. Do you remember that? Well, he learned the lesson. Why didn't you? Why didn't you listen to those who sought to warn you?'

Taurus, wounded but still on his feet, put a hand on Rufius's shoulder. 'That's enough, Corvus. What's done is done. Now we have to try to survive. Maybe we still have a chance of getting out of this hell. If we do, we'll reach Castra Vetera by marching due west. Lucius Asprenas, who commands the garrison, will come to us; he'll come to our aid and chase off the Germanics. We will march in close formation. Once we're on the open field I don't believe they'll try to attack us.'

'But how will we get there? The enemy is everywhere!' said Varus.

'There's some pitch in the bottom of one of the carts down there,' replied Taurus. 'It was meant for creating a barrier of fire if one was needed. We'll wait until the Germanics come back to attack us, then we'll set the pitch and the carts on fire and hurl them at the attackers. This will achieve two results: it will stop them for a while, and give us time to escape. We'll be able to move more quickly without the carts, with only the pack animals. We need to find fire, to make embers . . .'

Rufius Corvus widened his arms. 'And where are we going to find fire, Taurus, in this swamp, in all this damned mud?'

No one answered Rufius. A leaden silence fell over the group.

Almost immediately, Taurus heard something. 'There's someone out there,' he said. They could all hear it then, the sound of a gallop, very close. Then they saw a small meteor fall from the sky, plowing through the thick darkness. A tiny sphere of fire that fell into the middle of the circle of wagons.

Taurus looked astonished. He turned to Rufius Corvus: 'Run, get that before the mud puts it out.'

Corvus rushed to pick up the firebrand sizzling on the ground. He propped it up in a dry place and added some straw soaked in the pitch.

The sound of the gallop was lost in the night.

'What was that?' asked Corvus.

Taurus took a deep, deep breath. 'Someone paying back a debt. A flame for a flame. That's it; nothing else will be coming our way.'

'So you know who it could be?'

'I certainly do. I can tell one gallop from another. Every horse is different. This one is very different and he even has a name. He's called . . . his name is Borr. Now we have a chance. At least I hope we do.'

'You hope?' shrieked Varus. 'So that's your whole plan? Don't you have anything else in mind if this one fails?'

'I do have another plan, in fact.'

'So what's that?'

In the reflection of the burning firebrand, Taurus stared fiercely at him. 'To die like a Roman, Governor.'

Then he turned to the legionaries who were sitting in a circle around him. 'There will still be some salted food in the holds of the wagons. Eat and drink, even if it revolts you. Have your men do the same. Then find a dry spot on the carts, or underneath them, and try to sleep. What we'll have to face tomorrow will be no less difficult than what we've done today. We're going to find a way out, if there is one, otherwise we'll see each other in hell, boys.'

Sergius Vetilius stepped forward. He was covered with mud and blood and in the dark no one had recognized him; no one had seen him for such a long time that they were all sure he was dead.

'Well, well . . . the commander of the Eighteenth!' exclaimed Rufius Corvus.

Taurus had one of the legionaries hand him a piece of smoked meat and he tossed it over to him. 'Eat up, Commander. We're going to crack some heads tomorrow.'

'You don't say!' laughed Vetilius. 'And here I was, planning to take a little stroll.' Meanwhile he had drawn his gladius and was using a whetstone to sharpen it like a razor. Taurus watched him, knowing well who he was preparing that blade for, when he would no longer have the strength to fight.

The prefect of the camp showed up as well. He was a lad of twenty named Ceionius once destined for a dazzling career. 'Do you have a bite for me, Centurion?' he asked.

'Have some, son,' replied Taurus. 'There's still a bit left.' Ceionius ate with appetite and took part in the conversation as if he were an old friend of each of those present. They all felt equal in front of impending death, without any difference of rank or social standing.

Varus watched them in amazement. They were frightening to look at: bloodied, tattered, filthy with mud, limping, wounded. And yet sitting around that wretched little fire, surrounded by thousands of ferocious enemies, exhausted, mourning for the friends they had lost that day, and almost certainly destined to a horrible death in just a few hours' time, they still felt like joking.

Then their voices, one by one, fell silent, the remaining chunks of meat were thrown onto the fire and, lying one alongside another in the warmth of the flames, the legionaries and officers of the Eighteenth, utterly worn out, fell asleep.

THE REFLECTION OF a leaden dawn drew from the dark a squad of Germanic cavalry who were slowly advancing towards the wagons. Ceionius woke Taurus. 'Centurion . . . come and see this.'

'Damn,' cursed Taurus. 'So early?'

He strapped on his *balteus*, hung his sword from it, and followed Ceionius; hundreds of warriors were advancing on horseback towards the wall of wagons and each one of them carried a javelin on which he had stuck the head of a Roman soldier.

'Powerful gods,' he muttered.

The Germanics were advancing slowly. The surviving Roman officers, aided by their men, started helping Taurus to manoeuvre the carts and wagons so that they were pointing down the slope. As the Germanic horsemen got closer, the scene became more horrifying. In those severed heads, with their mangled, distorted features, many of the Romans recognized their friends, companions of many adventures and comrades of many battles. Some wept in silence, others boiled over with rage.

At that sight, something broke inside Ceionius, who had seemed so cocky and fearless until then. Before Taurus could stop him he pushed his way through the wall of carts and started running like crazy towards the Germanics, shouting, 'We surrender! We surrender, spare our lives!' He fell to his knees with his arms raised and open.

Taurus was beside himself, and shouted, 'Turn back, boy! Turn back!' But when he saw his words were useless he turned to the surviving group of archers. 'Kill him. In the name of the gods, kill him now.'

The archers let fly with their arrows but it was too late; they only hit the Germanic shields. Ceionius disappeared, dragged off towards atrocious sufferings.

Taurus startled the men with his curt orders: 'What's there to look at? What are you doing? There's work to be done here. Move those carts, men. Go, go!'

He turned to the civilians who had found shelter in their encampment: 'There's nothing we can do for you. Wait here. The Germanics have nothing against you. They'll take you as slaves but you'll live. Especially the women. Good luck.'

The torches were already aflame and all of the vehicles were set on fire. When they started to burn, they pushed them down the slope towards the Germanic cavalry. The smoke was soon thick enough to hide the Romans from sight and Sergius Vetilius ordered them to retreat towards the wood, heading west. There was a little more room in that direction, enough to form up the units in sufficiently compact order, and incredibly the Germanics did not attack en masse as they could have done. But the respite did not last long. It became increasingly difficult to manoeuvre between the large trees in the wood. The units advanced with difficulty, often splitting up due to the obstacles they found in their way. The Germanics, led by Armin himself, had soon slid into all of the passes. And the march of the legionaries quickly began to be seeded with dead and wounded soldiers. The cavalry of Numonius Vala, who had been sent ahead to reconnoitre and keep the passage clear, would not return . . .

The infantry tried to stay compact and for a certain time many of them thought they could actually reach the outposts of Asprenas in front of Castra Vetera, and survive. But the Germanic pressure was incessant. The Romans, guided by their most courageous and valiant officers, tried continuously to keep rank, but the terrain made it nearly impossible to stay in battle formation. They resisted nonetheless until nightfall. They finally reached a clearing and assembled into a circle to ready for their last, desperate defence.

26

THAT WHOLE NIGHT, the forest shuddered with the sinister rumble of the hammer of Thor. No one closed an eye. The sentries scanned the darkness to understand where the attack would be coming from. There were noises: twigs broken, the cries of night birds. The forest was crawling with invisible ghosts.

The news of Armin's success against the Romans had convinced even those in doubt to throw themselves into the final fight. The powerful army of Varus had been decimated and the survivors were exhausted, pinned down with no hope of getting away. What better chance to gain favour in the eyes of the victor? Thousands more warriors had marched all night to arrive in time for the final carnage. The strongest had danced the dance of death and massacre, had drunk the sacred beverage that erases pain and fatigue, naked, until they achieved a delirious state of fury, roaring like beasts, their eyes flaming with hallucinatory folly. The Berserkers.

But cruel fate was still not satisfied by the thousands more warriors pouring in, in a bloodthirsty frenzy, to fill Armin's ranks. The hostile sky unleashed a violent storm at dawn, with a wild wind that agitated the leaves of the ancient trees. Lightning tore into their enormous boughs and sent them crashing to the ground with deafening cracks. There was no hope left, besides a miracle, and Primus Pilus Centurion Marcus Caelius had something to tell his soldiers. An exhortation and also a goodbye to his weary men. The storm raged and the rain fell in torrential sheets from the sky, as if the floodgates of the heavens had opened.

'Men of the Seventeenth, Eighteenth and Nineteenth Legions!' he shouted. 'I am only a humble soldier and no words are adequate to express the immense admiration I have for you. I've done battle on all the fronts and regions of the Empire, but I've never seen men of your mettle. You have been fighting for days and nights without pause, without complaint, putting up with hunger, thirst, pain, lack of sleep, and the fury of the weather! You deserve victory, and you will not have it. But it was betrayal, deceit and adverse fortune that brought you down, not any want of strength or valour.

'The time has come for the final battle. It will be a fight to the death, without any glimmer of hope. You will die and I will die with you, but we will fall as soldiers and as Romans, dragging to hell all the enemies we can. Your sacrifice will be remembered for centuries, even when the Empire of Rome no longer exists.'

The legionaries listened to him in silence. In their eyes Taurus saw the signs of the inhuman strain that they'd been exposed to and the grief for their lost companions, lying on the pathways and among the trees of the Teutoburg Forest, cadavers stiff in the mud.

Varus was there to listen to Taurus's words. He walked among the victims of his ineptitude and credulity. His men did not turn away, did not shun him. They gave him the respect due to their supreme commander.

Then, all at once, a solitary voice rose from the ranks, hoarse and powerful. He sang the notes of an old legionary song, the ones that soldiers sing at night around the campfire, on the eve of a battle. Bravado and melancholy premonition.

> *'Miles meus contubernalis*
> *Dic mihi cras quis erit vivus*
> *Iacta pilum hostem neca*
> *Miles es, miles Romanus!'*

Another voice rose to join the first, and then another:

> *'Miles es, miles Romanus!'*

Taurus's voice joined those of his soldiers, joined Varus's voice, weak and uncertain, but also the resonant voices of Rufius Corvus, Sergius Vetilius and Gaius Vibius, the young cavalry prefect who was Numonius Vala's right hand.

As Taurus and the other centurions ordered *'Suscipite . . . scuta!'* all of the survivors of the three legions raised their shields and closed ranks. They were still singing.

> *'Suscipite . . . insignia!'*

The standard-bearers raised the eagles and the cohort ensigns. The army sang as one, and the loud song spread through the forest and filled the gorges. It reached the formidable Germanic warriors crouching in the wood, impatient to fly at the enemy and annihilate them. It reached Armin, who felt in his hands and arms the force of tens of thousands of warriors waiting for his signal.

But that absurd, incredible song, that not even the crash of thunder nor the echo of the hammer of Thor could stifle, stopped for an interminable moment his order for slaughter.

Then something broke in him. That last shred of his Roman self was ripped clean from his ancestral Germanic soul and

Armin yelled out, in the language of his fathers, the order for attack.

A blinding flash illuminated the forest and for an instant the Roman soldiers appeared. They stood shield to shield, shoulder to shoulder, swords in hand, around their standards. From that distance, their compact formation, their wall of shields, the steel cuirasses that cast away the flash of lightning, the open-winged eagle . . . all gave the impression of an intact force.

But they were starving, exhausted, wounded.

All they had left was their courage.

They stood firm and waited for the onslaught of the Germanic deluge. Armin's ranks pounded like the waves of a storming sea against the wall of shields that held for a moment, but then began to fall back. Armin in person pushed into the Roman formation, searching, as the tradition of his people demanded, for the enemy commander so he could claim his head for himself. Taurus tried to stop him; for a brief instant his rocky constitution, his courage, his skill in duelling and the experience of a thousand battles at close quarters seemed to test the young Germanic warrior.

'Look out!' growled the centurion. 'I'm not dead yet!' And he dealt a clean blow to Armin's shoulder, drawing blood.

Armin flew into a rage and responded with a hail of sword and axe strikes, forcing Taurus to his knees.

'I'm not dead yet,' snarled the centurion, trying to drive his dagger into Armin's foot.

All around them, despite the winds of storm, the air boiled with savage screams, roars, blood rage, arms clashing against arms. There were so many Germanic warriors that not all of them could throw themselves into the fray they had so hungered for. Those among them who managed to capture a legionary alive dragged him into the forest, where many warriors were already crying out in victory and abandoning themselves to wild dances, gulping down Celtic beer. There the legionary would be tortured in every way possible. They would take off his hands, his arms, his legs, cutting him up until only the trunk remained.

The screams lured another person to the scene. He wore a mask of bronze and mounted a black stallion. No one noticed him, so like a ghost he was. He descended down the slope at a fast gallop, holding sword and axe aloft. He swept through the sea of semi-naked warriors, his massive steed running them over, his axe and sword dismembering their bodies.

He rode away from the battlefield, vanishing as suddenly as he had appeared.

Armin hadn't finished with Taurus; he delivered a cleaving blow from above, with the centurion bent over on his knees. Taurus shouted, 'No! Never to the back!' and with a final burst of energy he rose to his feet and threw himself at his adversary, taking the blow full in the chest. It pierced him from front to back. He clung to Armin as he was dying. 'Nice work, boy,' he sputtered. 'No one has ever . . . managed to kill Marcus . . . Caelius . . . Taurus.'

He collapsed. Armin found Quinctilius Varus standing before him, plunging his own sword under his breastbone straight through to his heart. When Armin's sword gored him, he was already dead. The victors fought over the corpse avidly, chopping it to pieces. Armin cut off his head with a clean blow of his axe.

Gaius Vibius had seen everything. He stood fast, unwilling to leave Taurus's lifeless body.

As the legionaries saw their officers falling one after another or being put into chains by order of Armin, they lost their last remaining strength. Many were thus captured alive, simply because they could no longer move, while others fell fighting. To the last man.

The storm abated. The thunder rumbled only in the distance now, and the Berserkers were able to give free rein to their fury on the few survivors. Only their screaming could be heard, and the dry snap of bones being broken.

Gaius Vibius, Numonius Vala's personal aide, who had never stopped hoping that his commander would return with reinforcements, awoke before dawn in Armin's camp, wrapped in chains. He had a deep wound in his right thigh that had clotted over. He realized he must have lost his senses.

A gigantic Hermundur towered in front of him. He made a barely perceptible movement with his hand towards a group of Cherusci who were torturing a prisoner. He said in heavy Latin, 'It's your turn next. That's why they kept you alive.'

The boy looked around him in distress, then turned back to the Hermundur with a question in his eyes. The warrior lifted his chin towards the chain that bound the lad to the trunk of a tree. Gaius Vibius understood and nodded. Before the Cherusci could get to him, Gaius grabbed the chain, spun it with every bit of strength left to him and he split his own head wide open, spraying blood and brains all around.

Some of the surviving officers were butchered on the altars scattered through that corner of the forest, offered up to the Germanic gods. Others were nailed to the trees through the empty orbits of their eyes.

The legionary standards and the eagle were soiled and desecrated in every way possible and then hidden so they could never be found.

The echo of Gaius Vibius's final gesture arrived all the way to Tiberius's camp in Pannonia, thanks to the Hermundur, along with news of Varus's rout. Velleius, the supreme commander's aide, was informed of this on the day in which victory against the Illyrians and Dalmatians was being celebrated and he decided not to tell Tiberius about it until the next day, so as not to spoil the joyful festivities.

In his diary, Velleius extolled the virtue of Caius Vibius and defamed Ceionius and Numonius Vala as cowards, but no one would ever know the truth about the cavalry commander, buried in the mud and in the murky waters of the swamp.

ARMIN WAS RECEIVED triumphantly by all the Germanic tribes; his was the credit for the crushing victory over the Romans and he was confirmed the supreme commander of the army. He started to let himself think about a great independent, unified Germania with a single army and a single leader. Him.

He sent Varus's head to Marbod, king of the Marcomanni, with a message that referred to the favour that the sovereign had done for him when he had been caught crossing his territory in Bohemia.

Marbod put the head in a jar of salt and sent it to Augustus who had already had news of the defeat. The emperor was so shocked and so shaken that he stopped shaving. He took to always dressing in mourning robes and it was said that he wandered through his palace on sleepless nights crying, 'Varus, give me back my legions!'

Varus's head was buried in the family mausoleum.

27

AFTER THE TEUTOBURG massacre, Armin felt invincible. One by one, he would take by force the defensive structures and the legionary forts that stood at the Roman border beyond the western bank of the Rhine.

The first wave of assaults had been successful because they were completely unexpected and because Numonius Vala's cavalry, which had been sent out to find reinforcements, had been intercepted near the swamp. Although they were decimated, the few men who managed to survive raised the alarm, so when Armin arrived with his warriors at the first legionary outpost on his path, the commander was prepared and ready to counter the Germanic attack. While in the forest and the bogs, the warriors' brute strength and ferocity – and even more so their complete familiarity with the territory – had made them unstoppable opponents, things changed radically in front of fort battlements packed with archers and artillerymen.

Certain that reinforcements were on their way, the garrison soldiers waited calmly at first. The Germanics, however, by order of Armin, had set up roadblocks all over the territory so no one could get in or out of the forts.

At this point many of the garrison soldiers, along with a great number of civilians, decided to try to pass the Germanic lines under the cover of darkness, risking another massacre.

They succeeded using a very simple stratagem: someone sounded the cavalry charge and got out the word that Asprenas's army was arriving from Castra Vetera. When Asprenas learned of the situation, he actually did show up with an army, effectively dispersing the Germanic attackers.

Armin made other attempts to force the line of legionary bulwarks which defended the Rhine border, but he had to back down as his warriors were mowed down by the Roman war machines and archers. Furthermore, he had no equipment suitable for staging a siege. There was also a rumour that Tiberius himself was arriving at a forced march with an army of heavy infantry, and Armin decided to suspend his plans for taking over the border strongholds on the Rhine. The victory at Teutoburg had been like a drunken rampage, but now he had to organize and manage his warriors, which was no easy feat.

He began to wonder how and when the Empire would react. For Rome, he was solely a deserter, an officer of the Germanic Auxilia guilty of treason. What would be their next move? When would they retaliate? Armin realized that he had enjoyed extraordinary success with traps and ambushes, but if he tried to cross the Rhine or to attack a fort or an entrenched camp, his enormous technical disadvantage would surely preclude any hope of getting away with it.

He managed to find informers in Rome. It wasn't hard as he knew so many people. He learned that the emperor had discharged his personal guard, made up of Germanics. He had sent them into confinement, in small groups, on islands in the middle of the sea, and enrolled new forces. He feared an invasion from the north like at the times of the Cimbri and Teutons.

Tiberius arrived in Germania a year later. Velleius came with him as his trusted personal aide, as did a young man who Armin knew of well: Germanicus. He'd seen him for the first time when he was little more than a boy, on the marble frieze of the Altar of Peace. They had crossed their weapons in training when they were adolescents and Marcus Caelius Taurus was instructor to both of them.

Thinking of Taurus made him remember his two freedmen, Privatus and Thiaminus; Armin had noticed them on the field of slaughter at Teutoburg. They'd surely been killed themselves as they were trying to carry off their patron's body to perform funeral rites and give him a proper burial. This was vital in the Roman conception of *pietas*. They certainly had not been allowed to succeed in their intent.

Tiberius did not immediately cross the Rhine, nor did Armin do so from his side to invade Roman Germania and Gaul. They simply studied, observed and spied on one another. Armin had fought with Tiberius and knew what a formidable foe he made. Tiberius knew that Armin would almost certainly never accept a conflict on the open field because he was aware that he would lose. He thus reinforced the garrisons, repaired the roads and bridges and made sure that the commanders of the legions and the cohorts were worthy of the tasks they'd been assigned.

Armin kept an eye on everything Tiberius was doing, but at the same time he was busy recovering control over the various territories. He went as far as the Weser, but he didn't try to engage the various tribes in battle and he was careful never to allow himself to be lured into a place which would favour an ambush. Tiberius on the other hand took to burning villages and devastating territory so that the Germanics who were contrary to war with the Romans would have something to blame Armin for.

Perhaps Augustus would have preferred conduct that was more prudent, but he was also conscious that a catastrophe like Teutoburg could not remain unpunished.

Armin used that time to unite as far as possible the tribes which had been part of his alliance against the Romans in Teutoburg, putting in chains anyone who threatened to betray the cause. He realized very quickly that although that kind of coalition could be put together for a limited time, it tended to unravel once the objective was achieved. His efforts were also hindered by Thusnelda's father Seghest, still a mighty and powerful warrior, who remained hostile towards him; he had never stopped accusing Armin of the abduction and even the rape of his daughter.

After the first confused reactions from Rome, there was reassuring news for Armin: Augustus was apparently realizing that it was impossible to turn Germania into a Roman province and that the border could not be moved to the Elbe river. The frontier would stop at the Rhine. Forever.

Armin reflected at length on the recent turn of events and he felt increasingly at a loss about how to proceed. One important thing was clear: the victory was not due solely to him. It was nature herself that had fought alongside his warriors. The land of Germania was wild and fierce. This was thrilling from one point of view but discouraging from another. The Romans had never feared nature; they drained swamps, chopped down forests, dug canals, built dams to keep the rivers from flooding. He often thought of the day that he and Flavus had gone to see the road that never ends, which seemed so very long ago now. Roman soldiers were indefatigable and well used to hard work: they were the ones who built the roads and the bridges when they weren't fighting. Even when the arrows were raining down on them, Varus's armies had cut down trees, built footbridges, turned paths into roads.

He remembered his father's stories about his secret meetings with General Drusus, and he knew well that such a bond could never exist between himself and a Roman commander. Teutoburg had cut the bridges between Germania and the Empire forever.

Armin's plan for uniting Germania was very difficult to put into action. Even his own relatives were against it. His uncle Ingmar had not joined the coalition and had allied with Seghest, Thusnelda's father and Armin's worst enemy; it was lucky for Armin that Varus hadn't listened to Seghest's warning about the ambush waiting for them in Teutoburg.

Armin had heard that when Seghest was asked to account for this humiliating and even contemptible move, he said that he hadn't done it for personal reasons, but because he thought that peace was preferable to war and that the interests of the Romans and those of Germania were one and the same. Armin could imagine that his brother Flavus felt the same way. He'd been there, at Teutoburg. One of them could have killed the other that day. It didn't matter who. When brother kills brother, does it matter who dealt the first blow, or the final one?

Another person he thought about was the Hermundur: who was the titanic tattooed warrior who drifted in and out of his life? He never really tried to find out. He might have been a god of the forests, a solitary, invulnerable giant who passed from one world to the other, from one universe to another. Did he delight in deviating the course of events and then standing back to watch the consequences?

Years went by without anything very unusual happening. Had Augustus managed to forget Varus's debacle?

'No,' replied the Hermundur. 'Augustus is simply very old and he doesn't have the strength to react any more, not even against the most atrocious offences. He's tired and sad and you know why: his daughter languishes on a small desert island for having plotted against him. His only surviving grandson, Julia's lastborn, is confined to another small island and he will almost certainly die there. His only blame is that he was considered violent and thick-witted as a boy, but he has actually never harmed a living soul. Augustus went to visit him once, accompanied by his best friend. They embraced, grandfather and grandson. They wept in each other's arms. A journey that should have remained a secret but didn't and this means only one thing: the young man will die. It's only a question of time. If it hasn't happened already.'

'Who will be Augustus's successor?'

It was the day of the winter solstice. The Hermundur turned around, mounted his horse and disappeared into the fog.

HE TURNED OUT to be right on all accounts. Augustus died the next year, in the month that bore his name, and was entombed in the mausoleum where Varus's head had been buried. In his will he stated that the border between the Empire and Germania must be the Rhine.

Tiberius succeeded him.

A ruthless, indomitable soldier, thought Armin. *He'll want revenge for Teutoburg.*

But in the meantime, a mutiny had broken out among the legions of the Rhine due to their miserable living conditions, and Tiberius had decided to send Germanicus – his adopted son and nephew by blood – to quell the revolt.

So would Germanicus be the man designated to avenge Teutoburg as well? Or were there other reasons behind the move, besides dealing with the legionaries who were asking for more humane living conditions? In the crucial moment of succeeding Augustus, what were Tiberius's priorities? To avenge the dead? To kill more of the living and give a boost to the new monarchic order? To deal the final blow against residual Republican institutions?

The Hermundur later informed him that after Tiberius took power, a centurion landed on the island of Planasia and, not without difficulty, killed Augustus's remaining grandson. He was part of the Julian family, while the new emperor was Claudian. The two situations could not co-exist. The young man was murdered, but he had a fine funeral and was buried in the family mausoleum.

Germanicus thus left for Germania. His soldiers adored him because he was the son of General Drusus. He looked like his father and even had the same personality: he was friendly, affectionate, even-tempered and a formidable combatant. He travelled on the Via Flaminia and passed through Ariminum. As he proceeded with his escort of a hundred praetorian guards, people lined the roads to cheer him on.

He reached Bononia, where he found a much larger crowd than he had expected. It felt a bit odd to be receiving such acclamation, which would have been more suited to an emperor.

All of a sudden, he heard a voice shouting, 'Germanicus! Take me to Teutoburg!'

Germanicus scanned the crowd and couldn't pick out anyone in particular. But the shout was becoming louder and more insistent, until it drowned out the other voices: 'Take me to Teutoburg! Take me to Teutoburg! Take me to Teutoburg!'

Germanicus stopped, and then he saw him; he was the only one running through the crowd, apparently so he would stay within earshot. He called over one of the centurions of his guard and said, 'Do you see that man running and yelling?'

'Certainly, Germanicus. And I hear him.'

'Bring him here to me.'

The centurion obeyed and led the man who was shouting to Germanicus.

'Why do you want me to take you to Teutoburg?'

It was a rather corpulent man of about sixty with thinning hair, and a bristly two- or three-day-old beard. He said, 'Germanicus, my name is Publius Caelius and I run an inn here in Bononia.'

'Your name isn't new to me,' said Germanicus.

'I'm the brother of Marcus Caelius, known as Taurus, first-line centurion of the Eighteenth Legion . . .' He dropped his head to hide his emotion. 'Fallen at Teutoburg.'

'That can't be . . .' murmured Germanicus.

'It's the truth.'

'I can see that,' replied Germanicus. 'You look like him.'

Publius Caelius gazed at him without understanding.

'Your brother was my instructor. He's the one who taught me to use this,' he said, putting his hand on his gladius. 'And to be a soldier. There are very few men of his stature. It was a terrible loss. But why would you want to go to Teutoburg? It's a cursed place.'

'I want to find the remains of my brother and give him an honourable burial.' His voice was cracking now. 'I've been told that . . . he was cut to pieces. It won't be easy.'

Germanicus felt a knot in his throat and he couldn't say a word, but he embraced Publius Caelius like an old friend who he hadn't seen in a long time.

'You'll come with me to Teutoburg, Publius Caelius,' he said in the end. 'And we will do all we can to render honour to Marcus Caelius, known as Taurus, your brother and a hero of the Empire.' The crowd was mute; they were seeing the son of General Drusus in tears embracing an innkeeper in the middle of the road in Bononia.

That innkeeper was invited that very evening to dinner by Germanicus, next in line to become emperor of Rome. The next day Publius left with the troops, a mule carrying his tent and personal belongings.

Armin learned from one of his men serving among Germanicus's auxiliaries that there had been a mutiny among the legions in Pannonia and Illyricum, and that the revolt had spread to the legions of the Army of the North, which was under Germanicus's command. This situation was all to Armin's favour. He could boast to the other chieftains who were members of his coalition that this terrible crisis of the imperial army was the consequence of the harsh defeat suffered by Varus at Teutoburg, at his hand.

He met with his informer among the ruins of an abandoned village on the right bank of the Rhine. 'The situation was getting out of control,' he reported, 'but then the commander arrived and realized that the legionaries were right. These men were living and toiling in quite cruel conditions, much harsher than military service would warrant. Many of them were convinced to revolt and demand what they were owed: a small increase in salary and a reduction of their mandatory enlistment from thirty to twenty years. They were exhausted and desperate, but most thought of the army as their only home and wouldn't dream of actually leaving. I saw a veteran take Germanicus's hand and put it in his mouth. With my own eyes! He didn't want to bite it. No, he wanted the commander to touch his gums and see that he had no teeth left. He'd lost them all in twenty years of service under the Roman standards.'

'Well? Is it true that he put down the revolt?'

'It is. Most of them were convinced by his promise to guarantee the increase in wages with his own personal holdings. The firebrands found themselves isolated and they suffered for everyone: whipped in front of the drawn-up legions until their bare bones were showing, then decapitated.'

'*Divide et impera*,' concluded Armin. 'Divide your enemies, set them one against the other, and then conquer. And you're free to exercise your power. They do the same thing with us and they'll continue to do so until we manage to become a single people. What else do you have for me?'

'His wife is here as well. His beloved Agrippina, Julia's daughter and Augustus's granddaughter. She's six months pregnant. It seems they fell in love as adolescents and they've become as inseparable as General Drusus and his wife Antonia. She's expecting, as I told you, and she's brought little Gaius Caesar as well, Germanicus's first son. This has bound the legionaries even more greatly to their commander.'

'What else?' insisted Armin.

'Once he had re-established discipline among the ranks, the legionaries offered to follow him to Rome and proclaim him emperor in Tiberius's place. He refused, of course.'

'Why?'

'Well, the emperor is his uncle, his adoptive father, and was his commander in Illyricum and Pannonia.'

'So you mean to say he's loyal.'

'That's what it looks like. He's a man I would trust.'

The informer got back into his boat and departed from the shore to return to the left bank of the Rhine. Armin remained to ponder what he had heard, wandering among the gutted houses and burned beams of the village. He then called Borr with a whistle and the stallion ran up to him and made a smart half-turn, reins falling loose over his chest. It was all clear to him now: Germanicus was the man sent by the emperor to avenge Teutoburg. The togaed boy of marble on the Altar of Peace was now a man. They were the same age. This time they wouldn't be fighting with wooden weapons. It would be iron against iron and in the end only one of them would survive. He felt like going home, to Thusnelda, but he stopped first to see his mother. Her house was not far away.

'Be careful,' said Siglinde. Nothing in his actions or his words escaped her. 'Your victory is a kind of treasure that you've collected thanks to your bravery and your intelligence. You have to spend it wisely. Don't let anyone see that you're so proud of it. The envy of others is your most dangerous enemy and it could destroy you.'

Armin didn't answer, but he knew his mother was right. How could he use his prestige without giving rise to jealousy and rivalry?

'There's something else, my son. Germania has never existed before and no one knows where this word comes from. You learned it in Rome, and it means something to you, but not to the rest of us. You father knew what it meant; he'd learned the word from General Drusus, I believe. It means that all the peoples that live between the Rhine and the great eastern plains are one people, on a single territory. But it also means that that people and that land have to have a single leader. You know who that is.'

'Me?'

'Who else? Who else forced three legion commanders to their knees? Who decapitated the governor? Who exterminated half the Roman Army of the North?'

'What must I do now?'

'Nothing more than what you're doing. I'm just telling you to be careful: the Romans haven't forgotten Teutoburg, and you have bitter enemies among our own people who would like nothing more than to kill you. Don't let yourself be caught between two fires.'

'I know. I'm alone. I can't even count on my brother.'

'Try to see him if you can. In secret would be best. Tell him that I want him to join us.'

'I will, Mother. I hope that your words convince him to make the right choice, but I'm afraid it won't be easy.'

He thought of the bronze mask, so dark that he couldn't see the expression of the eyes behind it.

28

ARMIN RODE ON TO the secret place he'd made for Thusnelda and he spent the night there with her. There was love, and fire, but not only that; it was a sad night, even though the sky was clear and filled with stars. He confided his hopes, and the fear that Seghest's continued hostility kindled in him. He would have liked her father to be on his side; he respected him and appreciated his strength, his courage and the influence he had over their people.

'Your father wasn't there at Teutoburg . . .'

'I know. His men were burning to be part of the coalition, but his will prevailed. He is inflexible.'

'Can't you do anything to convince him?'

'If he so much as sees me, he will take me away with him and you would never see me again.'

'I'm tormented by doubts. After Teutoburg, I thought that all of our peoples would join me in my plan for unity. Join me in building a single great nation. But I'm realizing now that this nation doesn't even have a name. I have to find a way to make our victory a beginning, not an end. But if the Romans remain on the other side of the Rhine, where's the reason for us staying united? We'll just start fighting among ourselves again.

'I have to find out what intentions the Romans have. I'm

setting up a system to learn what they're doing and what they're thinking. Men who have eyes and ears everywhere.'

He hadn't finished speaking when they heard the sound of a gallop drawing near. He went outside to receive the man as he jumped to the ground.

'Germanicus has unleashed his legions on this side of the Rhine.'

'That can't be. His legions are still stirred up by their own revolt.'

'It started three nights ago. Germanicus convinced them that it was time to redeem themselves in the eyes of the emperor, to prove their loyalty. They set out from the forts that were built or repaired by Tiberius, the same ones you attacked . . .'

'That I failed to seize . . . Go on.'

'They fell on the Marsi, who had just celebrated the rites of spring, and it was a massacre: men still half drunk, old people, women and children. They devastated an area fifty miles wide and now they're making their way back to their base through the forest.'

'We have to attack them now, while they're still in the forest. Let's go.'

'The neighbouring tribes have already reacted. The Bructeri, Usipetes and Tubantes are already on them.'

'We'll make this another Teutoburg!' shouted Armin. He rode off with the messenger without a moment's delay.

He disappeared before Thusnelda's eyes. She stood watching the clear, star-filled sky with a heavy heart.

THEY ARRIVED AT dawn and made contact with the warriors of the tribes who were already in the fight. The chieftains held council but did not invite Armin to assume command.

'How are you carrying out the attack?' he asked.

The Usipete chief, a warrior nearly five cubits tall, wearing iron mail, sword and shield, answered: 'We've attacked them continuously on their flanks to make them believe that is our objective, but the real offensive will come from behind, once they've entered the forest. We'll attack in great numbers.'

'Good. Wait until they've disappeared into the forest,' said Armin, 'and then strike with everything you've got.'

'I know what I need to do,' retorted the Usipete chief. It was clear he wanted to claim his part of the glory; he wanted another Teutoburg as well.

The first legion at the head of the column had to keep the road open, and cohorts of auxiliaries and cavalry units rode ahead. The Twenty-First and the Fifth *Alaudae* protected the baggage trains from the right and left. The Twentieth was the rear guard and was followed by light allied troops. The Usipete chief waited until the entire column had entered the forest and then ordered the attack.

Suffering the brunt of the assault of tens of thousands of warriors, the allied infantry at the column's end were quickly routed, collapsing onto the Twentieth on their march. It looked like everything was going well for the attackers, but Armin was worried. There was something wrong. The rush to win such an easy and resounding victory had tricked the Germanic commander into ordering the attack too soon, without waiting for the Roman marching column to be deep enough in the wood.

In that moment, Germanicus, at the head of the column, must have been informed of what was happening at the rear because be pulled hard on his horse's reins and raced to the end of the column, along its left flank, at top speed, personally taking command.

'Twentieth!' he shouted. 'About-face!' And the legion, with

a sharp metallic sound, reversed their march, by simply turning to face the opposite direction. The eagle alone seemed to fly from the first rank to the last, transforming into the new front line. The legionaries, led by the supreme commander in person, unleashed such a powerful attack against the Germanic warriors that they pushed them out of the forest and into the clear. There the Twentieth had all the space and time to draw up eight deep with a front more than two thousand feet long. These were no longer the exhausted, bleeding combatants of Teutoburg, but an avalanche of iron and fury that poured over the enemy front.

Armin spurred Borr on at full force to throw himself into the fray, into the vortex of screams and blood raging in front of him. He wanted to infuse courage into the Germanic warriors; but he could sense that it was too late to change the course of the battle. There was a moment in which just one hundred steps separated him from Germanicus and he could clearly hear his voice, shouting 'Avenge Teutoburg!' He saw a little disc of gold shining on the Roman's chest – the same one he had worn as a boy depicted on the marble frieze and as an adolescent in Taurus's training ring. For an instant, hit by a ray of sun, it nearly blinded Armin, and he took that flash as a warning from the gods.

Thor, help me! he thought, before he was completely surrounded. Borr's dilated nostrils inhaled the stench of death and he reared like an ardent pegasus and leapt over the circle of enemies, carrying his horseman to safety.

Late that night Armin returned to the field, lit by the moon. It was littered with pale blond lifeless bodies.

IN THE AUTUMN, Germanicus returned to Rome. He crossed the forum in triumph, his children riding on his chariot and his prisoners in chains trailing behind him, between two lines of deliriously cheering Roman citizens. It was as if General Drusus had come back in the flesh. Now his name was no longer simply an inheritance from his father; his coat of arms had been earned on the battlefield. Germanicus was the Empire's hero.

On the day of the autumn equinox, Armin met with the Hermundur in the big clearing near the lake.

'Augustus's daughter is dead,' he said. 'Beautiful Julia. He showed a little pity in the end, moving her from that black, rocky island to a decent house of the Strait of Sicily. But only until Tiberius, who had long suffered the humiliation of her betrayals, had her locked up in a single room where she died alone, in agony and anger.

'Germanicus is preparing a new campaign, but it's being kept very secret. Impossible to say when and where it will be. Farewell.'

He disappeared.

Armin joined Thusnelda in the bed he'd built with his own hands for her, and in her arms he forgot his anguish. An embrace of flames, their bodies tangled in the spasm of desire, their passion swelling minds and hearts. After, he thought of her in the procession of spring, flowers braided in her hair, Freya appearing behind her soft eyelids.

'I'm pregnant, I will give birth to your child. It will be a boy, like you.'

Armin rose to his feet and his body shone in the glow of the moon. 'How do you know?'

'Didn't you know that the girls who see Freya can foretell the future?'

'When will it be?'

'Soon, at the beginning of spring.'

'I can't believe this good fortune. Your words have lifted the darkness that's been plaguing me. I find myself at the spring of life, after having given death to thousands. I will always protect you; the beating of my heart will reach him through your skin when I hold you in my arms. I'll love you forever, beyond death.

'I'll have to leave soon, to rebuild our Germanic forces and to raise a wall of spears against the invaders. My every moment and every thought will be for you until I see you again.' He paused. 'Did Freya tell you what would happen after the great battle?'

Thusnelda gave a half-smile, but didn't speak.

Three days later Thusnelda heard Borr whinnying and the drum roll of his hooves on the wooden bridge that crossed the torrent. She didn't have the heart to watch Armin leave from the threshold of their house.

'You will win the great battle,' she said softly, to herself, 'but you will lose your wife and your son.'

ARMIN TRAVELLED FOR hundreds of miles through the woods and along the rivers, over the forested hillsides and down the endless shores of the ocean, mustering the Germanic forces in light of a new invasion. One night, as he was nearing the ford on the Weser River, he heard a pounding gallop of the planks of the bridge: a squad of Cherusci. They'd ridden day and night to catch up, collecting information about his whereabouts as they went.

'Bad news, prince,' said the chief guard. 'Seghest has taken advantage of your absence and has seized Thusnelda. Your sentries fought bravely but they were slain. Someone betrayed you. It's hard to protect such a big secret for such a long time. Come back with us now. No one can predict when the Romans will decide to attack.'

Armin flared up with anger and indignation but he was soon gripped by a dark despair – the mere thought of never seeing Thusnelda again broke his heart. He returned to the house of his parents in Cherusci territory and waited there for more news. From there he continuously sent out messengers to all the other Germanic tribes, but his efforts were mainly concentrated on the liberation of his wife.

One day his informer, the boatman of the Rhine, gave him an appointment at the abandoned village. Armin arrived escorted by a squad of horsemen who remained out of sight. He knew that Seghest's killers were always looking for him; now that his daughter was back in his own hands, he would have no scruples about striking.

A soft lapping announced the arrival of the boatman and Borr greeted him with a snort. Armin dismounted and approached the man, his hand on the hilt of his sword.

'News?' he asked.

'This is news that's worth a lot.'

'You've always been given what you asked for. I don't deal with such matters. Speak up now or I'm leaving and that won't be a good thing for you.'

The boatman spoke: 'Germanicus is preparing a campaign for the summer. He'll cross the Rhine before the solstice.'

Armin dropped his head, scowling.

'Too soon?' asked the boatman.

Armin had heard enough. He jumped onto Borr's back and rode off at a gallop.

The news passed by word of mouth among the chiefs who were part of the coalition, on the condition that they kept this secret. Armin feared that the massing of forces could be delayed; the summer was still far off. He continued to gather information from other sources. The same news everywhere: a Roman attack in the summer.

Thusnelda also managed to get a message through to him: 'Your son will soon be born. He can wait no longer to see his father! He will be beautiful, and look like you. I think of you every day and night. I have to see you, at any cost. What name shall I give our son?'

'Tumlich,' Armin replied. 'It's the name of one of my ancestors who the Cherusci still venerate as a hero.'

TAKING EVERYONE BY surprise, Germanicus crossed the Rhine three months earlier than expected, with four legions. He was followed by his second in command, an officer of ancient Etruscan lineage, Aulus Caecina, with four more legions and an equal number of Germanic and allied auxiliaries from the left bank of the Rhine. An enormous force for a simple act of retaliation and, furthermore, in blatant contrast with the intentions of Augustus first, and then Tiberius as well, to establish the border on the Rhine. But at that point Germanicus had grown to enjoy such great popularity that he could not be denied anything he wanted.

He attacked the Chatti first. They had been members of the coalition that had taken part in the massacre of Teutoburg. They were annihilated, and their capital Mattium was razed to the ground. Germanicus then withdrew to the Rhine to let his engineers build the bridges and roads that would enable a long-term occupation of Germania. Armin saw his chance then to create a great alliance of all the Germanic tribes. He launched his own Cherusci into an attack, but they achieved nothing against the army of Caecina, and were forced to retreat.

The face-off between Germanicus and Armin had turned into a fierce duel, fed into by a burning passion for what each believed in and by their many similarities. They were the same age, each was strong and ambitious, but it went even further than that, extending to their personalities and the women they loved. Each had fallen in love with a beautiful woman at a young age, and each of these women were not only deeply in love with their husbands but also incredibly ambitious. Each of them was pregnant, about to give birth. Thusnelda couldn't bear being a prisoner of her father any longer, and she continuously sent messages to Armin begging him to come and free her. He'd instructed a slave on how to refer her words, and the girl had become so good at what she was asked to do that she could impersonate her mistress extremely well. She even imitated Thusnelda's voice perfectly: 'I can no longer live a single moment apart from you and I long for the time when I can put our son in your arms.'

Armin had worked long and hard at urging the men of Seghest's tribe to lay siege to the stronghold where their chief had taken refuge, in the hope of liberating Thusnelda and taking back total control of his people. In the end they obeyed him. But Seghest knew that Germanicus had crossed the Rhine once with a very strong army and had soundly defeated the Chatti and he soon discovered that the Roman was said to be advancing again, with two armies this time, one led by him personally and the other under the command of his deputy, Aulus Caecina. Seghest sent Germanicus a message asking for his immediate intervention to break the siege his own men had laid on him.

Germanicus held council.

Lucius Asprenas, who commanded the garrisons on the Rhine, was the first to speak. 'We must respond to this request at once. If we capture Seghest's daughter, pregnant with Armin's child, we'll succeed in weakening that dirty traitor, if not breaking him. No one can understand what I'm saying better than you: imagine how you would feel if your beautiful wife Agrippina, seven months pregnant, were to fall into Armin's grasp.' Germanicus frowned. 'You know how the "king's game" is played. Whoever takes the queen already has the king in his hands and knows he'll win the game.'

'Lucius is right,' said Quintus Florius, legate of the Twentieth. 'We'll seize the girl and Armin will have to play our game.'

Germanicus nodded. The next day he diverted his army from the objective he had decided upon, and went to liberate Seghest from the siege. The besiegers scattered quickly and Seghest paraded out surrounded by his friends and supporters, by his family and his women. The man had a huge build and he had put on his most beautiful armour for the occasion. Ingmar was the only one of his followers to abandon him; he was disgusted by Seghest's behaviour and promptly went over to his nephew's side, joining the coalition.

The person who had caused Germanicus to deviate from his route emerged from the stronghold as well: Thusnelda. She didn't say a word, asked nothing, did not cry, but she spat into her father's face when she passed in front of him. In a single moment she had lost everything, except for what she carried in her womb; she guarded her unborn child like the treasure he was.

She was handed over to a military tribune, as if there had been a tacit agreement. 'This one is coming with us,' the officer said, but his tone was not rough; Germanicus had ordered that she be treated with respect.

In the aftermath of Seghest's release, many of the men of his retinue declared their willingness to give up the spoils of the Battle of Teutoburg that they had kept as plunder. They hoped that the gesture of handing them over to the Romans would save their lives.

Publius Caelius, the innkeeper from Bononia who had always stayed close to Germanicus's men, asked if he could look at those objects to see if he could find anything familiar. He stammered out a few words in the natives' language that he had practised, hoping for information about his brother. All to no avail.

The Roman army moved on to attack the territories of the other Germanic tribes. They burned down their villages, destroyed their crops and put to the sword any man of arms-bearing age. In the land of the Bructeri they found that everything had already been destroyed by the inhabitants themselves, but they discovered the eagle of the Nineteenth Legion that had been exterminated at Teutoburg. The eldest centurion washed it until it shone again and delivered it personally to their supreme commander so he would be able to take it back to Rome when the time came.

When Armin learned that his wife had been taken prisoner by Germanicus and that his son would be raised a slave of the Romans, he thought he would go mad. But he did not give up. He sent no one to Germanicus to offer to pay a ransom for his wife, knowing well that his grovelling would only give the Roman leader greater satisfaction.

He gathered his people instead, and gave a rousing speech. 'This is what they call a hero of the Roman Empire: a man who uses his eight legions to capture a single, harmless pregnant woman. I instead brought three legion commanders to their knees in front of me, and my warriors killed the best soldiers of Rome, one on one, sword against sword! This is the difference between a Roman and a Germanic!'

For all the time that remained to him, Armin did nothing

else but roam the land far and wide in his effort to unite all the tribes in a single undertaking: to force out the Roman invaders. His gaze was always enflamed with passion and his words vibrated with enthusiasm for freedom. Only at night, when he fell onto whatever makeshift bed happened to be available, did he weep bitter tears in silence for his lost love and for the son he would never see.

GERMANICUS LED HIS troops on to devastate the territory between the Lippe and the Ems rivers, the region near Teutoburg, where it was said that the unburied remains of Varus and his legions still lay.

'Don't do it, Commander,' said Asprenas when he understood that Germanicus wanted to lead the army to the field of death. 'Don't take your soldiers among those restless ghosts. It will destroy their morale, many will take fright . . .'

'No,' said Germanicus, 'on the contrary. They'll become more ferocious and more ruthless. They'll be even more anxious to avenge their fallen comrades who were butchered like animals.'

When he learned where they were going, Publius Caelius started to tremble. For years he'd been searching for news of his brother who'd gone missing in battle. He had been saving all that time for the day in which he would journey to that bloody place and build a funeral monument in his honour, but now that he was there, he was deeply in pain. He was afraid he would succeed in finding and recognizing Taurus's remains, and he'd have to see the mark of the atrocious tortures he must have suffered. He didn't want to see that.

Germanicus often found himself observing Publius Caelius because he saw him as a simple citizen whose heart held the values of an entire civilization. He noticed how the innkeeper loved to buy wine from traders so he could offer some to the soldiers, saying that he felt somehow that he was pouring a cup for his brother Marcus.

'Publius Caelius of Bononia,' Germanicus said to him one day, 'don't be afraid. We will give burial to our comrades and we'll fight on with renewed vigour to avenge them. We'll bring peace to their vexed spirits. No one will dare to stop us. Just let them try! We'll hunt down Armin until we've caught him and strangled him, like the criminal he is.'

Publius Caelius thanked him for the great honour bestowed upon a simple innkeeper by the son of legendary General Drusus, and he joined the march as if he were a soldier. He'd even bought a sword that swung at his side.

The army, guided by a very small group of survivors, started down the same road that Varus had taken six years before. But this time Aulus Caecina was advancing at the head and sending his scouts forward on horseback. They widened the path where the road was obstructed or narrow, they built footbridges across the streams and the stagnant waters, they cleared fallen trees and boulders dragged there by ancient torrents. When Germanicus finally reached the passage between the mountain of rock and the Great Swamp, he found Caecina's legions drawn up to the left and right of the place of massacre. He recognized the hastily dug trenches of the camp improvised by Taurus on the second day. The entire stretch of land was covered by skeletons that shone white in the afternoon sun. Thirty thousand legionaries were mute and a leaden silence fell on the field of death. Publius Caelius covered his face with his hands to hide his despair, but he kept his back straight in honour of the fallen.

He started to search then, running from one spot to another. He barely stopped at the lone skeletons scattered here and there, lingering instead when many bones together showed the will to resist. That's where his brother would be. Time and plunder had done their work, however, stripping clean the bodies of the fallen and making them unrecognizable. Publius Caelius would not give up; he feverishly went through the bones with his fingers, trying to find anything he could recognize, but he realized that the abandoned bodies had become prey to wild animals, who'd left the marks of their fangs and mixed the legionaries' bones with those of their enemies and with the pack animals. Many of the soldiers who were present had friends and family who had fallen in those cursed days, and seeing the scene of the massacre up close made them shake with grief and outrage. Some of them took up shovels and pickaxes and started burying the bodies scattered here and there over the plain, without knowing whether they were burying the bones of their own relatives and comrades, or of the enemies that had been dragged to hell by Varus's legionaries in their last desperate stand.

For the first time in six years, a Roman army had returned to the Teutoburg Forest, to lay to rest their fallen comrades. But the horror had no end: it was in the forest that they found the skulls of the centurions and the high officers nailed to the tree trunks through their eye sockets and the skeletons of others chopped to pieces on the altars of the Germanic divinities.

The time had come. Germanicus gave an order and tens of carts drawn by mules arrived and were loaded with the remains of three obliterated legions. They would be buried in a single grave. The supreme commander threw the first grassy clod of earth and then, one by one, legionaries, centurions, tribunes and legates, tossed clumps of dirt on those bare bones until they were covered.

Germanicus donned his parade armour and the red cloak of

command. He signalled to Legate Asprenas. The legions drew up in a single formation, unit by unit. A monumental standard-bearer from the Fifth *Alaudae* took three steps forward and raised the eagle of the Nineteenth that had just been recovered. The legate ordered the troops to present arms and twenty thousand swords were drawn.

Another order: '*Percutite . . . scuta!*'

And twenty thousand legionaries started to pound their gladii against their shields all together, at a steady beat. A deafening din rose from the formation, a roar of thunder that echoed through the valley.

One hundred beats. The thunder would shake all of Germania.

Publius Caelius never dropped his hand from its salute and held his sword forward towards the burial mound: a green hill that the rains would water with tears from the sky.

Then, the silence that always accompanies death.

29

GERMANICUS DECIDED TO hunt down Armin wherever he was, and began making his way through the most impervious regions of Germanic territory. He felt he was finally closing in on him, in a flat area between the forests and the bogs of the north, and he sent his cavalry out in a surprise attack. The Germanic forces counter-attacked and the Roman heavy infantry had to be sent in, on swampy ground that was not viable for their style of combat. Germanicus ordered his men to retreat to the area of the *pontes longi*, the roads bridging the bog that Armin and Flavus had so admired as boys. But the structures had been damaged in part and the enemy troops were constantly at their heels.

The Romans found themselves in serious difficulty. They were sinking into the mud and could not manage to react effectively to their attackers. Discouragement and panic spread; the conditions were terrible, the area hostile and unfamiliar. On the contrary, the Germanic troops – who had no need for a baggage train, with wagons submerged up to their wheel hubs in sludge, and who knew the area so well – were more agile in their movements. They were lightly but effectively armed and they were becoming more aggressive by the moment.

Despite this situation, Caecina managed to cover Germanicus's troops as they pulled back and made their way to the river

Ems. There the legions would embark onto the fleet and be removed from harm's way.

Caecina remained, and the spectre of Teutoburg loomed large on the exhausted ranks of his army. It hung in the shouts of Armin: 'Forward, men! Onward! We're going to see a new Teutoburg! They're sinking into the swamps. We can win this and we'll be free forever!'

But Aulus Caecina was a thick-skinned veteran: he didn't know what fear was, his tongue was as salty as any jailbird's, and he never lost heart. At the price of incredible strain, risking their lives repeatedly, he and his men managed after two days of marching to reach dry ground on open terrain. But the enemy was pressing from all directions and Armin narrowly missed killing Caecina, disembowelling his horse instead.

Late that night the old soldier spoke to the legionaries and succeeded in instilling trust and calm: 'Men! Do you really want to die in this slime and let that son of a bitch traitor who led your comrades into the slaughterhouse at Teutoburg have his way? Don't you want to get back to your army quarters? Don't you want to see those girls you left there, fuck those pretty whores? You're not interested in some decent food, good wine, a dry bed and a nice fire to roast some tasty game?'

No answer.

'By Hercules! Did you hear me?' cursed Caecina.

'We heard you, Commander!' one soldier piped up. Another snickered.

'I'm ready to wager double what you earn, down to the last penny, that tomorrow we win!'

'Deal, Commander!' someone shouted.

Caecina was bluffing, but he got the results he'd hoped for.

It was still a dark and harrowing night. They had no tents, and no fire to dry out the damp. They were trying to work up their courage, but no one felt like talking. No one was sleeping that night in either camp, some for one reason and others for another. In fact, the Romans could see the fires of the Cherusci close by and hear the laughter and victory songs of the warriors.

'Right, sing, sing,' growled Aulus Caecina. 'We'll see if you're in the mood for singing tomorrow.' He knew they were surrounded by the enemy on every side, but he also knew that he could still be a threat to them. He called his officers to council.

'I've learned from a secure source that these barbarians have two options. Armin wants to let us pass and then, when we're back in the middle of the swamps and forests, just like at Teutoburg, they'll attack from both sides until they've bled us out. His uncle, Ingmar, wants to attack us here at camp directly so that they can lay their hands on everything we have. His plan will prevail as it appeals to the Germanics' nature. So, if that is indeed the case, they've got a big surprise in store.

'Four of you,' he said, pointing at four cohort commanders, 'will go out with four thousand men and you'll lie in wait . . . there, where that patch of oak trees is, and there, behind that mound of earth. You'll let them approach our defensive wall and when they're close enough you'll hear trumpet blasts. That will be your signal. You'll attack them from behind with complete force. In the meantime, we'll come out from inside and we'll squeeze them in the middle. The four of you will leave now.'

They made their way out without a sound and took position. The Cherusci were so sure of victory and so drunk they didn't notice a thing and the Romans were even able to get some sleep, under the watchful eyes of their sentries.

At dawn, the Cherusci poured out of their camp en masse,

heading for the modest defence structure built by Caecina's army. They tossed down boards to cross the trenches and readied for the final battle. At that moment trumpets blared and horns echoed through the valley. The Roman troops who had been hiding came out into the open, closed ranks in a single formation and attacked, while Aulus Caecina burst out of the camp with the rest of his army. The Cherusci and their allied warriors found themselves being attacked from front and back.

A furious fray ensued and incredibly the Romans made a show of willpower and physical strength that was nearly miraculous. Ingmar was gravely injured and Armin barely managed to save him. By midday the battle was over. The surviving Germanic warriors had fled into the woods. The legions of Aulus Caecina marched over the *pontes longi* until they met up with Germanicus's ships. They were taken on board and delivered back to their fort on the Rhine without suffering serious losses.

GERMANICUS'S EXPEDITION closed with mixed fortunes, although substantially in favour of the Romans, and it served to make him understand the enormous difficulties involved in conquering a land like Germania. His first enemy was nature. The obstacles put in their way in terms of geography and climate were practically insurmountable for an army like Rome's that had to be continuously supplied with an enormous quantity of materials and that needed open spaces in order to exploit their force. Swamps, impenetrable forests, quicksand, ocean tides in the coastal areas which could swallow up entire armies: crossing such treacherous terrain cost immense effort and resources; even just building a camp was often impossible. The summers were very short, the winters long, damp and icy. And the natives were indefatigable. They defended their territory fiercely and they were well equipped to blend in with the natural surroundings that they were well familiar with. They could strike and vanish instantly, but they were also able to mass multitudes of warriors capable of fighting like lions against the Roman armies. When the legions had finally reached the area of operations, they were too challenged by all these other aspects to think about making those lands more accessible with roads, bridges, water drainage systems and riverbanks – all of the elements that would counter the adverse nature of climate and territory.

Germanicus thought long and hard about how he could get around these obstacles and manage to make it to the operative phase in full force and in the best conditions of troop strength and morale.

The answer was a fleet.

A thousand ships.

The vessels of each sector were designed according to the use they would be put to in the shallows, rivers, lakes or the ocean. The ships destined to navigate in the ocean were built with two prows with a helm at each end, so that merely switching the direction of the oars would suffice to change direction, without wasting time in manoeuvres. They were equipped with decks wide enough to accommodate hundreds of men in full battle order as well as provisions, rigging and sails. There would be ample room for heavy and light artillery machines: ballistae, onagers and catapults.

Shipyards were spread along the entire coast from Gaul to Germania for building the hulls and masts. They relied on hundreds of other construction yards where trees were chopped down, debarked, cut and shaped to craft them into frames for the skeletons and planks for the sides. Thousands of carpenters and ironsmiths went to work day and night in the yards, which were constantly being supplied with all the necessary materials:

tall piles of oars, winches, anchors, coils of rope, stacks of hemp fabric for the sails and masts to support them.

Once completed, the fleet was so huge that if all the ships had been lined up in a single direction, they would have stretched out for more than twenty miles in length. As the immense fleet was assembling, Germanicus sent Silius, one of his lieutenants, to attack the Chatti who were besieging a fort on the Lipias River. He managed to disperse them, but the bad weather blocked further operations, forcing him to linger. On a bleak and rainy day, Silius had to take note that the mound Germanicus had erected over the bones of the fallen in Teutoburg had been demolished.

The fleet was ready to enter the canal that Drusus had excavated for over thirty miles, connecting the Rhine to a coastal lagoon. From there, once it had sailed into open waters, it began to make its way up the River Ems. Their Batavian allies, who had always lived along the ocean, made a show of diving into the water from the ships' sides and swimming against the waves of the ebb tide. A number drowned doing so.

Armin was informed that Germanicus was sailing upriver with a thousand ships and eight legions. Germanicus had heard that Armin was preparing for a massive attack.

The armies faced off on the two shores of the Weser: the Germanics on the right bank, the Romans on the left. Armin and several chieftains stood on the right bank, observing the movements of the enemy troops. At a certain moment, seeing a group of Roman officers walking along the shore, he yelled out in Latin, 'Is it true that the commander is in camp?'

'It's true all right,' replied one of the tribunes.

'I want to ask if he'll let me talk to my brother. I've heard he's in camp as well. His name is Flavus.'

The officers exchanged a look, realizing that the man

standing on the opposite shore was Armin, the leader of the Germanic coalition. 'Wait,' the tribune answered. 'We'll go and see.'

'You wait!' shouted Armin. 'Hold back your archers when I approach.'

'You bastard,' one of the three officers grumbled.

A short time passed and Flavus appeared accompanied by Stertinius, one of the lieutenants of Germanicus's general staff. He stood to one side and allowed Flavus to go forward.

'Hail!' shouted Armin. 'How are you?'

'Not bad, or good.'

'What did you do to that eye? That's why I barely recognized you under that mask in Teutoburg.'

'Don't you dare mention Teutoburg!' Flavus cut him short.

'How did you lose that eye?'

'In battle. Fighting for Commander Tiberius.'

'What did you get for it?'

'That's my business. It's my eye, not yours.'

'You haven't changed. So quick-tempered.'

'Is that what you wanted to tell me?'

'No. I thought I could talk to you. We used to be brothers once . . . I have a message for you from Mother.' Flavus said nothing. 'She says, cross this river and join us. It's your side too. Your people and your land. You can't betray us, you can't be a servant to the Romans!'

'I'm not a servant to anybody! I gave my word and I kept it, like the Romans do. Germanicus promised he would treat your wife and your son humanely and he has kept his word. You? You accepted Roman citizenship, the rank of *Eques*, you wore a toga. And then you betrayed them. It's you who are the traitor, you! Not me! Do you know how many of my friends died at Teutoburg? Friends who had saved my life, more than once, in battle. Their heads were ripped off! And Taurus? You killed him, didn't you? And Thiaminus, Privatus? They brought food to our table, remember? What did you do to them? Cut out their tongues? Gouge their eyes out? Varus? You ate his bread, drank his wine, you won his trust and then you cut off his head. You are not my brother! You are a bastard! My word is my bond, yours is worth nothing!'

Armin responded with insults of his own and both became livid with fury. The two brothers raced to the ford, urging their horses on, ready to make it a duel to the death, but they were pulled back, one by the Roman officers and the other by the Germanic chieftains.

'Don't you ever cross my path again, Armin!' yelled Flavus while four men were struggling hard to drag him off. 'Do not do it, or I will have no respect for the memory of our father, or of our mother either!' He grabbed the reins of his own horse then, spurred him on and disappeared in a cloud of dust.

GERMANICUS RECEIVED the spy in his tent in the middle of the night.

'Armin has decided where the final battle will be. The second Teutoburg.'

It was a level area, with wooded hills at the southern edge. The wood was full of big trees called something like 'Idstwis' in the local language, which the Romans renamed 'Idistavisus' to be able to pronounce it.

'He's put together a powerful army,' continued the spy. 'Armin reminds them constantly of Teutoburg, to give them the certainty of victory. He disparages the Romans for using the fleet instead of going on shore to fight. It's evident that such a huge show of Roman force has greatly shaken his men. In any case, all the chieftains have given him the high command this time. Seven tribes have contributed all of their able warriors to the fight.'

'If that's the place he wants, it's fine for me as well,' replied Germanicus, and dismissed the informer.

Germanicus left nothing to chance; he did not want to expose his men to any risks that could be avoided. When the spy came back, once again in the middle of the night, to say that the enemy army was just a short distance away and would attack the following day, Germanicus had already had two bridges built and placed hundreds of archers to cover the ford. The spy was still talking when Stertinius's cavalry and the Batavian squads were starting to take up position on the eastern bank, while the heavy infantry passed over the bridges in silence.

The first to attack were the Batavian auxiliaries, led by their chief Cariovalda who unleashed them against Armin's tribe. The Cherusci feigned withdrawal only to lure their assailants into a closed space where the Batavi found themselves completely surrounded. Cariovalda tried to break through the encirclement, but there was no way out for him or his men. The Batavian chief was riddled with stab wounds, and he died crushed under his own horse that had been gutted by the Cherusci warriors.

Stertinius's cavalry arrived just in time to prevent the complete extermination of the Batavi and managed to bring the survivors back in. But the bulk of Armin's Cherusci warriors hung back in the forest, waiting for Germanicus's army to advance: first the Gallic and Germanic auxiliaries, then the archers, then four legions one after another and then Germanicus in person with one thousand two hundred praetorians and a hand-picked cavalry squad behind. These were followed by another four legions, with assault infantry, mounted archers and even more cohorts of allies. The mere sight of them behind their segmented *loricas* was frightening. Their officers wore muscle cuirasses, red cloaks and helmets with crests of the same colour. The standard-bearers, one for every legion, held their eagles high and shining in the sun.

Armin, crouching in the forest, was searching for the point where he could break in two that apparently invulnerable mass of steel on the march and get at Germanicus. He had to hold back the warriors that he had until just now been firing up. They were perfectly primed: laden with ire and dying to get into the fray. Now that he saw the entire column was offering its flank, he launched the order for attack. He led the charge himself, whipping Borr up into a wild gallop down the slope of the hill. The forest was thick enough to hide them and yet the trees were sparse enough to allow them to race on at full speed.

But the Roman officers knew what to do; they had been instructed countless times. Every legionary was as taut as a bowstring, waiting only for the command to pass from parade order to combat order. The order arrived in unison from all their officers: 'right, face' and 'ranks in close order'. They turned as one towards the enemy cavalry charging at them. The archers let fly clouds of arrows, and then the heavy infantry hurled two waves of javelins that downed great numbers of the attackers and their horses. And Stertinius hadn't even had his moment yet; he was hiding in the forest at the Romans' backs with his heavy cavalry and with the surviving Batavi wild to avenge their murdered chieftain.

His orders arrived, brought by a horseman, clear and precise: the cavalry would attack the Cherusci on the flank, and then immediately afterwards Stertinius and the Batavi would circle behind them and push them onto the plain. The supreme commander with his praetorian cohorts would then intervene.

Stertinius ordered his men to charge forward at full speed. They penetrated the Cherusci column in a wild rush and broke it neatly in two. The Batavi were right behind them.

Furious brawling started. Armin, who had taken a sword blow, fought on with interminable energy, even as blood poured out of his wounded shoulder. He was aiming at the spot where the archers were drawn up because it was there that he could open a breach and get to Germanicus, but the Raetians, Vindelici and Gauls, Roman allies all, realized what he was intending to do and raced to counter the attack, blocking his manoeuvre. Germanicus spotted him and sprang at him at the head of his praetorian cohort. The superiority of the Roman forces was crushing and what remained of the Germanic army had not yet even engaged the Roman heavy infantry, with its wall of shields and deadly hedge of gladii extending from the front line.

Combat continued for nearly ten hours, until dark, and in the end Armin ordered a retreat to avoid a total debacle. He covered his face with the blood of his wounded shoulder and managed to escape unrecognized. His uncle Ingmar did the same. Many of their men tried to swim across the Weser, but these were easily picked off by the Roman archers. The riverbanks had collapsed at spots and other men fell into the current. Those who had sought shelter in the wood had climbed up onto the trees and were hiding amidst the leafy boughs but they too became easy marks for the Roman archers and they dropped one after another onto the ground.

The bodies of the fallen and the cadavers of their horses were spread over an area ten miles wide. The officers of Germanicus's army decreed that a mound be erected on the field, with an inscription listing all the peoples who had been defeated, to stand as a trophy and as retribution for the demolition of the mound of Teutoburg so soon after it had been raised.

Armin did not give up the fight. He stitched up his wound himself and would say to everyone he encountered, 'Not all is lost!' He continued to send messengers everywhere, to call to arms anyone who could give their contribution. He told them about the inscription of the Romans declaring their defeat and naming the peoples put to rout to prolong their shame for all of eternity. This was the one thing, more than any other, that convinced them to react. Men poured in from every quarter, many of them still boys, warriors on foot and on horseback.

Such a multitude gave him hope that their defeat could still be avenged.

He concentrated them all in a place further north, at a point where there was a narrowing between the wood and the swamps, fortified by a high dirt embankment which was called the 'Angrivarian Wall' because it had been built by the Angrivarii as a barrier between their territory and the Cherusci lands. It was a steep earthwork that included a palisade, and it had been well maintained. Many chieftains who were already thinking of passing to the other side of the Elbe changed their minds, and showed up with the full strength of their forces. The infantry was deployed to hold the wall, while the cavalry was hidden in the woods.

The Roman commander was immediately informed of what was happening and he ordered an attack on the wall. The Germanics were offering fierce resistance and Germanicus realized that getting too close to the wall would mean big losses, so he decided that instead of risking the lives of more men, he would draw up the heavy artillery. The Roman war machines began to incessantly rain down projectiles of every sort on the bastion. Incendiary bales of straw soaked with pitch disintegrated into a deadly blaze, throwing the defenders into such a panic that they abandoned the wall.

The battle shifted to the area remaining between the wall and the forest where the Germanics, massed in such great numbers in such a narrow space, could not use their agility and speed in striking to sufficient advantage. They had to face the compact formation of the legions and had no choice but to throw themselves at the wall of shields and the thousands of sharp sword blades sprouting between one shield and the next. Protected by neither helmets nor cuirasses, their losses were terrible.

Although Armin was wounded, he had been fighting on relentlessly, without stopping to eat or rest. He could barely stand and in the end he collapsed. He could hear Germanicus riding by on his horse, shouting, 'No prisoners! Take no prisoners, kill them all! Avenge Teutoburg!'

The slaughter went on until dark. Ingmar, who had fought valiantly, racing on his horse from one point of the battle to another, felt his strength failing him; he was forced to fall back, to save those of his men still alive.

Armin came to his senses late that night because Borr found him in a pile of corpses and was trying to wake him. He did all he could to straddle his horse's back but he kept falling. Only when Borr lowered himself to the ground did he manage to pull himself astride. He rode off slowly in the thick darkness of a moonless night. Before dawn he had found a shelter where other comrades had gathered. He fell into a profound torpor. He was awakened by a Cherusci warrior who shook him as day was breaking.

Armin opened his eyes. 'How many are left?'

'Enough,' replied the warrior.

30

PUBLIUS CAELIUS HAD brought his mission to completion, as much as he would be able to.

There was now a funeral monument at Castra Vetera that commemorated his brother Marcus, Primus Pilus Centurion of the Eighteenth Legion *Augusta*. He had him depicted on the facade wearing his dress uniform and cuirass, the decorations he'd earned in battle and the vine-shoot switch that stood for his rank. He also had the carver add his birthplace, Bononia, and his age when he died. Fifty-three. Just short of being discharged.

His freedmen, Privatus and Thiaminus, were included as two busts mounted on pedestals just behind him. They had a ghostly look to them. They certainly deserved to be there, for serving him with such loyalty. Thiaminus had jug ears, as Publius had requested; he liked a realistic portrait.

Publius Caelius paid the stonecutter what he asked for, without haggling over the price. He'd done a good job. He bequeathed a small sum as well to the Army of the North for maintenance of the little memorial even after he died.

He'd decided to raise the monument there in Germania rather than in Italy so the soldiers guarding the extreme limit of the Empire would always have an example to look to. He missed his brother terribly, even though they'd seen each other so little in their adult lives. But whenever they'd had the chance to meet up, usually at his inn, it had been a joyous reunion for both of them. He remembered well the day Marcus had shown up with those two boys; who would have said that one day one of them would have become his murderer?

The innkeeper hadn't managed to say goodbye to Germanicus, or to congratulate him on his victory at Idistavisus. He'd been told that the commander had descended the Ems with his fleet and sailed out onto the northern ocean in order to regroup and safely re-enter the ports of the great oceanic lagoon and then navigate up the Drusian channel and the Rhine.

Publius paid for passage on board a wagon loaded with timber to be used for building purposes; it was part of a convoy of ten vehicles that would cross the Alpine passes into Italy.

He reached Mediolanum after a journey of about a month and was greeted by bad news. Terrible news. Commander Germanicus's fleet had run into a severe storm and its vessels had been scattered far and wide. Many ships were lost and many men, horses and pack animals had died. A number of the survivors, those who had managed to make their way ashore with their damaged vessels, had been taken prisoner by the riverine populations and sold back to Germanicus, who used his own money to ransom them. It was a consolation to hear that this disaster had not broken Germanicus, who had proceeded to attack the rebellious tribes and had convinced them to see reason.

One evening, after Publius had watched all the timber being unloaded, he approached a military messenger and asked him if he'd accept an invitation to dinner at the exchange station tavern. He accepted; he was from Interamna and his name was Rutulius.

'Where are you travelling from?' asked Publius Caelius.

'Magontiacum, in Germania.'

'I've just left Castra Vetera myself. I followed Germanicus to Teutoburg to give a proper burial to our fallen.'

Rutulius regarded him with considerable surprise. 'What kind of work are you in?'

'I'm an innkeeper.'

'An innkeeper . . . so you had a friend, or a relative who was killed in that massacre?'

'A brother. My only brother.'

'I'm sorry. It was terrible.'

'Do you think all of this will ever be over?'

'Germanicus remains convinced that it can be. He still feels he can rout the Germanics once and for all, but the problem is that Tiberius is insisting that he return to Rome. This war is costing a frightening amount of money: one thousand ships, eighty thousand men, thousands of horses . . . it's unbelievable. The situation is nowhere near resolved. It's going to take further campaigns and enormous resources, huge investments . . .'

He was only a messenger, but he had a point. Germanicus in reality had full power in Germania and could do as he pleased. He could even choose to ignore all those letters Tiberius was no doubt sending his way, with a single order: 'Withdraw!'

Publius Caelius nodded and they went on talking until very late. He thought of Armin. When he'd seen him in Rome he would have sworn that young man was completely assimilated but he'd turned into a wild wolf. What was he doing now? Where had he gone to lick his wounds?

ARMIN HAD BEEN secretly brought to his mother's house where she could care for him and nurse his many injuries. Only his most loyal men knew where he was. The chief of his guard, a

Sicambri called Herwist, came to see him as soon as he learned about his condition and his location. He could see that Armin had lost weight and had dark circles around his eyes, but he wasted no time telling his commander what he was thinking. 'Germanicus thinks he's won but he's very wrong about that. He's lost his fleet and a great number of men as well. His expeditions against the Marsi and Chatti are nothing more than propaganda. He just can't wait for the historians to start singing his praises; they're already doing just that. But the emperor's not convinced. I don't think there's much truth behind these latest so-called victories at all.

'What is true is that we have suffered heavy losses. We can't hide that. At least we don't have historians to worry about. Our bards will one day sing of your deeds, but that's not worth much. You're not in good shape and the fact is that many of our allies are tired of waging war and dealing with such massive losses. Remember this: the Romans can recruit men and find money anywhere in the Empire. We have a very limited territory. You may not know that Mallwand, the Marsi chieftain, was captured at Idistavisus, and he told Germanicus where the eagle of the Eighteenth *Augusta* had been hidden, allowing him to recover it. Recovering a lost eagle is like finding a whole new legion, so great is its power and its importance to the Romans. It's as good as winning a battle . . .'

Armin listened in silence for a while and then asked with tears in his eyes, 'Where is Thusnelda? Where is my son?'

'No one knows. I've tried everything to find out, including bribing government officials and army officers, but no one's talking. Germanicus would never forgive a leak of information. He hasn't managed to kill or to capture you, so they're all he's got. He'll have to put them on show in Rome, when he enters in triumph.'

'Showing that he's triumphed over a woman and child?'

'He has no choice. They say that his wife Agrippina is preparing an unforgettable spectacle, including enormous panels painted with the most striking scenes of the war. There will be music, trumpets blaring . . . and in any case, you know the people adore Germanicus. That's not true of Tiberius, who is grey, cautious, taciturn: not the type of man who thrills the crowds.'

'Can you get a message to Thusnelda from me?'

Herwist fell silent. 'Maybe,' he said after a while. 'But I can't tell you when she'll get it. It may take years.'

'You know, I'd always hoped that my brother could help . . . if only I could have convinced him to come over to our side of the river. Instead we were ready to rip each other's throats out. But he did tell me that Thusnelda and the child were being treated well.'

'It's likely that he was telling the truth. What's your message?'

'My message is: "You are the only love of my life and you will be until the day I close my eyes. There will never be another woman at my side, nor will I ever have a child with anyone else." '

Herwist silently repeated Armin's words, trying to commit them to memory. He embraced Armin then, and said, 'Remember, all it would take is a nod from you for all the peoples of this land to rush to take up arms under your command. Farewell.'

That night Armin dreamed of Germanicus's triumph.

It was a terrible dream, worse than the vilest of nightmares, made even more real by the memories of his life in Rome and by Herwist's words. First the senators in their laticlave togas, then the buglers, then a sample of the meagre spoils taken from the Germanic peoples, then the white oxen with their gilded horns ready to be sacrificed, then the lictors who he had ranted against so often – 'Their fasces and the axes, their togas – out of our land!' – and finally the prisoners: half-naked Germanic warriors in chains, chieftains that had surrendered and were being paraded around like actors in a tragic play. And there, at their centre, his Thusnelda, pale and proud, holding the hand of a little boy who'd just learned to walk. Armin ached to burst out, weapons in hand, to liberate his family or die, but he himself was in chains, incapable of moving. He realized that he was a prisoner as well and that he was being forced to watch the parade. The victor, wearing a gold-trimmed toga and a laurel crown on his head, was accompanied by his own children on a chariot drawn by four white horses. Armin met Germanicus's eye, as had happened so often in the past, but neither of the two said a word. Then came the elite troops and the praetorian guard, so magnificent in their parade armour, and then the legionaries marching behind the standard-bearers carrying their legions' eagles. Next flew the two eagles of Teutoburg, soaring above all else. They were preceded by a solitary horseman on a black war stallion, his face covered by a bronze lamina mask.

Armin woke up screaming, dripping with sweat. Had he been dreaming all night? A pale dawn glimmered at the horizon.

THE TRIUMPH THAT Armin had seen in his dream, and which was actually executed with a great show of pomp, had turned into a trap for Germanicus. In order to go to Rome, he'd had to interrupt his plans to conquer Germania, and instead of being allowed to return, he was sent East.

At that point Armin no longer had an adversary, and nor did Germanicus. Armin found himself wishing, unbidden, that

Taurus were around to interpret the situation that had emerged. Clearly only the emperor himself could tip the balance. But like all true soldiers, he hated war. Armin had fought long enough at Tiberius's side to imagine what he was thinking: *The time has come to end the wars of conquest; too many resources have been squandered with scarce results. If we leave the Germanics to their own means, they'll immediately start fighting one another and fall without any help from us.* But Armin had understood that things could be different, if only he could manage to convince the tribal chiefs that fighting against each other amounted to suicide.

In the end Armin did manage to gather the Germanic nations around him in the name of freedom, thanks to his reputation as the victor of Teutoburg and his aura of command; he was the man who'd never stopped fighting for independence. He did have a rival, however. Marbod, a hateful, power-hungry man who cultivated ambiguous ties with the Romans with whom he'd actually lived as a young man.

For a long time, the two men vied for Germanic allegiance, neither succeeding in winning over more tribes than the other. This changed when two powerful peoples, the Lombards and the Semnones, switched to Armin's side, giving him a clear superiority over Marbod's forces and greatly enhancing his prestige. Armin let himself dream once again of achieving his mother's goal of becoming the sole leader of a great Germanic empire. He had begun to plot a raid of the place where Thusnelda and his son were being held prisoner. There was only one obstacle to realizing his dream, and his name was Marbod.

Armin joined all the chieftains in a great assembly and addressed them. 'For more than twenty years we've been fighting the Romans and their gigantic armies on land and on sea.

We may have lost a few battles on the way, but we can proudly say that we've won the war. The Romans have completely given up their plans to extend their empire to the Elbe River. They know that we are willing to fight to the last drop of blood, and the memory of Teutoburg is still very much alive for them. Emperor Tiberius prefers defence to attack. He believes that once the Romans have withdrawn, we'll battle one another while they sit and watch. They're wrong this time. We are like a single people now and I'm here to tell you that no one can beat us if we stay united! Tiberius thinks that he has Marbod in his pocket; he's been playing both sides. But our Lombard and Semnone brothers have realized what he's up to and they are with us now!'

A cry of ardent enthusiasm burst from all of the coalition chiefs and, one by one, they embraced the heads of the two tribes that had come over to their side. Armin resumed his appeal: 'You've all honoured me by accepting me as your head and the commander of our army. It's not thirst for power that has put me here, but passion. The scars that you see on my arms and my chest are a mark of that passion. I'm asking you now to renew the promise that allowed us to annihilate Varus's legions. I swear to you that by next spring we will have united Germania from the Rhine to the Elbe, from the ocean to the Danube. Our territorial confines will be in direct contact with the Roman Empire itself. They will have to fear us. They will have to tremble with fear when they hear that we are on the move!'

Another roar burst from the assembly of chiefs and from the ranks of the veterans of Teutoburg. Armin was proclaimed supreme commander of the Germanic forces.

A great dinner was held to cement their alliance. After-wards, Armin ordered sentries and guards to take position, establishing camp discipline quite similar to that of the Romans.

In the heart of the night, Herwist, his Sicambri guard, approached Armin, who jumped out of his bed, thrusting his sword at the man's throat.

'Take it easy. It's just me,' said Herwist in a whisper.

'What's going on?'

'Your uncle Ingmar is leaving with all his men. What do we do? To me it seems like a good chance to arrest them and take them into custody. Even if he resists, I'm sure all his men will come back over to our side. They are excellent combatants.'

'No. Let them go. I don't want to hold anyone back by force. I can understand him: he's my father's brother, and he won't take orders from his nephew. I'm too young and inexperienced in his eyes. He's always fought valiantly and he deserves respect. Tell the sentries to let them pass.'

'He'll inform Marbod of our plans,' protested Herwist.

'Nothing changes. We'll still have to defeat him.'

'As you wish,' replied Herwist. He went to deal with the guards.

Ingmar and his men proceeded to reach Bohemia and join up with Marbod's army.

At the beginning of the following spring, Armin went to see his mother, the only person left of his family. He wanted an embrace and a blessing.

'Take care of yourself, son,' she warned him. 'Trust no one but your most devoted veterans. Only those who have fought with you and have seen your courage and your spirit of sacrifice.'

'I promise, Mother,' he said. 'I'll return to you unharmed.'

'No news of your brother?' she asked with shiny eyes.

'Not much, all bad.'

'If you should ever get your family back, do not have another child. There's no greater sorrow for a parent than to see hatred among his own children.'

A guard had arrived on horseback but he was waiting until Armin had finished visiting his mother. When Armin noticed him, he lost no time in approaching and asked for permission to speak.

'I have good news for you, Commander. Our greatest enemy has died. It happened more than a month ago, but we've just found out. The Roman cities of the Rhine are all in mourning. Black drapes hang from the towers.'

'Germanicus?' asked Armin incredulously.

'Yes. He died in Syria. In Antioch.'

Antioch. That name evoked a season in his life he would never forget. 'How did he die?' he asked.

'It seems he was poisoned.'

'Poisoned . . .'

Armin could not rejoice. He thought of the image of the little boy sculpted in marble. They had been born in the same year. They'd battled against each other but they'd also trained at the same hand. Germanicus had indeed taken his son Tumlich and his wife Thusnelda into his custody but he'd treated them humanely. Or so his brother had told him that day on the Weser. He took no delight in his enemy's end. He would have preferred a death worthy of a warrior.

He was struck by the thought that perhaps death would be another thing that he and Germanicus would share: two young men who had learned the principles of life together in Rome from the same man. Perhaps they were destined to lose those lives together as well.

As he had promised, Armin invaded Bohemia in the early

spring. His army had been perfectly trained and fought in closed ranks, following their commander's orders to the letter. Marbod was no less battle-ready and the war between brother nations was no less fierce than war against the foreign enemy. The two armies met on an open field and fought on relentlessly all day until events took a turn and Marbod's forces were routed and fled into the forest. Most of them promptly chose to desert and go over to Armin's side.

Marbod was alone now. He abandoned his kingdom and took shelter in the Roman province of Noricum. From there he sent letters to Tiberius asking for help. In the end he was admitted to Italy and housed in a luxurious residence in Ravenna. There he forgot all about affairs of state and of war and he decided to enjoy life: the climate, the food, the flowers and the women of that enchanting corner reserved for Rome's most illustrious guests. He lived there without regret for eighteen years.

Armin remained the only ruler of the entire Germanic nation.

His newfound ascendency attracted the best warriors and counsel to him. He honed his skills in weaving relations between the chieftains, formally recognizing their authority but exercising his own power effectively at the highest level. He created an army based on Rome's, disciplined and obedient, and he turned it into his own instrument of power, certain that it was the only way of keeping Germania united and saving it from discord and internal strife.

Then word got out that he was plotting to become king. King of Germania.

BEFORE LONG, a letter sent by the Chatti chieftain to Rome was read aloud to the assembled senators:

From Adgandestrium, the chief of the Chatti, to the Senate and people of Rome.

Armin's arrogance has become unbearable. We fought so many years against the Roman people to regain our liberty and we will certainly not give it up now to an ambitious man who pretends to be our king. If you have a poison strong enough to kill a brawny man with a robust build, send it to me through the man who has delivered this letter and Armin, son of Sigmer, prince of the Cherusci, will soon have ceased his life.

The Senate replied that the Roman people were accustomed to avenging wrongs face to face, with weapons in hand, certainly not by means of dark, poisonous plotting.

ONE EVENING TOWARDS dusk, Flavus was returning to his quarters at Castra Vetera after having participated in a general staff meeting when he found himself suddenly facing the Hermundur whose face was striped with black tattoos.

'You scared me,' he said, returning his sword to its sheath, 'and that can be dangerous. Is it me you're looking for?'

'Yes,' replied the Hermundur. 'It's about something important . . .'

Flavus motioned for him to continue.

'Three days from now Armin will find himself on horseback at dawn together with his personal guard, now commanded by Herwist. They'll be riding from the bridge over the River Kreis towards what was once called Drusus's road, which has been abandoned. It's an isolated spot, surrounded by a dense forest. There your brother will be assassinated. Herwist has sold himself to the chief of the Chatti.'

'I don't see how that would concern me,' replied Flavus curtly.

The Hermundur bowed his head in silence. He adjusted the cloak on his shoulders, tapped his reins on his horse's neck and set off at a gallop, vanishing from sight.

ARMIN WAS FIRST to cross the bridge over the Kreis; he was heading for the old Drusus road. Borr slowed his step as if he could smell something and he started moving sideways, snorting impatiently.

'Good boy, Borr, be good . . .' said Armin, stroking his neck. He turned to Herwist. 'Something is spooking him.'

Herwist drew close as if to provide cover but instead pulled out his sword and drove it into Armin's side. Armin did not fall from his horse; he unsheathed his own sword instead and cried out, fending off the attack of two more guards.

At that very instant a horseman appeared, armed with a Roman sword and a Germanic axe that he was whirling with a sinister roar. He raced from the forest at great speed, fell upon Herwist and slaughtered the man, while the others moved swiftly to close in on their prey. A cry burst out: 'Help me, Wulf, help me!' as Armin persevered in defending himself, even as blood gushed from his side. He managed to take one of his attackers down, while Flavus axed the other in two at his waist. Armin began to slip slowly then to the ground. Flavus jumped off his horse and drew near; his brother was gasping for breath and blood was pouring down his side.

Flavus bound Armin's wound tightly and made a litter using pine branches, which he secured to Borr's straps so it could be dragged behind the horse. He set off at once, in the direction of a village that he remembered was nearby.

He would turn often to see how his brother was faring. Armin was thrashing, and calling out; this reassured him. There would be a shaman in the village who could take care of him.

He stopped once or twice and put his index finger to his brother's jugular vein to test the beating of his heart and then set off again. He was nearly there, by his calculations.

When he got to the clearing he was looking for, he realized that the village had been abandoned and that Armin was dead. He stayed at his brother's side until dusk, listening to the remote voices of two boys echoing through time who had once sworn never to leave one another. He took his axe and went into the forest to collect wood for the pyre. He set it aflame. He collected his brother's ashes in a clay jar and buried them in a hidden place. He let Borr run free and he mounted his own black horse and rode into the distance.

Epilogue

MANY YEARS PASSED, during which Flavus became a Roman citizen and was promoted to the highest ranks of the army. He never managed to learn where his nephew Tumlich, son of Armin, could be found. Nor did he dare ask. He knew that Thusnelda was dead.

He thought that one day, sooner or later, the Hermundur would appear to show him the way, but he waited in vain. Maybe he'd died in combat in one of the frequent skirmishes among the Germanic tribes or maybe he'd simply vanished. Maybe he was only a ghost, a mysterious connection he'd once shared with his brother.

It was a dream that roused Flavus's memory. A dream in which he was alone in a place he'd never seen before, a ring-shaped building made of wood, with the voice of a Germanic auxiliary telling him, 'It's a school for gladiators.' He turned and heard the sound of a gallop and saw a blond horseman emerging from the fog on a black stallion that snorted puffs of steam from his nostrils. Then the horseman disappeared.

Recalling that image was like looking in the mirror for the first time. He was the blond horseman on the black stallion and the moment had come to join himself to that person in his dream.

He returned one night to the place where he had secretly buried the jar with Armin's ashes. He dug it up, placed it in the sack which held his personal belongings, and readied for a long journey.

He first passed through the headquarters of the Army of the North. It was dawn. He'd come to say goodbye to Centurion Taurus. His likeness was sculpted on an empty tomb, but he was present.

'Hail, Centurion.'

'Have a safe journey, son,' resounded a hoarse voice inside of him. As he walked away he heard the notes of an old legionary song that he'd never managed to learn well.

> *Miles meus contubernalis*
> *Dic mihi cras quis erit vivus*
> *Iacta pilum hostem neca*
> *Miles es, miles Romanus!*

Flavus travelled untiringly by day and night. He crossed the Alps over the same pass where he and Armin had once tried to run away and there he saw the old woman with the ointment. How old was she now, a hundred? He descended towards the great lake to the south and spent the night in the same *mansio* where he had met Iole.

Where was Iole?

What Iole – some whore? They'd never heard of any Iole.

'If you should see her, can you give her this bracelet from me . . . thank you,' said Flavus.

The innkeeper had given him a wide smile.

His destination was Ravenna, the great bay where he had once stood with his brother in wordless amazement as the immense quinquereme, the *Aquila Maris*, sailed in. He found the city enveloped in dense fog and he felt that the place of his dream was close by. He spurred on his horse and he heard a pounding of hoofs and, as if he were in front of a mirror, he saw himself emerging all at once from the fog and he knew he had to stop.

In front of him was the building shaped like a ring, made all of wood.

He waited until daybreak.

A servant came out from under one of the arches with a sack slung over his shoulder. Maybe he was a slave, heading out to the market. Flavus took the helmet from his saddle and put it on.

'I want to know when the school opens.'

'No one can watch the training.'

'I can. I'm the commander of the Twentieth Legion and I can go wherever I like.'

'Of course. Please forgive me, Legate. Training begins right after breakfast. You can enter when you like. I'll talk to the man in charge.'

Flavus waited a little. There was a small tavern opening nearby and he took the opportunity to get something hot to drink. When the servant came back with what he'd bought, Flavus took the saddlebag from his horse and entered the school with him.

At the entrance to the *cavea*, the servant showed him the way to the sixth row of seats, the best, and Flavus took a place. After a while, the *lanista* and trainer appeared with the servant alongside them. He pointed to the unexpected guest who was sitting all alone up on the sixth row.

Three pairs of boys played off, with the winner of each round continuing. In the end, just one was left standing: the strongest, the most handsome and the most violent.

It's him, thought Flavus. *His father's spitting image.*

He asked the *lanista* if he could meet the young man in private.

'He's not for sale, Legate, not even to an officer of your rank.'

'I know,' replied Flavus.

The *lanista* nodded and accompanied him to a room close to the ring. The boy came in; he was still covered in dust and sweat. He closed the door behind them and left them alone.

Flavus took off his helmet, releasing the blond locks that had given him his name. His left eye was covered by a leather patch.

'I'm your uncle Wulf-Flavus,' he said as he took a little ivory coffer from his bag. 'And these are the ashes of your father Armin, the first leader of the Germanic people. He made many mistakes, but he lost his life in the quest for the freedom and unity of his land and his people. He loved you infinitely, although he had never seen you. Do not forget him for as long as you live.'

The young man regarded him with bright eyes, without managing to say a word. He took the box and clutched it to his chest.

'Farewell, son.'

'Farewell, Commander.'

Flavus left. He felt a knot in his throat for the first time in his life. He jumped onto his stallion and galloped off, disappearing into the fog.

Author's Note

THE BATTLE OF Teutoburg Forest of AD 9 is one of the watershed moments of Roman and European history. It was one of the three greatest defeats, along with Cannae and Adrianople, suffered by the Roman army over nearly a millennium of history. This debacle was a devastating shock for Augustus, who had invested enormous resources in twenty years of war in Germania, and it prompted him to move the north-eastern border of the Empire back to the Rhine. His idea of extending the frontier to the Elbe was forever forsaken.

But why did Augustus so want the Elbe to be the Empire's border, six hundred kilometres east of the Rhine? It couldn't have simply been the desire to rectify the eastern frontier in such a way as to eliminate the wedge that stretched from the upper Rhine to the upper Danube; this alone could not justify the deployment of tens of legions and thousands of war and cargo ships. Over the twenty-year period, Rome's finest commanders, including Drusus, his brother Tiberius, Germanicus and Aulus Caecina, were put to the test there. There were many successes, but a great number of failures as well, especially if we consider that our sources are Roman and thus prone to exalt victories and to play down the defeats or draws, at least to some extent. In these cases, spin played a role at least as important as that of the legions.

Author's Note

From the *Res Gestae* we know that Augustus sent his deputies (*per legatos meos*) to the extreme limits of the known world. We also know that the Caspian Sea and the Baltic Sea were considered gulfs of the ocean which, according to the geographical beliefs of that time, surrounded the entire earth. In other words, what Augustus truly wanted to reach was not a river border (the Elbe) but the ocean itself, although he could have no idea of how distant it actually was. His intention, therefore, must have been to unite all of the earth's land mass under the aegis of Rome. The *Urbs* (the City) had to coincide with the *Orbis*, that is, the world. This narrative imagines a wider goal: to prevent what Horace feared and what eventually occurred in actuality. The destruction of the Roman Empire by the Germanic peoples.

Germania, at that time, had nothing to offer a potential conqueror: the land was covered by forests and swamps and the state of the economy was primitive. Agriculture was practically unknown, as was iron and steel working, although there have been sporadic finds of iron blades with traces of carbonitriding. Germanic settlements had not yet reached a pre-urban state, even according to the most recent archeological discoveries which classify communities inhabited by more than five hundred people as indicative of important development. The climate was terrible by Roman standards (*horribile coelum*, says Tacitus), with long, frigid winters and short rainy summers.

All this would lead us to believe that the founder of the Roman Empire saw the necessity of including Germanic ethnicities in the Empire, assimilating them through military enrollment. He most likely saw them as the most dangerous adversaries of the State and as potential invaders. Horace's lines ('The victorious barbarians, alas! shall trample upon the ashes of the city and the horsemen shall smite it with the sounding hoofs', Epode 16) represent an almost prophetic scene of barbarian invasion, already evoked by Scipio Aemilianus in tears before the ruins of Carthage (Polybius, XXXVIII, 21; Diodorus, XXXII, 24). All sources recall the invasion of the Cimbri and the Teutons who had invaded northern Italy, before being defeated by Gaius Marius in the Battle of Vercellae. Although prevention may have been foremost on their mind, it cannot be excluded that the Romans saw the Germanic peoples as bringers of new energies.

The true enigma is how Publius Quinctilius Varus allowed himself to be so completely deceived by his commander of the Germanic auxiliaries: Armin, Cherusci prince, Roman citizen and member of the *Equites* (knights), the second rank after the senators. In vain, Germanic chieftain Seghest warned him of the trap, exhorting him to put Armin and all of his friends in chains. Varus was unshakeable in his trust and led three elite legions, the Seventeenth, the Eighteenth and the Nineteenth, down an impassable route littered with boulders and crossed by brooks and rivulets, surrounded on all sides by thick woods that made it perfect terrain for ambushes. All without an iota of suspicion. Meanwhile, the lower part of the massif of Kalkriese had been fitted with a screen of grates covered with clods of earth, behind which twenty thousand Germanic warriors were hiding, waiting to hurl their javelins. It appears that the path itself had been deviated so that the Roman column on the march could offer their flank without defence to the warriors lying in wait behind the wall. This was no battlefield but a slaughterhouse, and the legions had no possibility of escaping. Both the deviation of the route and the presence of a wall disguised by clods of soil have been deduced by archeologists, who have thus interpreted the results of their findings, although the ancient sources are insufficiently clear on these devices.

It is also difficult to explain how Armin was able to win the trust of the chiefs of the great Germanic tribes, who must have known well how the Cherusci prince had earned Roman citizenship: by fighting in the Roman army against his own blood (Tiberius's campaigns in AD 4–6, Velleius II, 118).

This story respects the information provided by the sources as far as possible, although many gaps exist, especially in Tacitus. Other versions (Cassius Dio and Velleius Paterculus) are more complete. In any case, this story gives an emotional retelling of events, inspired by the cenotaph of Marcus Caelius currently on display at the Archeological Museum of Bonn, as well as by figures who are barely mentioned in the original sources but who have an important weight in the decisions and thoughts of the characters. Armin's mother is a prime example: we know next to nothing about her (PW RE, 1191); even her name is invented in this novel. Armin's beloved Thusnelda (Strabo VII, 292) was carried off by him at a non-specified time, and was later recaptured by her father Seghest who held her prisoner and then turned her over, while pregnant, to Germanicus. Mother and child were exhibited at Germanicus's triumph in Rome, earning the disgust and rage of Armin. Tacitus reports this in keeping with the rhetoric prevalent in his day and he cannot thus be taken literally. The same can be said of Tacitus's account of the encounter between Armin and his brother Flavus (who indeed remained faithful to Rome) on the Weser.

As far as character names are concerned, I've attempted to recreate the Germanic names (present in Latin texts as Segimerus, Inguiomarus, Segestes, Maroboduus, Tumelicus, etc.) in a purely phonological way. The Germanic name of Flavus is unknown and the name chosen here, Wulf, is pure imagination. Armin's Germanic name is also uncertain:

Hermann is generally accepted today in Germany, but many scholars have disagreed (PW RE 1190); Armin or Irmin have been suggested.

Armin's father died in AD 7 (PW RE 1192) while his mother lived until AD 16 (Tacitus II, 10).

The victory of Teutoburg must have turned Armin into a hero and almost certainly the unquestioned chief of the coalition of peoples who had joined in the fight. The destruction of Varus's army surely marked a point of no return. Rome could not avoid avenging such a defeat, but six years passed before another Roman army crossed the Rhine. Germanicus's expedition began with a journey to honour the battlefield of Teutoburg and to bury the remains of the Roman soldiers killed there. But despite the great victory of Idistavisus in AD 16, Germanicus had to cut short what he had hoped would be a decisive campaign a year later by obeying Tiberius's orders to return to Rome. Germanicus's subsequent deployment to Syria and his death there under mysterious circumstances contributed to definitively burying all plans for Romanizing Germania. Tiberius himself, the greatest soldier that Rome had ever known, came to the conclusion that the project was too costly and dangerous and that when the Roman armies withdrew to the west bank of the Rhine, the Germanic tribes would be forced to fight out their disputes against each other.

In his campaign against Marbod, Armin very probably wanted to achieve the union of all the Germanic peoples under his leadership. But the rumour was circulating that he was seeking to name himself their king (the first Reich?) and this must have set off a plot that involved poisoning him and which ended in his murder in AD 21 at the hands of his own men. Shortly before his death, Germanicus, his great adversary and peer in age also died, probably by poisoning. Armin's wife

Author's Note

Thusnelda died in Ravenna in AD 17 and his only son Tumelicus died as an adolescent, probably in a gladiators' arena.

It has been said that with the rout of Teutoburg, Rome lost Germania and Germania lost Rome.

VALERIO MASSIMO MANFREDI

THE LEGIONARY SONG

Miles meus contubernalis
Dic mihi cras quis erit vivus
Iacta pilum hostem neca
Miles es, miles Romanus!

O soldier, my comrade
Tell me who will be alive tomorrow
Hurl your pilum, kill the enemy
You are a soldier, a soldier of Rome!

THE IDES OF MARCH

March, 44 BC. Rome, in all her glory, has expanded her territories beyond the wildest dreams of her citizens, led by Caius Julius Caesar. He is a man in command of his destiny, who wields enormous power throughout the vast empire. However, his god-given mission – to end the blood-splattered fratricidal wars, reconcile implacably hostile factions and preserve Roman civilization and world order – is teetering dangerously close to collapse . . . His power is draining away. None of his supporters can stop the inexorably evolving plot against him; prophecy will explode into truth on the Ides of March and the world will change forever.

OUT NOW

EMPIRE OF DRAGONS

Anatolia, AD 260. The Roman outpost of Edessa is on its last legs after the Persian siege, and the Roman emperor agrees to meet his adversary to negotiate peace. But the meeting is a trap and the emperor ends up in enemy hands, along with the commander of his personal guard, Marcus Metellus Aquila, and ten of his most valiant and trusted men. Their destiny is sealed: they will rot away in a mine, forced into slavery.

But Metellus – legate of the Second Augusta Legion, hero of the empire – and his men break free and meet a mysterious, exiled prince. They agree to safeguard the prince's journey back to his homeland, Sera Maior, the mythical Kingdom of Silk – China.

And so they begin an extraordinary and epic journey through the forests of India, the Himalayan mountains, the deserts of central Asia, all the way to the heart of China – as the very survival of the world's greatest two empires is at stake.

OUT NOW

THE LAST LEGION

AD 476. The year the Western Roman Empire finally collapses. The last emperor of Rome is encamped and protected by the Nova Invicta Legion. But in the space of a few minutes a horde of barbarians sweep through the camp in the fog, kill the imperial family and take the young emperor captive . . .

But all is not lost. From the dust of battlefields emerges a small team of invincible warriors – the Last Legion. Their task is to rescue the emperor and his enigmatic tutor and to try to resurrect the glory of Rome. They must guide the last Caesar in a dramatic escape through a devastated Italy and Northern Europe to their ultimate destinies in the land of the Britons . . . and the beginning of a new legend.

OUT NOW

CHILD OF A DREAM

THE FIRST ALEXANDER NOVEL

Who could have been born to conquer the world other than a god?

Ancient Greece: mesmeric beauty, consuming desires, an insatiable hunger. Then premature death. This is the story of a boy, born to a great king – Philip of Macedon – and his sensuous queen, Olympias. It tells of the stern discipline of Philip and the wild passions of Olympias, and how, together, they formed Alexander, a young man of immense, unfathomable potential, capable of subjugating the known world to his power, and thought of by his contemporaries as a god. As a protégé of Aristotle, Alexander must become a man and soon begins his adventures to conquer the civilized world.

OUT NOW

extracts reading groups
competitions books new
discounts extracts
competitions
books new
events books
extracts new reading groups
interviews
events extracts
discounts
new books events
events new
discounts extracts discounts

www.panmacmillan.com

extracts events reading groups
competitions books extracts new